A PROMISE
TO ARLETTE

ALSO BY SERENA BURDICK

The Stolen Book of Evelyn Aubrey
Find Me in Havana
The Girls with No Names
Girl in the Afternoon

A PROMISE TO ARLETTE

Serena Burdick

ATRIA BOOKS

New York   Amsterdam/Antwerp   London
Toronto   Sydney/Melbourne   New Delhi

ATRIA
BOOKS

An Imprint of Simon & Schuster, LLC
1230 Avenue of the Americas
New York, NY 10020

This book is a work of fiction. Any references to historical events, real people, or real places are used fictitiously. Other names, characters, places, and events are products of the author's imagination, and any resemblance to actual events or places or persons, living or dead, is entirely coincidental.

First Atria Books hardcover edition June 2025

ATRIA BOOKS and colophon are trademarks of Simon & Schuster, LLC

Simon & Schuster strongly believes in freedom of expression and stands against censorship in all its forms. For more information, visit BooksBelong.com.

For information about special discounts for bulk purchases, please contact Simon & Schuster Special Sales at 1-866-506-1949 or business@simonandschuster.com.

The Simon & Schuster Speakers Bureau can bring authors to your live event. For more information or to book an event, contact the Simon & Schuster Speakers Bureau at 1-866-248-3049 or visit our website at www.simonspeakers.com.

Interior design by Davina Mock-Maniscalco

Manufactured in the United States of America

1 3 5 7 9 10 8 6 4 2

Library of Congress Cataloging-in-Publication Data is available.

ISBN 978-1-6680-7030-7
ISBN 978-1-6680-7032-1 (ebook)

For my grandmother Margaret

PART ONE

FIRECRACKERS

1952

1

No one ever put the pieces together. Even years later, swapping rumors that couldn't be confirmed, they were sure that whatever caused the Whipples' sudden departure, the house packed up and everything gone, it must have been Ida's fault.

They thought they knew her. They thought this because she showed up to their children's birthday parties with tidy packages and joined their bridge games and baked a mean pumpkin pie, even though she'd never eaten pumpkin pie until she arrived in New England, or so she said. They thought they knew her because she shopped at Jordan Marsh and wore kitten heels and small hats and tea-length swing dresses, just like the rest of them. They thought they knew her because it was 1952, and she participated in their silent agreement that the best way to put the war years behind them was to keep up tradition, to lay Thanksgiving tables, string Christmas lights, and set off firecrackers on the Fourth of July. All of which Ida did with a smile.

It never crossed their minds that she was slowly collapsing. That she was thinking, *Screw you, Norma Jean*, as she waved across the parking lot of Marvin's Grocery at the woman who knew less than nothing about her. It didn't occur to them that she'd lied about her fresh pumpkin filling— she'd never baked a whole pumpkin in her life—mixing up canned pumpkin with a wry smile, or that on the days when she wanted to suffer more than usual, she slid a photograph of a dead woman under her girdle and thought about the friend she'd betrayed.

No one had any idea that she was a good wife but not a good mother.

What they did know, and tittered about behind her back, was that Ida kept her front door locked even when she was at home. No one in the town of Lexington, Massachusetts, locked their doors. Which, after the theft, they agreed was careless. The thing was, everyone knew everyone, and the riffraff never strayed this far outside of Boston, so who was there to worry about? Their children played all over the neighborhood, and if one of them was thirsty or needed to use the bathroom, their mothers liked knowing that any door was open to them, even the ones in the pristine, historic homes with towering pillars and wraparound porches. So long as no one tracked mud over the carpet, all were welcome.

The other mothers expected Sidney to put a stop to the whole locked-door business. He had grown up in one of those pristine houses, where his parents still lived with their trusting, open door. Ida didn't begrudge them this, or Sidney his happy childhood. She just wasn't going to follow their lead, and Sidney, despite what the neighbors presumed, would never ask her to. Fear was a complicated creature. He knew how it inhabited the body, burrowed into every cell so your veins pulsed and your muscles twitched with it. It didn't matter how much time had passed or how irrational the locked door was—if it made Ida feel safe, Sidney wasn't going to deny her that. It was her silent acknowledgment of their past, her way of telling him she'd never forget what she had done and that she didn't deserve to. And as much as Sidney wanted her to forget, the truth was, he didn't deserve to either.

During the war, it had been impossible to imagine a life after it. Now that Sidney was in that life, even all these years later, he felt a sense of bafflement. Walking down his quiet street from the train station after work, or mowing his lawn, he'd find himself consumed with the absurdity of it all. How does a person bomb and shoot and maim other human beings and then come home and mow the lawn? No one talked about the images that flashed behind closed lids or the dreams that jolted a man awake. Coming home was the dream, but home looked different through marred eyes.

With his parents living down the road, church on Sunday, and roast for dinner, Sidney was forced to face the privilege and ignorance of his upbringing, a naivete that had driven him to believe enlisting was the bravest thing he could do. He'd wanted to fight so badly he signed up for the Air Force three months before graduating from Boston University. It was February 1941. Within a year, he'd pinned on his blue bars, was appointed flight officer, and received a direct commission from the Eighth Air Force, shipping out to England with all the excitement of a twenty-two-year-old who thinks he knows everything. Sidney had been the kind of teenager who punched other boys for no good reason, which was why he'd thought war would suit him.

It didn't. Two years in, he sat in a field in France watching his closest friend, Sergeant James Freedman—a Chicagoan, stonemason by trade, fiancé, son, and brother—bleed out from a hole in his skull. The sun was bright, the grass a stunning green, the blood from the man's temple a brilliant red. There was the scent of fresh hay and burning metal in the air. James had latched his hand around Sidney's neck with startling force and pulled his face down so that their noses touched. "Whatever you do, don't let me die," he'd said. Sidney had locked eyes with his friend and promised he wouldn't.

Sidney thought about that lie every morning on his train ride to work. He thought about his brothers who had been killed in the South Pacific and wondered why he was the one who got to live. He had come home a hero simply because he'd survived. No one cared how he'd done it. No one chastised him for bringing home a wife and child without officially breaking it off with his fiancée. They cheered him, and this dug his guilt in a little deeper.

His was a cowardly survival. For years, he had been telling Ida that there is no guilt in war. One's actions are excused in trying to stay alive. A person does whatever it takes. But this was just a game of words. Neither of them actually believed it.

Swept up in his hero status, in his role as the sole surviving son, in the whirlwind of domestic life and his love for his wife and children, Sidney was convinced that the past would fade. And it had, to a certain extent. His raw edge of feeling was healed to a tender patch of scars.

And yet, lies don't go away simply because no one knows the truth.

2

FOR THE PAST EIGHT years, Ida had been telling herself she just needed time, but on that Fourth of July morning, surveying her image in the full-length mirror, she realized that time was not going to do her any good. The instruction booklet given to GI brides by the Red Cross on *How Americans Live* had coached her in running a household. It told her what to cook, how to dress, how to raise babies, how to get along with other housewives—*You'll be welcome, but you're to be friendly the moment you arrive. There must be no "keeping yourself to yourself."*

It just failed to teach her how to keep her soul intact.

Cinching her belt tight around her skinny waist, Ida adjusted her breasts into perky formation, looked at her flared skirt and made-up face and fat roller curls, and felt the urge to do something drastic. Maybe she'd dress in her husband's trousers and a sleeveless shirt, dye her lackluster brown hair red and iron it straight, go without makeup. She wanted to shock people. To shock herself.

Growing up in Petersfield, England, with her aging parents and three older brothers, Ida had been convinced that she'd been snatched from her real family and placed with strangers. Even after she got away, slipped into an entirely different identity in Paris, the feeling of estrangement had followed. It was with Sidney where she had felt, for the first time, that she belonged in her own skin.

Only lately, that wasn't enough.

A week ago, her elder daughter, Bea, a willowy eight-year-old with blonde hair and blue eyes, had walked through the front door holding a violin case. It might as well have been a grenade. Ida's body seized. The blood drained from her face. The cords in her neck went wire tight, and her mind flipped backward as she heard herself shout, "Get that out of here!" She'd seen string instruments since the war—just not up close, and not in the hands of her daughter.

Startled, Bea held up the curved leather case as if her mother didn't understand. "It's a violin, Mom. I borrowed it from Ruth. Her mom said if I like it, she'll give you the name of her teacher."

"Like it?" Ida's hands shook. "You don't just start playing and decide you like it. It takes a lifetime." She yanked open the front door. "Put it on the porch. I'll call Ruth's mom to come get it."

"But I—"

"No!" Ida hissed. "You do as I say, and do not tell your father."

Since laying eyes on that violin, Mendelssohn's Concerto Op. 64 had been playing in Ida's head.

Twisting a loose strand of hair into the curl it had sprung away from, Ida went downstairs to brew the coffee. She hated this version of herself. She didn't want to be a mother who yelled for no reason or a wife who kept secrets. She took a deep breath, sat down, and counted to five. She had half an hour before Sidney woke, possibly fifteen minutes before the girls came bounding down the stairs.

She needed more time.

She ran a finger over the two small scars on the inside of her left arm, an absent gesture, a habit. *I can't do this*, she thought. *I just can't keep doing this.*

SHE DID, OF course, keep doing it. When Bea and Dora tumbled into the kitchen, Ida set their bowls of hot oatmeal on the table and managed a smile.

Bea was tall for her age, her skin pale and freckled. Dora, at five, still held her baby plumpness. Her cheeks were round and pink under her vibrant brown eyes and her dark hair was cut straight across her forehead and bobbed at her chin like a child from a 1920s storybook.

Bea slid into her chair, glanced at her mother, and said, incredulous,

"You're dressed in yellow?" She had recently begun questioning most things Ida did.

"What's wrong with yellow?"

"It's the Fourth of July," Bea stated, matter-of-fact, pouring syrup over the pool of melted butter in her bowl.

Dora, swinging her legs back and forth in her chair, said, "That's your Easter dress, Momma," smiling at such a silly mistake.

Ida looked down. She had indeed worn this dress on Easter. The fact that her children had noticed and felt the need to point it out, that every mother in town would most likely notice and feel the need to point it out too, made Ida want to scream.

"I like this dress," she said, dumping milk into her coffee with a little too much force, causing it to splash over the rim of the cup and onto the countertop. Ignoring the spill, Ida picked up her mug and looked at her girls in their matching red-checked dresses she'd ironed and laid out for them and felt a sense of panic. Their elbows were off the table, hair combed, socks pulled up. They were already losing the sturdiness of themselves, morphing into compliant, respectable, proper girls. It was her fault. She was the one who'd taught them to sit like that, to follow orders, to please. Why did they listen to her? Why were they so bloody obedient? Ida hadn't listened to her mother. When she was Bea's age, she'd chopped her hair to her ears with gardening shears just to be defiant. She'd hiked up her skirt and gone barefoot with the exact purpose of enraging her mother, to prove that no one, especially not her mother, could bind or break her.

When Bea looked up and said, "You should change" in that imperious little voice, Ida thought if her daughter was going to speak up, she should speak up for the right reasons. Not to box Ida in. Make her conform. Ida's own mother would have backhanded her across the face for talking to her like that. Ida wondered if a good smacking would knock some sense into her children. They had no idea how to rebel.

By the time Sidney came into the kitchen, Ida had wiped up the counter and was cutting wedges from a grapefruit with a tiny serrated spoon. Sidney put his hands around her waist, and for a brief moment, she let her head rest against him.

"Morning, love." He kissed her cheek.

"Morning." She offered him a spoon of fruit that he slid into his mouth before pulling away with a swat to her behind.

"Is that all you're eating? You're getting too thin."

"That's the point." She popped a tiny wedge of grapefruit into her mouth. Her latest diet was a single grapefruit in the morning and a hard-boiled egg for lunch, which left her guilt-free to eat whatever she wanted for dinner. Measuring waists and thighs was a pastime of most Lexington women, and Ida had begun to feel a particular sense of satisfaction being the thinnest in the room. *See?* her figure said. *I can be just like the rest of you. I can be better.* The truth was, she liked the subtle feeling of hunger all day. It felt like being on the edge of something.

Sidney poured himself a cup of coffee, heaped a bowl of oatmeal from the pan, and sat down. "Morning, girls."

Bea scraped the last of her breakfast into a neat mound at the bottom of her bowl and said, "Morning, Daddy," while Dora, her legs swinging with all their might, tucked her chin to her chest in silence.

"Dora, say good morning to your father." Ida dropped into her chair with her grapefruit and coffee.

An obligatory smile pinched the corners of Dora's mouth, but she kept quiet. "Dora," Ida started in, but Sidney cut her off with a shake of his head and said good-naturedly, "A smile is worth a thousand words," while Dora looked to her sister for reassurance.

Dora did not speak until the age of three. Not a single babbling word. Unlike Bea, who ran around shouting every word she knew, Dora had looked at things with a silent inquisitiveness, refusing to name them even though Ida knew she understood. "What's this?" Ida would point to the flower, or truck, or swing in the picture book the pediatrician gave her to help Dora associate words with objects. Dora would stare at the images as if trying to make sense of how they fit into her particular world. Eventually she'd look up, smiling but stubbornly wordless, determined to keep some inner secret.

When Dora did start speaking it was in short, clear sentences without the slightest hesitation. Ida wanted to tell everyone, *See, I told you she understood.* But Dora only spoke those words to her mother or sister. Ida couldn't get so much as a "hello" out of her to their friends, which was an embarrassment, but not nearly as cutting as the fact that Dora wouldn't talk to her own father. She spoke around him, always directing herself to Ida or Bea.

Sidney shrugged it off, saying she'd come to it in time, convincing himself that it was his daughter's lack of confidence, not his lack of affection that was the problem.

Deep down he wondered if it was more than either of these things. Sometimes, when his daughter looked at him with her wide-open eyes, he'd see the depth of her perspicacity and think that this child's silence was merely a reflection of his own, that it was possible in some unearthly way she knew what he and Ida had done and was punishing them for it.

Over breakfast, both parents watched as Bea reached out and gave the back of her little sister's hand a small pat. The relief of this gesture rippled through Dora's body as she lifted her spoon and dug back into her oatmeal. Ida and Sidney looked at each other, then into their coffee cups. There was a sting in Sidney's chest and a hot pulse in Ida's. The tart grapefruit made her jaw tight. She wanted to touch her hand to Bea's shoulder and tell her what a good sister she was. Instead, Ida finished her breakfast in silence, wondering if her eldest daughter would always be burdened with the need to protect and translate the world for Dora.

And in that singular thought, Ida could feel how she'd carefully removed herself from the picture. In her mind, she saw an actual line around her body, like a cutout, an invisible, scissoring hand delicately, silently, extracting her from them.

3

THE DAY WAS FILLED with noise. Marching bands and screaming firetrucks, imitation guns, bang pops, sparklers, firecrackers, anything that exploded.

Ida did not change out of her yellow dress. Keeping it on was her quiet revolt. She disliked this particular American holiday. "Bloody Fourth of July," she'd say in her thickest English accent, making Sidney and the girls laugh, even though she meant it. She found it impossible to believe all Americans were this gung-ho and patriotic. An excuse for fireworks was one thing, but Lexington's all-out pageantry was idiotic: parades, costumes, reenactments on the famous Battle Green, respectable men gunning each other down in a field while corseted women screamed in mock horror. *I'm the enemy, you know,* Ida had wanted to tell them, watching the redcoats collapse, much too realistically, to their deaths. Not that she cared. What bothered her was that no sensible person thought to say, *Oh, right, how does it feel to watch us shoot your countrymen in the head?* Ludicrous, of course. Especially after she'd seen men shot in the head for real, but no one wanted to talk about that.

And this, she understood, was the real wedge between her and these women. They were the ones who had stayed home nursing their fantasies and fears of war while Ida had been in the thick of it. These women thought they'd suffered because they'd lost brothers and husbands and fiancés—or knew someone who had—because they'd held scrap drives and waited for letters and planted victory gardens.

But those things had not blackened their insides.

When Ida first arrived in Lexington, she was grateful to be enveloped into their faultless reality. No one discussed the most concealed places to hide, or what to do with dead bodies, or how best to clean a bloodstain. Instead, they sat on park benches with their children perched in prams, discussing how to properly clean baby bottles, where to buy the best formula, and how to get a decent night's sleep. Ida paid attention to the creams one should use for stretch marks and how to lay sliced cucumbers over puffy eyes. She had stretch marks and puffy eyes, and there were bottles to clean and diapers to change and formula to buy, so for a time, it all made sense.

When did that change? Ida wondered as she stood in Lulu Johnson's backyard in her big sunglasses with a gin martini in hand. Tiny American flags lined the walkway from the brick house to the groomed lawn, where round tables and folding chairs were arranged under a large white tent. Overhead, the sky was dove blue, cloudless, the sun hot. Ida wrapped a hand around the back of her neck. A horde of children ran past blowing noisemakers. A frozen lemonade can whizzed through the air—launched with a cherry bomb by the Titterton boys crouched behind the shrubbery.

Ida glanced at the food laid out in silver urns, hamburgers and hot dogs, corn on the cob, watermelon, chicken casserole, white fish in flaky puff pastry, bowls of strawberries and whipped cream and pound cake. She imagined piling a plate high and eating whatever she wanted in front of everyone. How pathetic that gorging herself had become the most dramatic thing she could do. She watched Tom Bowler gnaw on an ear of corn, butter dripping down his chin. He smiled at her, and Ida dutifully smiled back, moving to stand near her husband who was rolling up his sleeves in preparation for a game of bocce ball.

Warm and woozy from her cocktail, she watched Sidney hook his cuffs over his elbows with an inextricable longing. She wanted to run her hand over the fine hairs on his forearm, to find the line of muscle on the inside of his upper arm and sink her fingers into it. This sense of craving the thing she already had came over her more and more these days.

Sidney positioned himself behind the foul line, glanced over his shoulder, and said under his breath, "Buck up, old girl, the vultures are descending."

Ida turned as Suzie, Lulu, and Carol Ann reached her on a single swish of fabric, drinks in hand, foreheads perspiring. "This heat!" Lulu slid an arm around Ida, drawing her into the shade under the tent. "No need to moon over your own husband. It's bad manners in front of us gals who are sick to death of ours." Lulu was a tiny-figured bottle blonde who masked her plainness in red lipstick and thick fake lashes. The only truly interesting thing about her was her knowledge of plants. Her house was filled with them, and she could recite the Latin name of every variety.

Carol Ann, a fleshy, towering woman, sank into a chair, flapping a hand in the air. "I swear it's the humidity puffing me up and not all that pound cake you insist on having around." She glared at Lulu, who laughed and said, "It's for the boys, Carol Ann. They need bulking up. My Billy is as scrawny as they come."

"They'll grow, don't you worry. Then they'll eat you out of house and home." Carol Ann pressed her drink to her forehead. Beads of water dripped from the glass. Ida liked Carol Ann, her directness, her bolstered body and voice, the way she'd lean in and nudge Ida with an elbow or wink at her from across a room.

"If only we had a swimming pool." Lulu sighed.

"I thought you'd convinced Bert to put one in?" Carol Ann dropped her drink to the table, her forehead a dewy pink.

Suzie, decked out in cat-eye glasses with sparkling rhinestones, squeezed in between Ida and Lulu. "Lulu, love, you must save us from the dreaded local pool. How tremendously fun it would be to lounge around, just us gals, at our very own backyard swimming pool?"

Carol Ann tapped a long red fingernail on the table. "We'll have to lay off the Tom Collins so our children don't drown."

"We'll hire a lifeguard." Suzie sucked dramatically at her tiny straw.

"The Lepley's oldest son would do nicely," Carol Ann said. "Have you seen the arms on that man?"

"Man? He's nineteen." Suzie slapped her shoulder. "Don't be vulgar, Carol Ann."

"Bert says a pool is too expensive," Lulu said.

Carol Ann jutted her thumb at the gazebo Bert hired a carpenter to put up in May. "Since when has that stopped him?"

Ida listened, said nothing. She was already dreading the long summer months ahead of gathering towels and swimsuits and hats and hauling her children around trying to entertain them with school out.

Lulu glanced at her watch. "It's almost three, ladies. I'm sure the others are already waiting in the living room."

"Why did you schedule the LCCA meeting today?" Suzie grumbled, shaking the ice in her empty glass.

"Ellen insisted." Lulu stood up. "Apparently, she has something to show us that couldn't wait. She said she's going to start this summer's topic off with a bang."

This caught Ida's attention. "Ellen's leading the topic?" She tried not to sound hurt.

The LCCA—Literature, Culture, Cuisine, and Art—was their personal ladies club, formed a year ago by Lulu in an attempt to keep up to date on current affairs. Lulu was the only one of them who had gone to college, and she said she refused to let her brain turn to pudding just because she had to stay home raising four boys. Lulu had chosen the first topic, American literature, and they'd spent the fall discussing Ayn Rand, Ernest Hemingway, and Steinbeck. Culture went to Suzie, who, fittingly, opted for the culture of Hollywood, which meant watching the latest Betty Grable film and reading gossip magazines, admittedly fun, if not very intellectual. Then there was cuisine, led by Carol Ann, who purchased them each a copy of *Betty Crocker's Picture Cook Book* and instructed them in weekly recipes. The final topic, modern art, had been promised to Ida.

"Oh dear." Suzie bit the corner of her lip. "We did say Ida could lead the topic."

"I mean . . ." Lulu looked from Suzie to Carol Ann. "I didn't think anything was decided, and Ellen's so excited she's already bought a stack of books." She flicked a stray piece of grass off the table. "Although, I'm sure you'd be the better woman for the job, Ida, given your background and all."

Carol Ann stood up. "We'll put it to a vote."

"That will tick Ellen off," Suzie said, not sounding disappointed by the prospect.

Lulu frowned.

There was a tight feeling behind Ida's eyes. "It's fine," she said. "It's not a big deal."

"It is a big deal. We should have been voting all along." Carol Ann dragged Ida out from under the tent, saying that if they were going to be an official club, a vote was the only way to go.

Crossing the final stretch of lawn, their heels sinking into the soft grass, Lulu whispered to Ida, "I'll make sure Ellen knows the vote was Carol Ann's idea so she won't blame you."

Ida was sure Ellen would blame her anyway.

Entering the living room through the patio doors, Ida saw Eula and Lottie, twin sisters, perched side by side on the enormous curved sofa. Fran, the quietest of the group, was wilted in a leather chair, pressing a napkin to her forehead. Ellen stood by the window, her hair slightly unkempt, her skirt and blouse just a touch wrinkled. Ellen was always a little less than put together, which people thought was odd given how much money she had, as if wealth and perfection were synonymous.

"Oh, goodie," Ellen cried as they entered. Her use of the words *goodie* and *golly* drove Ida mad. Everything about Ellen drove Ida mad. Mostly this was due to the fact that Ellen had been Sidney's fiancée when he left for the war. When he came home married to Ida, Ellen refused to acknowledge her existence, managing, whenever they found themselves at a neighborhood gathering, to flick her eyes upward and pinch her mouth shut. She ignored Ida so blatantly that even Sidney's father commented on it, and he noticed very little when it came to anyone but himself. To Sidney, Ellen was sugar sweet, laying her hand on his forearm and pressing her chest up against him, bursting into airy laughs as if they had some endless joke between them. Everyone gossiped. Ida swore it didn't bother her, but it did. Ellen's past with Sidney made her prickle with envy.

Arranging herself on the sofa next to Suzie, Ida noticed the book on the side table, *Symbolic Realism in American Painting 1930–1940*. Next to it was a vase of tiny pink roses interspersed with sprigs of lavender.

The scent of lavender made Ida queasy. A clawed feeling landed in her chest, and she turned her head away, trying to put the book and the lavender out of her mind.

Lulu burst in with a tray of glasses and set it on the coffee table. Her lipstick was worn at the center, the edges pencil thin. "Those waiters lounging outside are absolutely useless. I should never have given Iona the day off. She's Irish. What does she need the Fourth of July off for?"

Ida was the only one in the room who didn't have hired help. When Dora was born, Sidney's mother, Isabelle Whipple, an efficient, no-nonsense woman, had tried to convince Ida that she'd never manage without a girl around. Ida had managed just fine. Although it would make hosting less stressful, she thought, watching Lulu effortlessly pour iced tea into tall glasses, drop in a slice of lemon and a cube of sugar, and pass them out with a platter of shortbread cookies. The arrangement of glasses alone made Ida anxious, not to mention food and table settings. In Paris, there had been a haphazardness to the parties she attended, the guests too impassioned and drunk and caught up in themselves to notice a missing slice of lemon or an improperly placed utensil. In Lexington, a woman's entire reputation came down to the perfection of her hosting. She must have gleaming floors, flowers on the table, cold cocktails at the ready. She must empty ashtrays, never criticize her husband, and wear a perfect outfit that did not outshine her guests'. It was exhausting.

Carol Ann was waving a small stack of paper in the air. "Okay, ladies, we've decided to put this year's topic leader to a vote. Any objections?" Lulu glanced apologetically at Ellen, who opened her mouth, then shut it as Carol Ann barreled on. "The votes will be anonymous. Lulu, how do you want to do the nominations?"

Lulu said, "Is anyone interested in leading besides Ida and Ellen?"

Lottie, a square-jawed woman with dark eyes and bushy brows, said, "Does it have to be modern art? It's so unrelatable. I was hoping we could do baroque." She'd only joined the club because her twin sister had, and she always found something to complain about.

"Since the group was organized to keep up on current topics, yes," Carol Ann said, handing out the ballots and pencils.

Heat beat at the bay windows. A trickle of sweat dripped down Ida's stomach. She touched a hand to her abdomen, hoping a wet stain wasn't appearing across her middle. She hadn't anticipated this blatant competition. It felt particularly unfair that they were sitting in Lulu's living room, like a home-team advantage. Ellen and Lulu had been best friends since high school. Ida didn't stand a chance. *Why do I even care?* she wondered, looking around at the women dressed in their patriotic best. Engaging in their social games was part torture, part desire. These women bored Ida to tears, and yet she desperately wanted their approval.

Suzie pushed her glasses up her nose. "This isn't very formal. Shouldn't we at least say what qualifies each candidate?"

Fran perked up. "That seems like a good idea."

"You go first then, Fran." Carol Ann dropped onto the sofa, wanting it over and done with.

The tip of Fran's nose turned red. "Well," she mumbled. "I mean, Ellen's always talking about art, and she visits museums in New York with Allen an awful lot. Don't you, Ellen?"

"I do, monthly." Ellen smiled with the patience of someone who doesn't believe themselves capable of losing at anything.

Eula said, "Ellen's been boring us with her knowledge of art since we've known her. She was talking about abstract expressionism before any of us had even heard of such a thing."

"I still don't know what it is." Lottie laughed.

As hard as Ida tried not to, she couldn't help thinking about the bold, stunning woman who taught her everything she knew about art, the woman who slid art books from shelves and drew Ida into the lemon scent of her skin as she explained the meaning behind the work, the intention, the rebellion of form.

"Ida? Did you hear me?" Suzie touched Ida's arm. Everyone was looking at her.

"Sorry, no." Ida reached for her iced tea, steadying herself with the cold glass.

"Fran was asking what it was you did with art. None of us could remember."

"I was an assistant for an art collector."

"Oh?" Ellen said, spite beneath her sweet tone. "Who?"

Ida looked straight at her. "Peggy Guggenheim. She has a gallery in New York. Maybe you've been to it?"

Ellen shrugged. "I've never heard of her."

Suzie looked down at her slip of paper. Fran fiddled with her hair. No one asked Ida to elaborate.

"Can we vote already?" Carol Ann said. "I'm going to need something stronger than iced tea soon."

"One last thing," Suzie insisted. She had been class president. A cheerleader. "Tell us, Ellen and Ida, in one sentence, what art means to you."

"Good God, Suzie." Carol Ann slumped forward in a dramatic gesture of boredom.

Ellen leapt in, her voice low and theatrical, "Art is desire, pain, dreams, it is the culmination of a great mind into a materialized vision. It is all the things we cannot say out loud."

"Ida?" Suzie's glinting glasses turned toward her.

Ida looked around the room. "Art is the way out. It's an escape," she said, even though no one would understand her meaning.

Cupping the slips of paper in their palms, the women wrote out their votes. Lulu collected them, standing in front of the fireplace as she ceremoniously called out the names, "Ellen, Ida, Ellen, Ellen, Ellen, Ellen."

And there you had it. Home-team advantage. Ida plastered a sportsmanly smile on her face. There was no way in hell she was going to sit through a summer-long discussion on modern art led by Ellen Franzen.

Ellen didn't bother thanking her dedicated friends. Flaring her hands, she marched forward with her agenda. "Now that that silly business is out of the way, I'm simply bursting to show you what Allen bought at a gallery in the East Village. I was going to have you all over for a proper viewing, but I couldn't wait." She stepped aside, her wide skirt swishing to reveal the brown backing paper of her framed art piece. Breathless, she said, "It's an original."

"An original what?" Ida couldn't help herself. A vein pulsed in her neck. What she wanted to say was *Piss off, Ellen.* She'd wanted to say it since the first day she watched Ellen take Sidney's arm and croon "I'll never forgive you for breaking my heart" while Ida stood right there watching. Ida wondered what would happen if she told Ellen to piss off in front of these stiff women. Gasps? Shocked silence? God, how she wanted to crack their glazed surfaces.

Ellen enunciated her words as if speaking to a child. "It's an original Man Ray."

Ida's mouth went bone dry. Next to her, Suzie twirled her pencil like a baton and whistled. "Well, well."

Ellen raised her hands in mock humility. "I know! Allen won't be buying me another gift for years."

Eula reached for her second cookie and said, "What did Allen pay for it?" This made her twin, Lottie, swat her leg and hiss at her to be quiet.

Carol Ann said, "Who's Man Ray?"

"I've never heard of him either," said Lulu.

Ellen, patient and teacherly, said, "Man Ray is one of the leading figures in the Surrealist art movement."

Ida gulped down her drink, the sweet, cold liquid tamping the heat in her chest. To sit here and be shown an original work of Man Ray's was like being shoved off a mountain she'd spent the last eight years climbing up. It would all come roaring back—London, Paris, the war—and when it did, Ida's life in this town would be unbearable. The fact that it was Ellen doing the shoving made it all the more insufferable. Ida looked out the window, wondering what excuse she could give to get up and leave, but Ellen was already turning the frame around, the sleeves of her blouse riding up as she held the picture aloft.

Here were the gasps. Shocked silence. Stunned stares.

It was a black-and-white photograph of two naked women, their bodies pressed together in a partial embrace, shoulders angled outward, breasts touching. Alabaster skin. Dark curly hair. The women's faces masked. The masks painted with vines. Stalks ran up noses. Leaves jutted over cheeks. Petals outlined dark, wide-open eyes. Sealed-shut mouths.

The heat in Ida's chest burst as if a pot had boiled over. She stood up so fast the room went black.

Startled, Carol Ann rose with her. "Are you all right? You're red as a lobster."

Ida backed away. She bumped into the coffee table and set the glasses tingling. "I'm tremendously hot," she gasped, moving past knees and skirts to the door.

Outside, the sun exploded against her eyes and the world was bathed in a haze of light and color. Ida stood on the patio steps, trying to adjust her mind to the reality of what she'd seen. How that buried photograph had made its way out of France, out of the war, and into the hands of Ellen Franzen in Lexington, Massachusetts, was impossible.

And yet, here it was.

4

SIDNEY WAS RATTLED BY the stunned look he saw on his wife's face as she came down Lulu's back steps. He dropped his bocce ball and sprinted over, grabbing her hand as if she was in physical danger. "What's wrong?" he asked, old anxieties swelling to the surface.

Ida's face was flushed, her hair wild in the humidity. "Nothing. It's the heat." She gave a laugh, but it came out frenzied. Pushing him backward down the steps, she said, "Another martini will cool me off."

Across the lawn, Sidney's bocce ball opponent was waving him over. Sidney threw up his hands in a gesture of defeat. "You win!" He kept to his wife's side as she made her way to the cocktail table. He filled a tumbler with gin and ice, gave it a vigorous shake, and strained it into two glasses.

"All right, what's going on?" He stabbed an onion with a toothpick and handed the drink to Ida. "That you think you can hide anything from me at this point is ridiculous."

She took a sip, shifting her gaze around the yard. The heat in her face had settled into a soft pink, but the displaced look was still in her eyes—eyes just like Dora's, brown and flecked with gold. "If you stop speaking to me like our daughter, I won't be able to bear it," Sidney said.

"Stop?" Ida swirled her onion in the glass. "She never started." Her tone was void of the usual sympathy she showed him on the subject. "Do you think," she said, in a conspiratorial whisper, "that we're being punished? Or haunted?" Her eyes got very big. Heat blotches broke out on her chest. "I don't mean the memories, I mean literally. Arlette is literally haunting us, Sidney."

This was not what he'd expected, and he had no patience for it. "Goddamn it, Ida." He didn't want to be angry, but he was fed up. They'd worked so hard to put this to rest. They'd talk it out, ignore it, convince themselves they'd moved on, then talk it out all over again. Around and around they went, and always back to the same thing. "Why don't you get something to eat?" he suggested. "No one can sustain themselves on gin and grapefruit."

"I don't want to eat." Her eyes bore down on him.

"Your memories are the only thing haunting you, Ida."

She shook her head. "It's more than that."

"Can we not talk about this right now? It's a holiday."

"Does your guilt take a holiday?"

Sidney snatched up his drink, wishing he hadn't forfeited his game of bocce ball. Keeping his voice low, he said, "I'll eat for the two of us" and beelined it for the food table with a cavernous feeling in his gut.

Both considered stalking angrily home, but people would gossip, the girls would complain, Sidney's parents would ask questions. So they stayed, mingling and drinking and ignoring each other.

Watching Ida across the lawn, Sidney wondered if he'd overestimated her ability to move on. He thought it would be enough to leave France, to start a family, keep their heads up and their eyes on the future. He'd convinced himself they could manage a life of integrity as long as they remained unwaveringly honest with each other. He'd made a joke of it, coming home from work, asking for all the wives' gossip. In turn, she'd demand he spill every lewd detail of his coworkers' debauchery at the woolen mill—men who were very clear on what information women were privy to and what they were not. "Dish it, and we'll compare notes," Ida would say, leaning close to him, her breath warm on his lips, her eyes bright with the fun of hearing how Bob Duncan mysteriously moved away after getting his secretary pregnant, or how Peter Schneider hired another extraordinarily good-looking man, which raised suspicions, and how Patricia Olive was given an actual sales job and the men who once called her voluptuous now called her fat. They said if women were going to take over their jobs, the least they could do was look good in a skirt. Ida said men were pigs. "Except you, my love"—hand under his shirt—"but if you start sleeping with your secretary, I'll have to start sleeping with the mailman, or the lifeguard at the local pool, who is significantly better looking," which they agreed would get messy.

In reality, neither had eyes for anyone else.

It wasn't love at first sight. Theirs was a union of impossible loneliness. It was France. They were in hiding. Naturally, they found each other. It was not until their solitude broke that Sidney realized how hard he'd fallen for Ida. When he tried to pull away—resisting the urge to wrap her bird-boned hand in his or gather her into his chest—his sense of loss was shattering.

Love, then, was the feeling that you were losing your own soul. If it weakened a man to give a woman all that power, he was weakened. That Ida loved him back still felt like the luckiest thing that had ever happened to him. And she did. She told him every day.

And yet something had shifted. He tried to pinpoint it as he dug into his strawberry shortcake, listening to Ida's disingenuous laughter a few feet away. It was the way she smoked her cigarettes now, flicking the ash wherever she wanted, in the dust that collected in the corners of their living room and the laundry she'd forget to iron. In the way she'd remove her hand from his, subtle, slow, but a noticeable pulling away. Last week he'd found a row of moths and a single butterfly lined up on the windowsill, perfectly preserved, their powdered wings intact. He knew his wife, not his children, had done it. There was precision in the arrangement of those tiny bodies, antennas pointed upward. Their delicate beauty, how deceptively ready for flight they looked, disturbed Sidney. He'd thought about those moths for days, careful not to bring them up with Ida. Their unwavering honesty with each other didn't necessarily include confronting her on a meticulous arrangement of insects, so he wasn't breaking any rules.

The truth was, he didn't want to know. His wife's unrest, her general agitation, terrified him. If not for Ida, he wasn't sure how he'd get through the day. Walking through the door, seeing her at some task, straightening a couch pillow or pulling up her stockings, her dark hair springing over her shoulders, her cheeks flushed, he'd think that she was the only thing that made sense in the tedium of his daily life.

God, how he loved her. He had returned to his hometown for her, for the very purpose of starting over. Why, then, did he feel like he wanted to go back, to cling to their beginning, to have everything at stake again?

At least, that's what he thought he wanted. Until suddenly, everything was.

5

THE HEAT INCREASED AS the July day moved toward dusk. Sweat persisted on brows and indiscreetly stained the underarms of chiffon dresses and oxford shirts, the air weighty with humidity. The party became noisier, voices louder, the children rambunctious. Bang pops whizzed with a whine like a distant air raid. Between the alcohol and the heat and the irrational thoughts swirling around in Ida's head, nothing felt real. A pretend day in her pretend life. She plastered on a smile and flirted with Tom Bowler to make Sidney jealous, which it did.

By the time the sun dipped behind the trees, Ida was properly drunk. She made a show of being overly friendly to Ellen, talking at length with her about her new piece of artwork and asking Lulu when the next LCCA meeting was being held, saying, loud enough for Sidney to hear, that she was "simply dying to get started on their new topic," which he knew from her exaggerated tone was a lie.

After a while, their eyes met across the lawn. Sidney mouthed, *I'm sorry*. Ida lifted her glass in a cheers motion, swigged back her drink and mouthed, *Me too*. Swaying over to him, she drew a seductive finger up his arm, standing on her tiptoes to propose, in his ear, that they find an empty room to sneak off to. Sidney wrapped his hand around her waist, the idea tempting but nerve-racking with his parents seated under the tent eating cake and his daughters running past with sparklers in their hands.

"I'll make it up to you tonight," he whispered.

Ida pulled away, muttering "Old man," which he absolutely felt like in that moment. There was a time when he would have snuck off with her anywhere, no matter who was nearby. When had he gotten so stodgy?

"Don't be like that." He reached for her, but she swatted his hand away and left him standing alone in the oppressive heat.

Later that night, sitting on a blanket in the grass, Ida let him draw her into his chest as they watched the fireworks explode. The noise made Sidney edgy, the closeness of all these people piled on picnic blankets. At their feet, Dora perched on her knees with her head tilted up, a small gasp escaping each time a boom went off. Bea lay flat on her back, smiling up at the bright greens and blues and reds as they sparked and burned and fell around them.

Ida did not speak a word on the walk home.

While she tucked the girls into bed, Sidney showered, brushed his teeth, and put on his pajama bottoms, making a point to leave his shirt off even though he was sure there'd be no passionate groping of each other.

Ida came into the bathroom, wriggling her dress down over her hips and shooing him out so she could wash up. He climbed into bed, wondering if she was still angry with him for his lack of adventure earlier. He decided that if she came out of the bathroom with cold cream under her eyes and her hair in curlers, she was holding a grudge. If, however, she emerged with her face scrubbed clean and her hair loose, there was a chance he'd been forgiven.

It was the latter, which gave Sidney a hopeful pulse in his groin until Ida clicked off the light and dropped heavily onto her pillow with her back to him.

He moved closer, putting his arm around her and pressing his palm to the flat of her stomach. "Are you still angry with me?"

She rolled onto her back. "I'm not angry."

"What, then?" He touched his thumb to her lip, running it along her Cupid's bow. The room was dark but he could still make out the lines of her face.

"I'm sad." She latched her hand around his neck, her grip so tight her fingers dug into his skin.

For a long time, he had believed he could take this sadness from her. "I know," he said.

She gave a small sob and found his mouth with hers.

His hand slid down her thigh, and she pulled on his neck as she wriggled out of her slip, their bodies sticky in the heat. Sidney licked the salty skin between her breasts and navel, touching her gently, and then harder as she sighed and opened her legs to him. She was wet and warm and determined. Ida had always known exactly what she liked.

He wished he could remember falling asleep beside her, but after Ida orgasmed, he'd come so quickly he dropped into a soporific stupor he didn't wake up from until his alarm went off at six a.m., at which point he slammed his hand on the buzzer, pulled a pillow over his head, and promptly fell back asleep.

When he woke again, the room was bright and hot. Untangling his legs from the twisted sheet, he hauled himself into a sitting position, feeling hungover. Ida's side of the bed was empty, but she always woke earlier than he. Sidney envied morning people, the sort who went for jogs at four a.m. or wrote something at the inspirational hour of dawn or, like his wife, sat with a hot drink in a silent house, watching the shadows slide into light.

Ida had never slept properly, at least not as long as Sidney had known her. There was a brief time before children when she had been content to stay wrapped in the covers with him, but then Bea came into their lives, crying at all hours, and by the time she was sleeping through the night, Dora had arrived with her own wail that continued for years, her high-pitched screams so piercing Sidney would wake with his heart thrumming, Ida already out of bed, telling him to go back to sleep. She was so tense at night, she said getting up at five in the morning was a relief. Sidney, on the other hand, could sleep until ten a.m. if the day allowed for it. He'd practically done that now, he noted, glancing at the clock before heading to the bathroom.

By the time he'd showered and made it to the kitchen, breakfast had been cleared and the coffee pot on the stove was cold. He popped open the lid and peered inside. Ida hadn't even made coffee, from the looks of it.

"Ida?" He walked into the living room. Dora lay on her stomach, reading a book. Bea knelt at the coffee table, cutting out paper dolls.

"Where's your mother?" he asked. Bea shrugged and kept snipping. Dora didn't even look up.

Sidney poked his head into the dining room. The glass doors of the cupboard reflected squares of sunlight onto the long empty table. "Ida?" He knocked on the downstairs bathroom door. Nothing. Looping back to the kitchen, he looked out the window into the backyard, noting that the hydrangeas needed trimming. At the front of the house, he stood in the open doorway and took in the fact that their car was still in the driveway. Ida had never owned a car before moving here, and she rarely drove it, so that didn't mean much. Across the street, Mrs. Helmsley was deadheading her roses. She waved. Sidney waved back and picked up the newspaper that had been tossed on the front step. It was Saturday. Most likely Ida had walked into town for pastries.

It was eleven fifteen when Bea came into the kitchen and declared that she hadn't eaten any breakfast. Sidney pulled his eyes away from the newspaper, his unease notching up. "Your mother didn't make you breakfast?"

"No."

"Did you see her at all this morning?"

"No."

"What time did you get out of bed?"

Bea twisted a strand of pale blonde hair around her finger. "I don't know."

Sidney set down the paper. "Well, it's practically lunchtime now."

"Can we have lunch, then?"

Sidney had had nothing himself, other than a weak cup of coffee. "I'd say we'd better," he said, going to the refrigerator, only to realize that he had no idea what his children ate for lunch, which struck him as absurd, that he didn't know a simple thing like that.

"Where is Mommy?" Bea glanced around, as if Ida might pop out from behind the door.

"She went to the bakery," Sidney said, overly confident. "What would you like for lunch?"

"Peanut butter and banana." Bea opened the cupboard and stood on tiptoe to reach the jar of peanut butter. She set it on the counter, watching her dad carefully. "You don't know how to do it, do you?" she said, with the honesty of a child noticing a truthful thing.

"Don't be ridiculous." Sidney picked up the jar. "How hard can banana and peanut butter be?"

Bea watched as he cut the banana lengthwise and spread a messy strip of peanut butter on top. "Mommy cuts it into little circles with a dab of peanut butter and a raisin on each. It's much neater that way, but it's your first try." She took her plate to the table and called, "Dora, lunch!"

Rummaging in the cupboard, Sidney found a box of raisins, dropped it on the table, and said, "You're old enough to make it yourself."

Dora darted in from the living room, practically smashing into Sidney's legs before skirting around him to her seat.

Just then, the doorbell rang. All three of them looked at each other.

It was when Sidney opened the door that he launched into full-blown panic. A policeman stood in front of him, legs parted, hands at his sides. Sidney's heart seized. Ida was dead. This man had come to tell him that his wife was dead. He stood with the sun on his face, the heat curling like a cobra around the neck of the day as he watched the policeman take off his hat and tuck it under one arm. The officer's lips were dashes, his eyes squinty, cheeks flat.

"Sorry to bother you, sir," he said. "But there's been a burglary, and we're asking if anyone heard or saw anything suspicious last night or early this morning."

Sidney's breath released in a small gasp. "No," he said, an absurd smile crossing his face.

"Something funny, sir?" The officer's lips tightened.

"No, no, sorry." Sidney shook his head. "I didn't see anything suspicious."

The officer questioned him anyway, jotting Sidney's answers down on a pad of paper. Date of birth. Profession. Where did he work? Who did he live with? Was he at the Johnsons' party on 223 MacDougal Road yesterday?

The policeman's authoritative attitude rubbed Sidney the wrong way. He couldn't help noticing how similar the man's uniform was to a Nazi's, right down to the high boots, belt, and narrow strap passing over his right shoulder. When the officer asked Sidney what he was doing at the Johnsons' party, Sidney said, "You can't work that one out for yourself? It was the Fourth of July."

The officer's eyes shot up. "I don't appreciate your tone, sir."

"I don't appreciate yours." It was the man's self-righteous assumption of power that angered Sidney, the control he wielded, making Sidney stand in the bright sun answering stupid questions.

"I'm just doing my job, sir," the officer said.

"Why, exactly, are you questioning me?" Sidney had better things to worry about than a petty burglary. He glanced down the street, wondering if he should drive into town to look for Ida.

"We're questioning everyone who was at the Johnsons' party yesterday. A piece of artwork was stolen from . . ." The officer flipped through his notebook. "Allen and Ellen Franzen."

Distracted, Sidney said, "If the Franzens were burgled, why are you questioning people who were at the Johnsons'?"

"Mrs. Franzen said she showed the artwork at the party. She claims no one else knew she had it. Did you hear anyone talking about it?"

"No." A faint memory of Ida talking to Ellen about a Surrealist photograph was making its way into his mind. "Was it worth a lot?"

"A fair amount." The officer raised his eyebrows. "But not worth half as much as the other valuables in the house. Mrs. Franzen's jewelry, for one, or the crystal sitting right there in the dining room cupboard. None of that stuff was touched."

Sidney remembered the look on his wife's face as she came down the patio steps, her mention of Arlette, and how Ida had thrown her voice so he would overhear her enthusiastic remarks to Ellen about the artwork she'd purchased. Almost not daring to ask, he said, "Who was the artist?"

"Some guy named Man Ray. I've never heard of him. Did you see the piece?"

A tight, breathless feeling came over Sidney. He unbuttoned the top button of his shirt.

"No. No, I did not."

The officer smirked. "It was a photograph of nude women, apparently."

"I see."

"Is your wife home, Mr. Whipple?"

"No."

"When do you expect her back?"

"She's gone to her mother's in Connecticut." This was an absurd lie. Ida didn't have a single relative in Connecticut. Her mother lived in England, if she was even still alive, and Ida hadn't spoken to her since before the war.

"How long will she be gone?"

"A week." Sidney's face went red. He was a rotten liar.

"All on your own? Behave yourself, now." The officer cracked a smile, and Sidney responded with a foolish salute.

"Army man?" the officer said, pleased.

"Air Force. You?"

"Marine. Private first class, 289th Regiment."

"Battle of the Bulge," Sidney acknowledged, the war haunting him from all angles, it seemed.

The officer nodded, and both men fell silent, neither willing to embark on the topic of that bloody battle.

After a minute, the officer said, "If your wife has any information, have her call the station. She can ask for Officer Gifford. I appreciate your time."

"No problem," Sidney managed, standing on the step, unable to move as he watched the officer get in his car and drive away.

He now understood the stunned look on his wife's face at the party and her sudden need to talk about Arlette. He had never seen an original Man Ray, but he knew from the stories Ida told him that Arlette had been one of the artist's many muses. It was uncanny that a photograph of her would end up here, but not unimaginable.

What was unimaginable was that Ida had stolen it. And yet Sidney knew that that was precisely what she had done.

6

WHAT SIDNEY DID NOT know was that the other woman in the photograph, baring her breasts, was Ida.

After making love to her husband, she lay listening to the pop of distant firecrackers, recalling how easily she'd shed her clothes in front of the camera that day, how risqué and electrifying it had been. Seeing the photograph on Ellen's wall split her reality. There was that world, and then there was this one. They couldn't coexist. It was impossible. And yet there was her pearly skin in black and white next to Arlette's, their masked faces and naked torsos on display for everyone to see in Lulu Johnson's living room.

A breeze came through their bedroom window and cooled the heat on Ida's skin. Sidney's body was sweaty against hers. She took in the shape of him under the sheet, the width of his back and the rise of his buttocks, his leg bent over hers, heavy and uncomfortable. "I love you," he'd murmured before dropping off to sleep, and Ida had said, "I love you too" with a stab in her heart. She had to get up, and yet she didn't want to move. She wanted Sidney to keep her pinned exactly where she was for a little while longer.

She closed her eyes and ran her fingers through his hair. He wore it clipped short now, but she remembered how it had curled over his forehead and hung down his neck in France. How his face was always scruffy without any sharp razors. It was all coming back, the musty library, the velvet chairs and coarse rugs, the taste of rabbit and boiled carrots, her numb fingertips, the scratch of wool, the endless winters and undeserving springs, the warmth a trick, the peaches sweet and forgiving.

She thought of the first time Sidney made love to her under the bright sun, hurried, the sweat drying on their skin. And the second time, measured and purposeful, the evening washing them in shadow. On her plush bed in Lexington, Ida felt the prickle of a Persian rug against her back and heard the groans of the floorboards. There was Arlette bending over a trunk of clothes, the click of a key in a lock, the sound of a violin, the crack of a gun. There was the name, *Anna,* shouted in desperation. Spit in the air, white limbs, bare breasts. Knees to stone. A bee hovering. An empty pile of clothes.

For the first time, Ida closed her eyes and let herself remember all of it.

PART TWO

DENIAL

1938–1940

7

IDA WAS, SHE BELIEVED, a person who could sense danger. She learned this from her father and brothers, the men in her life. She had no memory of her brothers as children. She knew them only by their deep voices, thick thighs, and wide chests, by the scent of manure and sweat and barley they carried in from the barn. Her family lived on the outskirts of Petersfield, England. Her brothers were hardworking, obedient boys who Ida understood didn't necessarily want to hurt her, but were forced, at times, to teach her a lesson. They were the ones who taught her to swoop and dive under a swinging hand or a hard object, to be quick and clever and guarded.

Ida was not well behaved. She was precocious and loud and given to fits of anger when she was not taken seriously, which was often because she was the youngest, and a girl.

When she thought of her father, she thought of the slick sound of a belt sliding through pant loops, of the heavy sigh he gave right before the strap came down, and the tired way his shoulders dropped after a lashing, as if he'd beaten something out of himself too. She remembered how he, unlike her brothers, smelled of freshly laundered clothes, of soap, and a faint hint of tobacco. Mostly, she remembered the deep blue of his eyes, and how she learned to look straight into them and tell a bold lie.

She lied to her mother as well, a woman equally as dangerous as her father, just less obvious about it. Words were her mother's weapon, daggers she aimed straight at the bull's-eye of Ida's heart. As a child, Ida would stand stock-still as those sharp points of anger flew from her mother's mouth, hitting their mark every time. Her mother was quite skilled at it. There was never any preamble. She'd hurl the insults with deft precision under the strangest circumstances. They'd be walking home from church and she'd tell Ida she was daft, an idiot. "Why do you walk like that? What's wrong with you?" Ida would think, *Like what?* wondering what *was* wrong with her. She eventually realized she was doing the very thing her mother wanted: questioning her own worth, her decency, against her mother's.

Beatings were easier for Ida to understand. She was being punished because she talked back. She had not done her chores. She had spit on her brother's shoe or thrown dirt at the barn door. Whereas her mother's eruptions were abrupt and seemingly unprompted. It didn't matter what Ida did or didn't do, her mother always found a way to ridicule her. *Why be good?* Ida thought. Why strive for obedience when it didn't work anyway?

Instead, she armored herself, growing tense and steely so that by the time she was eighteen years old, her mother's scorn pinged off of her with empty, hollow thuds.

Most of the time.

Like all imperfect things, there were chinks in Ida's armor—weaknesses, vulnerabilities.

Perhaps that's why, when she glimpsed a world outside of her own, she sacrificed everything to grasp it.

IT WAS IMPOSSIBLE to imagine what would come from that chance meeting on a July morning in 1938, when Ida's mother asked her to pick up buttons for her father's coat. After a tedious day of work at the hat shop, the errand put Ida walking past a green pickup truck at the precise moment someone called out, "Excuse me. You, you there."

A woman stood behind the truck with her foot propped awkwardly on the bumper balancing a large box on one knee. "Help me with this, would you?" she said, her accent thick and French.

"Me?" Ida glanced over her shoulder.

"Yes, you, if you'd be so kind." The woman's face was flushed with effort. "Take the other side."

A bulky, squat man angling a large blanketed object through the double doors of a nearby building shouted, "Hold your horses, Arlette. What's the bloody hurry?"

"Don't listen to him." The woman edged the box farther out. "Just try not to drop it or I'll have that brute to contend with."

It seemed Ida had no choice but to step off the sidewalk, wedge her hands under the box, and help the woman slide it from the back of the truck. The weight of it made the cut on the inside of Ida's arm pulse. It wasn't a deep cut. She'd made sure of that when she grazed her father's razor over her skin earlier that morning. She had no desire to ruin her arm. As disturbed as it sounded, she felt compelled to memorialize the day in some private, albeit painful, way. It was exactly one year since she'd been forced to decline her acceptance into the Royal Academy of Music. On that day, she had marked the occasion with a similar notch. They were not self-pitying mutilations. They were reminders of her resilience and determination. Second year. Second notch.

In the doorway of the building, the man nudged Ida out of the way and carried the box to the back of the room where he and the woman eased it to the floor.

"*Merde*, those sculptures are heavy," the woman groaned.

The man wiped his brow with his sleeve. The room was muggy and airless. "Next time, leave the task to me," he said with a hearty smack to the woman's behind.

"Beastly!" She straightened with a cry, shaking her head as he exited the room. "Pay no attention to him. Men are savages when they want to be. Of course, we women can be too." She came toward Ida with a hand extended. "Arlette Lellouche."

Arlette was stunning, petite, and full figured with shiny, dark hair that curled around her almond-shaped face: chin sharp, cheeks round, skin clear as cream. She wore a white blouse tucked into blue-velvet trousers—later, Ida learned these were workman's trousers found in the markets of Toulan, but Arlette made everything look expensive. A box purse was slung around her neck, and the strap crossed between her breasts.

"Ida Davies." Ida shook Arlette's gloved hand, the leather kitten soft.

"Nice to meet you, Ida. You're a sport to come to a complete stranger's rescue."

"Happy to help." Ida looked around at the boxes and crates and large covered objects. "What is all of this?"

"Artwork. After Germany's invasion of Czechoslovakia, my boss decided it would be prudent to get her valuables out of London before a war breaks out."

Ida was about to ask what they planned to do with the artwork in Petersfield when there was the blast of a car horn from outside. Arlette squeezed Ida's arm, her grip startling. "That's my boss now. She's absolutely detestable and fabulous," she said, and dashed out the door, dragging Ida with her.

A shiny blue car with bright red hubcaps was pulling up to the curb. The engine rattled to a stop, and a woman got out wearing enormous sunglasses and a hat pitched so steeply on the side of her head it grazed one shoulder. She stepped onto the sidewalk, her shoes bone pale, the lizard trim like an actual reptile curled around her toes. Clamping a white-gloved hand to Arlette's shoulder, the woman kissed her cheek and said, in a crisp American accent, "Nothing's damaged, is it?"

"I am." Arlette wriggled from her grasp. "I can't believe you made me ride with those two." She indicated the man who'd taken the box from Ida and another who was hoisting up a framed canvas.

"I needed someone to keep an eye on things." The woman plucked off her gloves and moved toward the workers. "Edmond, watch what you're doing. Don't press there! Hold the edge. You'll bust a hand through the canvas. I'm not paying you to destroy my art, you big oaf."

It was disarming watching this refined woman command these stern, muscular men. In Ida's world, the men did the commanding.

Ida turned to go, and Arlette sprinted up behind her. "Wait. You mustn't leave without a proper thank-you. Peggy!" She called down the street, "I'm inviting Ida for drinks at Yew Tree Cottage to thank her for helping me."

"Fine, fine." Peggy moved across the sidewalk, flapping her arms. "Careful of the doorframe!"

"It's decided. You're coming to Peggy's for an apéritif." Arlette took Ida's arm as if she intended to walk her there that instant.

Unsure why she was being invited anywhere by this stranger who kept touching her, Ida said, "That's kind of you, but I really didn't do anything, and I'm afraid I have to get home."

"You did everything!" Arlette opened the passenger door of the car. "I would have dropped that box, the sculptures would have shattered, and Peggy would have fired me, so you've saved my job." She leaned in, her velvet pants stretched tight across her bottom as she rummaged through the glove compartment. "Regardless, I want you to come. I'm always the youngest at these things. Peggy's ancient—don't tell her I said that—and her and her friends still drink themselves senseless and all sleep with each other as if they were twenty years old. I *am* twenty years old, and I never drink more than I can handle, and I haven't gone to bed with a single one of them. Don't get me wrong, I will, I just haven't found anyone interesting enough yet."

Ida stood speechless. Here was this complete stranger—gorgeous, worldly—speaking of sleeping with people and inviting Ida for apéritifs. Ida didn't even know what an apéritif was. What's more, she'd never heard sex mentioned in any conversation, *ever*.

Arlette turned, her blouse fluttering in the breeze, and handed Ida a cream-colored card with the name *Peggy Guggenheim* swirled in green across it. "It's Peggy's, obviously. I move around so much it's useless to have my own made. You're to come whenever you can. I'm desperate for company."

That was all it took. A stranger on the street and a cream-colored visiting card, and Ida's compact world sprang open.

8

IDA GOT AN EARFUL when she arrived home without the requested buttons, which she'd completely forgotten about. Her mother was browning onions at the stove, her apron yanked tight across her middle. She had been thin once but was hefty now, her face round and beginning to droop. "I can't count on you for the simplest task. Is there cotton between your ears? I don't know why I bother. Do you listen to anything I say?" Her mother looked up from the pan. "Your father's meeting a new client at the Worthing Inn tomorrow, and his good jacket is missing three buttons. What do you expect him to do now? You'll have him to reckon with when I tell him it's your fault he has to wear his old jacket."

Shame spread through Ida. She hated that she was a burden and a necessity. She hated this house, the stink of cheese curing in the pantry, the drab shutters, the creaky floorboards, the endless banging of her brothers' boots up and down the stairs, her father's gruff laughter and her mother's endless rebuttals.

"What are you standing there for?" Her mother scraped the spatula over the bottom of the pan. "Set the table."

Ida pulled the plates from the cupboard and yanked open the cutlery drawer. She snatched the glasses from the shelf and slammed everything onto the table, provoking a fresh stream of insults from her mother. Her mother had never figured out just how much Ida enjoyed pushing her further into her anger with her own stony silence, denying her mother the tears and remorse she wanted. Even when her father beat her as a child, Ida refused to cry. The last thing she would do was give either one of them what they wanted.

When the table was set, Ida took her mother's sewing basket, went upstairs, snipped three buttons off of her eldest brother Henry's jacket, and sewed them onto her father's. Henry wasn't likely to wear his anytime soon. He'd given up church and was generally unable to keep from swearing, which meant he was stuck cleaning beer barrels while Charlie, the next eldest, accompanied their father on business meetings.

The only sibling Ida felt an inkling of warmth from was Leon, the youngest of her brothers, and still older than her by eight years. It was his job to look after the cows, which he did with surprising tenderness. Once, Ida stood behind the barn door, listening to him speak aloud to them, a dull grief rising in her at his gentle tone. "That's it, girl, you're all right. Let me just get this strap off your neck. There now, that's better." No one in their family talked to each other like that. The Davies prided themselves on hard work, not kindness.

Ida's father was a brewer and dairyman who put in fifteen-hour days, never missed Sunday church service, and believed no one, male or female, had any business being educated. He'd pulled each of Ida's brothers out of school at age thirteen and put them to work, proving his point, as Davies and Sons Brewer and Dairy was doing quite well for itself. With no help from Ida, her father liked to point out. Ida was allowed to attend school until the age of sixteen simply because she was useless and disobedient. "I'd rather you out of the house than in it," her mother told her.

She was also allowed to take violin lessons for reasons she never fully understood.

The day her mother presented her with the mysterious box, Ida was suspicious. At seven years old, she'd only been given Christmas gifts and a package on her birthday containing something practical like crochet hooks. "What is it?" she asked, almost afraid. When her mother did something out of the ordinary, it was not usually to Ida's benefit.

Her mother pressed a hand to her abdomen, and Ida wondered if she had a stomachache. After a moment, her mother said, "It's a violin.

It was my mother's. I never learned to play, but I thought you might, if you want to."

Ida looked up, confused why she was being given something so special. Her mother's jaw was slack, her eyes cautious. "Open it," she said, as if she, too, didn't fully trust this generous side of herself.

The clasps were rusty. They stuck, and then gave way. Her mother stepped closer. Together, they peered in at the sleek curved wood, at the taut strings and elegant bow.

After that, Ida took lessons twice a week from Mr. Fitz, who lived down the road and used to play with the Austrian orchestra. He was ancient, strict, and passionate. Ida was a good student. It wasn't hard to be good in that space. The sounds she first made on the violin were scratchy and earsplitting, but when Mr. Fitz played, the compressed feeling in Ida's chest opened up. The gloom lifted. Wings expanded inside her. They beat a rhythm. Soared.

If she could make music like that, everything would be different.

Over time, Ida learned about her violinist grandmother, Amelia Verhoeven. Amelia died before Ida was born, as did Ida's grandfather, Eugene Verhoeven. Before Ida began playing, her mother never talked about her parents, but the music seemed to jog loose her memories. On certain days, Ida's mother would offer up small, savory pieces of the past, like she was breaking apart a chocolate bar, making it last.

Amelia Verhoeven started playing at the age of five. She was exceptional. She didn't care that she lived in a time when people considered the violin an unfeminine instrument: the stance of the legs, the clamping down of the chin, the energetic bowing. She got up on stage no matter what they said, and by the time she was twenty, she was playing all over Europe. London, Moscow, Vienna, Paris. She met Eugene Verhoeven, a renowned violinist from Belgium, on a stage in Berlin. They were married six months later. On their wedding night—Ida's mother relayed it to Ida exactly as her mother had relayed it to her—Eugene took Amelia's violin from its box and asked her to tell him what it was shaped like. Amelia said it was shaped liked the letter C.

He said, "Wrong."

She tried again. "Like an hourglass?"

"Wrong."

He then told her it was shaped like a woman's body. He said a woman had no right to be playing on another woman's body. Putting Amelia's violin away, he informed her that the fair sex were encroaching on all men's privileges. He would not have her encroaching on his. If she wanted to play music, she'd have to find a more suitable instrument, like the cello.

"My mother did as she was told," Ida's mother said. "What else could she do? Back then, women did not leave their husbands for a thing like that."

When Amelia became pregnant, they moved to Petersfield to be closer to Amelia's family. Amelia was restless after Ida's mother was born. She did not want to play the cello, and the baby bored her. One Saturday afternoon, she went into her parents' root cellar, took her violin from its hiding spot behind a potato bin, hoisted her baby on her hip, and went for a walk. In the woods, she set her daughter in the leaves and played. The next Saturday, she played to her baby again. Saturday after Saturday, year after year, while her husband played for audiences all over the world, Amelia played for her daughter in the woods. She played in all weather, knit fingerless gloves, pulled long underwear under her and her daughter's dresses, layered shawls over their coats.

Ida listened to these stories in awe, stealing glances at her mother's hard profile, thinking how wonderful it would be to have a mother who paid that much attention to you.

Once, Ida dared ask, "Was your mother kind?"

Her mother's head snapped around. "Of course she was kind," she said.

Why are you not kind? Ida wanted to shout at her.

Ida did not stop to wonder what her mother's dreams were, or if her mother wanted to sit in the woods all those years as Amelia's sole audience, her single devotee. What Ida did wonder was how her grandmother had so much passion and her mother so little. Ida decided she would be nothing like her mother and everything like her grandmother. She would be exceptional. She would play all over the world. No one would stop her.

When Ida was accepted into the Royal Academy of Music in London, her father did not even look up from the clock he was dismantling. "Absolutely not," he said.

"Why?" He never wanted her around. She was useless. He said so himself. This was his perfect chance to get rid of her. "I have to go," she said. "They only accept the very best, and I got in. Do you have any idea what that means?"

"Yes." He squirted oil into the gears, unwound a spring. "It means wasted money."

Ida felt her temper rising. Controlling her voice, she said, "I'll pay you back. I promise. Every penny."

"By playing the violin? Look what happened to your grandmother. A woman can't make money playing an instrument. It's a pastime. One I've supported long enough."

"Mum?" Ida looked desperately at her mother, who sat hunched over her knitting in the lamplight. "Tell him he must let me go. Tell him how important it is."

"Don't be so dramatic," her mother said. "No one ever said you'd be going to a conservatory. You heard your father. It's a pastime."

This was a slap in the face. Staring at her mother's creased brow and hunched shoulders, Ida felt her anger recede into something far more dangerous. This had been her mother's plan all along, to give her only daughter a violin, to tell her all those stories, and then sit back and watch her suffer along with the rest of the women in the family.

That night, Ida notched the inside of her arm with her father's razor. First year. First notch. She would get a job, save money, and pay her own way through school. She would prove her parents wrong.

Within a week, she was employed at the hat shop on Woodbury Road. At first, the prospect of getting out of the house and meeting new girls was appealing. Ida imagined gossiping while cutting felt, looping arms with them on their way home, or heading off to a pub together. Sadly, none of that happened under the watchful eye of Mrs. Fletcher, a deceptively attractive woman with thick lashes and rosy lips who was ugly as sin on the inside. She walked around the room, inspecting every snip and cut, and allowed no talking on the job. She'd slap the backs of their heads if they so much as coughed. At the end of the day, the girls put on their hats—Ida despised hats now—and left their posts in silence. No one even tried to get to know one another.

Most likely it wouldn't have mattered if she had tried. Ida was never good at making friends. In primary school, the girls didn't want to play with her because she was loud and bossy. She tried to keep her mouth shut but found it impossible. She also had a temper, which didn't help. By secondary school, she didn't have time to gossip over who was taking whom to the dance or the latest hairstyles in *Vogue*. After homework and farm work, every spare hour she had was dedicated to the violin.

Boys, she might have made time for, but none ever showed any real interest. She'd kissed all of three. Michael behind a bush in fourth form. Willy in her final year of secondary school, a catch, who asked her directly if he could practice on her for his date with Patty Hamshaw. Ida was happy to oblige, closing her eyes and pretending she *was* pretty Patty Hamshaw. She'd also kissed Lesley, who was four years older than she and had arms the size of small barrels. He'd been hired to help with the cows and had taken Ida by surprise in the barn, easing her up against the stall and kissing her gentle and long before pulling away with a hasty grin. He never kissed her again, much to Ida's disappointment.

Since no boys worked at the hat shop, her prospects of finding a beau were slim. Ida decided it was better this way. In a few years, she would be in London at the conservatory with a whole new life ahead of her.

What she did not see coming was Arlette.

9

WHEN FRIDAY EVENING ARRIVED, Ida couldn't figure out how to slip away without her mother questioning her, so she waited until Saturday to tell her that there had been a large order of hats and she was needed for an extra day of work. "What about your work around here?" her mother said, hands on hips.

"I'll do it tomorrow." Ida calculated the wages her father would expect if she put in an extra day at the shop. As long as she lived under his roof, she was forced to turn over half her earnings. She'd have to dip into her school fund to account for the lie.

"Fine," her mother grumbled. "But you're to do the milking first thing Sunday morning and make sure every bottle is capped before church."

In her room, Ida tucked the only decent dress she owned into a roll at the bottom of her bag and hurried into the warm July morning. The air was filled with birdsong and the scent of sodden grass. The address on the card was in South Harting. As the bus required money, Ida decided to walk the four miles. The road was gritty and full of pebbles that kept lodging into the small perforated holes of her shoes. She resisted the urge to run, convinced something other than pebbles would rise up. At one point, she ducked off the road to change and found a run in her stocking that went clear up her calf. Suppressing her mortification, she walked on, arriving at the stone cottage with rings of sweat soaking her armpits and her hair stuck to her forehead. No matter. She'd come too far to let her appearance stop her.

The grass was short and neat and lushly green, the garden beds filled with bright red dahlias and spidery pink Cleome. Over the stretch of manicured lawn, Ida could see a gravel tennis court, a swimming pool, and a cricket pitch. She had never played tennis or cricket, and she'd only ever swum in a lake, which made these luxuries in one's own yard astonishing.

Further up the drive she saw a man lying on a rug that had been laid under an enormous yew tree. He was reading a book through round spectacles with his magnificent hair swept off his forehead. Roused by her presence, he looked up, gave her a lazy smile, and turned toward a slim blonde-haired woman who was coming across the lawn balancing a drink in each hand. She wore a dress so sheer it might as well have been a nightgown.

"Hello there," she said to Ida, kneeling next to the man, who plucked the glass from her, swigged it down in one go, settled his head onto the woman's knees, and resumed his reading. "There's a tray of sherry in the sitting room if you'd like one." The woman indicated the French doors at the side of the house as if Ida was a regular guest.

"Thank you," Ida said, walking boldly past them over the grass and through the double doors, amazed that neither one of them had even asked her name.

The room was faintly musty. It took her eyes a moment to adjust to the heavily furnished space: velvet sofa, leather chairs, sheepskin rug, chintz wall hangings, shelves of books. Huge beams ran the length of the ceiling, and the fireplace was so enormous Ida could have stood up in it. On the coffee table was a tray of crystal glasses shaped like tiny bowls. Ida picked one up, careful to not spill the amber liquid brimming to the top. It caught in her throat and she coughed, grateful no one was watching as she set it back down.

Just then, Arlette stepped into the room. Her hair was pulled into a tight bun, and she wore a rumpled sweater and riding pants. She stopped at the sight of Ida. "You came." It was hard to tell from her tone whether she was annoyed or pleased, and Ida felt morbidly self-conscious as Arlette looked her over, saying, "I honestly didn't think you would. Did you meet Samuel and Jacqueline?"

"Not exactly. They didn't give their names."

"They're the rudest." Arlette paused, then, making a sudden decision, crossed the room and pressed her lips to Ida's in a quick, warm greeting. "You'll find the members of this household shameless and self-absorbed. We are, however, easy to get along with. All you have to do is pretend to listen to the men—who won't know whether you've heard them or not because they won't ask you a single question—and adore the women, who won't care if it's sincere because it will inflate their egos regardless. Come, Peggy is still in bed. We'll drag her out and get this day started."

Feeling as if she'd passed some unspoken test, Ida followed Arlette out of the room and up a set of stairs while Arlette rattled on about Peggy's lover, Garman, who remodeled the house a few years back. "I never met him, just heard stories. It's impossible to keep track of Peggy's lovers. One she married, then divorced. One died. I think that was John? Anyway, there are far too many to count." Arlette stopped outside a closed door and whispered, "Her latest obsession is the man you saw outside, Samuel Beckett. He's a poet, or essayist, or something equally as donnish."

"If he's Peggy's lover," Ida whispered back, surprised how easily the word *lover* crossed her lips, "then who is the woman with him?"

"Jacqueline? Oh, they're not sleeping together. Or at least, I don't think so. She's André Breton's wife. She was an underwater dancer before she married André, but from a bourgeois family, so it's all very scandalous." Opening the door, Arlette marched into the room, singing, "Rise and shine, Miss Guggenheim!" With a yank, she shot back the curtains, and the room came to life in a waxy haze of sunlight.

Ida hesitated in the doorway. It didn't feel right being brought into the intimacy of a complete stranger's bedroom, or walking boldly around this magnificent house as if she belonged. It was only a matter of time before they realized she had nothing to offer them.

The lump on the enormous bed stirred, and a single fur glove appeared from under the damask coverlet.

"Good lord, Peggy. Are you sleeping in your gloves again? It's July." Arlette whisked the covers off of her.

Peggy moaned, "It's freezing," and curled into a ball, pulling a pillow over her head.

"If you'd open a window once in a while, you'd discover it's warmer outside than in." Rolling her eyes at Ida, indicating the ridiculousness, Arlette took a small oil heater from the corner of the room, lit it, and carried it to Peggy's bedside. "There you are, warmth."

With a great sigh, Peggy threw the pillow aside and sat up. Her silk nightgown bunched over her legs. She looked quizzically at Ida. "I see Arlette has made good on her promise of a cocktail. Have you had one?"

It surprised Ida that Peggy remembered her, much less anything about their encounter. "I have, thank you," she said, wondering if all rich people drank cocktails before breakfast.

"Oh, good." Peggy stood up, slid her feet into a pair of pompom slippers, and lifted the handle of the heater with her fur-gloved hand. "Send Gabriella up, would you, Arlette dear? I'm going to take a bath before breakfast, which I'll have on a tray in bed when I'm finished. Oh, yes, and tell Samuel to bring me the Proust book I left in his room last night," she said, and drifted out of the room with her nightgown trailing behind her.

They found Gabriella, Peggy's maid, eating eggs in the kitchen. Arlette gave her Peggy's orders, then went outside to untangle Samuel from Jacqueline's company. He was reluctant to get up, but Jacqueline said, "You'd better go or Peggy will be in a mood." To which Samuel replied, "Peggy's always in a mood."

After that, the day became a swirl of profundities, as if Ida had stepped through Alice's looking glass, her colorless life instantly, wildly vivid. By midmorning a car arrived, driven by Jacqueline's husband, André, a short, earnest man with hair that shot out in all directions. Another man accompanied him. "Bram van Velde, a painter," Arlette whispered in Ida's ear. He was wonderfully good looking, with a sandy mop of hair, startling blue eyes, and a cigarette perpetually dangling from his lips. "He's Dutch. Just starting to come into his own. I don't love his work. I'm much fonder of Tanguy and Man Ray." All this said under Arlette's breath as she moved toward Bram, planting a kiss on his cheek and introducing Ida as her "dear friend."

Bram squeezed Ida's hand, slid the cigarette from his mouth, and said, "A friend of Arlette's is a friend of mine. If there's anything at all you need, my love"—he winked—"you just let me know."

Ida had no idea what she could possibly need, but thanked him anyway.

People divided, some played tennis, or swam, the men in their underwear, the women in bathing costumes. Ida declined a swim and said she preferred to watch tennis rather than play it. No one cared. No one questioned or reproached her. No one judged her faded dress or the tear in her stocking. It didn't matter that she was nothing like them. Everyone here was unique and opinionated and loud, changing from their soaked swimming attire into whatever fashion they liked—Bram with a scarf wrapped around his neck in the heat of summer, André in a beret, Samuel in a white shirt, untucked and rolled at the cuffs. Jacqueline wore a full-length shimmering gown while Arlette put on her riding pants and replaced her sweater with a shirt that exposed the white skin between her breasts. Peggy sat most of the day in a lawn chair in her enormous sunglasses, wearing an embroidered skirt and a string of pearls that reached to her navel. It was clear from her cool, amused expression that she was the center around which they all revolved.

By late afternoon, the party had moved from the heat of the lawn into the shade of the living room. Ida sat next to Arlette sipping sherry, enjoying the heady feeling it gave her, the lightness in her limbs.

"Do you see that man over there?" Arlette gestured to the newest arrival, a man with bow lips and a wide forehead that stretched into his thinning hairline. "That's Victor Brauner. He's Romanian." Ida was beginning to realize that no one here was English. Even Samuel was from Ireland. Arlette went on. " If you get up close, you'll see he has a glass eye. A bottle was thrown at a Surrealist party and hit him square in the face. People say his paintings are better for it. I'd love a good shaking up so I could see the world from a different angle."

"You could put a patch over your eye." It sounded stupid the moment Ida said it, but Arlette laughed as if Ida had meant it to be ironic.

"I wouldn't be nearly as gorgeous, now, would I?" She pointed to a woman who'd come in with Victor. "Now that woman sees the world from all angles, with both eyes."

"Who is she?" Ida figured she must be an artist too. None of these women looked like they cleaned or cooked or raised their own children, if they even had any.

"Djuna Barnes. She's an American novelist." Arlette crossed her legs, the thin stem of her glass held between two fingers. "She wrote a fabulously successful novel called *Nightwood*. Have you read it?"

Of course Ida hadn't read it. She hadn't even heard of it. She looked at the writer in her tweed trousers, the collar of her jacket standing straight up, her deep red lips and her hat—a series of shimmering gold leaves wrapped so tightly around her head they looked painted on—and tried to imagine what it would feel like to be that confident and beautiful.

In any other circumstance, Ida would have lied, or at least made it sound like she knew what she was talking about. For some reason, she confessed, "I haven't read it. I have never read anything worthwhile, or done anything worthwhile, or been anywhere worthwhile in my entire life."

Arlette slid forward on the couch, angling herself so she could look Ida straight in the eye. "Did you know that I only asked you here to be nice? I'm overly friendly. That's what I do. I didn't think you'd actually come. When I first saw you this morning, I was annoyed at the prospect of having to entertain you because I thought you might be boring. Then I noticed your dusty shoes and sweaty dress and realized you'd walked here. All that way? I asked myself. Why? Not for a drink, surely." She leaned back, dissecting Ida with her gaze. "To walk past complete strangers and enter a foreign house alone, to go unquestioningly up to an heiress's bedroom and listen to my rantings all day with that wide-open expression of yours." She narrowed her eyes and pointed a finger at Ida. "You want something, and you want it badly. You'd think everyone wants what this room has to offer, but not everyone does. Most people are content. I prefer discontented people. Great things come from restlessness." Arlette knocked back her drink and pulled Ida from the sofa. She put her hands on Ida's hips and danced with her to the quick jazzy beat coming from the wireless. Into her ear, she said, "You must learn not to put too much of your heart into any one thing. Stay unattached. Independence is freedom, and freedom is the only way for a woman to soar."

Ida swayed, woozy and uninhibited. How did Arlette make the hardest things in the world sound so easy?

"Turn it up," Arlette shouted, and Jacqueline and André joined them on the dance floor, the four of them soft stepping in time with the music. Djuna stripped off her jacket and began to sing over the saxophones and drums in a voice as sultry and stunning as she was.

They ate outside at a table set in the grass, *boeuf en daube* with crisp bread and onion soup. Peggy sat at the head of the table. She was an unattractive woman, with a pudgy, misshapen nose, small eyes, and turned-down lips, but the self-assured way she commanded the space gave her a power more valuable than beauty. Midway through the meal, André asked her how she managed such lavish food in England, and Peggy told him she'd fired her English cook, who made nothing but Yorkshire pudding and roast pheasant, and hired a French chef. "No offense, dear." She looked at Ida. "But English food is absolute rubbish."

"No offense taken. This is delicious," Ida said, astonished, once again, that Peggy had the wherewithal to think of her at all, much less note that she was the only Englishwoman at the table.

Ida could have stayed there forever swooning into honeyed walnut cakes served in huge slices on thin china plates, into the intoxication of gin and the heady scent of lilies stuffed into short vases. There was the ruckus of voices, the low beat of drums from the wireless, the striking of matches, and the glowing tips of cigarettes.

Ida ignored the time, the cows, the milking, the hint of fear that laced her stomach at the punishment waiting for her. She sank into the seduction of Arlette, who was telling her how she modeled for an artist named Man Ray. "I'm a decent model." She draped an arm over Ida's shoulder, her breath sweet and alcoholic. "But I'm a much better photographer. For all the progress these women made in the twenties"—she waved at the women mingling around the yard—"they're still the ones getting naked for the artists. I'd love to strip down any one of these men and make them stand with their cocks in the wind while I photograph them. See how they like it." Ida was delighted to find that the brashness of this sentence did not surprise her as it might have earlier. She was already getting used to Arlette's outrageous company.

"Come." Arlette drew Ida from the cool night into the living room, explaining how she began modeling when she was fourteen and Man Ray paid her in photography lessons. "Did you know"—Arlette stood on her tiptoes reaching for a catalogue on the shelf—"that you can entirely change what one sees behind the lens in a darkroom?" She flipped through the magazine's glossy pages, landing on a photograph of a naked woman pitched forward on her knees, exposing her bare bottom, which was round and supple as a peach.

Ida had never seen anything so sensual or erotic. The rest of the party made their way into the room and Ida flushed as if she'd been caught in a dirty act.

Djuna walked by. "Is that your gorgeous ass, Arlette? Good God, it's a young one. None of us can claim anything that luscious anymore."

Ida stood in the heat of her embarrassment as Arlette flipped through more photos: curved hips, bare thighs, a face in shadow, lines rippling over a belly, breasts dipped in sunlight. When Arlette came to a photograph of a woman whose naked back was overlaid with f-holes of a violin, Ida put her hand to the page, her constricted world colliding with this new and tantalizing one.

Under the picture were the words *Le Violon d'Ingres, 1924.* Ida traced the f-holes, the curve of hip and waist and bottom. Her grandfather was right, a woman's body and the violin were one. Only this woman was not hiding in the woods. If she were to step off the page, pick up a violin, and play it stark naked to this room full of people, they would applaud and thank her. They would tell her that the violin is as beautiful as a woman is beautiful. They would tell her that she did not have to choose.

"Found yourself another admirer, Arlette?" Peggy stood in front of them. A thin line of smoke curled from the end of her cigarette.

"This one's not of me." Arlette's eyes slid away as if something across the room had caught her attention.

Peggy looked at the photograph. "Oh, that's Kiki, isn't it? Well, your curves are just as praiseworthy, my dear." She took a long, hard drag and reached around Ida to pull a magazine off the bookshelf. "If you're interested in Man Ray, these were taken for an article in the Swedish weekly, *Bonniers Veckotidning*, on influential foreigners in Paris." Peggy wormed her way between them and opened the magazine to a photograph of a younger, slimmer version of herself. She wore a scintillating gown, large earrings, and a sleek, tight headdress. In her hand was a cigarette holder as long as a limb. Her eyes were dark and penetrating, her expression both powerful and vulnerable and startlingly seductive.

"There's a series of them." Peggy turned the large pages, each revealing a picture of her in the same outfit with a slightly different pose. "Enjoy your youth, girls. What I wouldn't give for that waistline again." She gave a plaintive sigh and slapped the magazine shut. "Ida, darling, if you're ever in London, you must come to my gallery," she said, flicking her ash into the air and walking toward Samuel, who was eyeing her from the card table.

If you're ever in London. Words sweet as candy. Ida was a guest. A person invited for apéritifs. A person asked to visit galleries in London. There was an actual straightening of her spin as she tucked the invitation into the pocket of her unimaginative life. It was not an impossible reality. She smiled at Arlette and said, "I look forward to seeing Peggy's London gallery," as if saying it would make it come true.

10

IDA ARRIVED HOME AT the hint of dawn. Her father did his milk run early on Sundays so he could make nine o'clock church service, which meant she had to hurry. Sobering up, she went into the barn where she saw that the milk had already been poured over the straining gauze. The bottles were filled and sealed and lined up by the door waiting to be loaded into the back of the truck. Too exhausted to feel anything other than gratitude that her chores had been done for her, Ida crept up to her room and fell asleep fully clothed.

The truck woke her three hours later, grinding to a stop outside her window. Ida dragged herself from bed and shook the wrinkles from her dress. She'd have to face whatever was coming one way or another. It was most likely Leon who'd done her chores. Possibly her mother. Either way, it would end badly for her.

Her parents did not say a word when they saw her. In church, Ida glanced at their somber profiles through the entire sermon. Their expressions revealed nothing. Back home, she helped her mother in the garden and waited. No punishment came. By midafternoon, Ida went to her room and forced herself to practice the violin through a headache that split her temples.

At dinner, she ate with her head down, certain her father was biding his time. There was no chance her parents hadn't noticed her absence. She's been gone for almost twenty-four hours. She'd missed dinner with no explanation. Hadn't done her evening or morning chores. It occurred to her that making her wait was part of the torture, and that whatever form their discipline took, her parents would demand an explanation, one she was not willing to give. She would not mar the perfect world of Yew Tree Cottage by dragging it into this one. Even if she tried to explain, her parents would never understand. They were old and dull and knew nothing of the upper classes. To desire that life was an insult to theirs. Hard work was honorable. Did she think she was above them? High and mighty, her mother would say. Ida would have to lie, otherwise her father might take any number of things away from her. The violin. Her job.

"How's the Amons' baby?" her mother said, and Ida looked up.

There was a swift kick to her calf, and Leon, in a too-loud voice, said, "You were gone the whole night taking care of him."

Ida swallowed. If any brother was going to defend her, it was Leon. He'd just never lied so boldly before. "He's better," she said.

"Good." Her mother set the salt dish down. "Does Mrs. Amon need help tonight? Leon can do the milking again if need be."

"The baby's fever passed," Ida said, smoothly. Lies had always been easy for her. "Mrs. Amon said she'd be fine on her own."

"I'll stop over anyway, just to check on them."

Ida cut her fork into her potato. "I asked her if she wanted me to stop in again, and she said she'd rather not be disturbed. I can check on them tomorrow, just to make sure, if you think that's best."

Her mother nodded. "I'll send you with a loaf of tea bread."

After dinner, Ida found Leon raking out the stalls in the barn, the muscles of his back flexing beneath his shirt as he worked. He was the strongest of her brothers and the least aggressive.

"Thank you," she said. He did not turn around. "Was the Amons' baby sick?"

"Don't know." He shrugged.

"Well, it was a good lie, so long as Mum doesn't ask Mrs. Amon about it." Ida stepped onto the first rung of the fence rail and leaned into the stall in an effort to get her brother to look at her. "Don't you want to know where I was?"

"No."

"Why not?"

Leon did not answer.

"Why did you lie for me?"

"Don't know," he said again, his eyes on the hay.

"Did you make it up on the spot when I didn't come home for dinner? How do you know you'll get away with it? What if they find out?" Leon raked in silence. "What else have you lied about?" Ida prodded. "Do you have a secret life I don't know about? Do you have a girl?"

"Stop it, Ida. Go away." Leon put down his rake and began shoveling manure out of the stall door.

"You're no fun." She kicked the fence. A cow snorted.

"You're scaring the cows." He moved past her. "Get on out of here, and don't make me lie again."

"You'd lie for me again?" She jumped down. "Goodness, what else could I get away with?" If only he'd look at her. Ida wanted the moment to be something she could hold on to.

"Go on," Leon grumbled.

In bed that night, Ida thought of the gentle voice her brother used when he spoke to the cows, and it carved a hole of sadness in her. They were, each of them, Henry and Charlie and Leon, her mother and father, entirely alone in their family of six. None of them knew how to talk to each other, much less love one another.

In the dark, Ida made out the deep crack in the beam on her ceiling. She used to be afraid that splintered wood would come crashing down on her. As a child, in her dreams, she'd hear the snap and boom, feel the crushing weight and scream, terrified she'd be pushed through the bed, through the floor, and down under the house. Only once did someone come for her, her father, who told her if she didn't shush up, she'd find herself sleeping in the barn.

Awake, dreamless, Ida realized that she hadn't cried out because she was afraid of being buried alive, but because she was afraid of being buried alone. She had always carried this fear of loneliness. Her whole life she'd watched her brothers grab and punch and wrestle each other. She used to squeeze her hands together, praying they'd look up and notice she was right there, begging to be a part of their game. If they were in a good mood, Ida might get a startling slap on the shoulder, but this was as far as their attention went.

Before last night, no one had ever curled their palms over her hips and pulled her from the sofa and danced with her. The memory made Ida smile in the dark. Affection passed so naturally between the people at Yew Tree Cottage it was impossible to tell friends from lovers. They kissed in greeting, slung their arms around one another, sat on the sofa with their legs entangled. Closing her eyes, Ida dared to imagine what it would be like inside their intimate circle, to touch and be touched so effortlessly.

11

THE WEEK CHURNED BY, each day clutching Ida a little tighter as her flat, gray, commonplace life stretched ahead of her. Everything became insufferable: the stuffy hat shop, Mrs. Fletcher's sickly perfume, the snipping scissors and the felt that stuck to Ida's fingers. Home was even worse, her mother's grating voice, her brothers' banter and her father's insipid stories.

When Saturday arrived, Ida was up before the sun. She kicked off the covers, dressed in the floral dress she'd worn the previous week, and slipped out the back door. She walked quickly, the stones hard under the soles of her shoes, the meadow phlox sweet in the air. No one was on the road, which was a good thing, as any old neighbor could drive by and ask Ida why she was walking out of town at six in the morning. With her eyes on the pink horizon, Ida kept a steady pace and tried to quell her nerves. Arlette said she was welcome anytime, but what did that mean?

By the time she walked up the drive, Yew Tree Cottage was aglow in sunlight. It was a relief to see the yard empty and the doors latched. It gave Ida a moment to collect herself. Brushing the dew from the iron slats of a patio chair, she sat down and pressed her hands into her lap. She understood that it was critical for her to appear at ease here, airy and carefree—emotions entirely against her nature. Normally, she was tense and edgy. Tense and edgy wasn't who she wanted to be around these people. She wanted to exude breezy and fun.

Tilting her face to the sun, Ida let the bright strands fall on her closed lids for what felt like an eternity before she heard the double doors un-latch. She opened her eyes to Arlette walking toward her in wide-legged trousers and a sleeveless shirt, her arms pale and long. Her hesitation dissolved as Arlette said, "What a gorgeous sight you are. I wasn't sure you'd come again, and here you've arrived at the crack of dawn." Ida did not bother telling her it was well past the crack of dawn. Instead, she let Arlette kiss her sun-warmed cheek and felt beatific.

"I'm going to the kitchen to see that breakfast is brought out to us," Arlette said, and with a swish of her trousers, disappeared into the house.

It was that easy, arriving to sunshine and breakfast on a lawn.

THE SUMMER WENT on like this, weeks of suffocation followed by a single Saturday of fresh air. Ida's parents believed she was working weekends due to a busier-than-usual summer season of hats. As long as Ida made sure the milking was done, showed up by dinnertime, and turned over an extra four shillings a week, they had no reason to suspect her. It meant less money for her school fund, but it was worth it.

She and Arlette were a good twenty years younger than the rest of the people coming and going from Yew Tree Cottage, which separated them but also made them worthy of attention. "They love that we're young," Arlette said. "We're impressionable, malleable." To be young was to be eager and enthusiastic, ready to soak up ideas, to ask questions these seasoned artists were dying to answer. "Didn't I tell you all they want is to be adored?" Arlette said one afternoon as she and Ida sat in the living room listening to a passionate argument between Samuel and Bram on the topic of making love to a woman. Samuel said making love without *being* in love was like coffee without brandy, and Bram argued that love and sex didn't necessarily go together at all.

The forbidden nature of these conversations captivated Ida, the tingling discomfiture she felt listening to Djuna tell them about a woman who fell in love with her at a brothel and tracked her down with a bouquet of peonies. Or the story of a man Peggy used to sleep with who tied her wrists in ivory bracelets and made love to her under a Surrealist painting of naked, large-breasted women growing out of trees. Ida learned about the frescos in Pompeii that depicted people having sex in various positions, of the countless affairs between artist and muse, of the romantic relationship suspected between Samuel and Bram.

There were less scandalous stories—but no less compelling—of Peggy's mother gifting her either a yearly fur coat or a new automobile, depending on her mood. "This from a woman who refuses to tip," Peggy snorted, telling them how the concierge at their hotel would put an X on their suitcases to warn the other staff. "Oh, my poor mother." Peggy shook her head, and Ida wanted to laugh too and say *Yes, our poor mothers*, as if their mothers were equally frivolous.

In a very short amount of time, Ida's life outside the company of these people became ridiculous to her: her provincial parents, her fatuous job sewing hats, the absurd task of yanking a cow's udder, sitting in church listening to the sins committed daily at Yew Tree Cottage preached of with genuine terror.

It was a relief that Ida's new friends knew nothing of her family. At Yew Tree Cottage, she was not boring or insignificant. She was beautiful, or so Jacqueline said, dressing her in flowing skirts, sheer blouses, and clinking bracelets. Arlette dabbed lipstick on Ida's mouth and let her wear her tiger-claw necklace like they were best friends. Ida's opinion mattered, Arlette told her, walking through the gardens, showing off her latest Leica II with a built-in rangefinder. She let Ida hold the camera up to her eye, explaining aperture and shutter speed and how to position objects through the lens. Peggy confided in Ida that she believed Samuel's poetry was childish, but that she was drawn to his sardonic humor and morbid ideas. Djuna took Ida aside and said that the way Ida watched people made her wonder if she wasn't a writer herself, and wouldn't she like to try it one day?

When Ida let it slip that she played the violin, Djuna turned to the room with a dramatic sweep of her arm and said, "There is a musician in our midst!"

Peggy, seated at the card table with her cards flared like a small fan, said, "You must play for us."

Arlette's eyes shot up from her magazine. "How did I not know this about you?"

Bram slid his wiry arm around Ida and tucked her into his side. "Next week, you're to bring your violin, or else I'll track you down in whatever secret place you reside and drag you out with it."

Ida couldn't possibly explain to them the difficulty of sneaking her violin out of the house. No one had any idea she worked a regular job and had regular parents who would throw her into the street if they knew she was lying to them about toiling away at the hat shop while she paraded around in lipstick drinking gin martinis.

Under the warmth of Bram's arm, looking at their eager faces, Ida realized that life, for these people, was not about the past and what hindered them, but about the future and what they planned to do with it.

The violin was her future.

"I'll bring it," she said.

THE FOLLOWING WEEK, Ida stole from her room before sunrise with her violin case pressed to her chest. The morning sparkled with the thinnest of rains. Ida lifted her face to it, thinking of her grandmother sneaking off to play in the woods all those years ago. She wondered if it was the violin or the women in her family who were cursed with secrets.

When Ida arrived at Yew Tree Cottage, she found the house shuttered and quiet. The drizzle had stopped and the clouds were breaking up. Standing in the wet grass, Ida took out her violin and played a Bach sonata under a veil of fog. She was not nervous or jittery. She was playing to an invisible audience with dahlias at her feet. She was playing to no one and everyone. The music dissolved the world around her and made her feel invincible. She played as a window opened and Bram stood in his nightshirt shouting, "Bravo." She played as Peggy and Samuel emerged onto the upper balcony, as Arlette came out on the lawn in bare feet and a thin nightgown, the mist cloaking her shoulders.

When the piece ended, there was a tremendous silence, and then Arlette said, "That was the most stunning thing I've ever heard," and Bram shouted, "I expect to be serenaded out of bed every morning. Nothing else will do." Peggy said, "Splendid, my dear," and Samuel told her she must play again over breakfast.

Ida had only ever known the silent praise of her mother and the occasional "Well done" from her teacher. Real praise, encouragement from people whose opinions mattered, gave her a stunning sense of accomplishment.

Every Saturday after that, Ida brought her violin. Often, she and Arlette broke off from the others to an upstairs bedroom where Arlette would drop onto the bed and say, "Play a song that matches the mood of the day," and Ida would feel that something exceptional was required of her, as if she alone could shape the day before them.

If the sun was out, she'd play a vibrant, fast-paced piece. If it was raining, something in a minor key. Arlette swayed in time to the music, absorbing it with her whole body in the same way that Ida absorbed it with hers. Now when Arlette spoke to Ida about art, it was as a confidant, an equal. She told Ida music was the epitome of abstraction. "I want to photograph sound," she said. "How does one freeze the notes and make them something concrete? Visible? How do we see a melody? What do you see when you play?"

Ida had never thought about music as anything other than scores on a page, a right and wrong note, and yet she understood what Arlette meant about the inability to hold on to it. A photograph lasted forever. A note vanished the instant you let it go.

Sitting on a high bed in a room filled with dark furniture and threads of sunlight, Ida described how she saw her fingers on the strings and bow, but it was as if they didn't belong to her, like she was seeing someone else's hands. With Arlette she was able to articulate the contradictions she felt when she played. The sensation of vulnerability and exposure like she was turning herself inside out, coupled with the feeling of complete protection, as if nothing could touch her. To play was to be utterly present, grounded, and yet filled with a detached weightlessness.

When she said these things, Arlette's eyes lit up. "Yes, yes," she said. "You are a true artist, Ida Davies," and Ida felt a swell of pride. She had proven herself. She was no longer a restless woman, but a restless artist, which was a critical distinction.

Her mistake was in believing that this made her one of them.

12

THAT SUMMER, IDA LEARNED what it was to be respected and admired. She learned how to appreciate jazz, to dance the Lindy and drink straight gin. She learned to listen to poetry and read excerpts of novels aloud. She learned that abstract art does not refer to anything outside of itself, while Surrealist art draws from the irrational. She learned to recognize a Brâncuşi from a Cocteau, a Tanguy from a Calder, to find meaning in the Surrealist images, to use words like *the unconscious mind, illusion, sensory, desire.*

In that singular world, Ida became what she wanted to be: confident, genuine, knowledgeable.

But it was a shaky identity, one that wouldn't last.

ON OCTOBER 8, 1938, Ida turned off the road and found the cottage empty, the doors locked, the windows shuttered. It was a clear, warm autumn day, but the place was as cold and silent as if blanketed in snow. The tennis net was down, the pool covered, the lawn chairs stacked on the patio. A week ago, the British and French had signed the Munich Pact with Germany, averting the outbreak of war and abating fears, Peggy's included. Arlette told Ida there was a gallery show to prepare for and they'd be moving the artwork back to London.

She just hadn't said when.

The emptiness stabbed Ida in the ribs. She found it hard to breathe. What had she thought? That this would last forever? That they'd take her with them? She wanted to collapse on the flagstone and stay curled there until someone came back for her. But no one was coming back. In the same breezy way they'd arrived, they'd all gone. No one had said goodbye or left a forwarding address or a telephone number. There was no promise of return, or even a note tacked to the door saying, *Au revoir!* As readily as Ida had been welcomed, she had been dismissed.

Standing in the quiet chill of Peggy's empty lawn, Ida wondered about people who could gather you and shine on you, and then disappear as if you were nothing. How did their hearts not break? Hers cracked open in her chest.

THERE WAS NOTHING to do but walk home.

As she neared her house, Ida saw the solid, impenetrable mass of her mother, legs planted, sleeves rolled up, forearms flexed as she tipped the slop bucket into the pig trough. Ida wanted to believe that she was nothing like her mother, but she had her height, her hair color, her high cheeks and round face. Ida's hips weren't as wide, nor her chest as hefty, but they would be in time. She would never escape this life. She'd marry an underwhelming man and find herself saddled with children she didn't want. Her hair would pepper with gray and her face would take on the same sheen of age as her mother's. Ida's future stood right there in front of her.

She climbed the stairs to her room, changed out of her dress and into her linen skirt, and went back outside. Taking the bucket from her mother, Ida told her that the hat shop no longer needed her on Saturdays.

Her mother said, "What did you do? Have you been sacked?"

Ida pitched the bucket over the fence—eggshells and potato skins and apple cores sliding into the trough—and said nothing.

LIFE RESUMED.

Ida cleaned the barns and baled hay. She attended church, milked the cows, set the table, and went to work with a feeling beyond loneliness. Her banal life ground her into particles so small her soul felt indiscernible. She was a husk of skin and bone. She did not try to feel better. She wallowed, letting the memory of Arlette consume her: Arlette's shining dark hair, firm voice, and buoyant laughter, the way she'd lean in and whisper in Ida's ear, her bold questions, the smell of her skin, a mix of floral and lemon, the feel of her hands on Ida's hips.

Ida was not sure whether she was in love with Arlette or if she simply wanted to be her. Why hadn't Arlette said goodbye? Why hadn't she asked for Ida's address so she could send a letter? Had she meant any of the things she'd said? Ida had believed it all, that Arlette adored her and they would be friends forever, that she'd bring Ida to Paris and introduce her to all of her friends. Ida would model for Arlette, and Arlette would model for Man Ray. Ida would be Arlette's muse, and she would be his. Arlette had described the light on the Pont Neuf at sunset, her favorite pastry shop on rue Montorgueil. "There is nothing like Paris," she'd say. "You have not lived if you have not eaten a *mille-feuille* or drunk Pernod at Le Monocle."

She told Ida that she'd teach her how to properly smoke and kiss and fuck. She had used that exact sordid word. Ida had heard it before from her brothers. She used to think they were talking about the cows, until she understood they were talking about women. It was a filthy word. And yet when Arlette said it, leaning her long arm on the table, it became both tantalizing and unremarkable.

Without her, Ida would learn none of these things.

WINTER BROUGHT NIGHTS of cold, bright stars and days of even colder sunshine. Ida ate little and shivered constantly. She couldn't stand the sight of her mother and readily gave up the warmth of the kitchen for her cold bedroom, where she curled under her blanket and let her tears freeze on her pillow.

By February, her bones ached like an old woman's. At eighteen, she was going to die of a broken heart and the bloody chill of Petersfield.

It was Monday. Ida hated Mondays. At work, she cut the rim of a hat too short and was told she'd have to make up the cost from her wages, after which she accidentally stabbed a needle into her thumb and bled all over the bright blue ribbon in her hand. She managed to shove the soiled satin into her skirt pocket unnoticed, but Mrs. Fletcher would find out anyway. She counted every feather and flower and inch of ribbon, and always found something missing.

When Ida got home, she tied up her ponytail with the blood-stained ribbon and went downstairs to prepare dinner. If her mother noticed the stain, she said nothing. In icy intimacy, they chopped, scraped, and poured, anticipating each other's moves from habit, never bumping elbows or crossing paths, darting up and over and around each other until the meal was laid out and the men served.

Ida's father looked haggard. Bags pulled at his eyes. Henry was out again. Where to, Ida had no idea. Charlie sat hunched over his plate, shoveling his food in his mouth as if he'd never eaten before, while Leon talked in excited breaths about the calf that was born last night.

After a few minutes, Ida's father said, "I don't give a damn about no calf, Leon. What I want to know"—he laid down his fork, slow and calm, and looked at Ida, his blue eyes revealing nothing—"is why, when I ran into Mrs. Fletcher, she said she was relieved orders had finally picked up." He ran a finger up and down the handle of his fork. "She was mighty surprised when I mentioned how busy she'd been this summer, keeping you all those Saturdays."

There was a long, empty silence.

Ida's mother looked at him. "What do you mean?" And then at Ida. "What does he mean?"

Ida locked her eyes onto her plate. Her carrots swam in gravy. Her heart thumped. She was a rabbit in a trap, and her father was going to skin her alive.

His hand was on the back of her neck before she even heard him get up. Ida looked at her brothers for a wild, hopeful moment, but they kept their heads down, Charlie's jaw slowly working his food, Leon silent and white-faced.

It was her mother's expression that stayed with Ida. Maybe because it was the last time she looked into her eyes. Or maybe because it was the first time Ida saw compassion in them, her mother's body rising ever so slightly, her hand reaching out as if to stave off her husband. In all the years Ida had been beaten, her mother had never lifted a finger to protect her. Why defend her now?

As their eyes met, Ida understood that it was because she was no longer a child, but a woman. Her father did not beat women. He had never raised a hand to her mother, and he hadn't touched Ida, or her brothers, in years. The blows stopped when they grew up, which seemed a natural progression. You hit children for bad behavior. Adults you punished in other ways.

Despite her mother's forward motion, she did not stop her husband as he dragged Ida from the room, his iron fist latched to the back of Ida's neck as he pushed her down the hall and out the front door.

FROST CRACKLED BENEATH their feet as Ida's father hauled her across the lawn. At the barn, he gave a final shove, and Ida stumbled into the sharp scent of feed and dung. Blades of moonlight cut through the slats in the walls. In their white glow, Ida saw her father reach into a bucket and sprinkle chicken grain over the floor. Her pulse raced. She couldn't imagine he'd put a strap to her, but he moved in the same deliberate way he always did before a good walloping.

She considered running straight out the door, but it was too late. Her father's hand snaked around her wrist.

"Take off your knickers," he said. Ida tried to yank away, but her father's grip tightened. "You can make this as difficult or as easy as you like."

Ida knew well enough dragging it out only made it worse. Tingling with humiliation, she reached under her skirt with her free hand and pulled down her knickers.

"Kneel," he ordered. Ida stiffened. She was a grown woman. Her father couldn't do this to her. "Kneel," he said again, shoving her so that she dropped to the floor. Her bare knees slammed into the chicken feed and she let out a small gasp. It hurt less if she kept still, so she clamped her jaw and tried to stop trembling. There was the resounding click of her father's belt buckle, and then the slick swish of leather against fabric.

There was no coming back from what happened next. In a single motion, Ida's father knocked her forward and her palms landed on the gritty floor as he flipped up her skirt. There was a hissing sound and then the sharp, cutting lash of the belt. Ida gritted her teeth and tried to keep from crying out. It was not the thrashing that debased her, it was her nakedness. She was a woman on all fours, exposed, her skirt tossed over her back, seed grain digging holes into her skin as her father whipped her like a child, beating what shred of self-worth she had left into dust.

Ida pictured the smooth perfection of Arlette's photographed bottom and thought how vulgar she, Ida, was. This was where she came from. These people. It was beyond demeaning. It was the most heinous thing her father could do, and Ida would never forgive him.

13

ALONE ON THE FLOOR of the barn, Ida thought of the small, mean things she occasionally did: stealing from the hat shop, a feather or a spool of thread, telling herself Mrs. Fletcher was the one fibbing about it, groaning with the rest of the girls at the injustice of their docked pay. Once, Ida stole a silver hairpin right out of her co-worker Sally's handbag. She told herself Sally deserved it. Sally was so irritating, unable to keep her mouth shut and always whispering under her breath even though she'd get them all into trouble. Only Ida felt wretched walking home with the cool silver piece in her pocket. There were twelve children in Sally's family, and they hardly managed to keep a roof over their heads. The next day, Ida pretended to find the pin on the floor and asked if anyone had misplaced it. Tears gushed down Sally's face. It was her grandmother's, she said, hugging Ida, never suspecting a thing. After that, Ida only stole from people who were no better than she was. The butcher, a surly man who Ida had seen fix the scales, cheating even the poorest of them, and the baker, a woman with a broad chest and thin lips who regularly swatted children out of her shop. When the baker's back was turned, Ida would slip a hot bun into her skirt pocket, justifying her actions as she sank her teeth into the soft dough on her way home.

In the chill of the barn, with her skinned bottom on fire, Ida recognized that she was no better than her father. She did not take things from others because they deserved it, but for the rush and satisfaction of getting away with it. She did it because she was bored, because she spent her life waiting for something to happen. Because, like her father, Ida did not want to be small. She wanted to take up space. To be important.

Ida stood, slowly, painfully. She pulled up her underwear and stockings and gave a vengeful kick to the unlit kerosine lantern on the floor. It clattered and rolled across the wooden boards, leaving a dark stain of oil in its wake. Kicking something in a fit of anger was precisely what her father would have done. In the same way as Ida had been born with her mother's hair and the curve of her hip, she had been born with her father's temper. Ida's parents were in her bones. She would never escape them.

The lantern came to a slow stop, oil pooling from it. A single match would light the whole place up, Ida thought, picturing the streak of blue flame racing across the boards and up over the hay bales. In seconds, she could ruin everything.

The simple fact that Ida did not have a match may have been all that prevented her in that moment. She left the barn, her underwear chafing as she picked her way across the lawn. In her room, she lay on her side—the only possible position—and thought of who she had been at Yew Tree Cottage. She had considered pocketing a small book or a tiny silver fork, but she hadn't done it. In that space, she had wanted to be the person who helped a stranger on the street for no reason, the person Arlette believed her to be.

Ida tried to imagine any one of the women at Yew Tree Cottage in her situation. None of them would tolerate it. They were women in control of their lives. They did exactly as they pleased, not what was expected of them. Ida did not have to take it either. Her father may have ground her into dust, but dust was not nothing. In a storm, it could blind you.

Ida did not sleep. In the middle of the night, she got out of bed, took a canvas bag from its hook, stuffed some clothes and her savings inside, and slid on her shoes. There was no last, nostalgic glance around her room, no trinket or memento put into a pocket. With her violin in hand and her bag on her shoulder, Ida walked down the hall to her parents' room. Her father lay on his back, face up, mouth open, his breath a faint grating noise in his throat. Her mother lay on her side with her braid coiled across the pillow like a snake.

All Ida intended was to say into the dead air over their heads, *You cannot beat me.* But something snapped inside as she stared at their sleeping forms: the mass of her mother's back, the powerful wave of her hip, her father's sharp, stubbled face and Herculean chest. They did not look tranquil or vulnerable as people do in sleep, but tense, their mouths and eyes ready to spring open.

Ida took her revenge against her parents in the only way she knew how.

The money was in a red labeled coffee tin on the top shelf in the kitchen. Since "the slump" after the war, Ida's father hadn't trusted banks. Whatever wasn't spent to keep the dairy and brewery running was stowed right here under their noses. Hiking up her skirt, Ida kneeled on the countertop, pulled the tin from the shelf, and stuffed her pockets with every last quid. It was odd her father didn't hide his money. She supposed he considered himself a fair man, paying her brothers a decent wage at the end of the week. They'd have no reason to take from him.

He just forgot to be fair to her.

14

I DA WAITED ON THE train platform in the dark, glancing at the large clock and praying her parents didn't wake up before the first train pulled in. She was beginning to regret taking the money. Not out of guilt but because it was occurring to her that her father would probably let *her* go without a fight, just not his savings.

Ida had no idea how often he dipped into that tin. She imagined it was daily. She pictured him getting an early start, combing his beard with his fingers as he set his coffee cup aside and reached for the tin, needing a little something to pay for the hops he'd run out of or petrol for the truck. He'd look in, his face filling with momentary confusion before cracking with rage. The tin would hit the wall with a clatter and he'd charge upstairs, discover Ida was gone, and fly out the front door. At any moment, he'd appear on the platform, roaring, grabbing. He'd drag her home through the streets. Or else, he'd see her empty bed and his rage would morph into a devilish smile. He'd saunter downstairs, pick up the telephone and contact the police, let them do his dirty work. They'd easily find Ida in London, and then what? She'd be arrested for stealing from her own parents. Her name would be in the newspaper. Arlette and Peggy would read about her and know exactly what kind of a person she was.

For a brief, horrible moment, Ida thought of hurrying home and returning the money before she was caught, but the sky was already hinting of daylight. Her mother would be in the kitchen getting the stove lit. Ida wouldn't be able to put the money back without being noticed.

It didn't matter. The thought of returning to that house set her gut churning. She'd never go back. Jail seemed a better prospect.

In front of her, the tracks vibrated and the train arrived in a screech of metal, the smell like a scorched pan. Ida couldn't get on quick enough, her heart racing, her mind irrationally charged. Her father was the wide-backed man coming down the aisle, the man who bumped her putting his bag on the rack. His was the voice shouting from the platform, the gruff cough behind her. Ida dropped quickly into a seat, forgetting about her torn-up bottom. Wincing, she shifted onto her hip to ease the pain. If the police came for her, she'd show them what her father had done. She'd tell them she took the money for revenge. Maybe they'd take mercy on her.

Minutes ticked torturously by before the train lurched forward. Ida's breath slowed as the brick houses dropped away. A tree flashed past and a field rose up, the immediate distance, the speed, a relief. Exhausted, Ida closed her eyes and slept.

AT THE EUSTON train station, she asked directions to the Tate Museum and from there acquired a list of galleries, Guggenheim Jeune among them.

Ida had never been to London—her audition for the Royal Academy had been held at her school—but she wasn't entirely ignorant. She listened to the radio and read magazines and was savvy enough to follow the directions the receptionist at the Tate gave her. Any worry she had about her father coming after her vanished in the frosty metropolitan air. It seemed impossible that she could be found in a place filled with this many people. Every new sight and sound thrummed with possibility: the shuffle of bodies on the sidewalk, the grind of car engines, the flutter of snow settling on hats and coat sleeves, the scent of hot chestnuts and popcorn and petrol mingling in one sweet, accosting scent. The money jostling around at the bottom of Ida's bag meant she could pay for a hotel, eat a decent meal, even buy an outfit from one of the sparkling shop windows.

More miraculous was finding Arlette in the West End of London in a high-ceilinged room on the second story of a building on Cork Street. When Ida opened the door, her friend was sitting cross-legged on the floor, arranging photographs like puzzle pieces.

Arlette did not hear her, or if she did, was too absorbed in her work to look up. Ida waited, buzzing with exhaustion and nerves as she took in the white plaster mounds balanced on black pedestals and the liquid shapes dripping over the canvases on the walls.

When Ida finally managed a cautious hello, Arlette stared at her, blank faced, as if trying to register who she was. Ida's heart dropped to her feet, her thin-skinned hope pricked and deflated with a single look. Why had she come? It was stupid. She did not belong here. Arlette would want nothing to do with her outside of Yew Tree Cottage. Flattened, Ida remained in the doorway, wondering what she was supposed to do now. She couldn't go home, not after what she'd done, and yet without Arlette none of this made any sense.

Narrowing her eyes as if trying to interpret something, Arlette slowly unpeeled her legs and stood up. She wore socks the color of lavender and a black sweater that fell loosely over her shoulders.

Glancing at the photographs scattered at her feet, she said, "I can't get it right. I sat here until three a.m., fell asleep on the floor, and was up with the sun. It's just not right. Do you see what I'm trying to do? Can you make sense of it?" Her tone was convivial, as if Ida had just stepped out, and now here she was, ready to converse with again.

Ida's heart picked itself up. Arlette was not dismissing her; she was simply consumed with her work. Dropping her bag to the floor, Ida went and stood beside her, the citrus scent of her friend's skin as reviving as spring.

To Arlette, Ida's arrival was unsurprising. Ida had materialized in this city as breezily as she had materialized at Yew Tree Cottage, as breezily as everyone came and went from these spaces. Ida's appearance in London was exceptional only to her.

"Do you see it?" Arlette said, intense and preoccupied.

The photographs were a series of pale limbs floating against black backgrounds: a hand, an arm, a toe, a leg, the top of a head, an eye, a belly button. "Body parts?" Ida was unsure what she was supposed to be seeing, exactly.

"A self-portrait." Arlette squatted down, balancing on the balls of her feet as she scrutinized her work. "I am trying to arrange them as a singular piece, but something is not right."

It was disturbing to see a body—Arlette's body—deconstructed and rearranged in this malformed way. And yet, there was a detached dreaminess in the brightness of her skin swimming in these pools of darkness. "What if you put them back together as a whole?"

"That's boring," Arlette said.

"It's truthful."

"It's the opposite of what I am trying to do. I am disentangling the body, making a point that we are not our whole selves."

"It's upsetting."

"Yes. That's what I want."

Ida dropped next to Arlette, and was reminded of kneeling on chicken feed. Here she was on a smooth floor in London with the wounds of yesterday still lashed into her skin. It didn't seem possible that was less than twenty-four hours ago. "It's more truthful if you at least try and put yourself back together." Ida wanted—needed—the woman scattered on the floor to be whole, to be real. "What if the photographs were saying that we can't escape the skin and bones we were born into. That it's more than a body, it's identity, heritage, a lineage you have no control over. No matter how you rearrange yourself, you're still the same person."

Arlette rocked on her heels, head down, eyes on the floor. She stared for a long time. "Let's try it," she said, and her acknowledgment sent a surge of adrenaline through Ida.

It was an exhibit that would never be seen, but that night they created something spectacular, arranging the photographs on the wall of the gallery in silent anticipation. Up close, each image held a pearlescent curve of skin buoyed in black, but as you stepped slowly backward, the photographs merged into an astounding, larger-than-life Arlette: arched back, legs splayed, arms flung wide, head tilted, eyes upward. Before them, a towering ghost-skinned woman floating in darkness.

When they finished, they lay on their backs on the floor with their hands propped under their heads as the sun tipped away from the windows and the image slowly darkened.

"Where's Peggy?" Ida asked.

"Away on holiday." Arlette rolled onto her stomach and propped on her elbows. "I'm starving."

Ida was too. The last thing she'd eaten was a boiled carrot right before her father's hand landed on the back of her neck. "Should we eat?" she said, even though she didn't want to move.

Arlette gave her a curious smile. "What are you doing here?" she asked, as if just realizing Ida hadn't been there all along.

"I came to find you."

Arlette's smile widened. "I'm glad," she said, and in a single, graceful motion, leaned over and kissed Ida.

It was different than a boy's kiss, their roaming, urgent tongues thrust into Ida's mouth, their need boiling up in small groans. This was a kiss all its own, drawn out and tender with a chalky taste of lipstick coming from Arlette's soft mouth, her tongue slippery and tangy. There was an impulsivity to it that produced a reckless pleasure in Ida. The kiss was unexpected and yet unsurprising. Like everything Arlette did, it seemed like the most natural thing in the world.

15

IDA SLEPT ON THE couch in Arlette's elegant spare flat, waking to the smell of coffee and the news broadcast on the radio. It seemed as if Arlette never slept. She'd be up when Ida fell asleep, reading or fiddling with her camera, and up when Ida woke, bumping around the kitchen in her rumpled sweater, her bangs falling straight over her forehead, a cigarette and coffee in hand, somehow seductive and gorgeous no matter the hour.

There was no kiss after that first one, and Ida wasn't sure what Arlette's intentions were or why she was letting her stay. It didn't matter. Living with Arlette was more than Ida had hoped for, and she wasn't going to risk her luck by questioning it. It did hurt a little that Arlette no longer asked her to play the violin. Arlette had moved on from the subject of sound to the subject of light. Light was the elusive, impossible thing to hold on to, the invisible, changing element she would capture on photosensitized paper in a way no one ever had before.

In close quarters, Ida found that there was something equally intimate and out of reach about Arlette. She was both direct and evasive. She knew exactly what she wanted for her future—success as an artist above all else—and had no interest in discussing the past. Neither spoke of their families. Once, Ida asked Arlette about her parents, and Arlette said, "My mother lives in Paris" in a tone that made it clear there was nothing more to be said. Ida liked the idea of her family dropping away to a single sentence. If asked, she would say, "My parents live in Petersfield." End of story.

Ida felt no guilt over vanishing into the night with her father's money. He had taken her earnings, and she had taken his. Scores were being kept.

Living without her family was easier than she thought it would be. To be unattached was to be free, Arlette had told her, and it was true. Arlette did exactly as she pleased without asking permission from anyone. As did Peggy and Djuna and Jacqueline. These women were not just married to or sleeping with artists; they were artists and art patrons themselves, taking what they wanted from the world without apology.

Money helped. Arlette was only twenty years old and had a full-time job with Peggy and an apartment all her own. The only women Ida knew in Petersfield who worked were either too young for marriage or too old, and poor as dirt, even with a job. The ease with which money flowed from Arlette's small clutch was astonishing. She'd see a pair of shoes in a window and tell the shop clerk she'd take them without even asking the price. Silk dresses, gold bracelets, lace underwear, satin slips, all bought on a whim. The money she spent on food and wine for a single meal would have cost Ida a week's wages.

Ida offered to pay her share, but Arlette flat-out refused, which only highlighted what Ida lacked. There was no way Ida could keep up, even if she had wanted to. Her father's money would be gone in a week. She calculated that if she didn't spend more than twenty pounds, she'd have enough money for a year of tuition at the music conservatory.

Ida had walked to Marylebone Road and stood in front of the high brick building of the Royal Academy of Music, watching the students make their way up the front steps, clothes neatly arranged, instruments in hand. She imagined herself among them, discussing who might be chosen for concertmaster and who would be left with second chair. When they entered the building and the huge wooden door shut behind them, Ida stood for a long time, wishing it wasn't midwinter and the windows were open so she could hear them play.

She practiced diligently, preparing to audition as soon as applications opened. Arlette was encouraging, even while she believed school was a waste of time. Art, Arlette said, was about formlessness, not structure, about breaking rules, not being taught how to follow them. Assisting her in the studio, Ida paid close attention to how Arlette set up ordinary objects—a string tied around a wad of fabric, a pair of gloves, a metal cap—and transformed them in the darkroom. A hat pin became a man standing at an odd angle with wire flowers in his hands. Hardwood floors became liquid. Shoes floated in blue skies. Rippling sunshine turned to stone.

One day, Arlette eased Ida in front of the window and said, "Let's see what we can do with you."

"No." Ida squirmed, but Arlette held her firmly.

"No one will see them but me, and they won't even look like you. Trust me."

The problem was, as much as Ida admired Arlette, she didn't trust her. How could she, after being dropped so effortlessly in Petersfield? There was an impermanence to Arlette. Being with her was like testing the too-thin surface of an iced-over lake. The risk was worth the thrill, but you had to be prepared for the ground to crack beneath you.

Forcing Ida into a chair, Arlette unbuttoned the top three buttons of Ida's blouse and drew her sleeve off her shoulder. Ida wanted her to keep going. She wanted to feel the cool tips of Arlette's fingers on her skin. She wanted her to kiss her again, to break the surface so they could sink all the way under.

Arlette stepped back with her eye to the viewfinder, adjusting the lens of the camera with her finger on the shutter button. "Tilt your head to the left. A little more. Now, look right at me."

Ida did as she was told.

WHEN PEGGY RETURNED from holiday, she was as unfazed to find Ida in her studio as Arlette had been. Kissing Ida's cheek, she said, "Lovely to see you, darling" and launched into a story about how she'd spent the last week in hospital getting an abortion. "My physician in Petersfield wouldn't do it, so I had to find a German doctor, who confirmed that I was far too old to be having a baby and, who, thank God, didn't kill me in the process of getting rid of it. I should never have gotten involved with that English artist. His wife and I were pregnant at the same time. Can you imagine? She was lucky enough to have a miscarriage. Although she didn't see it that way. The poor thing actually wants a child. Snobbish old English money can't buy you that. I offered to give them my baby, but Llewellyn said his wife wouldn't stand for it, and anyway, he said he could just make more." She threw up her hands, her skin pale in the cool light from the window. "Have I appalled you?" She cocked an eyebrow at Ida.

Most things out of Peggy's mouth were appalling. "Only a little." Ida smiled.

There was no reaction from Arlette, who busied herself at the desk. A distinct mood had come over her, her photo installation at the back of the gallery an unspoken pulse in the air.

When Peggy finally crossed the room to it, she said, "Let me guess. This monstrous body of work is your creation, Arlette."

Arlette stopped shuffling papers. She dropped into a chair, watching as Peggy inspected the pictures at close range, moving from one to the other as if they were individual images, missing the point entirely. Ida wanted to tell Peggy she was viewing it all wrong, but the aggressive way Arlette stared Peggy down made Ida think that Peggy's misinterpretation was the very thing keeping Arlette quiet. She'd told Ida no artist should have to explain their work. It was not an intellectual understanding. It was an instant reaction, a gut feeling.

"They're good," Peggy said. "Well executed, but I don't think they're right for the gallery. Do you?" It was not a question.

Rejection did not come easily to Arlette. Her eyes squinted as if trying to shield the wounded look that had come into them. "You're right. They're not ready," she said, and with a tortured smile, crossed the room, and began plucking the photographs from the wall.

Something tore at Ida with each blank space that appeared. It was all she could do not to rush over and stop her. How could Peggy so easily dismiss Arlette's work? It reminded her of her mother, these wildly different women impeding their futures. What right did they have?

"I'm closing the gallery anyway." Peggy moved around the room, inspecting her canvases, reassuring herself of her good taste.

Arlette gave no indication she'd heard as she peeled the photographs away to chalky plaster.

Pausing in front of a sculpture, Peggy flicked her eyes up at Ida. "Do you like this?"

Ida thought the lump of white clay looked like a malformed baby, but she said, "It's lovely," assuming that was what Peggy wanted to hear.

"Would you buy it?"

"I suppose."

"Well, then you're the only one." Peggy swirled around. "How come we never sold this piece, Arlette?"

"Buyers are finicky," Arlette said.

"How much money have we lost this year?"

"Six hundred pounds."

A photograph slid from Arlette's fingers, and Ida watched it float to the ground like a tiny sail.

Peggy sighed. "It's all those publicity parties. They result in a lot of wild, drunk jealousies and never any sales. If I'm going to lose money, I might as well do something useful. Which is why I've decided to open a modern museum. What do you think?"

Arlette climbed onto a stool to reach the higher photos. "Smashing idea," she said, notably indifferent.

"Don't be sore about your work. I'll show it one day. You said yourself it's not ready. You'll thank me when it is." Peggy went to the door, slid on her fur coat, and plucked up her handbag. "In the meantime, the museum will be brilliant. We'll open it here in London. I'll make you registrar. Does that please you? First, we'll need to go to Paris to procure the work, which I know for certain will please you."

Arlette gave a weak smile. "I'd love nothing more."

"Good, because I've already rented us an apartment on the Ile Saint-Louis."

Wait, no, Ida wanted to cry. The conversation had taken a swift turn. She wasn't ready to be abandoned in London. It was only March. School wouldn't start for six months, and she still had to audition for a spot.

Peggy prattled on. "After what I've been through, I'm going to need a holiday before we charge ahead with this whole affair. I should visit my children. If only my ex-husband hadn't bought a house in that wretched ski village. I detest it. Maybe I'll stay with Nell in the south of

France, but I do want to get this thing going. Arlette, how do you feel about going on ahead to Paris? You could manage without me for a month, couldn't you?"

The last photo fluttered to the floor, a jumble of body parts. The wall loomed white behind Arlette as she climbed off the stool. "I'll need help."

Peggy brushed at the sleeve of her coat. "A museum is costly. I'm trying to cut expenses, not acquire more. I've decided to stop buying clothes, and I've already sold my gorgeous car and bought a Talbot. Cheap little thing, but it runs. I am going to live a monastic life." She gave a determined shake of her head.

"Peggy." Arlette's tone said, *Let's be reasonable.* "A museum is a huge endeavor. You can't expect me to do it all on my own. Hiring someone would be a business expense, not a personal one, and a necessity if you're going on holiday and leaving everything to me." She crouched down and began gathering her photos from the floor. "We should hire Ida."

Peggy looked at Ida as if it had never occurred to her that she could be useful. "Do you have secretarial skills?"

Ida hesitated, and Arlette quickly jumped in. "Anyone can answer the telephone and make calls and take notes. I'll train her and keep her busy."

Peggy sighed. "I can only spare ten dollars a week."

Ida had no idea what this converted to in pounds, but it sounded like an enormous sum. It took her a month to make ten pounds at the hat shop.

"Brilliant." Arlette didn't look up from the floor as Ida tried to register what had just happened. How effortless these women made everything seem. In an instant, she had a job and was going to Paris.

Only later would it occur to Ida that she was never asked. It was assumed she would want the position. Arlette's seduction was in her confidence that she would be followed and worshiped, like any good leader. Ida went willingly, exultingly. She left music school behind and told herself there was plenty of time. Her dream could wait. She'd be back. Paris was temporary.

16

❧

SHIMMERING IN THE RAIN or drenched in sunshine, the streets of Paris were as lavish and magnificent as Arlette said they would be. Eating a tin of chocolates on the Champs-Élysées or sitting under the heavily scented roses in the Tuileries, Ida learned what it was to live a life of privilege.

Three months before Hitler invaded Poland in June of 1939, she and Arlette moved into an apartment on the seventh floor of a building overlooking the Seine. It was owned by an American Surrealist named Kay Sage who knew enough to get out of Paris while she still could. With a toss of her gorgeous hair, golden and curled like a movie star's, she said, "The apartment is all yours. It's going to be bombed to smithereens anyway, darlings" and stepped into the lift with her suitcase in hand, the cage door sliding shut with a bang.

Ida barely heard her. She was thinking how fantastic it was to live in a place where a lift opened right onto a terrace, the river sliding away below as one walked across the tiles and through the French doors of an airy, light-filled apartment. It was unreal, the pitched ceilings and silver-papered walls, the claw-foot tub languishing like a large, lovely creature in the bathroom, the copper handles tinged green, the marble floor petal soft under Ida's feet as she padded across and slid into the belly of water, pretending she was as bold and beautiful and rich as Kay Sage.

When Peggy came back from holiday, she slept in the master bedroom attached to a dressing room with a vanity full of glass perfume bottles and tortoise shell combs. Arlette and Ida slept in a smaller room off the terrace that had a double bed and a large armoire where their clothes hung side by side, Ida's newly purchased.

Arlette had taken her to a department store with high mirrors and hovering salesladies, watching from the seat of a tufted divan as Ida modeled a pleated skirt with a matching tunic, a rose-colored blouse, trousers with tiny pockets and tapered ankles. When Ida stepped from the dressing room in a black-and-white silk gown, a saleslady slipped a bolero with stiffened shoulders over her arms and turned her toward the mirror. Under the glittering lights, Ida didn't recognize herself.

Arlette joined her in the mirror. "Hemlines have come down," she said. "I like it." She lifted Ida's hair from her neck. "I'll take you to my hairdresser. Just a few inches off. Don't you think?"

Ida didn't know what to think. She felt grateful and ashamed for her lack of style and sophistication.

"It's too much," she said, but by that time the clothes were already being folded into tissue paper.

Arlette added a pair of leather heels and a pink-velvet saucer hat that was placed in a box with a satin bow. Sliding a wad of franc notes across the counter, she tucked the hat box under her arm and said, "There's no such thing as too much. You're in my home country now, and you are my guest."

Ida tried to imagine Arlette as a young girl ordering up hats and dresses from these slender perfumed salesladies. She wanted to ask Arlette where she'd shopped as a child. Did her mother take her? What street had she lived on? Where did she play? How did children spend their time in a city like Paris where all anyone seemed to do was eat and drink and shop?

Ida did not ask these things. Even here, Arlette's family felt like a taboo subject. When she handed over the luxurious bags, all Ida said was, "Thank you. I'll repay you one day." An ambitious, impossible promise.

Under Arlette's tutelage, Ida expanded. Her French improved. She learned how to walk in heels and drink straight absinthe and seduce a person from across a room. She learned which fork to use and which glass to drink from at their champagne dinners where flaky fish floated in cream and lemon. Wine came in goblets, sherry in thimble-sized glasses. Dessert was tiered chocolate or *crème pâtissier* wrapped in crumbling pastry.

Artists and actors and writers rotated through their apartment in droves. When a familiar face from Yew Tree Cottage appeared, they greeted Ida with a cry of delight and a kiss on the cheek as if she'd always been among them. At some point in the evening, someone would put on an album or sit at the piano, and the dancing began. Inevitably there was a shout for Ida to play, and she'd join the pianist and dancers, the air heavy with smoke and perfume and the warmth of the summer night.

These were the hours when Arlette's eyes were the most brilliant. Ida could feel them on her, dark and glittering and a little sad. To have Arlette's attention, her extravagant applause, even her sadness, made Ida play with purpose. These were no longer private concerts. They were public declarations to Arlette, and public admiration from her. It was the only time Ida felt like her equal.

When the evening died down, she and Arlette would stumble to their bedroom, strip into nightgowns, roll their hair in curlers, and drop onto the bed. Drunk and inspired, they'd talk of their futures. They were going to be successful, unbound women. No children. No husbands. They'd have careers and take multiple lovers. Ida would go to the Conservatoire de Paris and play for the Orchestre de la Société des Concerts du Conservatoire. Arlette would get a gallery show in Paris, then London, then New York.

It was easy to believe these things back then. Ida had not yet learned that deception could be used as a tool to survive, that to dream was to keep one's head above water.

17

A T FIRST, THE LOOMING war mattered little to Ida. She was nineteen years old, living in a glittering city where money flowed around her in chartreuse cocktails and anchovy toasts, in sable coats and sumptuous bedding, in canvases splashed with color and worktables towering with bronze sculptures. She gave the war a mere nervous glance. It was a lion atop a hill, a thing of danger, but far away and uninterested in her. There was no war in France. It had other prey to devour.

But it would come, that slow, stalking beast. It would gorge on them without pause and spit out their bones.

A WEEK AFTER Germany launched their surprise attack on Poland, Arlette brought Ida to meet her mother. Ida did not ask why the sudden visit. It made sense in a time of uncertainty. Even Ida had drafted a letter to Leon. It was still folded on her desk, but it seemed important to reach out to at least one member of her family now that England was officially at war.

Madame Lucienne Lellouche was a petite woman who sat with a tight, unrevealing expression as they sipped tea from bone china and ate finger cookies that crumbled on their tongues. The apartment was opulent, the surfaces shiny and filled with fresh flowers. There was an overhead pendant hung with crystal and a wall of books Arlette said used to be her father's. There was no mention of where he was now, or of the framed photograph on the mantle of a young man who looked vaguely like Arlette, but with lighter hair and a harder face.

Arlette did all the talking while Madame Lellouche looked Ida over with heavily made up eyes. Her pencil-thin brows arched into her forehead and her lips were candy-apple red. Arlette spoke in a reserved tone, as if visiting an old acquaintance. She told her mother about Peggy's museum plans, about the gallery in London and the hassle of transporting the art back and forth from Petersfield. When she mentioned the war, Madame Lellouche flapped her hand in the air like she was swatting away a fly. This was their cue to leave. Arlette stood up. Their teacups were empty. The cookies gone. Stiffly, Madame Lellouche pushed herself from her chair, clasped Ida's hand, and said, with great feeling, "*Au revoir, ma chère,*" and kissed Ida's cheeks with her waxy lips. She then kissed her daughter and said it was all too much, she was going to lie down.

Walking away from the building, Ida found the courage to ask, "Where's your father?"

"Dead." Arlette pulled the collar of her coat tight around her neck. The September wind pinched her cheeks red. Ida couldn't read her mood. She was not entirely collapsed, but something had shriveled.

They were crossing a bridge when Arlette stopped and lit a cigarette. She leaned on the rail, smoking and looking into the water. Out of nowhere, she said, "If you want to pass as French, you'll have to perfect your accent and pronunciation." She handed Ida her cigarette.

"Why would I want to pass as French?" Ida took a drag and handed it back.

Arlette finished the cigarette, flicked it over the rail, and said, "It will be useful one day."

Ida ignored the remark, and the subtle unease that went with it.

AS THE WAR pawed at the ground, its voracious appetite just beginning, Ida thought only of how to fit into Arlette's world, how to be both disarming and fierce. Arlette's skill in getting what she wanted was her ability to shower affection on everyone, making them feel singled out and adored.

This was why Peggy employed her. Ida learned this in the first few weeks she worked for her. The only women Peggy could stand to be around for long periods of time were women who made her feel significant. When Peggy stumbled across Ida in the apartment, she regarded her in the same manner as the Persian cats Kay Sage had left behind, pinching her face as if Ida were somehow bothersome and confusing.

The shine of Arlette's attention, however, set Peggy's cheeks aglow.

Arlette played this up, making Peggy look like the ingenious one, even though it was Arlette who secured a location for the museum, as well as organized the collection that was to be sent to England in the fall: borrowed paintings from the first abstract and Cubist works from 1910, along with Cezanne, Matisse, and Rousseau.

In addition to organizing the opening of a museum that would never be—the war would ensure the collapse of Peggy's well-laid plans—Ida quickly learned that being employed by Peggy not only meant managing her art but also her lavish dinner parties, breakfasts, luncheons, and love affairs. One had to be quiet in the morning, make sure spirits and food were always on hand, learn to lie to a distressed wife, to give vague answers to strangers on the telephone, and to head off one lover if Peggy had gone to meet another.

One night, when they were out to dinner, the wife of an art patron—Ida was never sure which one—walked up to Peggy and threw a whole fish in her lap, shouting epithets until the woman's mortified husband dragged her out. Straight faced, Peggy picked the fish off her dress and asked to see the dessert menu.

Arlette also had lovers, but these she silently managed on her own. For a while there was a woman named Giselle with astonishingly large eyes, lofty cheekbones, and skin the color of caramel. She'd come over in the evenings, and Ida would sit with them listening to the radio and drinking wine before the two slipped off into the bedroom. Ida tried to imagine what they were doing in there. She was certain Arlette's kiss was different with Giselle. With Ida it had been tender, innocent, someone Arlette was guiding into unknown territory, whereas Giselle looked like she knew exactly what she was doing.

Lust and jealousy rose up in Ida. In an attempt to satisfy herself, she kissed a sculptor's apprentice who'd been tasked with the job of convincing Arlette to come for a studio visit. While Arlette was upstairs checking her schedule, Ida pressed her mouth to Vernon's. He was a scrawny boy of no more than sixteen with a narrow chin and lovely eyes. They were parted by the time Arlette returned, and Vernon left flushed and speechless.

Ida did a lot of kissing after that. Only with boys. They were easy and willing. It never went past a squeeze of her breast or a hand over her bottom. It wasn't that she was scared of sex, she just couldn't shake the warning of unmarried sex her mother had hammered into her. Ida no longer believed she'd go to hell for it—if she was going to hell, the Parisian artists would be there with her—it was the idea of being damaged goods that worried her.

Eventually, Arlette took a new lover, a tall man with a trim mustache and neat hands who took her out to dinner and brought her back in the morning. Seeing Arlette with a man made Ida feel less confused about her own attractions to both men and women, but no less jealous. On the nights Arlette was gone, their bed felt cavernous, the cool emptiness a sinkhole. It didn't matter that Ida had lopped off her hair and curled it fashionably, or that she'd spent a week's earnings on Kayser silk underwear and leather gloves; she still felt like she was skimming on the edges of a life that wasn't hers.

She tried to emulate Arlette, the breathy way she answered the telephone, how she pinned the receiver between her ear and shoulder as she scribbled down an address. Ida paid attention to the jut of Arlette's hip and the tilt of her head as she inspected a piece of artwork, the way she threw her arms around men and women alike, kissing their cheeks and making them feel singular.

Every artist they visited, Yves Tanguy, Constantin Brâncuşi and Man Ray, received Arlette eagerly—as a buyer for Peggy but also as an artist and model herself. She was useful to them in more ways than one. Arlette molded herself into whatever these men needed her to be. With Tanguy, she wore pants and a tailored jacket, laughed boldly, told him that the hair standing up on his head was more interesting than his art-work, the insult confusing him just enough for her to get her hands on the exact painting she wanted.

With Brâncuși, she was as cold and glossy as his sculptures. He greeted her with a jerk of his head and went back to heating a tool in the furnace while Arlette inspected the smooth bronze pieces in his dust-covered studio. There was no smile, no kiss or banter, just a few choice words from her bright red mouth, a casual mention of the monument she'd heard he built for his native country of Romania, a squint of her thickly lashed eyes, and Brâncuși nodded and said he'd sell Peggy *Birds in Space*—a sculpture that looked like an enormous sleek quill pen—for four thousand dollars. Arlette raised a single plucked brow and said he'd already insulted Peggy with this price. In the end, it was agreed they'd pay in francs, which meant, with the exchange rate, Arlette saved Peggy one thousand dollars.

With Man Ray, Arlette was relaxed. She kicked off her shoes, kissed his lips, and gave him an irresistible smile. He was short with bushy brows and earnest eyes he couldn't take off of her. He barely glanced at Ida. She sat in a leather chair, watching him slide his hand to the small of Arlette's back while showing her an oil painting he'd done of a nude woman stretched above a fish in a sea of pearly waves. Arlette, wearing the same blue trousers she'd worn the day Ida first met her, let his hand roam where it wanted. Ida looked away. She took in a portrait of a woman with tiny ears and a trim nose, a coffee pot, dirty cups on the counter, a plate of uneaten cheese. Out the window, the clouds closed in. When they left, Arlette said it was a good thing Ida had come or Man would certainly have gotten her into bed with him.

"Have you been to bed with him?" Ida asked.

"Not yet."

"Do you want to go to bed with him?"

She shrugged. "Maybe."

Arlette's indifference, her ability to turn her impassioned personality compliant and appeasing in an instant, bewildered Ida. It was like living with a stranger and a best friend at once.

Ida was never sure what to believe.

18

⁓

IN THE SPRING OF 1940, a year after Ida arrived in Paris, she stood
on the sidewalk with her violin and bag in hand as Peggy ordered her
into the car.

"Hurry up," Peggy said. She held the Persian cats propped on her
hips like small children.

"We can't leave without Arlette." Ida scrambled into the passenger
seat as Peggy dumped the cats in her lap.

"We most certainly can." Peggy got into the driver's seat, slammed
the gear shift forward, and pulled the car into the street. She was un-
nervingly calm for the state of emergency they were in.

Until that morning, she'd ignored the air raids and radio bulletins.
All winter, Peggy had kept right on throwing dinner parties and collecting artwork as Germany invaded Poland and Stalin took the Baltic
states. Peggy chose to believe it was a "phony war," as the news declared,
drinking in cafés and barreling forward with her museum plans.

Arlette, on the other hand, had stopped going to restaurants, or putting her hair in curlers, or wearing lipstick. Over the last few months,
her breezy manner had turned sharp and focused. The girls who tied
bows to their gas masks disgusted her, as did news reports of anything
other than the war. She'd sit at the dinner table looking around with a
hard, raised brow as if the frivolousness of eating and drinking was taking things too far.

The worst thing was that Arlette had started disappearing in the
middle of the night. Ida would fall asleep next to her and wake to an

empty bed. She hated the silence and the heavy darkness. Out the window, Paris no longer sparkled. No couples traipsed under the shrouded streetlights. There was no laughter, no drunken shouts, just the occasional lone figure slinking past or a car crawling by with its single headlight painted blue. It felt, to Ida, as if a great winged creature hovered over the city sucking the life out of it.

One night, Arlette said to her, "Do you know why there are no longer crossword puzzles in the newspapers?"

"No." Ida was changing for dinner. Arlette had decided it was a waste of time to get dressed up and sat on the bed in her trousers reading the newspaper. "Are you going to tell me why?" Ida said, struggling to button the back of her dress.

Arlette tossed the paper aside and stood up. "Turn around," she said, and began buttoning Ida's dress for her. "There are no longer crossword puzzles because they are trying to prevent coded information from being sent through French newspapers. Not German or Polish newspapers. *French* newspapers. Has anyone asked why?" Securing Ida's last button, Arlette went to the window and pulled back the black cloth that hung over it. "Is anyone questioning why we now need an identity card for the simple act of using a public telephone? Or a certificate of residence signed at the police department in order to receive a telegram? If it's a diplomatic war, as everyone claims, why are we so wary of civilian spies? Unimaginable horrors are happening, and Parisians are still drinking champagne and gallivanting around as if it's a joke."

"The Germans have nothing on the French army," Ida said. She believed the stories she'd heard were isolated incidents, exaggerations, things contained behind borders. "We'll be all right here."

Arlette turned to Ida with an incredulous expression. "You will be. You're not Jewish."

Ida faltered, unsure how to respond. Arlette had never pointed out this difference. Peggy was Jewish. Almost all the artists they knew were.

"The Jews are safe in France," Ida said, as if she knew anything.

Dismissive, Arlette brushed past her. "People seem to think so," she said.

The day Hitler invaded Norway, Arlette refused to accompany

Peggy on her daily studio visit. "I'm not going." She stood in the open doorway of the apartment with her hair tucked into a black cap and her camera around her neck. She was jumpy and agitated. "I have something to do."

"What could be more important than procuring a Léger?" Peggy genuinely wanted to know.

"This is no time to be shopping for art, Peggy. Have you not heard what Hitler is doing in Poland? We are both Jewish. Do you have no idea what that means right now? Or do you not care? Do you think your money will protect you?"

Peggy's posture straightened. "I think my American passport will."

"Right, well, I don't have one of those." Arlette used a sharp tone of voice Ida had never heard her take with Peggy before.

White-knuckling her handbag, Peggy said, "I know what it's like to be discriminated against. I was turned out of a hotel in Vermont once. You can't imagine how humiliating that was."

This only flamed Arlette's anger. "Humiliating? There was an article yesterday about an eighty-year-old Jewish man who was chased down by a mob and beaten to death in front of his wife. After, they beat her too. Not to death, which she begged for, but enough so that she'd die slowly. It's gone beyond humiliating, Peggy. It's down to torture."

When Arlette turned to Ida, her face was full of contempt. She said, "Do you have traveling papers?" in a voice that implied Ida was at fault for something.

"No," Ida faltered.

"Do you have your passport on you?"

"No." Ida felt a growing panic. "It's up in my room."

"All foreigners residing in France are now required to carry identity papers. You'll be stopped and asked for them." Reaching into her brassiere, Arlette drew out a photograph. "This is the Stade Colombes where we saw a tennis match a month ago."

The photograph showed a line of men heading through the darkened door of the stadium dressed in hats and top coats. They might have been going to a football match, if not for the rifled men corralling them. "Our own government has rounded up over fifteen thousand German nationals. They're even taking Austrians and Czechs. They're isolating them right here in Paris, forcing them to sleep on the ground without food or water or latrines. These are renowned authors, musicians, scientists, doctors. It doesn't matter who you are anymore. If you're an enemy alien, you're being imprisoned or shipped off to an internment camp. Reporters can't get near them. Pétain is making sure of that. He doesn't want to tarnish his reputation with your precious Americans."

"How were you able to get close?" Ida asked.

The photograph disappeared back into Arlette's blouse. "I know people."

Peggy said, "They released Max Ernst." As if this was proof things were in order.

"He had connections. Others have not been so lucky, and there's rumor he'll be arrested again."

Over Arlette's shoulder, Ida suddenly noticed two people outside watching them. It was Giselle and the tall man Ida had also believed to be Arlette's lover.

"I have to go," Arlette said.

Without a backward glance, she joined the two in the street, and Ida knew that they had never been Arlette's lovers. Something else was between them.

When Arlette turned the corner, Ida had an urge to run after her, but this new thing alive in Arlette's body, the courage and rage, frightened Ida.

She stood watching Arlette go, and did nothing.

PEGGY BOUGHT A painting that day, a 1919 Léger she paid one thousand dollars for. The next day, she bought a series of rayographs from Man Ray.

While Peggy was in his back room choosing what she wanted, Man poured Ida a glass of sherry and asked where Arlette was.

"I don't know," Ida said. The world had shifted, and Arlette had gone with it.

Man looked Ida up and down openly, as if this was a perfectly normal way to observe a woman. "Has she photographed you?" he asked.

"She has." The sherry was smooth on Ida's tongue, expensive.

"Would you like me to photograph you?"

Ida thought how casually Arlette took these things. "Sure," she said, her stomach tensing. She did not want to get naked for this man no matter how famous he was.

"Bring Arlette and I'll photograph the two of you." He smiled and tipped his glass in a cheers motion, as if his proposal was worthy of celebration.

Poor Man, trying to lure Arlette through her. "Aren't you afraid of the war?" Ida said.

"Terrified," he answered.

Ida would say goodbye to Man that day and not think of him again for twelve years. She would not even wonder if he made it out of Paris alive until that photograph showed up in Lexington, Massachusetts. Ida finished her sherry and left with Peggy, telling herself that Arlette would return and they would pose for Man and life would go on as it had been.

BETWEEN ARLETTE'S SUDDEN departure and the mass exodus of almost every artist Peggy knew, Ida became her default companion. Together they packed up Peggy's art collection. Originally it was to be stored in the basement of their building—until the landlord told them that the basement was being used as an air-raid shelter. "Human lives are more important than your art," he said. Peggy said she'd beg to differ, and the man said he didn't care what she thought, there was no room, and that was that. The Louvre then agreed to give Peggy one cubic meter of space where they were secretly storing paintings, only to decide at the last minute that the work she patronized was too modern and not worth saving. Peggy told the curator he was an imbecile. In the end, her collection was being sent off to a chateau in southern France, where it was to be hidden in a barn.

Two days after the boxes were loaded onto the truck, German soldiers broke through the supposedly impenetrable defense barriers at Sedan.

The beast had leapt and landed. Denial was no longer possible.

OUT THE CAR window, Ida watched the current of bodies pushing wheelbarrows and wagons move in a strangely uniform fashion as Peggy drove. There was no chaos, at least not yet. An old man helped a child into a cart, wheeling the boy over the cobblestones with steady arms. A woman hoisted a bag onto her back. A man took her hand. They held on. The young and old, the middle aged. They walked side by side, unhurried, but with a sense of urgency, pacing themselves, as if deep down they knew how long of a road it would be.

Earlier, as Ida helped Peggy load the *bidons* of petrol into the boot of the car, she asked what they were going to do about their lack of papers. Peggy had recently discovered her traveling permit was expired. When she tried to renew it, it was denied. Ida didn't have one to begin with. Flicking the hair off her forehead, Peggy said, "Do you see all these people pouring out of Paris? Trust me, no one is checking traveling permits."

This was not reassuring. Peggy was an American. The Americans were not at war with Germany. The Brits were.

Ida tucked her violin between her feet and held her bag in her lap. Her father's money was still stuffed into her socks at the bottom of it. She had no idea how, or where, to exchange it. Her wages had been paid in francs, most of which she'd spent. How much would it cost to leave the country? She didn't have an exit permit or a traveling visa. Ida scanned the street for Arlette, picturing her leaping from the throng of people, waving and shouting for them to wait for her.

Peggy drove on in silence. The cats mewed and clawed at the seats. Arlette did not spring from the crowd. By the time they were on the main road to Fontainebleau, the line of cars laden down with household goods, boxes, suitcases, and bedrolls was endless. They crawled along in first gear, the air black with smoke and the smell of petrol. Swearing under her breath, Peggy veered onto a side road, and then another, the car bumping over rocks and grass. At one point, a man flagged them down with his walking stick, his face dirt-stained, his clothes filthy.

"I wouldn't go this way if I were you," he said. "Italian soldiers are coming over the border to the east."

"Thank you for the warning," Peggy said, rolled up the window, and continued on.

PART THREE

CONCERTO, OPUS 64

1940–1945

19

PEGGY WAS RIGHT. THE exodus of two million people out of occupied France meant no one was checking papers. Within a day of their departure from Paris, driving east and avoiding the general madness on the main roads, Ida and Peggy landed in Annecy, where Peggy's children—spoiled teenagers—lived in a house on a lake with their father, Laurence, a pudgy middle-aged man who drank too much, and an artist couple named Jean and Sophie Arp whom Peggy knew from her early Paris days.

The Arps were tolerable, the rest of the family impossible.

Ida spent the summer typing in a hot room overlooking the tennis courts where Peggy's son, Sindbad, and her daughter, Pegeen, swatted a ball around with a relentless pop and thunk. When they weren't playing tennis or swimming in the lake, Pegeen was sprawled on the sofa in an airy dress with a scowl on her face, Sindbad flung into a chair, both of them moaning about the heat and boredom. They'd ask Ida to fetch them a cold drink or turn on a fan. Ida did it begrudgingly. They were naive and overindulged. She supposed you couldn't expect them to mature in an instant just because a war was on.

She had no such excuse for Peggy. What was glamourous in Paris looked like madness in Annecy.

Gathered around the radio at night listening to war news, Peggy would shake her head and cry, "What a disaster! How absolutely tragic it all is," pour herself another drink, and launch into her museum plans, the "disaster" a temporary setback. The worst of it was her taking up with her hairdresser, a fact that did not bother her ex-husband in the least. After reading D. H. Lawrence, Peggy decided that "sex with a lower-class man would be a romantic way to pass the time," first dyeing her hair a hideous red, then blonde, then back to brown as an excuse to see him.

It was like living in a house of illusions, these people somehow carrying on with affairs and tennis and cocktails while the news reported bodies left by the side of the road, entire towns destroyed by bombs. Phone lines were cut off. Railroads were down, and here they were, saturated in the luxury of boredom.

The indulgence was shameful. Ida could see why Arlette had turned her back on Peggy. It was November now, and Peggy hadn't even tried to find her. When Ida asked about it, Peggy said, "Arlette is the most resilient woman I know. And she left *me*, remember?" Even if she were to send a letter, there was no mail from the occupied zone. People were losing each other every day. There was nothing she could do.

Letters from America, however, were still getting through. Peggy squinted at the one on her tray from Kay Sage. "Read this for me, would you?" She had misplaced her reading glasses again. Peggy sat up in bed, gloves on, heater cranking.

Ida slid the paper from the envelope.

Kay scolded Peggy for remaining in Europe, bemoaned her gorgeous apartment falling into the hands of the Germans, and insisted that if Peggy was going to risk staying in France, she might as well be heroic and help her rescue and finance the passage of five distinguished artists who were certain to be captured and sent to concentration camps. *I am begging you. We must do something*, she wrote.

"Five distinguished artists?" Peggy cracked the shell of her hard-boiled egg with the edge of her spoon. "I know a lot more than five on the Nazi wanted list. Does she say who the five are?" She spooned a wobbly bit of egg into her mouth. Ida read the names: André Breton, Jacqueline, their daughter Aube, Max Ernst, and the Surrealist's doctor, Mabille. Peggy scoffed, "Dr. Mabille is not an artist. Neither are Jacqueline and Aube. That makes exactly two distinguished artists."

Ida said, "You can't expect André to leave without his wife and daughter."

"I suppose not." Peggy moved the tray aside and swung her legs off the bed. "Hand me my robe."

The robe was silk, printed with tiny colorful fans. Peggy slid her arms into the sleeves and yanked the tie around her waist. "Last week, I got a letter from Victor Brauner asking for my help. He's hiding in the mountains. How does one choose whom to save? If I can even save any of them. It's my own skin I should be worrying about, and my children's. Does Kay think I'm not *trying* to get out? Our passports haven't been renewed, and we're at risk of being cut off without money. One can't travel on a whim anymore." She dropped into the chair in front of her vanity and began dabbing cold cream under her puffy eyes.

In the end, though, Peggy was someone who liked to be needed.

IDA HAD NO idea what was in her valise when she stepped off the train in Marseille. The entire ride, Peggy had kept her face to the window, her body angled away from the commotion. Ida sat across from her with her valise wedged between them, less wary, but still nervous. It was startling to be packed in with so many people fleeing the occupied zone, their lives reduced to a single suitcase, their faces tight and guarded. When the train pulled into the Gare Saint-Charles, Peggy bolted off so fast Ida had to scramble not to lose her in the crowd.

It was a magnificent station high on a pavilion overlooking Marseille. The city was washed in cold December light, the sky bright and clear. Wrapping her scarf over her mouth, Ida hurried to catch up with Peggy, who was barreling toward the stairs, when a policeman stepped in front of Ida. He was young, smooth faced, with a cap pushed off his forehead.

"Papers." He hooked a thumb into his belt loop.

Ida dropped her valise and began fumbling in her purse. She'd done nothing wrong, and yet it was astonishing how his authority rattled her.

Peggy was beside her in an instant. "Is there a problem?"

"I'll need to see your papers too," he said.

People ducked and moved aside, a fearful pocket of air opening up around them.

Ida handed the policeman her passport and travel permit, looking him in the eye as she used to in her stealing days. Not that she had anything to hide. Her passport was in order, and Peggy had assured her that the Vichy weren't arresting civilians for being British.

He held her passport up. "Pull down your scarf."

Ida obeyed. The wind bit her lips. He looked from her face to her photo, checked her travel permit, gave a nod, and handed them back. Peggy was still digging in her purse, making a show of it.

"Oh, here they are!" she cried. Earlier that morning, Peggy remembered she still hadn't renewed her expired travel permit, and Ida had watched her confidently scratch out the old date and write in a new one.

At a single glance, the policeman said, "You've changed the date."

"I've done no such thing!"

"Right here." He pointed to the pen mark slashed over the numbers.

"Oh, that." She swatted her purse. Her coat whipped around her legs. "Some incompetent official at Grenoble wrote in the wrong date and then scratched it out and changed it. I don't see how that's my fault." The ease of her lie was impressive.

"You're staying in Marseille?"

"I am."

"Why haven't you registered in Marseille?"

"I just arrived!"

"Guggenheim? Is that Jewish?"

Peggy grunted. "My grandfather was a Swiss from St. Gallen. I'm as Catholic as they come."

Militantly, the officer folded Peggy's papers into his breast pocket and said, "I'm going to need you to come with me."

Peggy rooted herself to the ground. "Do you know who I am?"

"I don't care who you are. Your travel permit has been tampered with."

"I am a Guggenheim! I am an American citizen. You cannot detain me."

Without a flicker, the policeman said, "You can walk or I can drag you. Your choice."

Peggy clamped her jaw, shoved her chest forward, and said, "I'll walk, thank you very much."

As the policeman turned toward the stairs, Peggy squeezed Ida's arm and whispered, "Go to Villa Air-Bel. Tell them what's happened, and by God"—her voice dropped so low Ida barely heard—"bury the money in your suitcase."

"Hurry up," the policeman ordered, and Peggy fell in step beside him.

Money? Why was the money in Ida's valise?

Marooned, she watched Peggy's small back disappear down the stairs, realizing she hadn't been on her own since she'd stepped off the train in London over two years ago. It was idiotic to leave the safety of Annecy. Why had they thought this was a good idea? Ida snapped up her valise and started down the stairs, wondering what the charge was for carrying black-market money. The plan was to see the artist Max Ernst hand over the money for the emergency visas, and get back on the train to Grenoble. How was Ida supposed to do that on her own? She had no idea where Villa Air-Bel was. And why bury the money unless Peggy thought Ida was in danger of being caught with it?

At the bottom of the stairs, there was a startling touch to Ida's shoulder, and she jerked back, stumbling into a small man in a tweed jacket. "I beg your pardon," he said, catching her arm. "I didn't mean to spring up on you. Are you all right?"

Ida pulled out of his grasp. Behind him was an enormous sculpture of a woman lounging in the sunshine, her expression haughty and commanding, as if she pitied the smallness of everyone who looked at her. "I'm fine," Ida said, wishing she had a crumb of that statue's impregnability.

The man peered at her from behind wire-rimmed glasses. "It's just that I was wondering if you were, by any chance, traveling with Peggy Guggenheim?"

"Who is asking?"

"Varian Fry." He put out his hand. Ida did not take it. Peggy had never mentioned him.

Varian gave an embarrassed smile. "Peggy informed me via telegram that she was arriving on the four o'clock train. I was heading up the stairs when I saw that." He pointed to a small red X on the side of Ida's valise. "I've never met Peggy, but I was to know her by the mark on her luggage."

"It's my luggage," Ida said, defensive. Peggy had not only hidden money in her valise but marked it up? Had she planned on being arrested? "You spoke English to me from the start. How did you know I wasn't French?"

"I assumed. I take it you are Peggy's companion?" He smiled and extended his hand again, his equable attitude persuasive.

Ida shook it. "Ida Davies. I didn't mean to be rude, it's just that Peggy never mentioned meeting anyone. She's been taken to the police station, and I don't know whom I should be speaking to or not."

This news did not elicit the alarm she anticipated. Varian sighed heavily, looking more put out than anything. "That's what I get for running late. I'll drop you at my office. It's on the way to the station. The chief of police knows me well by now. May I?"

He picked up Ida's valise, and she nodded, grateful to follow him down the quiet boulevard. She had never been to Marseille, but the deserted streets put her on edge. For whole stretches, the sidewalks were empty, the air briny and frigid, the roads carless. The windows without signs were the Jewish shops, run by French business owners who were no longer allowed to call themselves French.

A wagon rolled past, followed by a horse-drawn carriage, and Ida wondered if all of France was out of petrol. Under the New Order, people said life in the free zone would be tolerable, but Ida had learned from radio announcements that women were no longer allowed to wear shorts, that knee-length bathing costumes were required at beaches, that divorce was no longer legal, and that the price for an abortion was the death penalty.

Tolerable was relative, as far as Ida could tell.

A few blocks from the harbor, Varian turned into a narrow alley and led Ida through the back door of a two-story building. Down a hallway and up a flight of stairs, they entered a room furnished with three tables, four chairs, and a single lamp at each. At the far end of the room, a dark-haired woman sat writing furiously, while the woman closest to the door raised her head, her concentrated expression softening into a wide smile.

"You found her." Arlette's chair scraped over the floor as she stood up.

20

JOY, AND THEN ANGER, swept through Ida. It was disorienting how unapologetically Arlette presented herself, coming over and wrapping Ida in a hug, whispering, "We have so much to talk about," her tone intimate, devoted.

Ida was furious with Arlette for abandoning her a second time, and yet the moment she pulled away, Ida drew toward her, the feeling instinctual. It didn't matter what happened, or how much time passed; under the shine of Arlette, Ida forgave her anything.

"Where's Peggy?" Arlette turned to Varian. The hollows were gone from her eyes. She looked well rested and healthy.

"The police have taken her to the station."

"No! Do you think they'll search her?"

Varian took off his glasses and wiped them on his coat sleeve. "They might," he said. "I'm headed there now. Hopefully I can intervene in time."

They were worried about the money, Ida realized. She should tell them Peggy had put it in her valise, ease their minds, but a needle of control was threading through her. Why was she, the one transporting the banknotes, the last to know about it? Did they not trust her? And why hadn't anyone told her of Arlette's involvement? Peggy must have known she was here. Were they all using her? Did they think she was too naive to see it?

Arlette stalked to the door. "Good God, Varian, get going. What if you're too late? What would we do then? Peggy would not survive long in prison."

"*We* will do nothing." Varian returned his glasses to his nose. "I will do what I always do. Figure it out." He left with an exasperated look at Arlette and a polite nod to Ida.

"He is frustratingly reasonable. No melodrama where that man's concerned." Arlette sat back down in front of her scattered mess of paper. "Tell me everything that's happened since I last saw you."

Ida lifted her chin and said nothing.

"You're angry with me."

"Of course I am."

"I had to leave. I had no choice." Arlette leaned back in her chair, steepling her fingers.

"Which means I should forgive you for abandoning me with Peggy for six months without an explanation?"

Arlette dropped her elbows to the table. "I never ask anyone's forgiveness. I'm not beholden to you or anybody else. I do what I please, when I please. We make our own choices, Ida. The sooner you learn not to apologize for them, the better off you'll be. Anyway, I found you, didn't I?"

"You didn't find me. Peggy brought me here."

"Who do you think told Kay Sage to write to her? I knew she'd bring you."

This was so like Arlette, manipulating everything behind the scenes. "Why not send a telegram asking me yourself? At the very least, you could have told me you were safe. Does Peggy know you're here? Has she been lying to me too?"

"Peggy has no idea I'm involved. She thinks this is all Kay's doing, and I didn't send a telegram because it isn't safe."

Ida touched the leather handle of her valise. "What if I hadn't come? What then?"

"I would have found another way to get you here."

"Why do you care if I'm here or not?"

"I do care about you, Ida."

"Or you need something."

"Well." She smiled, openly guilty. "That too." Raising her voice, she said, "Lovely Lena over there is firing me."

The woman at the other desk gave Arlette a fed-up look. "You can't fire someone you never hired in the first place."

"They refuse to keep me on, even though I'm the best they've got."

Sharpening her pencil over a waste bin, Lena said, "You're the worst we've got. You've been caught twice in the street roundups."

"And released twice because I am a French citizen with a valid residency permit in Marseille."

Lena looked up. There was an alluring intensity to her: eyes small, nose sharp, lips wire thin. "Your being here puts us in danger. Varian's allowed it this long because, like everyone else, he can't refuse you."

Arlette thrust her chest forward and rose from her chair. "I know. It's my gorgeous tits. They get me whatever I want. If you knew what was good for this organization, you'd realize how useful they can be."

Unimpressed, Lena said, "I didn't realize you'd shown them to him," and began making marks in her notepad.

"Oh, I haven't. Not yet."

The pencil slashed across the page. "Why don't you do what you're told for once, and let me focus."

"You're no fun." Arlette sat on the corner of Lena's desk. "You will be pleased to know that I am officially no longer your problem. Ida's your gal. She's fabulously discreet and utterly controlled."

Lena looked at Ida. "Do you want to work here?"

"Work here? I don't even know what *here* is." Ida held her valise against her legs with the urge to back herself against the wall. "I have a job, remember? I work for Peggy, in case you've forgotten."

"Don't be sour." Arlette went into the next room and came back with a bottle of scotch. Wrestling the cork from it with her teeth, she took a swig and handed it to Ida. "Let's start over."

"Varian will not like you drinking his liquor," Lena said.

"He won't know if you don't tell."

Ida took the proffered bottle and drank from it, the liquor hot and biting. Arlette made her want to break all the rules.

"That a girl." Arlette recorked it and said, all business, "We need you, Ida. This isn't a joke. It's serious, necessary work, and I know you're not staying with Peggy out of loyalty."

The gravity with which both women looked at Ida made her pay attention.

Lena said, "This is the Centre Américain de Secours. It's a rescue committee set up by the Americans to get emergency visas for artists in danger of being sent to concentration camps. Varian Fry runs it, and Arlette helps fund it."

"You fund it?" Ida looked at Arlette.

"Do you see?" Arlette set the bottle on Lena's desk. "Ida lived with me for over a year, and she doesn't even know who my father is, which is why I trust her. We're practically best friends, and she's never told me a single thing about her family, or asked about mine. Whatever secrets she's got, she hasn't spilled them. It's a rare quality."

Arlette was complimenting Ida to get what she wanted, and it was working. To be needed was not something Ida was used to. She liked the way it made her feel, not exactly powerful or in control—Arlette took those for herself—but valued.

"Come on, I'll convince you as we walk," Arlette said, sliding on her coat and pinning her hat to her head. She opened the door, shouting over her shoulder, "Have a drink, Lena. It will do you good."

They went down the back stairs, through the alley, and out onto the open street. Under her breath, Arlette said, "Keep your head up and walk with confidence. When we get onto the streetcar, don't sit down. We might have to change cars quickly."

"Why?" Ida asked, knowing she should be cautious but feeling only relief anchoring herself to Arlette again.

"The Kundt Commission likes to follow me."

"Who are they?"

Arlette waited for a tall man with a mustache to walk past before speaking again. "A branch of the Gestapo who roam around gathering information on anti-Nazi refugees."

"You're not a refugee."

"No, but they're after me all the same."

21

THERE WAS NO QUICK changing of streetcars. They rode to the last stop. The car emptied, and the passengers scattered off in different directions. Unhurried, Arlette walked down one road and then another, leaving the city outskirts behind. Brown fields stretched to dark forests. A few people pedaled past on bicycles, but for the most part, the road was empty. It reminded Ida of her walks to Yew Tree Cottage. In the crisp sunshine with Arlette beside her, she could almost feel the expectancy of those days again.

Arlette reached for Ida's valise. "Let me. You've been lugging this around all day."

Ida let her carry it. Her arm was tired, and she wore impractical pumps that caught on the loose stones. She hadn't planned on walking into the countryside. "Where are we going?"

"Home," Arlette said, which took Ida by surprise. It was not a word she associated with Arlette, who seemed to live only in other people's worlds.

"We can talk freely here," Arlette said. "The Vichy have tapped Varian's phone lines and who knows what else. Can you imagine suspecting that mousy American in his tweed jacket of criminal activity? Poor thing. He arrived believing he'd be running a perfectly legal organization. Turns out an honest man is the best kind to run an illegal one."

"It's not a legal organization? I thought the Americans sent him here?"

"They sent him on an impossible mission. The Vichy are turning over any foreigner on the Germans' list, no questions asked. There's no time for the bureaucracy involved getting people out of the country legally. The only way is with forged identity papers or by taking them over the border into Spain, all of which involves black-market money exchanges." Arlette gave Ida an excruciating smile. "Which is where you come in."

Ida stopped walking. She was fairly certain Arlette did not know she was currently carrying black-market money. Even if she did, Ida was no longer willing to be ordered around. "I haven't agreed to anything," she said.

"And you shouldn't unless you're absolutely sure you're up for it and you know what's at stake." Arlette glanced at the shuttered cottage behind them. No smoke came from the chimney, but she dropped her voice anyway. "Varian thinks I brought Peggy here for her money, when it was *you* I wanted all along." There was a shimmer in the word *you*, as if Ida were a prize.

Ida held her ground. "What is at stake?"

"Our lives." Arlette said this with an ease and directness that made it clear she was willing to die, if it came to that.

This didn't surprise Ida as much as she would have expected. She'd sensed her friend's fearlessness the day Arlette left her standing on Peggy's doorstep, and Ida wondered if this was the real reason she hadn't run after her. Ida was no martyr. Her life up to this point had been a series of selfish acts, really. And yet this time Arlette was seeking her out, asking for help as if she saw something in Ida that Ida couldn't see in herself.

"If I said yes, what exactly would I have to do?" Ida said.

"Your cover job would be working in the office interviewing refugees, when the real task would be bringing Varian small sums of money when he needs it. It's not safe to keep large amounts at the office in case it's searched."

"Why me? Why don't you bring him the money?" Ida said.

"Because I'm too conspicuous."

"Why?"

The sun dipped behind the tree line and the air grew colder. "We should keep walking," Arlette said, resuming her pace as she explained that her father, Emile Lellouche, had been an outspoken anti-fascist who helped fund the printing and distribution of hundreds of anti-Nazi pamphlets. He was not only a rich Jew, she told Ida, but an outspoken one who openly railed against Hitler and Goebbels in the French newspapers. The Lellouches were powerful. Her father was the last male heir of a line whose family name had a coat of arms that dated all the way back to the 1500s. They made their money in banking and railways and accumulated enough wealth to become politicians and philanthropists.

"We rivaled any Guggenheim," Arlette said. "Can you imagine?"

Ida couldn't. Peggy's wealth seemed immeasurable. "What happened to your father?"

"Did you ever hear of the assassination of the king of Yugoslavia in '34?"

Ida had not. The king, Arlette told her, was killed right here in Marseille by a Bulgarian revolutionary. He was on a state visit, parading through the streets with the French foreign minister. Her father was in the crowd. At the precise moment the king's car rolled past him, two shots were fired. The king died almost instantly. Emile died hours later in the hospital. The government claimed the revolutionary Vlado Chernozemski fired the shots. They said it was an accident. Arlette's father was an innocent bystander. Only the coroner told Arlette's mother that her husband was shot by an 8mm modèle. A standard-issue French military revolver.

"The French killed him?" Ida said.

"Technically, but the Germans were behind it. That they organized his assassination while another high-profile assassination was going on was obvious."

Turning off the road into a corridor of cypress trees, Arlette told Ida that this was where she grew up, and Ida tried to picture Arlette playing here as a child, making the natural world bend to her will.

The house they came to at the end of the drive was made of white stone and reached three stories high with single-story wings flanking it on either side. The windows were dark. The grounds neglected but regal. The flower beds had gone to seed. Dormant rose vines snaked up trellises. Stray shoots stuck up from hedges that had been pruned into flat circular walls. Past the house, Ida could see a low brick building and a domed glass conservatory. Arlette turned a key in the sapphire-blue door, and they stepped into a hallway as big as a living room. The floor was covered in triangular black-and-white tiles. Overhead, a chandelier dazzled. Under it was a round table and an empty vase the size of a small child.

Arlette set Ida's valise on the floor. "The humble Chateau Lellouche."

The austerity filled Ida with a strange dread. She could not have known at the time the blood that would stain the grout, or how the marble walls would hold the tiny sprays of red for weeks. Yet in that initial moment of entry, she wanted to flee.

In the chilled hall, under the glare of the chandelier, Arlette said, "The real reason Varian and Lena don't want me working for them is because I am part of an early Resistance group that was formed long before the French Resistance." She paused to let Ida take this in. "We predicted what was coming when Hitler's government required all Jews in Germany and Austria to register every asset they owned—property, bank accounts, paintings, furniture, jewelry. Have you heard of Aryanization?"

"No." Ida was still trying to work out how Arlette was a part of something that sounded so dangerous, and for so long, without her knowing.

"The Nazis are cataloging our belongings in order to take them from us. It is only a matter of time before they strip the French people too. There is no free zone. It is not freedom when you can't travel from one city to another without proof of identity. When an exit visa is required to leave and yet is impossible to obtain. Last week, the citizens of Marseille cheered Pétain as he strode through the streets, believing he's saved the South of France from the Germans. Meanwhile, his police force is rounding up Jews and immigrants and throwing them into prisons. There is no order. It is a game without rules." Her voice was hard and filled with resentment.

"Peggy is here because Varian is going to ask her to take over the rescue committee. The American government suspects his illegal activity and has demanded his return. And do you know what Peggy will say? She'll say no. She'll say no because she only serves herself. She'll fund the artists she wants to fuck or buy paintings from, but she will risk nothing. The Americans gave Varian a list of people they deemed important enough to save. Who are the Americans to decide whose life is worth saving and whose is not? Varian has taken matters into his own hands. He can't save us all, but he's trying, and he won't leave despite the danger he is in because he is the absolute opposite of a person like Peggy. He thinks—"

Arlette suddenly stopped speaking. They heard the distinct sound of footsteps coming up the path. Putting a finger to her lips, Arlette flattened them against the wall as the footsteps approached the front door. They held their breath. The doorbell rang. There was a moment of silence, and then it rang again in a quick three-ring pattern.

Arlette threw open the door to Varian, who stood with his hat in his hands. She pulled him inside. "You scared me to death."

"That's not easy to do." His manner was lighter than when he'd left them. "I came to tell you that Peggy is all right. The chief released her with an apology. The French do not wish to anger the Americans by detaining their heiresses in case they enter the war, and possibly win it, for the British."

"What about the money?" Arlette said.

"No worry on that front either. It's right there." Varian pointed to Ida's valise.

"In your luggage?" Arlette looked at Ida. "Did you know?"

"Yes."

"And you didn't tell me?"

"No."

Arlette smiled, pleased. "Your ability to deceive is an asset, even if directed at me," she said, swinging the valise onto the hall table and unclasping it. The banknotes were tucked into the inside pocket. Arlette handed them to Varian. "Did Peggy agree to your request? Is good old Miss Guggenheim the head of Centre Américain de Secours?"

"Unfortunately, no," Varian said.

"I told you she wouldn't do it. She's not as tough as she puts on."

His glasses slipped down his nose, and he pressed them back up. "You can't blame her, especially not after today. She told me the American consulate warned her not to get involved with me. It's good advice." He shrugged, his heroics more of an embarrassment than anything. "I'm grateful she's given us money for the passage of the Breton family and Mr. Ernst."

Arlette snapped the valise shut and set it on the floor. "You should strap the money to your leg and not have it right there in your pocket."

"It'll be fine. I'm on my way to Villa Air-Bel. I'll have Daniel bury it in the forest until we need it. I sent Peggy on ahead with Max. Will you ladies be joining us for dinner?" In that grand hallway, with his white handkerchief tucked into his breast pocket, it was hard to believe Varian a man capable of the slightest infraction.

Arlette turned to Ida, her jaunty self restored at the prospect of a party. "Shall we go? It's only a few kilometers away, and André and Jacqueline will be there. It'll be like old times."

22

THE GATHERING WAS HELD on a terrace in front of a large house with a crumbling stone façade. A long table littered with glasses and wine bottles had been set under a plane tree, its bare limbs slashed across the sky. In the distance, rugged limestone mountains were silhouetted against a deep blue.

André embraced Ida, his pipe clutched between his lips, his mane of hair falling into his eyes. Jacqueline kissed her cheek while her daughter, Aube, peeked out from behind her legs. Gliding over with a cool smile, Peggy said, "That was quite an arrival, yes?" Her expression was unruffled, but her skin ashy, as if the event had leached her of color.

Similar to her time at Yew Tree Cottage, Ida was introduced to artists and writers she had not met in Paris—Max Ernst, Victor Serge, and Victor's son, Vlady. The son was not much older than Ida, with dark, scrutinizing eyes. At one point, he leaned over and asked her if she wanted to go up to bed with him. A flattering prospect she politely declined. There was a beautiful woman named Laurette with a narrow chin and arched brows, a poet called Benjamin who wore a mustache and a necktie, a painter named Remedios, a woman with jet-black hair and an unsmiling face. There was a plain-looking American named Mary Jayne—an heiress, Arlette told her—and a British woman, Theo, whose husband, Daniel, had worked for the Préfecture de Police in Paris until the Germans took over. Now he worked for Varian.

Only it was not like old times. Everything had changed. Ida watched Arlette circle the crowd and understood that she was dangerous. To trust her was impossible. Where once Ida saw mystery and charm, she now saw deception. That's what truth did. Opened you up to the lies. When Arlette slid her arm through Ida's and drew her from the patio to the edge of a frozen pond, whispering, "Have you made up your mind?" Ida knew that saying yes, even for a righteous cause, would end badly.

Instead of answering Arlette, she said, "If you're so rich, why did you work for Peggy?"

"To get my art in front of her. If Peggy likes it, everyone else will." Arlette lit a cigarette. "All she's ever respected is my name, not my art. I thought if I stayed with her long enough, I could change her mind, but it doesn't matter what I create. These people want an artist who's pulled themselves up by the bootstraps, fought all odds, struggled in a sea of pain and poverty. Rich-girl artists are not sympathetic enough." She exhaled, smoothing the base of her thumb across her forehead. "If my father had lived, he'd have made sure Peggy liked my work. She would have seen it his way and loved what she saw because he's a man. Men do the most horrible things to Peggy, and yet it's women she dislikes. Did you know her ex-husband was known for stripping her in front of people and attempting to make love to her? One of her lovers made her stand naked in front of an open window in the middle of winter while he threw whiskey in her eyes. To hear Peggy tell it, she thought he'd kill her, and yet she stayed with him. Adored him. She adores them all, in one way or another. I can't stand women who are too stupid to take responsibility for themselves."

Ida saw exactly what Arlette was doing. "Peggy's not stupid," she said.

"She's not." Arlette shook her head. "Which is why it's so enraging. She's smart enough to know better."

"Like me?"

Arlette picked a bit of loose tobacco from her lip. "I don't know. Are you?"

"What? Smart enough to risk my life for you?"

Arlette laughed. "That's where you're stuck, love. Nothing is for me, or for you, anymore. It's not about us." She dropped her cigarette to the ground and stubbed it out with her heel. "If I know you, you'll do the right thing." No gratitude, just righteous expectation.

Ida said, "I haven't decided what that is yet," and left Arlette standing alone by the pond.

They stayed up late. A new moon rose and oil lamps were lit. Max suggested they have an impromptu art auction in Peggy's honor, and paintings were strung from tree branches and propped against trunks. People picked at the stale bread and sausage. They laughed, shouting out bids meant to spur Peggy on.

Nothing was as it should be. There was not enough food. They were outside because it was just as cold inside. And yet, they knew what they were doing. It was a charade of normalcy, an auction meant for one. Money was needed to escape the beloved country that had turned against them. They were not in denial.

Gathered with exiled artists and the people trying to save them, Ida could not have predicted that this was the last time she'd play the Surrealists' games or join in their heated discussions. She didn't know that it was the last time she'd see Peggy Guggenheim. Sipping wine with her back against a tree, it did not even cross Ida's mind that the art would survive, but some of the artists would not.

23

THREE DAYS LATER, ARLETTE and Ida were seated in the dining room at Villa Air-Bel when the paddy wagons drove up. They'd walked over from Arlette's villa to see Peggy off but had missed her by an hour. "Downed her tea and flew the coop," Jacqueline said, offering them a watery cup.

Ida had spent a restless three nights at Chateau Lellouche, wavering between staying and returning with Peggy. Her decision felt momentous. For once, Arlette needed Ida, and it was clear Arlette didn't like depending on someone in any real way. Ida wasn't holding out to be cruel. A part of her was eager to do it, but a bigger part was terrified of failure. This was not stealing a hat pin from a co-worker; this was real danger.

In a way, Ida was glad Peggy left without her. It made her staying circumstantial and less about pleasing Arlette. Ida was finishing her tea, half listening to Jacqueline explain how Peggy insisted Max Ernst drive her to the train station, when there was a sudden shout of "Police!" and Theo thrust her head through the dining room door. "There's a car and two paddy wagons coming through the gates. Why paddy wagons? Why two of them?"

There was a commotion in the hallway, and Varian and André barreled into the room. Danny came from the kitchen with his two-year-old son in his arms, and Victor sprang in from the back door.

"What's going on?" André said.

"A raid?" Jacqueline asked.

"Why here? What could they possibly have on us?" Theo said.

Varian said, "Everyone to their rooms. Burn any compromising documents."

Danny dumped the child into Theo's arms and rushed out. Frantic, Jacqueline said, "Where's Aube? Aube?" The little girl came running down the stairs into her mother's arms.

It was then Arlette stood up and drew a small pearl-handled revolver from the waistband of her skirt. "Stay calm and keep drinking your tea," she said to Ida.

"My God, Arlette, what are you doing with that?" Theo said, crouching in front of her boy, who buried his face in her chest.

"Put it away already," said Jacqueline, hoisting her daughter onto her hip.

"Do you trust me so little?" There was a stubbornness to the way Arlette looked at these mothers holding on to their children. For the first time, Ida saw the difference between them. Arlette, unlike Jacqueline and Theo, had nothing to lose. The war had hardened her into a revolutionary. Or maybe that's what she'd been all along.

Disobeying the order to drink her tea or stay calm, Ida stood up. "Do you mean to shoot them? You will get us all killed."

Outside, the vehicles ground to a stop.

"Put it away, for Pete's sake," Theo said.

"I'm not entirely out of my mind." Arlette went to the mantel and slid the gun into a porcelain vase. "None of you have done anything wrong, so stop acting like it."

A fist pounded the front door, and uniformed men barged in without waiting for a response. Within minutes, the household was rounded up and ordered into the dining room, where Varian was handed a piece of paper from a squat man who kept his hand on his holster. André whispered, "Who put the stick up his fat arse?" Jacqueline shushed him with a swat.

Red-faced, Varian read the paper. "What is this nonsense?"

What the inspector lacked in stature, he made up for in his booming, arrogant voice. He practically shouted, "It's an order from the chief of police to search all locations suspected of being involved in communist activity!"

Varian tossed the order on the table. "It's not even signed."

This did not matter. The inspector ordered his men to search the house while he circled the room collecting everyone's papers. The two-year-old wailed. The inspector shouted at Theo to shut the child up. She shushed him into her shoulder, but the boy only cried harder. It wasn't until the inspector stood in front of Arlette that Ida remembered what Lena had said about Arlette being caught in the street roundups. What would stop them from arresting her now?

Just then, Lena came in from the back door with a satchel in her hand. When she saw what was going on, her face went sheet white.

"Stand with the others," the inspector ordered, and Lena slid in next to Ida.

"Papers," he demanded, palm up in front of Arlette. She took them from her skirt pocket and handed them over. The inspector glanced at them, slid them into his coat, and moved on to Victor. "Ah! Monsieur Serge, the dissident socialist. How many times have you been arrested?" Victor tried to respond, but the inspector barked, "Be quiet. I forbid you to speak."

The other officers returned, throwing the confiscated items onto the dining room table. The inspector picked up a revolver, and André quickly laid claim to it. He said he was authorized to carry it as a medical doctor. Ida had no idea André was a doctor. She only knew him as a writer and theorist.

The inspector didn't care who he was. "If you don't have a permit, it's an arrestable offense." He dropped the revolver onto the table and picked up a collage of a woman's face. "What is this?" Squinting, he read the title. "Pétain?"

"You're misreading it." André stepped up, looking the inspector square in the eye. "It's *putain*. Whore. The correct title is *This damned idiot of a whore.*"

The inspector looked ready to spit in André's face. André looked ready to welcome it.

While this was happening, Arlette was slowly making her way over to Lena. Ida watched the satchel pass with eel-like slickness from one woman's hand to the other. Smooth and silent, Arlette circled Ida's wrist with her cool fingers and backed her noiselessly out of the room.

Around the corner, Arlette set the satchel on the floor, smothered the latch with her bunched-up skirt, and clicked it silently open. She pointed to a painting over the mantel, indicating Ida should take it down. Ida couldn't help feeling that she'd been dragged into this as a test. With a line of sweat beading down her neck, she eased the painting from the wall. They worked quickly, removing the back of the painting and hiding the franc notes from the satchel behind the canvas as they listened to the inspector in the next room ask Monsieur Serge about his typewriter. What was he writing on it? A manuscript. Where was the manuscript? Upstairs. Whose journal was this? Danny's. Why were there notes on internment camps written in them?

With the painting back on the wall, Arlette and Ida slipped into the dining room in time to see the police loading the confiscated items into canvas knapsacks. No one noticed their absence, and the thrill of getting away with it beat breathlessly through Ida.

Varian was saying, "You have no search warrant and no right to these. They are our personal property."

The inspector ignored him. He told Theo and Jacqueline they were to stay behind with their children. Everyone else was to go with them. No one panicked. They put on their coats. Danny and André kissed their wives and children goodbye. Arlette glanced at the vase, reluctant to leave her weapon behind. Victor was the only one who'd packed a bag. "I know the drill," he said as they were ushered outside and made to climb into the backs of the trucks.

Varian refused to get in. As an American, he still thought rules applied. "I am not going anywhere until you show me a warrant for my arrest."

The inspector smiled, suddenly cordial. "I'm not arresting you, monsieur. I need you as a witness. You have my word of honor. I'll have you back here within the hour."

"What about the others?"

"They're only being questioned. You'll make this a lot easier if you comply. Do you think we want to arrest an American here on official business? That would make us look very bad, now, wouldn't it?"

Reluctantly, Varian climbed in next to the others. The doors slammed shut. Dappled sunlight came through the bars of the truck like a trick of beauty.

"What is happening?" Ida asked.

"Fascism," Victor said.

24

A POLICEMAN'S WORD OF HONOR, apparently, meant nothing. They were taken to the police headquarters and detained for hours in a bare room with an armed guard at the door. On arrival, Arlette said her name was Amelia Moreau, and Ida realized the inspector didn't question it because her papers were false.

The women were instructed to sit on a wooden bench while the men were led into a windowless room and interrogated. Varian assured them they'd be released before the end of the day, but the hard line of Arlette's jaw and Lena's stony silence were not encouraging.

By nightfall, Varian, André, Victor, and Danny came out subdued and pale with anger.

"What is going on?" Lena's tone was low.

Varian shook his head. "I honestly have no idea. They have nothing on us."

The guard shouted at them, and they were herded into a room filled with hundreds of detainees. The residents of Villa Air-Bel dispersed in the crowd, and Ida sank onto the trampled floor with her back to the wall. For some reason, her family sprang into her mind. If she disappeared, they'd never know what happened to her. She'd been arrested before she'd had the chance to do anything heroic. Did the Vichy think she was a British spy? Did it matter that she wasn't? The lack of logic to it all was terrifying. What was society without laws? What prevented those men from coming in here and gunning them down with no explanation?

A hand patted Ida's forearm, and she looked over, the gesture intimate and unexpected. A woman wearing a colorful silk headscarf sat on the floor next to her. "You'll be okay," the woman said.

By then, Ida was crying noticeably. "I'm not sure I will be. Turns out I'm not very brave."

The woman slid a photograph from her bag and handed it to Ida. The picture showed three girls in pinafore dresses smiling from a large living room sofa. The woman pointed to each girl in turn, reciting their names. "Isold. Nadia. Sabina." She held her finger on the youngest, a child of maybe three, with apple-round cheeks. "This one is my sunshine. Right before they pulled her from my arms, she said, 'Hold me forever and ever, Mummy, don't let go.'" The woman looked at Ida from tearless, deep-socketed eyes. "You are not a mother yet, are you?" Ida shook her head. "There is no greater pain in this world than losing your children. And yet, here I sit, speaking to you. My soul is not the same, but I can attest that one survives." The way she said it made Ida feel ashamed. What did she know of real suffering? This woman was enduring a war Ida was only just beginning to understand.

At midnight, they evacuated the police headquarters. The detainees were herded into a courtyard and engulfed by the fumes of idling trucks. Cold moonlight fell around them. In the chaos, Arlette found Ida's hand, the tension in it rope tight. Her strength was reassuring. What Ida had read as silent stoicism was Arlette's anger brewing. Her face held edges of it. Her body quaked with its intensity.

Their names were called, and they were pushed to one side with the others from Villa Air-Bel, watching as the rest of the crowd was ordered into the backs of the trucks. One by one the courtyard emptied, the confused faces disappearing into the police wagons with unsettling efficiency.

It was disturbing to watch in silence as the iron gates clanged open and the vehicles drove out. That there was nothing any of them could do was beside the point. They looked at each other in the strange moonlight. The gates had been left wide open, and there was not a soldier in sight. Afraid to speak, they walked noiselessly out, their sudden release as inexplicable as their imprisonment.

25

THE ARREST CHANGED IDA. There was something unbearable in the memory of the daughterless woman, in the people she'd seen packed into those trucks, and in the reality that she had walked away while they had not. To do nothing made one culpable.

The day after their arrest, Ida agreed to work for Varian transporting black-market money.

Peggy sent Ida's belongings—her violin and Parisian wardrobe—to Chateau Lellouche, where Ida slept in a plush bed in a pink-papered room with gold-legged furniture. The house was a mix of luxury and discomfort, everything shiny and big and cold. There were five bedrooms on the second floor and four on the third, all adorned with enormous beds, marble fireplaces, and intricately carved armoires. The reception rooms, library, dining room, and kitchen were on the ground floor, their windows overlooking various portions of the grounds: gardens or hedges or views of the mountains.

To sit in a blue-velvet chair, brush out one's hair in front of a gilt mirror, or read an original copy of *Les Misérables* in the dark-walled library might have been enjoyable if there had been heat, or gas, or a working telephone line. "Life in the countryside," Arlette mocked. "Lavish and provincial. One has great feasts and hunting parties and ignores the necessity of heat and telephones." They at least had electricity for now, a modern amenity added at a point when the only option was to lay the exposed wires over the beautifully papered walls.

Ida would exchange working lights for a stove that lit properly.

More than anything, she missed small heated spaces. Even Varian's office was freezing. In the morning, she brought whatever money was needed from Arlette's hidden stores, after which she sat all day at a frigid table interviewing refugees, their wan, desperate faces staring at her through the dismal lamplight.

They were still trying to get people out legally if they could, but since no ships were sailing from the unoccupied zone, the only way was through a port in Lisbon. To get there, one needed a conduct pass to the French border, an exit permit out of France, transit visas through Spain and Portugal, and a valid passport, all of which took a great deal of time and paperwork. After that, they still needed a visa to whatever country they were trying to escape to, which required affidavits of support, a testimonial of character, and, of course, money.

Varian and Lena approached the refugees with the utmost calm, but Ida felt helpless sitting there explaining to yet another person in danger of being rounded up and sent to an internment camp that yes, their travel document had come through, but it had taken so long that their other documents had expired. "What does that mean?" they'd say, the woman with cool green eyes, the boy with a scar on his hand, the man in thick glasses. It was always the same: "What do we do now?"

"Start over," Ida would say. Some would cry. Others would smash their fists into their palms. Some would nod and walk out, heads high. It took resilience to survive and resilience to die. Either way, they kept on. What else could they do? France did not want them, and yet the French government was making it impossible for them to leave.

It was a gruesome game of scatter and run. Every one of them had a target on their backs.

Arlette was right. There was no use playing by the rules.

ON A FREEZING day in January, Ida lifted her skirt as Arlette secured a thin layer of money to the inside of her thigh with a stretchy stocking. "Good and tight. How does it feel?"

"Fine." Ida pulled her wool stockings over it, wiggled into her girdle, and shook her skirt down. Three layers to search, if it came to that.

Arlette had assured Ida it would not come to that. "You're not on any list," she had said. "You're not Jewish. You are a British woman with a valid passport waiting for her paperwork to travel home. There'll be no reason for anyone to search you."

Ida looked out the frost-covered window. It was four a.m. and the moon was still up. The temperature had dropped ten degrees overnight. People were saying it was the coldest winter they'd seen in this part of France.

The knot in the stocking tightened around Ida's leg as she crouched in front of the stove. They were out of rationed coal and had to scrounge for wood in the pine forest, fallen branches and rotting logs, most of it wet and impossible to burn. Ida lit the newspaper under the layered twigs and smoke snaked into the room. When the wood finally caught, she latched the door and opened the flue, grateful for all the fires she'd started back in Petersfield.

"It's utterly sexy how handy you are." Arlette was at the sink filling the tea kettle. "I would freeze to death without you."

Their friendship had matured beyond wardrobes and dinner parties. Even beyond art and music. They were dependent on each other to ward off suffering, and this gave rise to a level of devotion neither of them predicted.

Ida took the kettle from Arlette and set it on the stove. "It'll be noon before the water's hot enough for tea."

"Tea?" Arlette took the tin off the shelf. "Where's the coffee?"

"No more coffee. I could only get four hundred grams of tea, and that's the last of it."

"If my cigarettes run out, I'll have to turn myself in," Arlette moaned.

"Don't joke."

"How do you know I'm joking?" Arlette shoved her feet into her boots and began lacing them up over her trousers.

"I'm worried about you," Ida said.

"It's safer for me in the mountains than walking the streets of Marseille."

"Then don't walk the streets of Marseille. Stay here."

"And do nothing?"

A socialist Arlette knew in the Resistance had drawn her a detailed map of a smuggler's route out of Banyuls-sur-Mer over the Pyrenees to the Spanish border. Against his better judgment, Varian was letting her take refugees as long as their contact was strictly through Ida, and as long as Arlette promised to leave France the moment her emergency rescue visa came through. Her forged transit visa had arrived weeks ago, but without a proper rescue visa, she'd be turned away at the port in New York and sent straight back.

Ida touched the side of the teapot. Out the window, a layer of snow crusted the lawn. The chill under her skin, her inability to get warm, made her feel desperate. "Why not take yourself over the border into Spain? Why come back at all?"

"Are you trying to get rid of me?" From behind, Arlette wrapped her arms around Ida.

Arlette was intimate with Ida in a way that inflamed and confused her. "What will I do if you're caught?" she said, resting her hand on the coarse sleeve of Arlette's wool shirt.

Arlette assured her she would not be. The people she was taking all had their travel documents, just no exit permits out of France. A small detail the Spanish border guards were easily bribed to overlook.

Ida slid out of Arlette's embrace. She'd seen Varian's list of *important artists*. "The United States is powerful enough to get everyone at risk out of France if they wanted to. Why is your visa taking so long?"

"Governments fail people all the time. Why do you think we're doing what we're doing?" Arlette hovered her hand near the stove, testing its warmth. "No tea today." She took her heavy coat from its hook and her pearl-handled pistol from the shelf over the stove.

A band of tensions shot across Ida's eyes and she massaged a finger over her temple.

"I'll be fine." Arlette gave her a bright smile. If she was afraid, it never showed. "Head in to work as usual. Varian will take care of you. He's a lot more heroic than he looks."

With a toss of her head, Arlette tucked her pistol into her waistband, pulled her fur cap over her ears, and opened the door to a blast of cold air.

26

LIFE CONTINUED ON, THE hours filled with an imminent sense of loss. Each one that ticked by without incident, a lucky break.

Arlette would leave for a few days at a time while Ida stayed behind working for Varian. When instructed, she took money from the armoire, strapped it to her thigh, and headed into the city. Every policeman she passed made her pulse race, and yet the feeling of getting away with something right under their noses electrified her. When she made it to Varian's office, she'd toss the money on his desk like she'd won a race, her body buzzing for hours.

Alone in the chateau, Ida and Arlette teased each other about "letting themselves go," not bothering to squeeze into girdles or brassieres or put their hair in curlers or cold cream under their eyes; luxury items were impossible to find anyway. They layered on trousers and sweaters and kept to the kitchen, listening to the news or reading aloud. Sometimes Ida would play the violin for Arlette as she had at Yew Tree Cottage, the warmth of those summer days in England a lifetime ago.

One overcast afternoon, Arlette came into the kitchen with a pot of paste, tubes of paint, scissors, and a stack of newspaper. Dumping them on the table, she opened the cupboard and asked if there was any flour. Ida dug the bag out from behind their ration of sugar and salt, watching as Arlette filled a shallow bowl with the last of their flour, added water, and mixed it into a goopy paste. Cutting strips of newspaper, Arlette instructed Ida to lie flat on her back on the floor while she dipped the newspaper into the flour mixture and placed the cold, gummy pieces over Ida's face. The uneven tiles were frigid beneath her, the strips of paper slightly suffocating. She was grateful when the mask hardened and Arlette pulled it off, the sensation like a layer of skin cracking away.

"Now do me." Arlette lay on the floor, arms crossed, eyes closed.

Ida smoothed the coated newspaper into the soft divots of Arlette's eyes and over the mounds of her cheeks and lips. The typeset words ran into each other and turned the paste cement gray. When the mask hardened, Arlette pulled it off, and they sat at the table with dull kitchen knives, cutting out eyes and poking holes in nostrils. Arlette squirted a tube of paint directly onto the tabletop, and they dipped their brushes and covered the blurred news with an unrelenting white. They worked in silence. Holding their blank expressions in their hands. A clean slate. A do-over. They could block out the headlines of the world and start again. With tiny strokes, they painted green vines and purple flowers over molded cheeks, encircling lips and framing eyes, their faces a bloom of possibility: spring and youth and new beginnings.

When the paint dried, they tied their masks to their heads with string and moved around the room like Shakespearean fairies, with only the sound of their shuffling, stockinged feet. They were trapped in a dreamlike reality called war. They were fiction. They were myth. They were violinist and photographer waiting to become themselves.

Ida moved with Arlette from the kitchen to the living room as if pulled by an invisible rope. Arlette propped open the legs of her tripod and secured her camera to it before lifting her sweater over her head. The way she undressed was more deliberate than the usual scrambling in and out of clothes they did in front of each other. To gaze on Arlette's pale-as-bone breasts, her soft stomach and jutting hipbones, to understand that Arlette wanted to be looked at, empowered Ida. Arlette was unashamed. Afraid of nothing. Ida eased her own sweater over her mask. Goose bumps freckled her skin, but she did not hug herself warm. She stood in the full sensation of her nudity, letting her nipples rise and a tingle spread across the wings of her shoulder blades.

Going to her camera, Arlette carefully pressed the spring attached to the shutter timer, turned a knob, released a button, and arranged herself next to Ida. The heartbeat and murmur of Arlette's skin in the cutting cold burgeoned against Ida. She wanted to stay there forever. Chests pressed together. Arlette's body a river of pleasure. Their eyes black holes. Lips sealed in silent expectation. The timer counted down. The box buzzed. Reaching up, Ida wove her fingers into Arlette's hair as the shutter clicked.

27

SPRING CAME IN A burst of peach blossoms. The pond thawed and the grass sprang green over the lawn. Honeysuckle sweetened the air and birdsong woke them at dawn. Arlette dragged a table onto the terrace, and they ate their stale bread under a canopy of pink petals. There was no milk or salt or butter, but the bread filled them.

"We should start a vegetable garden," Ida said one morning, looking at the plots of sprouting tulips and budding rose bushes.

"I'd give anything for a fresh vegetable right now." Arlette poked at the center of her bread. "Or some meat and champagne. An egg would be nice."

"Chocolate," Ida said.

"Why hasn't Peggy sent us any?"

"I suppose even Peggy can't get the things she wants anymore. I'm surprised she hasn't visited."

"I think her being arrested when she first arrived in Marseille scared her more than she'll admit. I'm surprised she's still in France."

There was a shout from the driveway, and they saw Varian walking toward them, waving an arm in the air.

"This can't be good." Arlette waved back, and Varian broke into a jog, his paisley tie swinging.

At the edge of the patio, he stopped to catch his breath. "Morning, ladies."

"I've never seen you run anywhere," Arlette said. "I'm almost afraid to ask."

Varian had lost a considerable amount of weight, and his eyes were ringed in shadows.

Ida said, "Would you like something to eat? I'm afraid all we have is stale bread and an unforgivable coffee substitute."

"I'm fine, thank you."

Arlette said, "At least sit. You're making me nervous hovering like that."

Varian perched on the edge of a chair and set his hat on one knee. He gave Arlette a firm, almost-angry look. "There was an attempted raid on the office last night."

"By who? The police?"

"No. By the young fascists, the Jeunesse Populaire Française."

"Did they get in?"

"Luckily, no. I had the locks reinforced, and they weren't able to break down the doors."

"What were they after?"

"I believe they were trying to plant illegal documents on us. The police mysteriously showed up first thing in the morning to search the place. Clearly, they are in cahoots."

"Did the police find the money?" Ida asked. She'd brought him two thousand francs yesterday.

"No, thank goodness I'd already sent Daniel off with it. They did, however, ask about you, Arlette." Behind his round lenses, his small eyes were beady and hawkish.

Arlette crossed her arms. "Do they know about the escape route?"

"Not yet. If they did, I'd be in prison right now."

"What do they want with me, then? I've made sure not to be seen at the office, or Villa Air-Bel, for months."

"They have files on everyone who officially works for me."

"I've never officially worked for you, and Lena made sure there was no file on me."

"Correct." He cleared his throat. "She did, however, create a file on a woman named Anna Bacri. A woman I had never heard of until this morning. A woman who is, according to the police, one of my employees, and consequently, the owner of this estate."

Ida was not following. She looked at Arlette, who plucked nervously at her shirtsleeve.

Varian pounded the table, a gesture distinctly unlike him. "Do you know what a mess you've gotten us into? I was about say, to the chief of police no less, 'Who is Anna Bacri?' when Lena burst in with a tray of coffee talking nonsense as she slid a piece of paper into my palm."

Without missing a beat, Arlette said, "Good old Lena saves the day. What did you tell them?"

"Lies. All lies I had to think up on the spot. I told them I knew who you were, but that we'd only met a few times and I hadn't seen you in over a year. I told them, yes, I employed an Anna Bacri, but that my employees keep their personal lives to themselves, and I knew nothing about the estate or that Miss Bacri owned it."

Ida had never heard of anyone named Anna Bacri.

Arlette smiled. "Well done."

"Well done, my foot! I'm under suspicion from all angles. We're barely hanging on, Arlette."

"You covered for me, so we're good."

"We're far from good. As of yesterday, the Vichy have frozen all Jewish bank accounts and are seizing their assets."

Arlette stood up so fast her chair teetered. She caught it right before it toppled over and walked to the edge of the patio with a hand latched over one shoulder. She was silent for a long time looking out over the tangled lawn. A robin swooped into the peach tree. It would be a perfect day, under different circumstances.

Varian and Ida stayed quiet.

When Arlette finally spoke, there was a self-possessed dignity to her voice. "What did the Vichy want to know, specifically?"

"They wanted to know how Anna Bacri was associated with the Lellouche family. Did she know your father? Did she know you? When did she acquire the estate?" Varian stood up. Ida had never seen him so upset. Red blotches dotted his neck, and he kept opening and shutting his fists. "Do you have any idea what kind of danger this puts us in?"

Arlette whirled around. Her eyes had a hard glisten to them, as if she could see straight through a person. "I had no choice. She was the best option for both jobs, and how was I supposed to know the police would question you about her?"

"You should have told me."

"You wouldn't have hired her."

"You're right. I wouldn't have."

"She's been useful. You needed her and I needed her, so what's done is done."

The sun shot out from behind a cloud, and Varian turned to Ida. "You don't know, do you?"

"Know what?" Ida was lost.

The look Arlette gave her was impenetrable and startling. "It's simple," she said, with an unnerving laugh. "Why every other idiot didn't think to do what I did is beyond me. I sent my mother to New York and liquidated our assets, all except for this chateau. The chateau my mother sold to Anna Bacri, a wealthy Aryan Frenchwoman who is in no way associated with our family because she doesn't exist."

Varian squashed his hat on his head. "Except she does exist. You made her real, Arlette. I can't believe Lena was in on this and didn't tell me. How is she more loyal to you than to me?"

"I don't understand," Ida said. "Who is Anna Bacri?"

"You. I gave you a false identity and put the chateau in your name." Arlette said this as if any sensible person should have seen it coming.

The sun was bright in Ida's eyes, the birds loud. "When?" she said, trying to absorb this information with a familiar, demoralizing unease.

"The day after you met my mother."

This landed hard. For a moment, Ida couldn't breathe. Things that had never made sense became clear: Arlette plucking her from the street and inviting her to Yew Tree Cottage. All those discussions about Paris and art and literature. Ida's wardrobe. Perfecting her French. Had Arlette been grooming her from the beginning? Poor little Ida in her dusty shoes. Poor little Ida desperate to become someone. The perfect Eliza Doolittle. *You want something, and you want it badly*. Arlette understood people. She knew how to get exactly what she wanted from them. She had abandoned Ida in England, knowing how desperate Ida was. Desperation is a powerful motivator. Following Arlette was like trying to eat light. It left one empty and craving. One might steal from their family. Run away. Chase the brilliance to London. To Paris. To Marseille. The extent of Arlette's manipulation, the years of planning, of secrecy, was staggering.

Ida closed her eyes. She pressed a hand to her forehead. "When were you going to tell me?"

"When I had to."

"Why not ask me directly?"

"I couldn't risk you saying no." Arlette reached for Ida's hand. "For what it's worth, I am sorry I didn't tell you sooner."

Ida jerked away, her face flaming. "We make our own choices, remember? The sooner you learn not to apologize for them, the better."

Arlette nodded. "You're right. I deserve that. In this case, maybe I didn't make the best choices. But I did what I had to." She folded her arms, bristling under the accusatory stares of Varian and Ida. "Neither one of you has any right to judge me. You have no idea what it is like to be looked at with pure violent hatred simply because you exist. Do you know how it feels to have your power stripped away to nothing? Power that is rightfully yours, that you've always had." She gave an ugly laugh. "Not power. Basic human rights. Your right to walk down the street. To go into a shop. To eat in a restaurant. Gone." She snapped her fingers. "They are taking everything. They are gutting our souls. We are less than animals to them. We are the dirt under their boots. This is *my* father's home!" she shouted, fury rising from her core. "Do you think I wanted to put it in someone else's bloody fucking name? I want it in my own goddamn name. A Jewish name. A name they want to kill me for being born with."

Her words clawed at Ida. They tore up her heart. She knew what it was to not be loved, but she had no idea what it was to be hated.

A breeze sent a piece of hair scuttering across Arlette's face. She brushed it away like she wanted to tear it from her head as she turned and stormed into the house. Ida looked at Varian. His chin was down, his eyes on the ground. The world had reached an unconquerable level of hopelessness.

When Arlette returned, she handed Ida a passport and a Marseille residency permit. "It may look purely selfish, but this ensures your safety as well."

The name Anna Bacri was typed in black next to a photograph of Ida. It was the photo Arlette took in London, the one Ida resisted. There was no unbuttoned blouse or bare shoulder, just Ida's face from the neck up. Arlette had not turned her into something unique, or interesting, or surreal. She had simply turned her into someone else.

Arlette said, "Being a young, attractive Aryan Frenchwoman is your best protection right now. When your real papers come through and you go back to England, well, then you're good old Ida again with a boatload of money I put in an English bank account in your name."

"I'm to be your money holder until the war is over?" Ida's voice was stripped of anger. She felt simultaneously used and guilty.

"Don't worry, as soon as I get out of France, I'll take it all back." Cold facts. No love. Arlette turned to Varian. "Where are we with that?"

Varian was no longer upset. He looked tired and apologetic. "I've applied for Ida's transit visa, but I haven't been able to secure you an American emergency visa. There's not a lot of logic to who they grant visas to and who they do not." He rubbed his chin. "It's complicated because the files the police have on you, Ida, are all under the name Anna Bacri. You'll have to stick to that identity for now. Where are your original papers?"

"In my coat pocket."

"You'll need them to travel, but you should hide them until then and carry your new ones. And I'm afraid it's too risky for you to come in to the office anymore. As soon as your transit visa comes through, I'll send a message through Theo."

Varian crossed the patio stones to Arlette, who stood with her hands shoved into her skirt pockets. Gently, he touched her elbow. "The gendarmes raided another hotel yesterday. I imagine they'll be out here before the end of the day. Your father's wealth was no secret, nor were his political views. They'd love nothing more than to strip the Lellouche family of its wealth. I'm sure they'll want an explanation for where it all went. Things are far worse than when we started out. I went to Camp des Milles last week. I will not repeat the horrors, but you do not want to find yourself there. Your best chance of survival is to take yourself over the border into Spain."

"What about the escape route?"

"I'm closing it. It's too dangerous."

"We cannot abandon Mrs. Blau and her son. I'm supposed to take them in two days."

Varian pulled off his glasses and rubbed his eyes. He looked spent. "We can't save them all, Arlette."

She took his hand in a pleading gesture. "These will be the last two, I promise. I'll go over the border with them, or hide at the vineyard in Banyuls, or Saint-Gingolph."

"Not Saint-Gingolph. You'll start pestering me about taking people over the Swiss route."

"You're not giving up. Why should I?"

"We should both be giving up. If you're arrested again, I can't help you." He looked at Ida. "Either of you. I've lost all influence, if I ever had any in the first place."

Arlette said, "Just let me take these last two and then I'll disappear."

"Can I really stop you?"

"No." They looked at each other, and an understanding passed between them.

Varian planted an awkward kiss on Arlette's cheek. "In spite of your stubbornness, it's tremendous what you've done. We couldn't have saved nearly as many without you." Making his way over to Ida, he offered her a stiff handshake. "Thank you for your service, Mademoiselle Anna Bacri. If you need anything, go to Villa Air-Bel. Theo and Danny will help you."

When he turned to go, Ida saw a premonitory expression of tragedy.

"Goodbye, ladies," he said, tipped his hat, and walked away.

28

T HE FIRST THING ARLETTE did after Varian left was remove the roll of film from her camera while Ida knelt on the floor, filling a box with the money from the armoire. If Ida felt betrayed or lied to, there was no time to dwell on it. Things were happening too fast.

"Why are you hiding your film?" Ida said.

"I didn't just take pictures of us." Arlette tucked the roll next to a small stack of gold bullion and a pile of franc notes. "Varian's not the only one who went to Camp des Milles. I hid in the trees and took photographs that I guarantee the French don't want anyone to see. Until I figure out how to get the film out of France, I can't be caught with it."

They buried the mahogany box in a square of earth just past the rose garden, concealing the freshly turned ground with dead leaves and grass before going inside to scrub the grit from their nails.

In the bedroom, Arlette pulled a skirt and blouse from the closet and tossed them onto the bed. "Put these on. You should look the part when the police arrive." It had been a long time since she'd ordered Ida around in that tone. Ida watched her shimmy out of her grass-stained trousers and shirt, Arlette's head halfway in the closet, hangers clicking as she swiped through outfits.

Dirt flaked from the knees of Ida's pants as she crossed the room to her, leaving a trail over the rug. Reaching out, she traced a finger down Arlette's spine to the birthmark that sat like a pink quail egg on her hip. The hangers stopped clicking.

"What do I really mean to you?" Ida laid the flat of her hand against Arlette's back.

Arlette dropped her head, her hair curtaining her face. "I wouldn't have made you Anna Bacri unless I trusted you more than anyone in the world."

"How can trust be so full of lies?"

"It's survival."

"I don't trust you."

"You shouldn't."

"Why did you tell me to, then?"

"Because I had to, and I am good at getting what I want."

Ida kissed the back of her neck. "I want you to make love to me. Why have you never made love to me?"

Arlette turned around. The sweater in her hand brushed against Ida's leg, soft as a kitten. "Because I didn't want you to think I was using you."

"A little late for that now."

They made love on the flat weave rug of blue medallions. Tongues between legs. Fingers. Wet warmth. Squares of sunlight fell on their skin. Arlette's mouth and hands covered Ida in a heat that came up from her bones, and Ida was lifted from herself, flung open.

After, they lay in unnatural brightness.

"I have to go," Arlette said.

"I know."

They dressed in silence. Arlette tucked her pistol into her pants pocket and stuffed a change of clothes into a canvas bag. She rolled franc notes and slid them into an empty tube of toothpaste. The zipper of Ida's skirt stuck, and she buttoned her blouse wrong and had to undo it and start again.

"Come here." Arlette helped her with the last button and turned Ida to the mirror. "You are beautiful," she whispered.

Ida's cheeks were flushed, her lips bitten red, her eyes clear. She was beautiful, but that was only because Arlette had a way of making everything true.

In the backyard, at the edge of the shrubbery abutting the pine forest, Ida buried her face in Arlette's hair. She thought of the first day they met, the way Arlette had crossed the room to shake her hand, her open confidence, her total acceptance. Was that all a lie?

"I can't do this without you," Ida said.

"Yes, you can."

"What will I say when I'm questioned?"

"We've gone over it."

"What if I forget? Or slip up?"

Arlette pulled away. "You won't. Remember to breathe slowly and count in your head like I showed you. The trick is to remain calm. When your transit visa comes through, you're to leave straightaway, even if you haven't heard from me. Promise?"

"And then what? How will I know where you've gone?" Ida's resentment had vanished in the wake of loss.

"When it's over, I'll find you," Arlette said.

"How will you know where I am? I don't even know where I'm going."

"I'll figure it out."

"What if you're arrested?"

"I won't be."

"How do you know?"

Arlette grinned. "Because there's no way I'm leaving you all my money."

Ida wanted to tell Arlette that she loved her, and that she would do anything for her.

"Don't be lonely," Arlette said, and Ida stifled a sob. "Close your eyes," she instructed. Ida did as she was told. "Now, take a deep breath."

Ida inhaled. She could smell the soap scent of Arlette's hair. Pine needles. Damp earth. Behind her closed lids, sounds were heightened, rustling leaves and creaking trunks. There was a whisper of goodbye and a snap of twigs, and when Ida opened her eyes, the forest stretched dark and empty before her.

29

THEY CAME THAT AFTERNOON. White-gloved men in blue uniforms with guns at their hips, their boots muddying the tiles. Looking into the hard core of their eyes, Ida thought of her father. She had looked straight into his eyes and lied. She could look straight into theirs.

They questioned her at the sleek dining room table. The young one, pink cheeked and eager, held her fake passport and residency permit while the other, slightly older, his lips cracked dry, asked how she came to acquire the chateau. In her best French, Ida told them the story she'd rehearsed with Arlette. Before the war broke out, her father bought the chateau as an engagement present. Her fiancé, Yannick Barbeau, died in Sedan near the Meuse River when the Germans first invaded France. Now, she lived here alone.

"Where are your parents?"

"New York."

"Why?"

"They left before the war and decided to stay until things settled."

"Why haven't you joined them?"

Ida leaned her elbow over the back of her chair, and the man's eyes slid down her chest. "One can barely get a travel pass to leave one's home, much less the country. Do you have any idea the paperwork involved?" She crossed her legs, her skirt tightening over her knees. Arlette was right about the outfit.

"You said your father purchased the chateau?"

"Yes."

"When did you move in?"

"Last summer. I left Paris when the Germans invaded."

"Did you meet the previous owners?"

"No."

"You have never met a woman named Arlette Lellouche?"

"No."

"And yet she was here."

Ida's pulse shot up. She inhaled slowly and fixed her expression into slight confusion. "I apologize, I don't know what you mean."

"Mademoiselle Lellouche was in Marseille last summer. There are records of her arrest. What I am trying to figure out is how she was so close to her childhood home, and yet you two never met."

"Why would we?"

The officer shrugged. "Seems natural."

Ida kept her head cocked in feminine befuddlement. "Monsieur, there are thousands of people in Marseille."

"People are sentimental. It's impossible for me to believe Mademoiselle Lellouche never once ventured out here. It would have been better for you if you'd told me she knocked on your door, had a look around the place, and went on her way."

"You would have preferred I lie?"

The officer put his hands on the table, leaning so close that Ida could see the chip in his front tooth. "I think you're lying now."

From his expression, Ida saw that it was her self-assured attitude he didn't like. This man wanted her to cower. After the day she'd had, it wasn't hard to bring tears to her eyes. She made sure he saw her welling up before she dropped her gaze into her lap and said, "I am a Christian woman. I have never been accused of lying."

The man removed his hands from the table. He rubbed the top of his short-cropped hair and looked away. The younger officer said, "Then you won't mind if we search the place."

"Of course not."

Alone in the kitchen, Ida filled the kettle with shaking hands. Upstairs, doors opened and closed. Cupboards slammed. Furniture slid across the floor. When the house went silent, she looked out the window and saw the policemen walking across the lawn toward the torn-up patch of ground. The disturbed leaves looked obvious. Why hadn't they planted something over it? Ida realized that she hadn't cleaned the dirt from the upstairs rug. Had they found the grass-stained clothes in the laundry basket?

The kettle whistled. She pulled it off the stove and spooned in ground chicory, her eyes fixed to the yard as she watched the men walk past the turned-over earth and enter the orangery. Next, they went into the caretaker's house, then into the carriage house, before making their way back to the chateau, the garden undisturbed.

They drank her chicory coffee. It was watery and bland, but neither complained. When they rose to leave, Ida followed them to the door and watched as they climbed into their vehicle and drove away.

When she turned back to the house, the emptiness, the silence, left her weak.

30

WITHIN WEEKS OF ARLETTE'S departure, André Breton and his family finally got on a boat bound for New York. Victor's Mexican visa came through, and he and his son were gone before Ida could say goodbye. The only people who remained at Villa Air-Bel were Theo and Daniel, who dedicated all of their time to the Emergency Rescue Committee. Even Peggy was leaving France. She'd sent a letter—via Theo, as instructed—saying that she was sorry she couldn't take Ida with her. *Or my dearest Arlette. There are only twelve spots on the clipper, and you can't imagine how hard it's been choosing who to bring. I've had a tremendous time getting my money from the Banque de France. They only allow $550 per person! It's outrageous. What am I supposed to do with that? It's hardly enough to get my own family out. Don't give up hope. Varian is working on Arlette's passport, and I'm sure your travel permit will arrive any day now. When you get to New York, look me up. Regards, Peggy G.*

It was the sort of letter Arlette would have scoffed at. She would have said, "Can you believe her? Self-consumed to the end. To deliberately write and tell you she didn't choose you or me!" Ida would point out that it was nice of Peggy to think of them at all. "She could have left without a word," she'd say, and Arlette would respond that it was only to ease her own guilty conscience.

These were conversations Ida had with herself.

ON JUNE 13, 1941, Ida spent her twenty-first birthday standing in a food line in Marseille waiting for the shopkeeper to clip her book and hand over whatever pathetic amount of food was on hand. Behind her, a cluster of girls murmured in low voices. A woman held a boy's hand. Ahead in line, an older man thanked the woman handing him a loaf of bread. He took another woman's arm, and they moved toward the door. These people had each other. That's how they kept on. How had Ida's world shrunk so small? She missed Arlette. She missed Lena and Varian. In an abstract way, she even missed her family. What had happened to them? Was her mother alone? Was she standing in a food line too? Had her brothers fought at Dunkirk? Was the dairy or brewery still running? Was Leon caring for the cows? Was her father at home, or had all the men vanished to war?

Ida walked home feeling tragic. Arlette told her not to be lonely. Had she known Ida would find herself more isolated than she'd ever been?

To distract herself, Ida played the violin. She read and gardened. She'd procured seeds from the sullen, but generous, farmer down the road, and now green beans sprouted from the old flower beds. Zucchini vines spiraled around turnip tops. Artichoke hearts and potatoes fattened under the dirt. Ida was grateful her mother had taught her to make use of her hands. Toil. Labor. Drudgery. Words she'd hoped to escape entangled around her days and became her livelihood.

Ida canned food for the winter with the jars she found in the cupboard. She thought of her mother with her hair up and her sleeves rolled to her elbows, showing her how to ease the jars into boiling water without burning her hands, how to tap the tops to make sure they were sealed, her mother's fingers dirt-stained, the cuticles torn. When Ida's travel visa came through, she'd go back to Petersfield. Not to stay, but to return her father's money, to offer an explanation.

In September, standing on the terrace under a blue sky, Theo told Ida that Varian and Lena had left for America.

"What about my travel visa?" Ida wrapped her arms around her middle. The first chill of autumn was in the air.

Theo shook her head. "I am sorry, but it hasn't come through. Honestly, with things as they are, if you haven't gotten out by now, you're not likely to."

They spoke in English, one British woman to another.

"No word from Arlette?" Ida asked.

"I'm afraid not. Daniel and I are leaving Villa Air-Bel. I don't know where we'll land, but I promise to try to get word to you if I hear anything." Theo glanced at the house. "You'll be all right here. You've done an excellent job keeping up your French identity. People say the new owner of Chateau Lellouche is uppity and keeps to herself." Her quick smile dropped into a frown. "If I were you, I'd keep it that way. Don't get close to anyone. It's impossible to know whom you can trust. At this point, the Vichy have no reason to suspect you, but that could change in an instant." Theo was not an affectionate woman, but she gave Ida a brisk hug before pulling away with a hurried goodbye.

Ida did not heed her advice. To be alone, indefinitely, was too much. After Theo disappeared down the drive, Ida took a jar of green beans and cucumbers and walked to the farmhouse a half-mile away. She'd met Jean only once when she'd asked for seeds, which he'd produced quickly and silently before shutting the door in her face. The house reminded her of her parents', a modest two-story set a few yards off the road. The gate was open, the path weedy. Brown paint chipped off the front door. Ida knocked twice, and the door swung open.

"Yes?" Jean had a shock of white hair, bushy brows, and a snow-white beard that stuck out in all directions.

Ida held out the jars of preserved vegetables. "To thank you for the seeds."

He looked at them with suspicion. "I don't need a thank-you," he said. There was an uncomfortable silence. Ida was wondering if she should leave when Jean said, "I don't recall your name."

"Anna Bacri."

"You're the new owner of Chateau Lellouche?"

"I am."

"Mmm." He looked at the vegetables again. The sun went behind a cloud, and the air cooled. Jean finally took them, weighing the jars in his hands like small dumbbells. "Hold on a minute," he said, and disappeared into the house.

He returned with a bottle of milk, proffering it with what seemed like obligatory sternness. "The Vichy don't know I have a cow." He glanced over Ida's shoulder as if the police might be standing behind her. "I keep her tied up in the woods so they can't find her when they raid the place. I milked her an hour ago. You'll want to drink it all so it doesn't spoil."

Ida took the slightly warm bottle. It might as well have been liquid gold. She couldn't remember the last time she'd had a glass of milk. "All we need now is a shot of brandy," she said.

Jean smiled, the corners of his eyes wrinkling. "We do indeed."

31

Fall turned to winter. If nothing else, Ida had the dependable companion of changing seasons. Cold air slithered under the doors and ice cracked over the windows like lace. With no garden to occupy her, she turned to her violin. She played musical scores from memory. She listened to the radio and played by ear. She cut the fingertips off her gloves, put on her coat, and took her music past the dormant gardens and untrimmed hedges into the pine forest. Under the evergreens, she played for the ghost of her grandmother. She played for the memory of her mother. For Leon. For Arlette. She played for the creatures scurrying up tree trunks and hidden underground. She played for herself.

On a clear day in January, Jean came to tell her that the cow had been confiscated. Once a week, she made the trip down the road to fill her bottle of milk, but she'd never stepped foot in his house, and he'd never come down the road to hers. Now, he stood in the front hall of Chateau Lellouche with his hat in his hands, unfazed by the grandeur of the place. "It was too cold to keep her outside. They were bound to find her in the barn, but I had no choice. I came to tell you so you wouldn't bother coming over for milk anymore. She wouldn't have produced much longer anyway."

"I enjoyed the company more than the milk," Ida said. "You're just about the only person I talk to."

Jean tugged at his beard. "I never talked to too many folks before, so not much has changed for me."

"Other than the general lack of food and freedom." Ida did not succeed in cracking a smile out of him. They stood in silence. She said, "If there's to be no more milk, you should at least share the last of mine."

Jean lifted his shoulders, dropped them. "Okay."

In the kitchen, Ida turned on the radio as she warmed the milk on the stove. Jean sat with his elbows on his knees, fiddling with his hat and looking at the floor. A song finished on Radio Londres, and the announcer came on, blaring his familiar, "Before we begin, please listen to these personal messages!" Ida poured the frothy liquid into two cups and set them on the table.

Jean had stopped fiddling with his hat. His eyes were on the speaker. Radio Londres was a French station broadcasted from London under Charles de Gaulle, the former undersecretary of state for defense, now a leader of the Free French Forces living in exile in England. It was not lost on Ida that she had no idea whose side Jean was on. He'd hidden a cow, but maybe that was only because he wanted milk. Now, he listened with a stony expression as the radio announcer read the bulletins everyone knew contained coded information meant for the Resistance.

When the messages ended and a woman's slick voice began to sing, Jean did not reach for his cup. He looked at Ida. "How did you come by this place? It's belonged to the Lellouche family for as long as I can remember."

Conscious of her French, Ida repeated the story she'd told the police. If he detected an accent, he didn't mention it. "I play the violin," she said. "I've found that this station has the best music. I listen to the pieces and try and play them by ear. What do you listen to?" She was trying to see if he'd say Radio Paris or Radio-Vichy, indications of loyalty to Pétain.

"I don't listen to anything," he said, and raised his mug to his lips.

JEAN BECAME IDA'S only companion. If he was spying on her for the Germans, so be it. She wasn't doing anything suspicious. She wasn't doing anything at all.

Jean would knock on her door with unimportant news: freezing rain was coming, his barn door hinge had come off, rodents had gotten into the last of his grain, and Ida would invite him inside. They'd sit on hard chairs drinking the crude milk she made by soaking oats in water. They kept the radio off and talked only of the weather, or how hard it was to come by fuel, or how scarce meat was. They spoke of these things as if they were the usual difficulties of life and not the war stalking the perimeter of their lives, caging them in.

His presence was a comfort. There was a sturdiness to Jean, a soft-spoken strength Ida found reassuring. She wondered what her life would have looked like if she'd had a father like Jean. Someone who cared about her opinions, who checked on her well-being, made sure she had firewood and food, who worried about her safety and told her to bolt her door at night. It didn't take much to care. It wasn't even love, just thoughtfulness.

She wanted to tell Jean about Arlette—her friend's absence was a constant nagging at the base of her skull—but Jean's conversations never went beyond the day to day, and he hadn't said a word against the Germans, which made her wary.

The day the Americans joined the British forces, Jean came over with a pot of sprouted tomato plants he'd been caring for in a sunny window. "They may not produce anything, but it's worth a try," he said. No mention of the US troops. Ida wanted to throw her arms around him and shout that this was it. The end. The Americans had joined the war! They would swoop in and pluck up the Germans like hawks diving for mice. They'd liberate the camps and Arlette would come back and life would resume.

But Jean's cool expression, the controlled way he set the plants on her table, kept her quiet.

She was wrong anyway. There was no swooping in. No saviors. The American defeat of the German armies in Africa only succeeded in angering the Germans into more action. They'd been generous with their "free zone." They were generous no more. Their arbitrary line of freedom was scratched out as easily as a line in the dirt.

The hard-bodied Germans with their pale, unforgiving faces arrived in Marseille in November, rumbling over the cobblestone in great iron tanks, in trucks, on motorcycles, on foot, marching in single file in their field dress: black boots, green jackets, metal helmets.

There was a ruthlessness to their presence that made Ida grateful for her false identity as Anna Bacri. Little did she know that in the end, it was her protective shell of a name that would save her.

32

JANUARY 1943. CLOUDS HUNG heavy, the air frosty. Ida's stove was out, and she'd scrounged the last of the fallen branches. Seeking warmth, she walked down the road to the farmhouse. Jean had logs in his barn. He was good at chopping trees, splitting wood. In the three months since the Germans had invaded the free zone, Ida had seen very little of him.

Mud cracked under her boots as she stomped to the front door. The force with which it sprang open startled her, as did the German officer filling the doorway. Her instinct was to turn and run, but that could get her killed. She'd seen this happen in the square in Marseille. She'd been a foot away from a man who suddenly sprang forward as if he had somewhere important to be, and a soldier had unhesitatingly raised his gun and dropped the man to his knees. Ida had screamed. The child next to her had burst into tears, his mother grabbing onto him as they all watched the soldier cross the road, step up to the fallen man, and put a second bullet in his skull.

It was the first time Ida had seen a person die. It would not be the last.

The soldier filling the doorway smiled a row of crooked teeth at her and stepped inside, indicating that she should follow. If she turned away, he could put a bullet in her back. He didn't need a reason.

The curtains in Jean's house were drawn, the rooms dimly lit by the light creeping around them. In the main room, a soldier with a wide, flat nose sat in a rocking chair with his hands propped on the armrests, the chair creaking. Another soldier stood with his elbow on the mantel, twirling a porcelain figurine in his hand. The hearth was a bed of coals. The chimney needed cleaning and a faint pall of smoke hung in the air. The soldier who'd met her at the door spoke to the others in harsh German. Ida couldn't understand a word. When Jean stumbled into the room, pushed from behind by a fourth soldier, the others leapt to attention. The rocking chair was abandoned, the figurine set back on the mantel.

The soldier who'd shoved Jean stopped at the sight of Ida. "Who is this?" he asked in French. He was older than the others, forty, maybe, his features bold, his face chiseled and smooth and uncomfortably attractive.

Jean said, "That's Anna Bacri. She lives at Chateau Lellouche. She keeps to herself. She knows nothing." He lifted his head, set his jaw, and met her eyes. Dirt covered his trousers and flecked his sleeves and hair as if he'd crawled from a hole in the ground.

"Chateau Lellouche?" The soldier whistled. "I've heard that's a grand old place." There was an unnerving air of calm about him. "What are you doing in this shabby home, my lady?"

It was ridiculous, the way he said *my lady*, as if they were playacting. "I came to see if Jean could spare some wood," she said.

The man looked at Jean. "Can you? Spare some wood?" Jean did not answer. "I asked you a question," the soldier said, saccharine, charming.

"I can always spare something for a person in need." Jean's voice was cutting, and there was hatred in his eyes.

This only encouraged the soldier's civility. "Ah, good man, helping a neighbor. But would you help a neighbor who did not support your cause, I wonder?"

"I told you she knows nothing." Jean stood tall, his back straight, his chest thrust out. Years seemed to have slid from his shoulders.

The soldier slapped his back like they were old pals. "Come, then, let's bring the little lady a bit of wood." He took Ida's hand as if he intended to waltz her around the room. "Lieutenant Franz Kunstler at your service."

His overt kindness set Ida's teeth on edge. "Anna Bacri."

He said something in German to the other men, smiled at Ida, and said, "Shall we?" His hand moved from her palm to her wrist. It was the same grip her father used on her the night he dragged her into the barn. Struggling would only make it worse. Keeping her arm limp, her hand slack, Ida let Herr Kunstler lead her from the house.

Jean trailed them. "She's not involved," he said, tripping frantically over the stones.

Later, she would think, *Why did Jean follow? Why didn't he stay behind?*

The wind lifted the edge of Ida's jacket. She'd forgotten a hat and her ears were cold.

No one carried any wood.

When they stepped into the front hall of Chateau Lellouche, Herr Kunstler let go of her. It was like facing a bear in the woods. Ida backed away slowly. He watched her, running his hand along the marble wall as if checking for imperfections, his fingers long and graceful. Jean stood behind him in the open doorway.

"Aren't you going to invite me in?" Herr Kunstler said.

You're already in, you bastard, Ida thought. The rage she used to feel toward her brothers and father rose up. Power looked so ugly on men. She wanted to shove him. To kick him to the ground. She wanted to be the lounging goddess she'd seen at the base of the Gare St. Charles. Her power vibrant and gorgeous and mighty.

Ida set her teeth and walked past Herr Kunstler into the living room. "Please, come in, sit."

With a wide stride, Herr Kunstler entered the room, his game of guest and hostess officially begun. "Do you play, Anna?" He indicated the open violin case on the coffee table.

"I do."

"How well?"

"Extremely well."

With a flourish, Herr Kunstler walked to the grand piano, removed his helmet and holster, and dropped them on the bench with a clang. He sat down as if she'd challenged him to a duel. Ida glanced at Jean, who kept to the far end of the room. He gave a quick shake of his head, cautioning her of something, she just didn't know what.

The piano key was in the fallboard. Herr Kunstler unlocked it and slid it back, brushing his fingers over the ivory keys, running them back and forth. It was a tactile play of power. Possession by touch. Ida's wrist, the wall, the piano.

A single note rang out, high C, and then another. Combing a hand through his fine blond hair, Herr Kunstler unbuttoned the top button of his coat, and his face filled with pleasure as he began a song in a minor key Ida had never heard before. It was beautiful. The notes trilled, sped up, became fierce, and then fell, feather light around them. An ache began in Ida's chest, an excavation of wounds. Music weakens everyone if you get it right.

After a while, the notes turned delicate as snow and drifted into silence.

Herr Kunstler stood up and gave a little bow. "Thank you for indulging me." He went to Ida's violin and lifted it from its case. "My sister plays. I haven't heard the violin in a very long time." Creases appeared in the corners of his washed-out blue eyes. "Music reminds me of home. Would you be so kind?" He presented the instrument like a gift.

There was danger in playing for this man. "My fingers are cold," she said.

"Please? I insist." His tone was irrefutable.

She held the neck loosely. "What would you like to hear?"

"Do you know Schoenberg's Opus No. 36?"

"No."

Herr Kunstler looked past her to Jean. "Do you know the piece?"

Jean did not move or answer. Everything was a trap.

"No?" Herr Kunstler pressed. "I was sure a Jewish sympathizer would be familiar with Schoenberg. It is a shame they banned his music." He gave a shallow laugh. "Don't tell anyone I said that." Chummy, personal, he sat down on the sofa and crossed his legs, one shiny boot rising into the air. "I don't agree with Wagner that all Jewish music is repugnant and shallow. Mendelssohn, Meyerbeer. These are great composers! You're a musician, Anna. You must agree?"

He was cornering her. "You cannot argue with the greats," she said.

His boot jiggled up and down. "Exactly! What composer said, 'To copy truth can be a good thing, but to invent the truth is better'? That's all we're doing here, inventing a new truth. It is my opinion, expressed only in the safety of like-minded company like the two of you, that we don't need to settle accounts with gifted Jews. It's the rest of them we need to do away with. Keep the talented ones, I say." He let this land, his face bright and smiling.

"Come, Lyam, sit with me." Herr Kunstler patted the seat next to him. It took Ida a moment to realize he was talking to Jean. "What instrument do you play?"

Jean sat with his back tight against the sofa. "I don't."

"Nothing? Well, I am sure you appreciate music. Who doesn't? What would you like to hear Mademoiselle Bacri play?" Silence. "Name your favorite piece. I insist."

Closing his eyes, Jean rested his hands over his stomach and tilted back his head. The cords of his neck bulged under his beard. "Do you know Mendelssohn Opus 64, Anna?" he asked in a soft voice.

"Ha! Good choice." Herr Kunstler beamed like a child. "Do you know it?"

Ida loved that piece. Why had she and Jean never spoken of it? "I know the first movement," she said.

"Go ahead," Herr Kunstler said. "We won't judge you too harshly."

Something terrifying was happening, Ida just couldn't see what. She lifted the violin and drew the bow along the strings. Notes rang out. Her cheek quivered. She fumbled. Started again. Closing her eyes, she reached for the score in her mind, the notes gliding out from memory. When she heard Herr Kunstler stand, she looked up. The music stalled.

"Keep playing," he said, walking to the piano bench. He did not pick up his helmet or belt, just his revolver. "Begin again."

She began again. Herr Kunstler moved his gun through the air like a baton. The violin screeched.

"No, no, no." He stopped her. "It was good. What happened? Start over. You." He waved the gun at Jean. "Stand up, old man."

Jean stood. His eyes were hard as steel.

The barrel swung toward Ida. "Play." Herr Kunstler's manner was no longer tempered.

Trembling, she managed a single note before dropping her bow. "I'm sorry." She fumbled to retrieve it.

"Who is this man?" Herr Kunstler demanded of her, pointing the gun at Jean.

"Jean Aubert."

Jean said, "Do you see? She knows nothing. She sat here every night and made me listen to Vichy radio. She is not one of us."

The lie was meant to protect her. His silence, their conversations about weather and tomato seeds, all meant to protect her.

Soft and low, Herr Kunstler said, "I want to hear the song from start to finish. I do not want a mistake. Can you do that?" There was a warning in his voice.

Ida's heart thundered. Her eyes blurred. Lowering the gun, Herr Kunstler put his arm around her shoulder. It was thick and strong. He smelled of the outdoors, crisp air, pine needles. "Come, play in the entryway. The acoustics are better in there."

He drew her into the wide-open hall, his gun beckoning Jean to follow like a friendly hand. Removing his arm from Ida's shoulder, Herr Kunstler looked up at the chandelier like he was gazing at the moon. "Try again, my dear." The tenderness in his voice was disorienting.

Positioning her violin under her chin, Ida thought of standing in her living room in Petersfield, playing while her parents argued in the next room. The louder her parents shouted, the harder she played. Her music had blocked out the filthy rug under her feet, the scent of manure, the house saturated in mildew and rot and anger, the sobs in her throat.

She heard Jean say, "It's okay, Anna. It is a beautiful piece. Close your eyes and see only the notes."

She closed her eyes. She began again. When the shot came, it ricocheted through her whole body. Her muscles spasmed. The bow fell from her fingers.

Jean was collapsed against the wall with his legs bent at a funny angle. He looked at her, his eyes steady, his voice thin. "Keep playing," he said. "Whatever you do, keep playing." *If you don't, Herr Kunstler will turn the gun on you*, his face said.

Frantic, Ida picked up her bow and put it to the strings, the notes all wrong. In her peripheral vision, Herr Kunstler tilted his head with a dissatisfied smile, aimed, and pulled the trigger a second time.

The noise cracked through the room. Ida doubled over. Jean slipped sideways to the floor, his kneecaps blown out. "Keep playing," he rasped, his teeth clenched with pain.

Gulping back sobs, Ida drove the notes into the air with detached madness. Her elbow dipped and rose. Her head jerked back and forth. Sweat pierced her stomach like a swarm of bees as Herr Kunstler timed the final bullet in Jean's temple with the final note of Mendelssohn's Opus 64.

The violin clattered to the floor, and Ida dropped to her knees, her body twitching and frenzied.

There was a deafening silence, and then the sound of boots clacking over marble, their shiny black toes coming into view. "Come, my dear, get up." Herr Kunstler extended his hand. It was not a work-worn hand, but the hand of a white-gloved officer, the skin baby soft. He pulled her to her feet.

"Lyam Babin, or Jean, however you knew him, was one of the most influential men in the Resistance. He was going to be killed one way or another." The creases around his eyes deepened. It was unnerving how handsome he was, this wicked man gifted with pillowy lips and cheekbones high enough to hold pools of tears. "We made his ending a pleasant one. You will find that I am generous when I want to be." Considering his options, Franz looked around and said, "I have a few things to take care of in Marseille, but if it's all right with you, I'll stay here for a while."

Letting go of Ida's hand, he stepped over Jean's body like a discarded pair of shoes and walked out.

33

WHEN THE SOLDIERS ARRIVED, Ida was sitting in the hallway with her back against the marble wall, praying to a god she no longer believed in. Blood pooled at her feet. Her violin lay where she'd dropped it, the heel of her bow resting near Jean's mangled knees.

The soldiers halted at the sight of her, prepared for a dead man but not a live woman.

"Are you all right?" one of them asked in French.

Ida almost spoke to him in English, remembering herself at the last minute. *"Non."* She didn't know what else to say. She was not all right.

They looked concerned. One propped an arm around her waist and helped her to her feet. A fuzz of hair crowned his upper lip. "You shouldn't have to see this," he said, leading her through the living room and into the kitchen where he helped her into a chair. "It's cold. I'll find some wood and start a fire." The kitchen door opened and closed. Voices came from the hallway. Out the window, the sky was a flat blue. It would be nighttime soon.

On some level, Ida understood that she was in shock. It was like being underwater, everything muted and slippery. The soldier returned with an armload of split logs. Jean's logs. He started a fire and put the kettle on. He went down the hall to help the others. They did not act like killers but well-raised young men, polite, deferential. They did not drink her tea or raid the wine cellar. They were sorry for their intrusion. They picked up her violin and wiped the blood from her bow. They shut and locked the piano and pushed the bench into place. They found a bucket and rags and cleaned up the blood, their heavy boots stomping back and forth from the kitchen to the hallway.

Ida never knew what they did with Jean's body. When the soldiers left, she sat in the kitchen until dark and then went up to bed, careful not to look at the place where Jean had died. Every time she entered or left the house, every time she ascended or descended the stairs, she would be reminded.

OVER THE NEXT few months, Ida learned how Franz operated. He could have stayed anywhere, he told her, but he liked the chateau, despite how out of the way it was. He was well spoken, indulgent, and cruel. He was generally cheerful, ready to sit and regurgitate his day, impervious to any emotion he might see reflected in Ida's face.

His acts of kindness were to please himself, as was his brutality. He missed his sister and would tear up when Ida played the violin for him in the evening. He spoke of his home with affection and watched men die with indifference. He was a hypocrite: unshakably patriotic and yet willing to break the rules for his own purposes. He brought Ida coffee and sausages and butter he'd purchased on the black market. He confiscated her radio and came home with a banned shortwave radio they listened to in the evenings.

When he left the house, he locked the radio in a cabinet and took the key with him. Only once did he slide his hand to the back of Ida's neck and ask her if she found him attractive. When she jerked away, he looked disappointed but did not force her. He played the piano beautifully, and regularly brought men to the house to be shot to the tune of Ida's violin. It was easier to bring them to the chateau, he said, than bring her to the Old Port. "We'd gather a crowd." He traced his hand in the air as if reading a marquee. "Anna Bacri of Chateau Lellouche plays for dying Jews."

He was in a good mood that night. He had brought Ida a prized chicken one of the SS officers confiscated from a nearby farm, tossing it on the counter as if he'd defeathered the thing himself. Over dinner, he told her that the raid on the Old Port was going well. In as little as two days, they'd sent thousands of Jews to camp Royallieu-Compiègne. Purging the neighborhood was gratifying. "Like scouring rusty metal into a bright shine," he said. The estimated number of removals was up to thirty thousand. The buildings were set to be dynamited in as little as a week.

Ida moved the meat around on her plate, questioning what it meant to eat the flesh of an animal. "If the Jews are being sent to camps, who are the men you are executing?" she asked. These sorts of questions did not upset Franz. He liked to talk about his work. Holding a chicken leg with both hands, he pulled the meat from the bone with his teeth and explained, between bites, that the men he executed were the dangerous ones. The ones helping the enemy.

Why he executed them to music, Ida never understood. He'd quote Schumann to her—"To send light into the darkness of men's hearts; such is the duty of the artist"—as if he was doing these men a service. Cleansing them, like God. He would stand beside them, serene, comforting, and ask what their favorite piece of music was. Ida hadn't decided whether letting them choose was kind or sadistic. If she knew the piece, she played it. If not, she played Mendelssohn's Concerto.

The ones who arrived angry and defiant, accepting their fate with heads high, she could put out of her mind. It was the whimpering ones who haunted her. There was one in particular. She never knew his name. She never knew any of their names. He couldn't have been older than sixteen. Scrambling from the car, he'd fallen to his knees and looked at her with wide, flat eyes. "Help me," he'd sobbed, splaying open enormous callused palms. Ida turned her head away as the soldier blindfolded the boy and tied his hands behind his back. She had learned not to watch. When asked what music he wanted to hear, he said, "My mother used to sing 'Au clair de la lune.'" It was a simple lullaby, cracked in three places. There were always three shots, one to each kneecap, and then a close-range shot to the temple. It was Herr Kunstler's way.

The music soothed him, Franz said. It was hard work. It took a toll.

When the boy's body was dragged away, Ida went upstairs and lay on her bed imagining the mother who sang to her son. She pictured her at a table in a kitchen, alone. Or maybe she was dead too. Maybe without her son, that's what she'd wish for.

That night, Ida locked her bedroom door and skipped dinner. After a while, she heard the creak of the mattress on the other side of the wall. Franz was removing his boots. There was the thud of each one hitting the floor, the groan of his bedsprings as he climbed in. The springs creaked every time he rolled over, which was often. He was a restless sleeper.

What once drove Ida—the desire to escape her family, to play the violin, to make herself over in the likeness of Arlette and become something worthwhile—fell away. She floated in a senseless world, thinking only about the men she played into the next one. Who were they? Who had they loved? Who loved them?

Ida stopped imagining a future. She stopped picturing a life with or without Arlette. She stopped pretending she'd go to music school one day. She had learned to play the violin to find freedom and make something more of her life. Through her instrument, she had tried to make sense of the world, and through it, now, had come madness.

34

I N MAY, THE EARTH sprang senselessly to life. Blood stained the grass, and it continued to grow. Shameless pink blossoms covered the peach trees. Buds came out on the rose bushes, tight, red, and oblivious.

One morning, Franz entered the kitchen with a bouquet of tulips. Ida pressed a hand over her eyes. Sparks of exhaustion ran through her. She hardly slept anymore. Her hands twitched and she'd developed a tick in her neck.

"Are you all right? Do you have a headache?" Franz asked.

"I'm fine." She turned her back to him, poured hot water over the chicory coffee—not even the black market could provide the real stuff anymore—and set it on the table next to a plate of roasted potatoes.

"Thank you," Franz said, like a husband who didn't take her for granted. He handed her the bouquet. "I am afraid this will be our last breakfast together."

"Oh?" Ida wasn't getting her hopes up.

"I have orders to be in Paris."

"I see." She kept her eyes on the flowers. Franz had picked them too early, and the buds were bound into fists of white.

"I will miss you." He took her hand, running a finger over her knuckles as if they were lovers. He liked to play out fantasies that had nothing to do with her.

Finishing his coffee, he rose from the table, went into the marble hallway where his packed bag waited by the door, and left.

Ida tossed the flowers out back.

That evening, she listened for the sound of his boots, for the clink of his belt buckle, his harmonious *"Bonjour"* as he came into the kitchen. That she would not have to hear his nauseating voice or see his pale eyes or severe cheeks again seemed impossible.

Days went by, and then weeks. Ida continued to sleep badly. She'd wake in the middle of the night not knowing where she was. Disoriented, she'd claw her way back to reality only to want to lose herself in the oblivion of sleep again. Thoughts became hard to hold on to. Tasks were performed with uncertainty. Ida would find herself wondering why she was filling a pot with water or what she was doing with the scissors in the living room. A vague confusion followed her everywhere.

In midsummer, Ida knelt in the overgrown garden, pulling weeds for no reason. The rosemary and sage had survived the winter, and last year's seeds had sprung up a few tomato plants, but there were no other vegetables. It didn't matter. It felt good to be under threatening rain clouds with her hands in the dirt. There was an earthy, wet smell to the air, and a bolt of lightning slashed across the sky. Ida looked up, watching another flash with satisfied detachment. What once frightened her no longer did. She welcomed the electrical currents and the cracks of thunder. It jolted something awake in her, made her feel alive.

It was in this alert state that her eyes fell on a man standing stock-still at the edge of the forest. His face was bone white. His hair plastered to his head. His gaze startled. There was another flash of lightning, and he was gone as instantly as he had appeared. Ida found herself staring into the dark patch of trees, convinced the ghosts of the murdered men were haunting her. *Fine*, she thought, brushing the dirt from her hands and walking straight across the lawn into the woods. *I'll give them what you want.* Thunder rumbled and fierce drops of rain pummeled her back as she snapped twigs and branches into manageable pieces. Ida did not look around for the dead man.

Back in the living room, she dumped the twigs on the hearth and unlatched the windows. Rain slid in. Not bothering to go into the kitchen for newspaper, she ripped pages from a book and balled them under the kindling. She struck a match. The paper flared, then fizzled out under the damp twigs. She needed something dry. Something that would burn hot.

In the carriage house, she found a rusty axe and hacked at an old chair until it splintered and cracked apart. Hauling the pieces to the living room, she crisscrossed the spindly wood in the hearth, struck another match, and blew until the fire roared to life.

Her violin was next to the piano. She had not played since Franz left. She had not even opened the case. She touched the clasp, thinking it would summon the ghosts of the dead men, but it was her mother who stood beside her, proud and cautious. "*Open it,*" she whispered. The clasp gave way. Ida lifted the instrument, and with an easy toss, fed Amelia Verhoeven's violin to the flames.

Heat sucked at the wood. It popped and crackled and hissed, dying in moans. The scars on Ida's arm pulsed. It was strange watching an object that had defined her whole life disappear within minutes. She thought of entire houses burning, every beautiful, symbolic item crumbling to ash, the abrupt cessation of one's ancestry, one's history. Everything gone in the blink of an eye.

Ida rubbed her scars. One, two strips. She had failed in so many ways.

The case went next, the bow strapped to the inside, her resin tucked into its pocket. The velvet turned the flames green. The bowstrings curled over the coals like shriveled worms. The metal clasps glowed red.

Dusk fell, a slow creeping of darkness.

A startling knock rattled the door, and Ida looked up. She had no idea how long she'd been sitting there. It came again. A hard thud. It was coming from the back. The Germans, in their polite superiority, always came to the front door. *Arlette*, she thought with a leap of her heart, and then realized how foolish that was. Arlette wouldn't knock.

There was a distant rumble of thunder, and Ida thought it must be someone looking to escape the storm. She stayed kneeling on the floor. She was not a savior. She was not Arlette. She could help no one. Rain continued to fall. Puddles formed on the floor under the windows. When she heard the unnerving thud of boots, she scrambled to her feet as the living room door swung open. A figure filled the doorway, tall, broad-shouldered, hair smoothed flat to his head. It was the man she'd seen at the edge of the forest. That he was not a ghost was only slightly reassuring.

In English, he said, "I'm sorry for the intrusion," then shook his head and tried to say something in French, but failed.

In the dim light, Ida couldn't make out his features. "I speak English," she said.

Her voice released something in him. The man's chest heaved as if he was taking a gulp of air and he pressed a hand to his eyes. Was he crying? "I'm sorry," he mumbled.

His raw emotion was disarming. Ida stepped closer. Water dripped from the shoulders of his oiled army jacket. "Are you hurt?"

He drew his hand down his face. "No."

"You're bleeding."

He looked at his stained jacket. "That's not my blood."

"Are there others?"

"No."

"You're an American soldier?"

"Yes."

They stood in silence.

Unsure what to do, Ida said, "Would you like to sit down?"

"If you've got something to drink, I'm parched."

"Of course."

He was blocking the doorway to the kitchen. Ida put a cautious hand on his forearm, and he looked down at it as if trying to work out what it was doing there.

"The kitchen is behind you," she said.

"Oh, sorry." He stepped abruptly aside, and her hand dropped away.

The man sat at the table while Ida lit the oil lamp and poured him a glass of water that he drank greedily, holding the glass with both hands as if he might drop it. He looked strong but unintimidating, and in this way, he reminded her of Leon. The wind picked up and the rain fell harder. Ida thought about closing the living room windows before the floors were completely ruined, but she didn't move to get up.

The man set the glass down and looked out the window. "I have no idea where I am," he said.

"You're outside of Marseille."

"Marseille?" He rubbed the stubble over his chin. "That's not where I was headed. Are you sure?"

"Pretty sure. Where were you headed?"

"Vannes."

"I'm afraid you're nowhere near Vannes."

He dropped his elbows onto the table. There was a calm solidity in his soft brown eyes. "How did I get so off course? I must have blown in the wrong direction."

Ida couldn't help smiling. "You blew here?"

He smiled back, and boyish dimples sank into his cheeks. "My parachute," he said.

Sidney Theodore Whipple, Twelfth Air Force, gunner for the 98th bombardment group, was shot down somewhere over the Tarn River, or so he thought. Bowing his head, he admitted that he wasn't prepared for war. "I thought I was. I suppose most of us think we are until we're smack in the middle of it."

This confession seemed obvious and extraordinary to Ida. Maybe he was bold enough to make it because she was a complete stranger and he had nothing to lose. Or maybe all Americans were this frank. Peggy had a similar bluntness about her. Whatever it was, Sidney went on to tell Ida that the comradery he felt for his fellow soldiers, the kinship, vanished the moment he was in real danger. When the bomber spiraled out of control, all he thought about was saving himself. "It was like tunnel vision. Like when you've got the ball and everything but the end goal fades into the background. When I saw the roll of black smoke engulf the bomber's wing, I didn't even wait for the bail-out bell. I ripped off my oxygen mask and headset and rolled out without looking back. My parachute opened at the last minute. I remember trees rushing up at me and then"—he slapped the table—"nothing. I woke with my face in the dirt. I couldn't for the life of me remember where I was until I turned over and saw my buddy James a few yards away, his head bleeding something fierce. I don't know whether he hit a rock, or if it was shrapnel, or a piece of the plane, but there was blood everywhere." Tears sprang into Sidney's eyes. "I crawled over to him, but what could I do?"

He looked into the palms of his failed hands. "Nothing. I could do absolutely nothing. I just held him."

Ida hadn't held Jean. She hadn't even touched him. "What did you do then?" she asked.

"I took his dog tags and left him there." Sidney didn't know where the plane had gone down or what had happened to the rest of the crew, but he did know he was in enemy territory and needed to get away from the crash site as fast as possible. Untangling himself from his parachute, he made his way into the woods and hid until dark. When the moon rose, he started walking, discovering, then, that he'd lost his escape kit, map, and compass. "Thankfully, I had a chocolate bar in my pocket." Sidney touched his hip. "And my pistol, although the chocolate ended up being more useful."

"When did you last eat?"

He whistled. "Gosh, not for a few days now. I walked for four. Slept a little, but not much. At one point I found some wild blackberries. Tiny ones. Sweetest things I've ever had, but they don't fill a belly." He smiled softly at her. "I'm pretty sure you're a hallucination."

The warmth in his expression caught Ida off guard. "Lucky for you, I'm quite real," she said, getting up to put a loaf of bread and a hunk of cheese in front of him. She was sorry she hadn't prepared a hot meal. She never cooked for herself anymore.

He ripped the bread and held a piece out to her. Ida took it, biting into the crust trying to remember if she'd eaten that day. "Why stop here?" she said.

He shrugged. "I couldn't keep on without food, and I figured I was as likely to be caught by the enemy out there as in here. I had a fifty-fifty chance walking through your door." He wiped the crumbs from his lips. "Truth is, I saw you in the garden, and then I saw you gathering wood in the forest, and I figured you were alone."

"You thought you'd be safe because there wasn't a man around?" If Arlette were here, she might have shot him before he got past the living room door.

He grinned, his dimples unsettling her. "Can you blame me?"

35

SINCE THE CHATEAU WAS regularly searched by Germans, they decided it was best if Sidney slept in the caretaker's house. It was furnished with a four-poster bed and a single chair that had to be swept of dust. Each morning, Sidney was to check for a green vase in the kitchen window: their signal that German troops had arrived. If he saw it, he'd slip out to the carriage house where they'd found a hidden room under the eaves. The room was full of cobwebs and moist, mildewing floorboards and was no good to stay in permanently, as Sidney could hardly stand up in it, but it would do in an emergency. The stairs leading to the room were behind a door that had a lock and key. The plan, if they could manage it, was for Ida to lock Sidney in and hide the key. Franz's company had left her with a questionable reputation among the citizens of Marseille, but a solid one with the Germans. If they asked what was on the other side of that door—no one had yet—she'd play dumb. It would take heavy implements to knock it down, which would be loud and time-consuming and give Sidney plenty of time to jump out the window at the far end of the room and flee.

"I could just run into the forest in the first place," he said, but Ida told him the soldiers were as likely to be prowling out there as anywhere. Best to stay hidden.

"As long as you don't forget about me in that locked room," Sidney said.

Ida would not forget about him. His sudden presence in her dim existence gave her a temporary reprieve from herself. He did not fit into this place, which allowed her, in a sense, a way out of it.

At night, she watched from her bedroom window for his light to wink out. In the morning, she watched from the kitchen window for him to cross the lawn, barefoot, his ankles showing below the short trousers she'd found for him to wear in one of the upstairs bedrooms. His shirtsleeves, also too short, would be rolled to his elbows, his hair spiked along his head. Walking through the kitchen door in sunlight, he'd ask how she'd slept, and she'd say, "Well. You?" A lie.

The destruction of Ida's violin had not eased her night terrors. She'd start awake, convinced she'd heard a scream, only to be met with an equally dreadful silence. Lying in the dark, she'd listen for the sounds of approaching Germans, her body stiff with exhaustion.

One morning, Sidney found her asleep at the kitchen table. When he put a hand on her shoulder, she jumped awake, embarrassed. When she went to stand, he pressed her gently back down. "Stay. I'll light the stove."

He made her chicory coffee and toast and insisted on doing the breakfast dishes. He did not mention her fatigue. He heated water, carried it up to the bathtub for her, and told her to stay in as long as she needed; he'd listen for anyone coming up the road. When it got dark, he didn't go to the caretaker's house but sat with her in the living room. The windows were open and the evening was warm and full of insects, their tiny forms swarming around the lamplight.

"What do you spend your time doing here all alone?" Sidney asked.

I was not always alone, Ida wanted to say.

She had told him about her false identity, touching loosely on her friendship with Arlette and Peggy, and the family she'd left behind in England. She had not told him of Franz Kunstler.

"I read." No need to bring up the violin. She was no longer a musician. "What books do you like?" She went to the bookshelf and roamed the spines for something in English.

"I'm not much of a reader," he said.

"Well, we have to do something to pass the time." She pulled a book from the shelf with a dragon sketched on the cover. *The Hobbit*. Inside, it said, *For Lucienne Lellouche, With affection, J.R.R. Tolkien.* "Shall we try this one?"

They read aloud, a chapter each. Sidney sat on the couch, Ida in a chair. Sidney's voice was deep and rhythmic. Ida watched him as he read, head down, shoulders forward, legs outstretched. She had a desire to touch him. To do the simplest thing of holding his hand. It had been so long since she'd felt the warmth of another person's skin.

When Sidney finished reading and set the book aside, he said, "If it's all the same to you, I might just sleep here on the sofa for the night."

Ida did not want him on the sofa. She wanted him to take her upstairs and wrap his arms around her and pin her into the darkness.

"What if someone comes?" she said.

"I'll hear them."

"What if they arrive on foot?"

"I can hear a twig snap in my sleep."

Ida brought down linens. They did not mention the numerous empty beds upstairs. The sofa was less of a commitment, and a straighter shot to the back door if noises were heard in the night.

Together they tucked the sheet around the cushions and shook out the coverlet. Sidney's hand brushed Ida's and sent tiny sparks up her arm. If she had not been a broken version of herself, she would have reached for him. Or not. It was hard to tell what she would or wouldn't do in any given circumstance anymore. That there was desire in her at all was questionable.

With a hurried goodnight, she made her way upstairs where she stripped naked and lay between the sheets, thinking how natural and absurd it would be to fall in love.

36

WITH VARIAN AND LENA gone, Ida had no idea how to help Sidney get back to his unit, or get word home. He was anxious to try. Both of his brothers had been killed in the Battle of Guadalcanal, and it tore him up to think his parents believed he was dead too. He pleaded with Ida to use her connections with the rescue committee. At the very least, he needed to find a way to get a letter out of France.

She said she'd try, but it was impossible to know whom to trust. A shopkeeper was just as likely to be a German informant as a Resistance fighter. Since the Nazi occupation of the free zone, signs hung from every window saying aiding or abetting an enemy of the Third Reich was punishable by death. People were terrified of each other. They walked with their heads down, backs tense, fists clenched. No eye contact. No small talk. The gleam of German helmets, the clack of boots, reigned over them all.

If not for her food ration, Ida would have kept out of the city entirely. The places she frequented were aware that Herr Kunstler had been billeted with Anna Bacri of Chateau Lellouche. People didn't know what part she'd played, but they knew that the men taken there never came back. No one trusted her. She saw it in their eyes, in their shut mouths and the hard lines of their jaws.

Sidney believed she was noble and rebellious. He championed her for working for Varian and safekeeping Arlette's chateau under a false identity. How was she to admit to him that she'd aided a German officer? Played music while he shot men in the head and dragged their bodies into the woods? How could she explain her compliance? She couldn't even explain to herself why she hadn't resisted.

THEY FINISHED THE *Hobbit*. Good prevailed over evil, a comforting fiction.

Now, in the evenings, Ida and Sidney talked. Without his head buried in a book, his eyes looked right at her, warm eyes that she wanted to crawl into. She wondered if it was pure physical attraction that drew her to him, his distinct jaw and broad forehead, the stubble of hair on his face, his dimples and squinty eyes. Franz was attractive—if you looked for perfection of features—but he had repulsed her. What was the difference? Trust? No one in Ida's life had been trustworthy. Not her parents or brothers. Not Peggy. Certainly not Arlette. For reasons unknown to Ida, she trusted Sidney. Maybe it was the honest way he spoke of his family or how openly he admitted failure. Or maybe it was simply how easily he asked and answered questions. He never seemed to hide anything.

Whatever the reason, Ida was soothed by his presence. His steady sensibility, his kindly, unjudging expression gave her temporary relief from her shame. When he spoke, she fell out of her world and into his.

Sidney was from a hardworking middle-class family. His dad went from sweeping the floors of a woolen mill to running it while his mother raised him and his two brothers. When Sidney was in his last year of high school, his mother became a fourth-grade teacher. She told him it was to stave off the loneliness of her boys growing up, but Sidney suspected she'd wanted to work all along. Her first and only grandbaby was born three weeks before Sidney's brother Peter shipped out to the Solomon Islands. "You could say it was a kind God who let my brother meet his son before he died, or an evil God who took away his chance of raising him. Or no God, just cruel luck. Peter sent me a photograph of his boy before he left. By then I was stationed in England. Still haven't met my nephew. Michael James Whipple. Ugliest thing you've ever seen." Sidney smiled. They were under the peach tree, gathering the last of the ripe fruit. "He looked like a wrinkly old man, and yet somehow, I felt love for that little guy anyway. How is it we can feel love for a person we've never met, simply because they're part of a family we already know we love?"

He said this as if it was the most natural thing in the world, and the idea fluttered in Ida's chest with a swarm of possibility. She did not tell him what it was like to be a part of an impossible-to-love family.

Sidney's shirtsleeve brushed her hair as he reached over her, testing the ripeness of a peach. "My parents have an apple tree in their yard. I used to climb it and chuck apples at my fiancée." He laughed. "When we were kids, that is. I don't know how she'd feel about me chucking apples at her now."

The tips of Ida's ears went hot. The nephew was forgotten, the brother, the beloved family. The word *fiancée* ricocheted in her head. How had he never mentioned a fiancée? She steadied her voice and said, "How long have you been engaged?"

"Two years, almost. I proposed right before I left. Most of us GIs did. Girls want something to wait for."

"What's she like?" Ida wanted to know everything about her.

The peach gave way with a tug. Sidney tossed it in the air and caught it in his palm. His shirt was open at the collar, his khaki trousers tight around his hips. It was too hot for socks and shoes, and their bare feet rested close in the spiky grass.

"Gosh, what's she like? Sometimes it's harder to say the longer you've known a person. I've known Ellen my entire life. She grew up three doors down from me."

As if this is a reason to marry her, Ida thought, hating Ellen Whoever She Was.

Sidney plucked the stem from his peach. "Let's see . . . she's stubborn, and very determined. She told me when we were ten years old that she was going to marry me. I couldn't stand her back then, but"—he grinned—"she grew up."

A light wind shifted Ida's skirt around her legs. She propped the bowl of peaches on her hip and started toward the house. Sidney followed, coming up next to her a little closer than she would have liked.

"Do you have a picture of her?" Ida set the fruit bowl on the patio table.

"I left it back at my bunker in Suffolk." He sat down on a chair, bit into his peach, and said breezily, "Don't worry, she's not nearly as pretty as you are."

Ida flushed. She put a hand to her chest trying to hide the red blotches she felt breaking out around her collar. Summoning the power of Arlette, she met his eye and said, "Prove it."

Sidney gave a startled laugh. He choked on his peach, coughed, and glanced away.

Ida kept her gaze on him, observing herself from a distance, curiously and without judgment, as if to see what this woman on the patio would do next.

Wiping peach juice from his lips, Sidney tossed the pit over his shoulder and stood up, walking toward her with an amused expression. When he was close enough for her to see the flecks of green dotting his brown eyes, he reached up and pressed the pad of his finger to the dip in her collarbone. She could smell the fruit on his hands and feel the slight stickiness as he traced his fingers over her skin. His touch, the nearness of his body, made the colors of the day suffuse, spread out, and whiten.

"You don't wear any jewelry," he observed. "Most women I know wear too much."

"Like who?"

"Like . . ." He grinned. "My mother."

"And?"

"And no one."

"Jewelry bothers me." The bracelets borrowed from Arlette, the clip-on earrings, the claw-foot necklace, had felt like tiny anchors on Ida's body.

"I like your skin bare." He bent his head and touched his lips to her neck, her earlobe, her mouth.

Hoisting her onto the table, he slid her dress up over her knees, and pressed his fingers into her thighs. Their clothes were quickly shed. There was his mouth over her nipple, the strangely erotic prickle of his facial hair, his hands under the soft flesh of her bottom, his shoulders in sunlight, the dizzying sky and the intoxicating force of him as he moved inside her. It wasn't like the rolling orgasm she'd had with Arlette, but there was a sense in the furious rhythm that she was headed toward pleasure.

It was over much too quickly. Sidney's head fell to her shoulder. The quick pulse of his wrist rested against her thigh. "I'm sorry," he mumbled into her hair.

For what? Was he sorry he had sex with her? Or sorry it was all so abrupt? She slid her leg out from under his. Her boldness had left her, and she felt embarrassed to look at him.

Exposed, vulnerable, they scrambled to put themselves back together, aware, suddenly, of the bright day, the outdoors.

Tucked in and buttoned up, they went stoically about their afternoon. Sidney brought in kindling and lit the stove while Ida chopped leeks and garlic. She filled a pot of water and dumped in a bone shank. They avoided eye contact. When Sidney left out the back door, Ida watched him walk across the lawn and enter the caretaker's house with her heart in her throat. He regretted it. He'd cheated on his fiancée and she was the cause. Multiple partners were a way of life for Arlette and Peggy, for everyone in their circle, as far as Ida could tell. She hardly knew Sidney, and yet the idea of sharing him sent a sharp stab of envy through her. She had never felt possessive of Arlette. She had been jealous of her lovers not because she wanted Arlette for herself, but because they made her feel inferior.

Snipping rosemary in the garden, Ida thought how effortlessly Sidney had lifted her onto the patio table and slid her underwear down over her ankles. He hadn't hesitated. She'd liked the urgency, the boiling over of desire. He made her feel irresistible. With Arlette, there was always something distracted in the way she looked at Ida or touched her. Even in their most intimate moments a part of Arlette was elsewhere.

Forcing herself not to look in the direction of the caretaker's house, Ida went into the kitchen and set the herbs onto the cutting board. What was Sidney doing? Did he mean to start sleeping out there again? The smell of his skin lingered on her body. She heard Arlette's words,

"All men want is a tumble," and wondered how often Sidney did this sort of thing. It was a known fact that soldiers slept with foreign women. They were far away from home with no one to answer to. Sidney had probably had sex with dozens of girls in England. Ida pictured one, a beauty with dark hair and green eyes, what table he'd lifted her up onto, how he'd torn off her blouse. She imagined his fiancée: blonde, wholesome cheeks, freckles, blushed red lips.

Jealous of these fantasy women, Ida aggressively chopped the herbs and dropped them into the pot. The soup boiled and the smell of beef steamed in the air. When the sun dipped below the horizon, she went into the cellar for a bottle of wine. The shelves had been cleared by Franz, but there was a secret wall panel that slid away to reveal Arlette's father's prized reds. Ida took a bottle and went upstairs to pour herself a glass.

When Sidney came in, she offered him one. He thanked her and sat down with his eyes on his soup. The wine was dry and smooth and warmed Ida's chest. Sidney did not ask her where it came from or what the occasion was. They ate in torturous silence. When they finished, Ida washed their bowls at the sink with her back to him.

She heard the scrape of his chair over the floor. He cleared his throat and said, "Do you want me to light a fire in the living room?" Polite, deferential.

"Sure." Ida shook the water from the bowl and set it in the rack. It was a warm evening, but a fire meant they'd sit by it. It meant he might sleep in the house after all.

"Ida?"

She tensed. "Yes?"

"Would you like another glass of wine?"

"Please." A breeze through the open window cooled her cheeks. There was the glug of wine into the glass and the clink of the bottle as he set it down.

"I'm sorry," he said.

She turned off the faucet and faced him, propping her arms against the sink. "For what?"

His face was as flushed as hers. It was the wine, or the moment.

"For today," he said.

"I find that insulting."

"Oh." This confused him. "I didn't mean it to be." Sidney twirled the stem of his glass. It looked delicately out of place in his large hands. "I don't want you to think I do this sort of thing often, or casually. I mean . . . I have done it . . . and I wanted to." A flustered smile crossed his face. He shook his head. "I don't know what I'm trying to say."

With the uncharacteristic confidence she'd felt earlier, Ida picked up her wineglass and said, "Yes, you do," wondering if it was Sidney who made her feel brazen, or if she'd simply changed.

He laughed. "I've never met anyone like you."

"What am I like?" The way he said it made her feel exceptional.

"Stunning, for one. You're absolutely stunning."

Now she laughed, spilling her wine, both of them nervous. Ida grabbed a rag and wiped up the spill. Sidney said, "I'll go light that fire."

They sat like blundering strangers. The outside of Ida's thigh touched the outside of Sidney's. Neither knew what to do with their hands. Sidney put his arm on the back of the couch, and then removed it. Ida fiddled with a loose thread on her skirt, thinking how easily she'd sat here with Arlette, drinking wine and feeling similar urges.

Out the window, the sky was velvet.

After a while, Sidney's hand settled on her leg. He kept it there, his fingers making tiny circles on her thigh that released a flood of delirium in her.

"What I was trying to say earlier"—heat radiated from his palm—"was that was not how I wanted our first time to go."

Our first time. Ida didn't move. She felt wide awake, solidly in her body in a way she hadn't been in months. Years. Maybe ever. "Then show me how you wanted our first time to go."

There was no uncomfortable laughter, no groping hands or frenzied movement. With the utmost tenderness, Sidney unbuttoned Ida's blouse, bottom up, a bead of navel appearing, soft belly, ribs and breastbone. His hands floated over her, sliding her brassiere from her shoulders, her skirt from her hips. Standing up, he looked at her with an expression of improbable devotion. No one had ever looked at Ida like that. She reached for him, and his scent fell over her, sweat and wood-smoke. She gripped the protruding wings of his shoulders, his weight a barrier against the world.

They slid from the sofa to the floor. Because of Arlette, Ida was un-ashamed to tell Sidney exactly what she liked, where to put his fingers, his mouth. When they finished, spent and breathless, Ida lay on her back with Sidney's head on her pelvis and her hand in his hair.

"You're never to apologize again," she said.

"For anything?" Sidney stretched out, gazing at her from the crook of his arm.

"For anything."

37

IDA AND SIDNEY APPROACHED each encounter like it was their last. Their isolation, mixed with the knowledge that any day they could be separated, made their sex urgent and secretive and heartbreaking.

Things in the outside world were easily ignored. Confessions in bed a natural occurrence.

At the pale end of the day, the sheet at their waists, chests bare, legs tangled, Ida told Sidney how she'd stolen from her father. "His money is still in my bag. I haven't touched it." She told him about the night she left, about the beating in the barn and how she'd stood over her parents watching them sleep, wanting revenge. When Sidney pulled her into his lap and put his arms around her, she realized it wasn't protection she was looking for, but forgiveness. Proof that she was not a rotten person. She did not disgust him. He did not recoil. When he kissed her shoulder and said, "I'm so sorry, Ida," a sliver of self-loathing fell away.

There were things they did not discuss. The fiancée was never mentioned, nor the intimacy of Ida's relationship with Arlette. She had no idea where Sidney stood on the topic of homosexuality. It was a crime in America, as it was in England. Best to leave it.

Ida was also careful never to mention her violin because that would require speaking of Franz Kunstler, and she refused to speak of him. She had banished him into a dark corner of her mind, convinced that silencing his memory made him forfeit his power over her.

"Is your father the reason you can't sleep?" Sidney said into her neck.

"I'm sleeping now." She burrowed deeper into him and felt him grow hard under her. "Who sleeps in wartime, anyway?"

He lifted her hair and kissed her shoulder and she turned around, straddling him.

"When it ends, the whole world will sleep again," he said.

Finding his mouth with hers, Ida suddenly didn't want the war to end. This would end with it, these arms, this solid bulk, this heart against hers. Time would ruin everything. In time, the Germans would return. In time, Sidney would be caught or escape; either way, he'd leave her. In time, this would be a memory, like all the moments before it, and she would be alone.

SIX MONTHS AFTER Sidney fell from the sky, two things happened on the same day.

Motorbikes revved down the driveway. Sidney and Ida heard them from the kitchen. Leaping from the table, Sidney flew out the back door while Ida scraped his food into the garbage before following him to the carriage house where she locked the door, buried the key in the hard-packed dirt of a planter, and ran back to the chateau.

The front bell was ringing frantically. She slowed in the hallway, catching her breath.

There were three German soldiers, young, easygoing. They asked Ida for her papers, checked the upstairs rooms, opened doors and closets and cupboards, and then sat down to tea. "A shame this chateau is in the middle of nowhere," one said. They spoke in broken French, for her sake. "Much better a lovely woman in a lovely house than the batty old matron we're staying with in Marseille," the other said. But petrol was valuable, as were horses. Daily transportation would be an issue. Securing their helmets, they thanked Ida for the tea, hopped back on their motorbikes, and raced off to check the next house for weapons, or radios, or hidden enemies.

Ida stood in the hallway with her stomach pinned under her ribs. She looked at the bloodstained grout at her feet. If these men took Sidney, if they did to him what they'd done to Jean, she wouldn't survive it.

In the carriage house, she wiped the dirt from the key and unlocked the door. "They're gone," she called up the stairs, her voice empty.

Sidney rushed down so fast he tripped and fell into her. The reality had hit him just as hard. "I love you," he said, his hand on the small of her back, her face buried in his shirt.

Ida's heart bloomed. Her ribs ached. She did not want these competing forces, fear and love. They were not supposed to go together.

Sidney's arms tightened at her silence. "I want to take you home."

"When?"

"When the war is over."

"That could be forever from now."

Behind them, a voice said, "Not forever."

They leapt apart.

It took a beat for Ida to recognize Arlette silhouetted in the doorway. It seemed impossible that she was here, and at the same time entirely predictable. Arlette had a way of appearing out of nowhere. Overcome, Ida burst into tears, sprinted forward, and threw her arms around her. She wanted there to be no question of loyalty.

Arlette was skinny as a sapling, her chest shrunken, her back bony. The hug took the wind out of her, and she gently pushed Ida away. Ida wiped her nose. She sniffled. "You've barely missed the soldiers."

"I am aware." The sleeves of Arlette's frayed coat hung past her hands. Her trousers were rolled at the ankles and her bare toes were crusted with dirt. "I've been watching the house. I figure they won't be back for a while."

Aware of Sidney, Ida quickly said, "He's not one of them."

"I know that too." Arlette's voice was dry as bark.

Sidney stepped forward. "Sidney Whipple, US Air Force." He put out a hand.

Arlette glanced down at it and laughed. It was a hysterical sound. "I think we're past formality." With an iron hand clasped around Ida's upper arm, she pulled her outside. It seemed as if all of Arlette's strength had condensed into those five fingers. The rest of her looked drained of life. Her eyes bulged and her cheeks rose like knuckles under her tight, raw skin that flaked like soap. Her lips were chalky, and what hair she had left stuck up in spikes over her scabbed scalp.

"Are you going to stand there staring at me, or are we going inside?" She dragged Ida toward the house like she was leading a horse. Sidney followed a pace behind them, and Ida hoped he wouldn't notice how helpless she felt.

In the kitchen, Arlette dropped to her knees and began rummaging through a cabinet. She emerged with a bottle of absinthe she'd conjured from the rubble of pots and pans and slammed it onto the table. "Thank God for small miracles."

Ida watched in disbelief as Arlette took three glasses from the shelf and poured them each a dram. Her best friend, her lover, the woman Ida had yearned for, was here, alive. Lifting her glass, Arlette said, "To beating death" and shot back the glinting green liquid. There was a startling hardness to her. "Go on." She nudged them. "Don't make me drink alone."

Ida had only had absinthe with a spoon of sugar and water poured over it. Straight, it burned like fire, and she coughed uncontrollably. Sidney put a hand on her back. Arlette poured herself another glass. Even in her tattered coat, filthy trousers, and shorn hair, she looked regal holding that tiny glass of emerald green.

In candlelight, over potato soup and boiled carrots, Arlette told them she'd been watching the house for three days. "I wasn't sure if you were a German." She pointed her spoon at Sidney like a weapon. "Until last night when I snuck in and heard you speaking English."

The thought of Arlette spying on them raised the hair on Ida's arms. "Why didn't you reveal yourself last night?" she said.

"I saw the troops making their rounds at the edge of the city and knew they'd be out here soon. Better to wait it out." Whatever Arlette had been through showed all over her skeletal face.

In a voice washed of emotion, she told them how she hid in Saint-Gingolph helping people cross the Swiss border before she was caught and sent to Camp de Gurs. "A year in that hell almost killed me. Women and children dropped like flies. Every day, another one down.

They'd lie dead for hours before anyone noticed. Even then, all the soldiers did was dump their bodies in the woods, so close you could see their arms and legs through the wire fence. And the stench of it." She ate her soup in tiny bites, not like a starved person but like a person afraid of being poisoned. "Why one body survives and another doesn't, I'll never understand. Somehow these skinny bones kept on." She shook her scrawny arm. She'd drunk another shot of absinthe and seemed completely sober. Ida had only had the single shot and her head was swimming.

Arlette went on to tell them how she escaped off a moving train while in transit from Gurs to Drancy. "Some idiot soldier forgot to latch the cattle car door. We hadn't gone half a mile when the train took a corner and the thing slid right open." Her eyes widened like the doors themselves. "Suddenly there was a field, trees flashing past, wind tearing through the stench and suffocation as if God had swept down his hand and was holding it out to me. I leapt without hesitating. If a bullet hit me in the back, so be it. I was sure everyone would jump. I imagined the train screeching to a halt, soldiers shooting at us as we ran. I hit the ground and rolled into a thicket as the train whizzed past and all went quiet. Not a single blessed soul came with me. A door slides open and voila, freedom. How do you not grab on to it?" She looked at Sidney, her eyes large and beautiful in her sunken face. "Was it that easy for you?"

"Mine was not a leap into freedom," he said.

It was the first time they'd really looked at each other.

"No? You seem pretty free to me."

"I am in enemy territory. We both are."

Jerking her head in Ida's direction, Arlette said, "Do you feel free?"

"No."

Arlette laughed loudly and then hunched over, hissing like a cat. "Do you know how ignorant you two sound? You think this is hard living?" She waved a hand in the air. "You don't know the meaning of imprisonment."

Sidney set his spoon down. "You're right. I have no idea what you've been through. All I meant is that we're not safe in this country."

"Ida's safe."

Arlette's bitterness was a pinprick. Small, painful.

Ida said, "If I'm caught hiding an American or a Jew, I'm as likely to be arrested or shot as either of you." She wanted to say, *It's not my fault I'm not Jewish*. She wanted to say, *I've done everything you asked*. She wanted to scream at the top of her lungs: *What more do you want from me?*

Arlette dipped into her soup. "If you haven't been caught by now, it's unlikely you will be. You're a natural liar, which puts us in excellent hands."

Ida felt Sidney's eyes on her.

"What do you mean?" Ida asked. *Say it!* she shouted in her head. *Say what you really mean.*

Arlette did. She said, "Don't get me wrong, it's not a bad thing. It's how I knew you'd pull off your false identity. Which you've done beautifully, from what I hear. Franz didn't suspect a thing." His name frothed in her mouth. "Rumors run hot in the Resistance. Did you enjoy his company?"

The selfishness that had always lurked under Arlette's generous impulses was splayed across her face. She did not care about the truth. She was beyond caring.

Ida poured herself another dram of absinthe. Sidney sat in silence. He did not ask *Who is Franz?* He was working over that bit about her being a liar.

Ida thought of Jean, remembering the way he tugged his beard and the soft wrinkles around his eyes. She thought about the boy who cried for his mother, the one who'd opened his hands and begged for mercy. She thought about all the nameless men with holes in their heads who haunted her dreams. She thought about her violin, how her fingers ached to play. How she'd never satisfy that ache again, and how that made them ache more.

The holes were in her too, and they hadn't started with Franz. She had been leaky and flawed from the beginning. Her depraved nature was what allowed her to play her violin for a man who shot people for enjoyment. If Arlette believed she was a liar, it was because she was one.

Ida raised her glass and drank her absinthe and decided that she would say nothing about what she had done with Franz to anyone. Ever.

Listening to Arlette and Sidney discuss escape, she felt certain that none of them would survive this war. Why were they even trying? Sidney insisted there must be someone who could help them over the border, but Arlette said it was impossible. All of her connections were either dead, or captured, or had fled the country. They talked about hiding in the carriage house together but decided it was safer to hide separately.

Rising from the table, Arlette told them to follow her to the basement.

The room at the bottom of the stairs was cool and damp and held the scent of rust and metal. Shoving aside an empty wine rack, Arlette showed them a crack in the wall that slid open to a rectangular space big enough for a single person to stand up in. "People needed hiding places long before this war," she said, flattening herself in and sliding the door shut to test it out.

The moment they were alone, Sidney ran his finger up the back of Ida's hand. She shuddered. The oil lamp flickered. A strained energy had risen between them.

The wall slid open, and Ida pulled her hand away. The mold in the air clawed at her throat.

Arlette said, "If anyone comes, Ida, you'll have to move the wine rack over the door so they won't see the crack in the wall if they search down here."

"Of course."

"And then you'll need to let me out again."

Ida laughed uncomfortably. "I know."

Sidney said, "She has to let me out too."

"Well, then, we're both at the mercy of Ida, aren't we?"

Sensing she'd been left out of an intimate moment, Arlette pulled Ida into an embrace and whispered "I'm sorry I was so beastly earlier," her breath cloying.

38

SIDNEY WENT BACK TO sleeping in the caretaker's house, and Ida and Arlette slept in the rooms they'd occupied when Ida first arrived.

The security Ida felt with Sidney vanished. A coolness came over him, and the truths she'd confessed scabbed over like wounds. He distanced himself, kept his hands and eyes off of her. Whether it was regret over professing his love or that he no longer trusted her, Ida didn't know.

Arlette's color returned. Her skin smoothed out and her hair grew in enough to soften the hard lines of her face. Her mood, however, remained frigid, restless. She paced. She wrung her hands. She ordered Ida into Marseille for a newspaper, and when Ida came home with *Le Petit Marseillais*, yelled at her for not finding her a copy of *l'Humanité*, which had been banned since the occupation.

One day, Ida came into the living room to find Arlette standing in front of the piano. "Where are the keys?" she said, accusation tight across her forehead.

"I don't know." It was the truth. Ida had no idea where Franz had put them. For all she knew, he'd taken them with him.

Arlette found fault with everything. Why hadn't Ida hidden a radio? How were they supposed to know anything that was going on? Did she at least have a rifle somewhere? Where were her grandmother's linens? Had Ida moved them? Why wasn't the silver in the top drawer? What happened to her mother's bedroom slippers? Had she let a German steal them? Where did Herr Kunstler sleep? And where were the keys to the piano? Had he played it?

"Well?" Arlette said. "Did he?"

Ida refused to answer. The sun came out and light sprang through the window. Not once had Arlette asked Ida about her violin. From the piano bench, Arlette shouted into the next room for Sidney to come break the lock with a screwdriver. Arlette rarely played, why was it so important now?

Ida watched Sidney kneel before the piano, remembering how he'd knelt before her. She ached. The lock gave way.

Ida left the room before the first note rang out.

Arlette did not play well, but she played often. She said it was to stave off her boredom, to relax her.

When the music started, Ida shut herself in her bedroom. The notes punctured her skin, slit open her belly. She saw Herr Kunstler's long white fingers moving over the fallboard, felt them at the back of her neck, saw them running over the marble wall.

Once, Sidney followed her, standing in the doorway as if he'd never entered her room, as if he'd never entered her bed or her body.

"Are you okay?" He kept a hand on the doorframe.

"I'm fine." She went to her closet and pretended to look for something.

"Does her playing bother you?"

How did he know these things about her? What right did he have to invade her privacy when he'd retreated so far away? The Germans had not taken him, like she'd feared. He had not been sent back to his unit, or back to his family and fiancée. He'd gone away all on his own.

Ida retrieved a sweater. "Why would it? It's beautiful," she said, pushing past him out the door.

The truth was Ida burned with jealousy. Arlette took everything for herself. It was only a matter of time before she took Sidney. In bed, at night, Ida listened for the creak of a floorboard. Was he sneaking into Arlette's room or was she sneaking out to the caretaker's house? Ida was sure she saw looks of mutual alliance pass between them. Everything became a sign that they wanted each other. If they brushed shoulders, if their eyes caught, if they greeted each other with a simple "good morning," Ida took it as betrayal. If she found them alone in the kitchen or in the living room, she imagined they'd just leapt apart.

At times, Ida would get out of bed and strip naked in front of her mirror, inspecting every inch of her body. She envied Arlette's large breasts and small waist, her wide eyes and button nose. At twenty-three, Ida looked haggard. Where had all her birthdays gone? The last one she'd celebrated was in Paris when she'd turned twenty and had gotten drunk on champagne and fallen asleep in Arlette's arms. Touching her nipple, Ida remembered how Arlette had put her mouth to it, how she'd stroked her stomach, how confident and sincere and assuring she'd been. Why was Ida being so petty? Here was her best friend, whom she loved, who'd survived, and all Ida felt was resentment and jealousy. She missed the Arlette of Paris. She missed Sidney. She missed her violin.

The war had sunk its teeth in. Ida could feel it at the back of her neck, a beast shaking its prey. It would either discard them or eat them alive.

39

A PORTION OF ARLETTE'S BRIGHTER self returned with the warmer weather. Sweet scents filled the air and colors sprang over the yard, and Ida's envy lost its zeal.

Sidney developed a habit of touching her whenever he asked her a question. *Do you need hot water carried up to the tub?* Palm pressed to her forearm. *Is there enough wood for the stove?* Hand on her shoulder. *Would you like to play a game of cards? Is there weeding I can do in the garden?* Palm. Fingers. Heat.

Ida took her time answering.

Tensions eased all around. They played cards and cooked and read aloud to each other, Sidney making a mess of the French text and Arlette palming her ears in mock offense. They took cautious walks in the forest and sat on the couch wishing wine into their empty glasses.

One warm evening, Arlette lugged a trunk of old clothes downstairs and made them dress up while she set up her camera. They undressed with their backs to each other. Ida slithered into the sequined gown Arlette tossed her, unhooking her brassiere and pulling it out from under the thread-thin straps. When she turned and saw Arlette wearing a full-sleeve shirt, bowtie, and trousers, she cried, "No fair. Why am I half naked?"

Arlette donned a hat with a pluming cock's tail and said, "Would you like me to take my shirt off and even things up?"

No, Ida would not.

Sidney tugged at the sleeves of the velvet jacket he'd been told to put on. "Is this some kind of a joke? Are you trying to humiliate me?" He looked like a boy who'd sprouted out of his clothes overnight.

"I'll call this series *The Fool and the Beauty*," Arlette said.

"Are you calling me a fool and yourself the beauty? Or the other way around?" Sidney teased.

Arlette smiled at him. "Hard to tell."

Ida bristled.

"Either way, I look ridiculous," Sidney said.

"Have you never played dress-up before?"

He laughed, and then said, "Oh, you're serious."

"There's a first time for everything. You're clearly a man who's never made fun of himself. Absurdity is necessary fun. I'll show you how it's done." Arlette took his hand and pulled him to the sofa, instructing him to sit with one leg crossed over the other. His velvet pants stretched to the point of bursting. Arlette arranged his arm over the back of the cushion. She tilted his chin up and straightened his shoulders. His military haircut had grown into a mop of brown curls she brushed off his forehead. It was like watching her direct a play, turning Sidney into a pompous man blind to his own absurdity.

Sidney squirmed. "This is worse than the holiday photos my mother made me sit through."

Arlette raked her fingers through his hair, tussling it into a wild halo. "Shout," she said.

"Excuse me?"

"Scream at the top of your lungs."

Sidney looked at Ida to save him. She threw up her hands as if to say the situation was entirely out of her control.

"Ida, come sit here by Sidney." Arlette beckoned, and Ida was reminded of their last photoshoot, the masks, the fairylike dancing, the nudity.

Instead of sitting next to Sidney on the sofa, she slid to the floor and let Arlette arrange her arm over Sidney's thigh. "Lean into him. Perfect." Arlette stepped back, squinting at them. "I'm still waiting for that scream, Sidney."

Ida looked up at him. "It's not like anyone will hear you."

"This is all very strange," he said.

"Artists." Ida shrugged.

He cleared his throat, let out a thin howl, laughed uncomfortably, and said, "I was taught it was impolite to shout in front of girls."

Throwing her head back, Arlette let out a piercing shriek, the sound primal. Ida jumped, and Sidney's thigh tightened under her arm. The scream left a ripple in the air.

Sucking in her breath, Arlette said, "And I was taught that it was impolite for girls to shout. No need to follow the rules, Sidney. Besides, we're not girls anymore. We're women, in case you hadn't noticed."

"Oh, I've noticed," Sidney said.

Their candor set off alarms in Ida. She couldn't read what was between them. Arlette's expression behind her camera was focused, Sidney's placid.

Turning the timer on the Autoknips, Arlette dropped to the floor, curled up like a child, and put her head in Ida's lap. Her cheekbone dug into Ida's thigh. Her hair had grown back thick and strong, and Ida wove her fingers into it. Under her left arm, Ida could feel the muscle of Sidney's leg under the smooth velvet of his pants.

They held still. They held their breath. They waited.

After the camera clicked, Arlette sat up, and Ida slid onto the sofa next to Sidney. She put her head to his chest and felt the steady rise and fall of his breath. His arm tightened around her. The lamps burned brightly, flickering over Arlette, who stood in front of them releasing the buttons of her shirt.

Ida wanted this, and she didn't.

Sidney sat perfectly still against her. She couldn't see his face. Did he want this? Probably. Wouldn't every man want this? The shirt fell from Arlette's shoulders. Her breasts hung heavy and low, her ribs tiny ripples, her thin stomach sagging at the bottom. She eased her trousers over her skinny hips, coy and provocative and confident. She wore black silk underwear, something from her Paris days. She walked toward them. The slope of Arlette's waist, her pale skin, the scar on her calf, and the birthmark on her hip, were achingly familiar. She touched Ida's knee. Under her hand, the sequins sparkled.

Then, out of nowhere, Arlette said, "Good night, you two. I'm dead tired. It's up to bed for me." Smiling impishly, she slapped Sidney's thigh. "You must learn, above all else, to be ridiculous. A serious life is much too tedious." Turning, she strutted out of the room in her underwear, giving a wiggle of her behind before disappearing through the doorway.

Arlette was more generous than Ida had given her credit for. She had done this for them, to arouse them and embolden them and give them permission.

When they were alone, Sidney pulled down the strap of Ida's dress, and she slid under him as he hiked the sequined fabric up over her hips.

They made love on the couch, in front of the window, on the rug. They did not care if Arlette heard them. Drowned in pleasure, they thought of no one but themselves.

40

ON JULY 20, 1944, the heat was at its worst.

Ida was at her best. They all were. The US troops had landed in Normandy. Thousands of American soldiers were flooding into the country. It was only a matter of time now.

That morning they spoke of where they would go when the war ended. Arlette said to New York City to find her mother. Ida would go to Petersfield, but only long enough to see if her brothers had survived. From there, she didn't know. Sidney said he was going straight home to Boston. He put a hand on Ida's leg when he said this, and she thought he was going to say something more, only he didn't.

The three of them agreed to meet up. "In Paris." Arlette winked at Ida. "It's the only place worth meeting up in."

Enlivened, they finished breakfast together, and then separated, Sidney to see if he could shoot a rabbit for their supper, Arlette upstairs to sort through her mother's oil paintings, and Ida outside to the garden.

Unlike the day Sidney stood at the edge of the forest almost a year ago, there were no storm clouds, just the blazing sun in a white sky. Ida yanked and pulled weeds. Sweat dripped down her sides. Dirt stuck between her toes. Mice had gotten into the seeds she'd saved, which meant lilies adorned their table instead of vegetables. Between her food ration and the rabbits Sidney shot, they were hungry, but not starving. Sidney was skinning one now. If Ida could find any herbs and maybe a sunchoke in this mess, they might have a decent stew for dinner.

She heard a low whistle and stood up, her straw hat pitching sideways. A shadowless man approached, the sun at its peak in the sky. Ida's heart froze in her chest. His uniformed frame was unmistakable.

Franz Kunstler stopped a few feet from her, smiled, and took off his hat. His hair was a white flame, his eyes blue marble, the pupils dilated to a pinprick.

"Hello, Anna." He squinted, and Ida's mind pitched forward.

He had come from the woods. The Germans always approached by the single drive from the main road. The forest was deep and thick, and there was no reason for them to arrive from that direction. Ida and Sidney and Arlette knew this. They'd talked about it. The drive was visible, open. Whoever was in the house warned the others.

Ida glanced at the windows of the chateau. There was no green vase. Arlette had not heard him. How could she have? Maybe she would look out and see them. Had Sidney heard the whistle?

"You don't look happy to see me," Franz said.

Ida forced her attention on him. She moved a step closer. Close enough to smell the sweat of his skin under his tight, belted jacket. Taking his hand from behind his back, he presented her with a bouquet of wild lavender. He looked like a schoolboy. He looked absurd. He had come from the forest because he was picking flowers. Ida took them, buried her face in their scent, and closed her eyes. In the shade behind the orangery, Sidney was skinning the rabbit. In the house, Arlette was not looking out the window.

Ida opened her eyes. She smiled. "Thank you." She reached for Franz's hand. His palm was cool, his face less resilient than it had been. The war had finally shaken him. His emotions—regret, pain, longing—showed right there on his beautiful, ugly face.

"I didn't think I'd ever see you again," she said. If he wanted a fantasy, she would give him one.

"I didn't know you wanted to." His voice was vulnerable and hopeful.

"Why would you think that?"

"You gave me no reason to think otherwise."

Another step closer, her face below his, his lips parting. She let him kiss her, his mouth plush as a woman's, tongue pungent with the taste of foreign tobacco. Her stomach roiled. She was buying time. But why? To do what, exactly?

His hand flattened on her back, and he pressed her against the bulk of his clothes, his hard belt against her stomach. His holstered pistol dug into her side. His tongue searched her mouth. Ida pulled away, resisting the urge to wipe her mouth on her sleeve. Heat beat at the top of her head. Her eyeballs were dry. She blinked rapidly and said, "I have something for you."

"Oh?" He held her terrifyingly tight.

"It's a surprise."

"I don't like surprises."

"You surprised me."

Cynicism crept into his face. "All that time under a roof together, and you gave me nothing. Why now?"

"I gave you my music," she replied.

"You did." His grip relaxed. His eyes roamed to the carriage house where all those men had fallen, and then back to her. "Willingly? Or did I force you?"

She pictured Sidney just out of sight. *Stay*, she thought. *Stay right where you are. Do not come out.* The sun was too bright. Her ears rang. Dead men rose from the grass and walked toward her. "I did not want men to die, but I always wanted to play." He would believe this. She needed him to believe her. To trust her.

"I shouldn't have made you do it," he said. "I'm sorry." She had not thought he was a man capable of apology. "I have heard you play in my mind hundreds of times since then. It has sustained me. There is little left to sustain a man these days."

Ida eased out of his arms, keeping her hand in his so he wouldn't lose sight of her. She could ask him to get her something in the carriage house, say she needed to put the flowers in water, go inside and warn Arlette. Or she could send Franz inside, slip behind the orangery, and warn Sidney.

It was an easier choice than she wanted it to be.

She turned her voice meek, feminine. "Will you put these in water? I need to get something from the orangery."

"My surprise?"

"Yes. The jars are in the kitchen. You remember your way around, don't you?"

"I do." He took the bouquet, the tiny purple flowers bobbing in his hand. "If you plan to shoot me, I should warn you that my men are arriving soon." He seemed to like the idea of her harboring some violence toward him. It enhanced his desire. "I walked from Lyam Babin's farmhouse. Did you know it's still empty?"

Unable to resist, she said, "You've killed so many, who is there left to move in?"

Franz gave an abrupt laugh. "I haven't killed them all," he said, offering her his arm, elbow bent like a gentleman. She took it. They moved across the lawn, the unkempt grass needling their calves.

Franz said, "Even if you do have a weapon in there, you're probably a terrible shot."

Ida thought of the pistol Sidney left on the hall table earlier, the limp rabbit in his hands. She saw her desecrated violin, the charred strings over the hearthstone. She heard music. Her music. She heard Mendelssohn. She heard Jean's voice, *Whatever you do, keep playing.*

Herr Kunstler reached for her hand. He squeezed it so hard her knuckles cracked.

Killing was not his true skill. His true skill was reaching inside a person and weakening their soul.

"I'll only be a minute," she said, afraid he might not let go.

A sprig of lavender fell to the ground, and he released her.

She walked slowly, the music screaming in her ears, her ribs catching with each step. It took all she had not to run. When she heard the chateau door open, she assured herself that Arlette would hear him too. She would hear his boots clomping in the kitchen, hear him rummaging for a glass jar.

Behind the orangery, the skinned rabbit lay abandoned, pink as a newborn, its spatter of blood over the grass like tiny red buds.

Where was Sidney? Ida flew to the carriage house. The door to the hidden room was open. "Sidney?" she cried, reaching the top of the stairs as he stepped in front of her with a bloody knife in his hands.

"Who was that?" he said, an accusation. Had he seen Franz kiss her? There was no time to explain.

Ida's heart throbbed in her throat. "Other Germans are on their way. I'll lock the door, but when it's dark, you have to run. Leap out the window, go to the road, and head east. There's an empty farmhouse about a mile down. Hide there."

"I'm not leaving you."

"You have to! I don't know how long they'll be here for."

"I'm not leaving you alone with that man." He held her arm.

"He won't hurt me." This, she couldn't guarantee. What she could guarantee was that he would blindfold Sidney, shoot out one kneecap, and then the other. He would make her watch. He would make her watch as he put a final bullet into Sidney's skull.

She sobbed, "Please, Sidney, goddamn it, you have to listen to me. Right now, he's in there with Arlette. I put her in danger to warn you." She kissed him, hard and fast. "I love you. I need you alive." Then she yanked her arm away and fled down the stairs.

Sidney did not follow.

The sun walloped her and took her breath away. She stumbled and pulled herself forward, running smack into the stone wall bordering the patio. Pain shot down her calf, followed by a warm trickle of blood. She looked into her empty hands. What surprise was she bringing Franz? He would suspect her. He would go to the carriage house. The air buzzed with heat and flies. Should she go back and tell Sidney to run now? No. Franz's men were on their way. If he suspected anything he'd send them into the woods. Better to risk hiding in the carriage house until dark.

She hurried around the chateau and through the front door into the entryway. The house was silent, the table empty. No pistol. Had Arlette taken it? Ida's calf throbbed as she moved toward the stairs.

"Looking for this?"

She jumped.

Franz stood in the living room doorway. In one hand, a glass jar of lavender, in the other, Sidney's pistol. He set the flowers on the table and waved the gun at her, shiny, black as pitch. "You're not supposed to have one of these. I could arrest you for failing to turn it in."

The table separated them. Ida was near the stairs. Franz near the door. She felt the same surge of rage she'd felt the first day he'd shoved her into this hallway, the last day Jean was alive. She put a hand on the table to steady herself. She was familiar with men like Franz. Arrogant. Insistent on being right. You, the woman, the daughter, the sister, at their mercy. The humiliation and anger she felt the night her father beat her came back in small waves across her eyes. The room undulated, heavy with the scent of lavender.

She said, "You could shoot me for not turning it in. Isn't that what the posters say? Punishable by death?"

Something close to enjoyment flashed across Franz's face. "I could. I could shoot you right here in this hallway. It's been done before." He flipped the gun in the air, caught the barrel in his hand, and held it out to her. "But I have no desire to." He gave the dramatic sigh of an actor. "We are losing France. First Normandy, then Cherbourg. Two days ago, we lost Saint-Lô. Defeat is not something I am familiar with."

Without a radio, the mouth-to-mouth buzz of information on the streets of Marseille had been hopeful but unreliable. To hear defeat from Franz, even in his disbelieving tone, confirmed that the end of the war was really upon them. It was a cruel trick, him here, now, when they were so close.

To reach the gun, to put her hands on it, Ida had to round the table. The closer she drew to Franz, the clearer it became that defeat had not softened him. He did not have feelings for her. He was incapable of feeling. He was here because he was losing. He was here to return to the scene of his power, to handcuff her the moment her freedom was in sight. His affection was a game. The gun a piece on the board.

He let her take it easily. Ida had never held a gun before. It was cold and heavy and did not feel natural in her hands.

"I don't believe you'd ever hurt me," he said, his voice plaintive. He did, and did not, want to be hurt. He reached aggressively under her blouse and clamped a hand on her breast. His fingers were clammy. "I want to hear you play again."

He knew she was lying to him about her affection. She was playing a game too, but that was also fun. The uncertainty. Would she or would she not give herself to him? He kneaded her breast like dough. She gritted her teeth and leaned into his hand, faking pleasure. "Why do I have to go first?" she said, breathy, like he was arousing her. "You could play for me."

If Arlette heard the piano, she would know for certain someone was in the house.

Franz kissed her. Ida's finger found the trigger of the gun. He had made it look so easy, but the reality of raising a weapon, of firing it, was harder than it looked. Franz knew this. He'd counted on it.

At the sound of quick, light footsteps, Franz leapt away, an animal primed for danger. He snatched his own revolver from his belt so fast Ida didn't have time to register what was happening. The footsteps died at the top of the stairs, and Arlette looked down at them, one hand on the rail, the other holding a small stack of envelopes.

"Who are you?" Franz's voice was bullet cracked. He had made it very clear he didn't like surprises.

Shock froze Arlette's expression. Her body tensed, the instinct to flee a powerful one. With a quick glance at Ida, she regained herself, descending the stairs with Franz's gun on her. Her figure had not returned, but she had a way of moving that made her look voluptuous. She smiled, and a flush of pink slashed across her cheeks. "Arlette Lellouche. This is my chateau, or it used to be. But I imagine you already knew that."

Franz lowered his gun and turned to Ida with a look of disgust and a new spark in his eye.

It was the spark that scared her. Ida gripped the gun by her side, fully aware that the small, cool object in her hand could end his life.

"I am disappointed in you," he said, and meant it. He had choices. He could take them out back and shoot them. He could arrest them. He could let them go.

"You must be Herr Kunstler." Arlette looked from him to Ida. "I've heard about the two of you."

"The two of us? What have you heard?" Franz's tone shifted. He liked the idea of being spoken about.

"That a German officer had taken up residence at Chateau Lellouche and that the new owner, Anna Bacri, had fallen in love with him. I just didn't believe it until now." With exaggerated contempt, she said, "Were you planning it all along, Anna? Waiting for your German to arrive so you could denounce me?" Arlette widened her eyes in fraudulent despair, and Ida realized that she too was playing a game, contorting herself for Franz, becoming the deceived friend, his one last Jew to take down. She was saving Ida, or at least trying to.

"Was this my surprise?" Franz said, bright and cheery like it was his birthday.

Ida's morals abandoned her. She became an animal willing to gnaw off its leg to survive. "Are you pleased?" They were starkly lit. Performing. Waiting for the curtain to fall.

"How long has she been here?" he asked. He didn't believe her, not really, but it was more interesting this way.

"A few months." Ida looked to Arlette for a sign of forgiveness, but Arlette's eyes had fallen on the gun hidden in the folds of Ida's skirt.

"Why not turn her in when she first arrived?" Franz said.

Ida shrugged. "I figured you'd know best what to do."

"I gave you no indication that I was returning."

"I still hoped you might." In her head, she said, *Raise the gun. Pull the trigger.*

Either Franz had forgotten about the gun—which was unlikely—or he really believed Ida incapable of firing it. Turning his back to her, he took hold of Arlette's arm, and the envelopes in her hand scattered to the floor. Arlette's eyes bore down on her. *Do it*, they said. Franz yanked Arlette toward the door. *Do it*. He dragged her out.

Ida raised the gun with her hand on the trigger. An engine roared down the driveway, wheels on gravel. She shook violently, unable to keep the barrel still. She was Jean convulsing on the floor of that small murderous room. She was the boy crying for his mother. She was the blood in the grass, in the grout, in the cracks of the walls.

The gun fell to Ida's side, and the look on Arlette's face as Franz dragged her down the steps was shattering. Arlette did not understand how Ida could not do the thing she would have done without hesitation.

The truck pulled to a stop, and two soldiers got out, equal in height and build and hair color, like a matching breed of man. Franz shoved Arlette forward, and she smacked the chest of a soldier like she'd hit a wall. Franz said something, and the soldier yanked Arlette back by her hair. With a grin, he tore off her blouse. Shirt, trousers, brassiere, and underwear fell to the cobblestones. Franz watched, unsmiling. Bored. The other soldier stood to one side toeing the dirt with his boot.

The expression on Arlette's face was no longer fearful. It was defiant. Justified. Vengeful. A look that said she'd do it all over again. The soldier let go of her, and Arlette did not run. She did not cover her breasts or shield the dark place between her legs. Rebellious, she flung her arms wide, lifted her chest and shoulders and grew enormous. She was the larger-than-life woman on Peggy's studio wall, a woman uncontained in this out-of-control world.

Throwing back her head, Arlette's veined throat exposed, she gathered momentum and aimed a glob of spit directly into the soldier's eye. He flinched, startled. Within seconds, Arlette was on her knees with a gun to her head.

Framed in the open doorway, it came to Ida like an image on a movie screen, the imperfect reel flecked with black. If someone had told her to run in that moment, she would not have been able to move. The terror of what was happening paralyzed her.

Franz barked an order in German that Ida didn't understand, and the soldier lowered his gun. He yanked Arlette to her feet and dragged her to the truck. Her bony spine and spindly legs looked frail and small and terrifyingly mortal as he shoved her under the domed green canvas.

Ida was never sure why Franz didn't kill Arlette right then and there. Maybe he was sparing Ida the trauma. Most likely he needed information, names. It didn't matter. Regardless the reason, he'd sealed Arlette's death.

Yanking open the passenger door, Franz turned to Ida. He looked disenchanted. Extending his right arm into the air, he said "Heil Hitler" and climbed into the truck. It backed away. Through the windshield his blue eyes turned to specks and then snapped from view.

In the magnificent marble hallway, in the heat of July, Ida collapsed to the ground. The gun clattered to the floor. Outside, the sounds of life continued. The branches of the plane trees rubbed together. A bird squawked. An unseen creature rustled the shrubbery. Over the stones, a puddle of clothes and a bee buzzing, searching for sweetness.

PART FOUR

ABSOLUTION

1952

41

IN THEIR BEDROOM IN Lexington, in the heat of July, Ida lay with her husband's legs crossed heavily over hers. The fake Man Ray photograph of her and Arlette swept through Ida like a riptide, pulling her into the past.

Ida pushed Sidney off of her and climbed out of expensive sheets and into fine clothes she did not deserve. She padded down the hall to her children's room.

To love her children too much would devastate Ida, so she had learned to love them just enough. The night she left, it hurt to look at them. Standing between their twin beds while her eyes adjusted to the dark, she thought of standing over her parents' beds in an entirely different lifetime. The thief in her, the runaway, was still there. What changed was the girl who thought that any of this was for her.

Leaving her husband was harder than leaving her children, which felt wrong, but also exactly right. He slept on his stomach, elbows bent, hands shoved under his pillow, his face smashed into creamy yellow cotton. When Ida pressed her hand to his shoulder blade, he didn't flinch. The feel of his skin, the sound of his breath as he slept, made her shed tears she hadn't for her daughters. Ida told herself that she had lived through worse, but that didn't help. Her heart split open anyway.

Logic told her that leaving was a choice, but it was the same useless logic that told her she could have prevented the killing of a woman she loved.

Choice was relative.

With her shoes and bag in hand, her hair a tragic mess, Ida left the house without locking the front door. There was no need. Her ghosts were coming with her.

42

~

THE DAY AFTER THE Fourth of July, Sidney sat in a kitchen chair with his head in his hands. He was hungover. The police were looking for a person who had stolen a piece of artwork from a neighbor. The neighbor, at one time, had been his fiancée. His wife was the thief and she was gone, and he had no idea if she was coming back.

Sidney's throat hurt. His head hurt. He got up and poured himself a glass of water. His daughter's lunch plates were in the sink. The peanut butter and raisins put away, the banana peel in the garbage pail, the counter wiped clean. He had done none of these things.

Upstairs, he rummaged through the closet. Ida's lime-green luggage was still there, along with her white leather handbag. Had she packed a bag? He had no idea how many bags she owned. For a beat, he thought maybe she hadn't actually left him. He listened for the front door. She'd walk in with a box of pastries and laugh at him for worrying, tell him she'd been at a neighbor's house and lost track of time.

He sat down on Ida's side of the bed. Her smell lingered, a floral-scented perfume he couldn't remember the name of. It was then he saw a folded note on the nightstand. Why hadn't she left the note on *his* side of the bed?

Facts, it read.

I told you to run, not Arlette.

I did not drop to my knees and beg that man to let her go.

I did not tell him I would do whatever he wanted.

I did not pull the trigger.

I have no right to mother Bea, hardly Dora, for that matter.
I have no right to love them.
I have even less right to love you.
The fact that I do love them, and you, makes no difference.
I lied.
I betrayed people.
I betrayed Arlette.
This is my chance to set one thing right.
Or at least try.
I love you. I love you. I love you.
That is not a lie.

Ida

Sidney choked back a sob and smashed his fist into the mattress. In the bathroom, he splashed cold water on his face until his skin went numb. He looked out the window, where his daughters appeared to be performing some sort of ritual. Dora squatted on the lawn, arranging tiny stones in a circle, while Bea ripped up clumps of his perfectly cut grass and sprinkled them over the rocks like she was casting spells.

I lied. About what? What about their pact of honesty? Their attempt to lead a life of integrity? That she was not here to ask infuriated him. The least she could have done was stick around to fight about it.

Sidney looked at their bubblegum-pink bathroom—sink, floors, bathtub tiles—and felt the irony of it. He hated this color. They'd kept the original decor because Ida insisted it made her happy. He scrubbed his face with a towel, hard, reddening his skin. Even the towel smelled like Ida. He wanted to break something. He wanted to cry.

An hour later, when the phone rang, he leapt at it, his heart hammering his ribs.

It was his mother. "Poor Ellen. Can you imagine? That piece must have cost thousands. I heard it came from a gallery in New York City. Some avant-garde artist. Highly regarded. What does Ida think? She must know the artist, what with her time in Paris and all. Did she see it?

I heard it was a nude. Who puts a nude on their dining room wall? Maybe it's best it's gone. Every teenage boy in Lexington would have found a way into that room." Isabelle Whipple laughed, a high-pitched sound. "I bet it was a coalition of mothers who stole it. As if their boys' heads aren't already filled with dirty pictures."

Sidney stopped her. "Mom, I have to go."

"I called to talk to Ida anyway."

"She's not here."

"Where is she?"

"I don't know."

"What do you mean you don't know?"

"Mom, seriously, I have to go."

He hung up, which was a mistake.

Fifteen minutes later, his mother's mint-green Buick peeled into the driveway. She walked in without knocking, wearing her belted polyester slacks and a short-sleeved blouse. Isabelle Whipple never wore anything but slacks, because they were practical. She kept a collection of antique clocks, because in a way, that was practical too. She called Sidney daily, wrote in her journal weekly, and threw dinner parties monthly. She believed raising good children was the only truly noble cause in this world. That and teaching, which was essentially the same thing. There was little difference between one's children and one's students, other than real love, which she liked to tell people got in the way of good parenting anyway. It left a person unobjective.

"What's going on?" She was also pragmatic, to the point, and frustratingly supportive.

Sidney had not calmed down. With every minute that ticked by, the realization that Ida had left him sank in deeper. What did she mean by *setting this one thing right?*

He was in an accelerating moment, pacing the living room. "If I could just talk to her." He picked up a magazine, set it back down. He was always talking Ida out of doing crazy things. He'd talk and talk, and she'd slowly come down from whatever emotional ledge she was about to jump off of.

Isabelle went into the kitchen, poured two glasses of lemonade and whiskey, and came back to her son, who was fiddling with a paper doll, flicking the poor thing's head. She replaced the doll in his hand with a drink. "Sit."

He sat. The drink calmed him, or at least cooled him off. The heat was smothering.

He told his mother what he knew about the photograph and his suspicions. The note, he kept to himself. The enthusiasm on his mother's face was aggravating, and he said as much.

"Can you blame me?" she said. "It's one thing that Ida knew the woman in the photograph—really, what are the chances of that?—but it's absolutely astonishing you think she stole it." She slapped her son's knee. "I'm not judging her. I'm sure she had a good reason, or at least an explainable one. I'd be lying if I didn't say it tickles me to know that she took it from Miss Priss Ellen."

Ellen had always annoyed his mother. Ida, she adored. She told Sidney that as far as she was concerned, Ida had saved his life. That they had lived in secret and fallen in love and returned with a child—precious Bea—was the war's fault. A mother can forgive anything when she thinks her son is dead for thirteen months and he turns up alive. The only thing that upset her was that they had gotten married in England in a registrar's office without her. But it was obvious Bea's conception did not line up with the wedding dates, and she wasn't going to lecture him on moral ineptitude. If he'd fathered a child in France and *not* married the woman, then they would have had a problem. She saw her son's devotion to his wife and family as a reflection of her own good mothering. Plus, they let her throw them a post-wedding party, and Ida graciously agreed to wear Isabelle's outdated wedding gown, which left very little room for complaint.

Finishing her spiked lemonade, Isabelle said, "Ida is not acting rationally."

Sidney looked into his glass. He'd watched Ida squeeze the lemons yesterday, putting her whole arm into it. Bea had filled the jar with sugar and Dora had stirred it up with a spoon while Ida poured in the juice.

His throat constricted. His mother kept talking. "If the authorities find out and Ellen wants to press charges, Ida will be in a great deal of trouble. Art theft is no small matter. The question is, why did she steal it? And where could she have gone with it?"

"Mom, if I knew I wouldn't be sitting here." Sidney had no patience for his mother right now.

Isabelle ignored his tone. "She'll call," she said, decisive. "When she does, you find out where she is, and you go to her. Don't make her come to you. I'll tell people you've gone on a spontaneous summer holiday."

This practical advice collided with the chaos inside Sidney. Was it that easy? Ida would call and he'd join her in whatever plot she'd cooked up? Somehow, he didn't think so.

His mother stood up, securing her scarf over her puff of hair. She wore it permed and short, which kept the heat off her neck but made it frizz uncontrollably in humidity. "Where are the girls?"

"In the backyard."

Isabelle called them from the screened-in back door. They came running, hugging their grandmother simultaneously. She picked the grass out of Bea's hair. "How about a night at Grandma's?"

Bea and Dora nodded in delight. There was grape candy and late-night television at Grandma's. There was also Dierdre, Grandma's maid, who baked tea cakes and told them Irish fairytales, and Grandpa Ed, who built Tinkertoys with them and let them drive his model train.

Kitten pajamas, toothbrushes, Puddles the Pig, and a book from the nightstand went into overnight bags. Isabelle marched around the room mumbling to herself as she gathered items. Stuffing in a final pair of underwear, she gave Sidney a reassuring pat on his cheek. "Don't worry. Ida is a rational woman, and rational women don't up and leave their children. It isn't natural. One night, maybe two. She'll call. She'll be back."

43

WHEN HIS MOTHER DROVE away with the girls, Sidney poured himself another drink and sat by the phone. It didn't ring. As the hours ticked by, he paced from the living room to the kitchen and back, remembering how charmed he'd felt when they first moved in. Within a month of arriving in Lexington, the GI bill had given him a zero-down, low-interest loan, and he'd found himself in this auspicious house with his beautiful wife and child and their exquisite life ahead of them. Ida was giddy over the kitchen. "Look," she kept saying, opening the refrigerator door for the umpteenth time. "It has a compartment for frozen food." She'd click the burners of the gas stove, marveling at the instant flame, and rearrange the dishes his mother gave them, in awe that it was all theirs.

There was a steadiness to Ida back then, a sense that she had landed on solid ground, and yet he never forgot the comment she made as they walked down the street Sidney grew up on about having, once again, entered someone else's life.

"It's *our* life now," he'd said, walking under the dappled light of a maple tree, thinking that's all it took, a new address and a new job, and a new life was made.

That first week when Bea stayed with his parents while they waited for their furniture to be delivered, he and Ida made love in every room in the house. On the living room floor. Upstairs on the twin bedroll. In the bubblegum-pink bathroom. After, he'd lain in the echoing space feeling the fullness of her next to him, wishing they could stay in that moment forever.

Time propelled them forward anyway.

Lexington wasn't the best choice. Sidney could see that now. In France, he and Ida had gotten used to doing things on their own. To be instantly surrounded by family and friends—at least his, which was partly the difficulty—was more stressful than they'd anticipated: his parents' neediness, the social obligations, the way everyone expected them to leap, full force, into their lives. No one wanted to hear what they'd been through. Better to tuck those dark memories away and get on with it.

The first day Sidney went off to work at the woolen mill, he came home to find Ida pacing the living room, smoking with a vengeance.

"I can't believe these women! The way they looked at me, side-eyes and whispers. And do you know what this awful woman, Mrs. Lulu Johnson, said?" Ida pointed her cigarette at him, scattering ash on the floor. "She made a remark about how her *Jew* plumber ripped her off, and this other woman said, 'What did you expect?' And do you know what someone told your mother?"

Sidney wrapped his arms around Ida from behind. She stayed rigid but didn't push him away.

"What?" He rested his chin on the top of her head.

"That my clothes were shocking! What's wrong with my clothes?" She swung around, flushed and radiant. He loved her clothes for the precise reason that she didn't look like every other woman in this town.

"What they can't stand is that you have a figure to wear them." He put his hands on her hips. Ida had cut her hair in a new style, and it curled against her cheeks.

She raised an eyebrow. "What these sodding women can't stand is that I stole one of their friend's fiancés."

"That too." He kissed her, tasting peppermint and tobacco. When he pulled away, the hard lines of her mouth had softened. "They'll warm up to you, it just takes time. You're an outsider with fashionable clothing and a funny accent."

"Funny?"

Just then, Bea toddled in holding her baby doll by one foot, the poor thing's hair dragging on the floor. Looking up at them, she said, "What's 'sodding'?"

Ida smiled and sat down, pulling Bea onto her lap. "The worst of it is our poor children are going to grow up with your funny American accent," she said.

He didn't register children, plural, until she tapped her stomach and repeated, "Children."

Now, with his drink in his hand, Sidney sank into the same chair Ida was sitting in when she told him she was pregnant with Dora. After that, it didn't take long for the wives to accept her. It was easier with a baby on the way. Ida joined their clubs and church groups, and her days took on a domestic routine that was fitting. What bothered Sidney was that he couldn't remember when she'd given up her Parisian wardrobe, and why he hadn't noticed. Ida had morphed into a proper Lexington mother, the exact thing she did not want to be. She was restless. She missed the art world. She missed Paris. She missed her best friend. Looking around at the oatmeal rug and peppered wallpaper and teak furniture, Sidney wondered why he'd ever thought this would be enough for her.

In the abnormal quiet, the weariness of their suburban existence in this boxy house with the maple tree in the yard and the Plymouth in the driveway sank deeper in. He was no longer satisfied here either. Cocktail parties bored him. Bocce ball bored him. Tom Bowler bored him. Corn on the cob and fireworks and stifling conversations bored him. How had he become so average? All anyone talked about was the new hospital wing being built and the A & P supermarket going up with a self-service meat department. Their town was booming. Money was flowing. They were blessed. Lucky. Comfortable in a way no one could have imagined ten years ago.

The problem for Sidney was that he no longer felt blessed or lucky. You can tell yourself you should be grateful, but you can't *make* yourself feel grateful, which was an awful thing to admit. He was spoiled. His parents spoiled him, and he let them. His brothers' deaths put a great deal of pressure on them. Their spoiling was to make up for the loss, and his acceptance was to make up for the loss. There was no question that he'd live down the street from them, attend their church, go over for Sunday dinner. His parents had purchased his furniture. His father got him a job. His mother introduced Ida to all her friends.

On the whole, it was a good life. A life he tolerated for his parents but lived for Ida.

Without her, none of it made sense.

MONDAY MORNING, SIDNEY'S alarm went off at five a.m. He got up, showered, dressed, plucked the newspaper from the front step, and made his coffee with military efficiency.

Opening the *Minuteman,* he read the headline: *Priceless Art Stolen from Local Couple.* Priceless was a bit of an exaggeration. That would be Ellen's doing. Under the headline, the photograph took up half the page. Sidney had pictured something more provocative, a pinup-girl image of Arlette, not these strangely masked women. Regardless, the mothers of Lexington would be up in arms this morning, scrambling to shield their children's eyes.

He looked at the image, inspecting the women's bodies as he tried to pull up the memory of Arlette stripping naked in front of him all those years ago in France. The details were fuzzy. He lifted the paper, moving it into the light as his eyes focused on a dark spot under one of the woman's nipples. He looked closer. It was a mole. It was a familiar mole. He knew the slope of those breasts, the rise of that stomach, the shape of the nose and the angle of those masked cheekbones.

He dropped the paper to the table. Right now, every man in Lexington was looking at his wife's breasts splayed across the newspaper. He had an urge to cover them and a competing urge to brag about them. They were gorgeous. He smoothed out the paper, shaking his head. This was insane. Ellen was lucky all Ida did was steal the photograph. If she'd burnt the woman's house down, it wouldn't have surprised him. To think that

Ellen owned a nude photograph of Ida and was displaying it on her wall? It was too much to ask anyone to endure.

Studying the image, Sidney wondered why, in all these years, with all the stories Ida told him about Peggy Guggenheim and Paris, she never mentioned modeling for Man Ray. Why wouldn't she tell him? What else hadn't she told him?

44

FOR THE NEXT SIX days, Sidney vacillated between despair and anger. He called in sick to work, left the girls with his mother, and poured himself a stiff drink at five o'clock. He kept the newspaper by his bed and stared at it constantly.

When the phone rang, he snatched at it. "Hello?"

"Hi." It was Ida.

The storm of emotion sloshing around inside him hurled outward at the sound of her voice. "Where are you?" She didn't answer. He shouted, "Ida! Goddamn it, where are you?" He should have known that an outburst would make her hang up, but he wasn't in a reasonable mood. There was a click, and then silence. "Hello? Hello?" He slammed the receiver down. Picked it back up. "Operator?"

"Yes?"

"A call just came through. Can you tell me where it was from?"

"Sorry, sir. Nothing came through my switchboard." The woman had a movie-star accent.

"Nothing?"

"No, sir. It must have been long distance."

"Is there a way to trace that?"

"No, sorry, sir. The operator in the city where the call was made would have put it straight through."

He hung up and found the wall with his fist. The ease with which the Sheetrock crumbled under it was unsatisfying. The ragged hole gaped at him.

An hour later, the phone rang again. This time, he took a deep breath. "Hello."

"It's me." Ida's voice was cradled against his ear. He wanted to touch it. He wanted to reach through the phone line and touch every part of her.

Sidney cleared his throat but found he couldn't speak.

"Are you okay?" she asked.

Her voice was undoing him. He was a mess.

She said, "It's unlike you not to have anything to say." Another pause. "Are the girls all right?"

"They're fine," he managed.

"Are they with your mother?"

"Yes."

The line crackled. Sidney thought he heard traffic. A car horn? "Where are you?" His desperation charged into the silence. "Ida, please, tell me where you are."

There was a long pause, a sigh. "Los Angeles."

"Los Angeles? My God." He had thought she might be in New York City, but even that seemed impossibly far away. They didn't know anyone in Los Angeles.

"It's not a Man Ray," she said.

"What?"

"The photograph. It's not a Man Ray. It's Arlette's."

Sidney didn't care whose photograph it was. "That doesn't explain what you're doing in California."

"It's complicated."

"Tell me anyway."

"I only have three minutes on the call."

"How did you get there?"

"Train."

"When are you coming back?"

"I don't know."

"*Are* you coming back?"

"I don't know."

His ability to talk her out of things left him.

They only had three minutes.

He should have said *I love, I love you, I love you.*

He said nothing.

There was a click. Ida's voice. "Sidney, I—" And the line cut out.

45

L OS ANGELES WAS NOT what Ida expected. It seemed like an unin-
spiring place for an artist like Man Ray to live. Nothing glittered.
If there was a street where women smoked long cigarettes in sable
coats, Ida had not seen it. The one she walked down had the melan-
choly of lost ambition. Bottles in gutters. Cigarettes half smoked. Low,
flat buildings. Hot wind. A discarded newspaper wrapped around her
ankle and her hair swept up in gusts. Her eyes smarted. She needed
sunglasses and a scarf but wasn't feeling generous with herself.

Hunger, both literal and metaphorical, took hold of her. This was a
bare-bones trip. It was penance and restitution.

The train ride there was already an indulgence. Leather seats.
Huge windows. Little tables where they served coffee and doughnuts
while you took in the view. The doughnuts, she left. The view, she de-
voured. When the train tipped and groaned through the Rocky
Mountains, it took her breath away. Conifers towered and sculptured
peaks ripped through sheets of clouds. Pitching and rising, the train
fell from cool greens and blues into bloodshot soil, the desert endless
and jagged.

Ida loved it. The scenery felt as wild and reckless as her state of
mind.

When she stepped off the train in Los Angeles, desire pulsed in her.
An ache. A longing to be that young woman who first stepped off the
train in London. Back then, she believed her depravity and determination were unique and untouchable and strong enough to propel her any-

where. She had been a musician, an artist, part of a scene. How did a person go back to a time before they'd given up their dreams, to a time before they'd become unremarkable?

From Union Station, Ida took a bus to Hollywood and Vine with her face lifted to the open window. The air was so hot it evaporated the sweat right off her forehead. Her blouse dried as quickly as she perspired. Stepping off the bus was like walking into an open oven.

Back in New York, it had taken some convincing for the gallerist on 10th Street in Manhattan—the smarmy man who sold Allen Franzen the Man Ray—to give up the artist's LA address. Ida had found the gallery name printed on the backing paper on the night she stole the photograph. It was a small place, nothing like the ones on West 57th Street where Ida had just walked from.

She'd gone uptown hoping to ally herself with Peggy Guggenheim, only to discover that Peggy had closed her gallery and gone back to Europe five years ago. It wasn't surprising. Peggy had never responded to the letter Ida sent from France, asking if she knew where to find Arlette's mother. Without Arlette, Ida was nothing to Peggy.

The 10th Street gallerist wore tiny glasses and a slick suit. When Ida walked in, he gave her a pitying look. She reeked of the suburbs. Lacquered pin curls. Pumps. Poodle skirt. Worse was the green duffel bag she carried with a cardboard wrapping paper tube sticking out of it. The photograph hadn't fit in her luggage, so she'd taken Sydney's old army bag.

Calling up her Paris days, Ida pulled out the tube and set it on the man's desk with confidence. She could do this. It was an attitude, not an outfit.

"What do we have here?" He smiled, humoring her.

"What we have here"—she slid the photograph from the tube and unrolled it— "is a forged Man Ray you sold."

"I beg your pardon?" the man snapped, caught off guard, but not letting a woman like this intimidate him.

Careful not to get her fingerprints on it, Ida laid the edges flat so there was no mistaking the image. "You sold this last week to a man from Lexington, Massachusetts. Allen Franzen. Only, it's not a Man Ray."

The gallerist pressed his lips into a tight smile. "I guess, then, that you are unfamiliar with Man Ray's work."

His mocking attitude infuriated Ida. The one benefit of the war was that she no longer tolerated men like this. She moved into the chalky light of the window. Outside, buildings shadowed other buildings. Freeing her blouse from the band of her skirt, Ida began unbuttoning it with swift, sure fingers.

Behind circular lenses, the man's eyes glistened with alarm. He stood up, his composure crumbling. "Excuse me, I don't know what is going on here, but I am going to have to ask you to leave."

Men were so easily taken down by a woman's breasts, Ida thought, exposing her left one with a yank of her bra straps. She pointed to the photograph. "That's me. Do you see the resemblance?" She propped a gloved hand under her nipple, drawing his attention to the dark spot on her skin. "Do you see this mole? It's the same in the photograph. Compare them if you like. Those are my breasts. My nipples. My mole." She walked over and propped her hands on his desk. "I was there when the photograph was taken. And I can tell you for a fact that it was not taken by Man Ray."

It was surprising how undramatic it felt to be standing topless in front of this stranger. Ida shifted toward the light, closer to the window, and the man flapped his hands, his face scalded red. "All right, all right. You've made your point. By God, cover yourself up before someone sees you." He moved to the window as if his skinny frame could block it.

Securing her breast back into her bra, Ida buttoned her blouse and tucked it in with a gratified sense of control. This was the closest she'd felt to Arlette in years. After Arlette's death, Ida found out about her liaisons with German soldiers, and she wondered if this was part of the reason Arlette slept with them, not only for favors, but to humble them, weaken their authority, make them crumble in her hands. It was a self-abusive, deformed power. But power is power.

The gallerist was inspecting the signature. Sweat beaded on his forehead. "How dare you. I don't even know your name and you march in here and—" He waved his hand at her chest. "For all I know, you're the fake." He loosened his tie. Unbuttoned his coat. He had the shocked look of a man inadvertently involved in an extravagant crime. "I sent the commission check to Man Ray myself." He took a book from his desk drawer, flipped it open, and drew a manicured fingernail along the page under the artist's name. "See? Right there. Man Ray. I've sold his work before. I don't have his telephone number or else I'd get him on the line and clear this up." He shook a finger at Ida. "This photograph is from his Paris days. Are you one of those street prostitutes? Are you trying to blackmail me?"

The insult did not land like he wanted. Ida smiled at the idea of being taken for a French prostitute. From her handbag, she produced a small photograph—a last-minute grab from a shoebox. "I was Peggy Guggenheim's assistant. I'm right there with Peggy, Max Ernst, and Samuel Beckett at a party in Paris." It thrilled her, just a little, to dust off her connections and roll out her red carpet of names.

The man sank into his chair, staring at the star-studded cast in his hand, the name Guggenheim chipping away at his disbelief. "I don't understand. If this is a fake, I swear I had no idea." He looked up at her, the snap gone out of him. "How did you get the photograph? It's no small matter, selling a fake. I'll be ruined."

"I stole it." Ida began rolling it back up. "You keep my secret and I'll keep yours. All I want is Man Ray's address."

Grateful for the bargain, the gallerist gave it to her, and Ida got on a train to California. A telephone call wouldn't do. Man could easily deny it. She needed to face him. To unroll the photograph and watch his reaction.

IN THE CRACKLING heat of LA, Ida walked down Vine Street with the address clutched in her fist. Her pumps were not made for walking. They dug into her heels. Her pencil skirt restricted her stride. Sweat gathered under her girdle. A tall blonde sauntered by in a tight dress, hips swaying. Two women teetered along in heels. They were, every one of them, bound and restricted by fashion. Ida had the impulse to rip the side seam of her skirt so she could at least take a decent step forward.

By the time she saw the sign for the Hollywood Ranch Market, she was parched. The building sprawled the length of the street, which smelled of hot tar and gasoline. A grimy sign read WE NEVER CLOSE, and there was a huge clock whose hands ran backward at a high speed. Ida was sure it was meant to be ironic, but it came off as absurd.

Inside, people hovered around the produce stalls, elbowing each other over peaches and plums the size of small pumpkins. The noise of the ping-pong machines, the metal turnstiles, and the buzzing voices made Ida woozy. She cashed a check and purchased a Coca-Cola, tempted by a sign that said JUMBO HOT DOG 18 CENTS. Hoping to find a decent meal elsewhere, she bought a pack of cigarettes from a machine and went back outside. The soda fizzed down her throat, ice cold and glorious.

She thought of her children. She thought of Sidney. Without them she felt an essential part of herself absent, a missing limb, and yet her independence was extraordinary. She could go wherever she wanted, eat whatever she wanted, sleep whenever she wanted. There were no needs to satisfy, no dinner to prepare, house to clean, bedtimes to follow.

She finished her drink, threw the bottle away, and lit a cigarette. From a pay phone, she called Sidney. Hanging up on him felt good. A fight was real. It meant they cared. When she called back, the strain in his voice, his attempt to control himself and keep her on the line, tore at her. She wanted to tell him everything. She just couldn't. Not yet. She needed to do this alone. It was selfish and impulsive, and Sidney might never forgive her, but she'd been hurtling toward some outlandish act like this for months. He just hadn't seen it. Or hadn't wanted to.

When the phone cut out, she grasped at reason. He knew she loved him. She'd explain herself later. The girls would be fine. They were with Grandma Isabelle, who excelled at mothering in every way.

Ida needed to stay focused. She was here to confront Man Ray and make him own up to his forgery. More than anything, Arlette had wanted to be a successful artist. If Ida could give this to her, even posthumously, it would mean everything.

Leaning against the phone booth, Ida smoked her cigarette, inspecting the four-story building across the street. A sign over the entryway said VILLA ELAINE APARTMENTS. A series of shops lined the first floor: hair salon, nightclub, florist. Through the archway, she could see a fountain and a burst of green shrubbery. She hadn't been able to picture Man in this hot, dry place full of stucco until now. The building, with its arches and brick, was a slice of Europe.

Ida flicked her cigarette to the ground. She felt unbearably hot and itchy. Kicking off her shoes, she reached under her skirt and wriggled her stockings off her suffocating legs. She didn't care who was watching. The air against her bare skin made her feel like she could breathe again. With her shoes in one hand, she shouldered her bag and crossed the street, the pavement burning the soles of her feet.

46

WHEN THE PHONE CUT out, Sydney waited five minutes before snatching his car keys from the hook and yanking open the door, startling Ellen.

"Oh!" She jumped, then laughed. "I was about to ring the bell. Are you heading out?"

"I am." He was in no mood for Ellen.

She swatted his chest with her gloved hand, plucky and energetic. "I came to check on that adorable wife of yours. She missed the LCCA meeting. Is she unwell? No one's seen hide nor hair of her since the Fourth of July."

Groping for a more believable lie than he'd given the policeman, Sidney said, "She's gone to visit an old friend in New York City."

"New York City? Ida never mentioned anything about it, but she is secretive, your wife. Do you mind if I come in for a moment? Where were you headed? Nowhere urgent, I hope?" Ellen was already pushing her way inside, setting her gloves on the hall table, and taking off her hat. She turned, pursing her lips into a tight smile as she waited for Sidney to shut the door behind them.

He did. Best to give Ellen what she wanted and get it over with.

"I was heading to my parents'," he said.

They stood uncomfortably close. Ellen's perfume was too strong, her lips too red.

"I won't stay long, only I expect you to mix me a drink before I go. It would be rude otherwise, and I have something I want to say to you." She spoke to him in the exact way she had when they were together, assumptive and breathy, her affection hinging on her orders being obeyed.

He poured her a gin and tonic with two limes while she sat at the kitchen table jiggling her foot up and down. The clasp on her strappy shoe clacked irritably. If it wasn't for the stolen photograph, he wouldn't have indulged her. He didn't want to give her any reason to think he was hiding something, but it was discomfiting having her in his house without Ida here. His culpability intensified as he set the mixed drink in front of Ellen and realized he hadn't asked what kind she wanted. He already knew, and her deliberate look of intimacy told him she was flattered he remembered.

He poured himself a shot over ice and sat down. "I don't have long, Ellen. What did you want to say?"

She took a sip of her drink, leaving a red ring of lipstick on the glass. "It's actually what you have to say to me."

He had no patience for her games. If Ellen knew what Ida had done, she could have out with it already. "Are you going to tell me what this is about, or are you expecting me to guess?"

As Ellen leaned over the table, Sidney could see straight down her blouse, which was most likely her intention. "Do you realize"—she tapped a pink lacquered fingernail in front of him—"that this is the first time we've been alone since the day you left for the war? That was almost ten years ago! How is that possible? Can we not be trusted together? Or is there some unspoken rule about the jilted not being allowed to speak to their ex-fiancé in private?" She sat back with a gesture of triumph, as if Ida's departure had been orchestrated for the sole purpose of this meeting.

Sidney didn't like where this was going. "I've been here all along. If you wanted to speak to me in private, all you had to do was ask."

"Somehow, I don't believe that." Ellen cupped the glass to her chest and the moisture spread out in a small ring over her blouse.

Sidney knew how Ellen operated. This had nothing to do with Ida. His wife was gone, and Ellen saw this as an opportunity to confront him. Sitting across from her, he was charged with a feeling of familiarity for their shared past and simultaneously confused by the sense that they were completely different people.

Asking her to marry him had been a mistake. Ellen was weeping in his arms when he made the declaration he never meant to make but was prepared to stand by, as he had enlisted and was leaving her. Their engagement was sanctified on his parents' bed in the middle of the day, Ellen's tight skin and warm mouth and curvaceous body something for him to hold on to. He had loved her back then, on the sheets in the sunshine. It just wasn't enough.

"I am used to getting what I want," Ellen said.

Sidney often thought this was the sole reason their breakup upset her. "What, exactly, do you want from me?"

"An apology. Are you aware that you've never so much as apologized? Although, to be fair, I did sleep with Bobby Dartsmore while you were gone, but I would never have thrown you over for him."

"Bobby? What did you see in him?"

"Absolutely nothing. I was young and bored, and he was just about the only man left in this town. Don't worry, he wasn't any good. Isn't that what men want to hear? If you'd married me, I never would have told you."

"How noble of you. That would have made for an honest union."

"Oh, please, men do it all the time. It's not lying. It's omitting the truth. Do you have a smoke?"

Sidney's cigarettes were in his coat pocket in the hallway. He brought her one.

"Light it for me, would you?" Her tone was soft and seductive and Sidney knew exactly what she was doing.

Before making love, they'd share a cigarette, passing it back and forth, their bodies coming closer together until the cigarette was finished, and he'd put his mouth over hers.

Seeing his hesitation, Ellen said, "What are you afraid of?" in a taunting voice she knew would spur him into putting the cigarette in his mouth, lighting it, and handing it back. It was only a cigarette, he told himself. After he lit it and passed it to her, Ellen took a long, hard drag and purposely held the smoke out to him. Sidney felt irrational. He wanted to go up to bed and close his eyes and touch the skin of a woman, just not Ellen's.

He did not take it. "No thanks."

Unflinching, she sucked her cigarette and smiled up at him. "I just might forgive you if you take me upstairs and apologize properly."

This bold proposal did not surprise Sidney. He felt like she was acting out some scene she'd seen in a movie. Ellen had always been dramatic and forward. When they were eleven years old, she let him put his hand up her blouse on the playground in broad daylight. When she suggested he put it up her skirt, he was the one who hadn't wanted to.

"If you're looking for an apology, Ellen, I am sorry for the way I broke it off with you, but Jesus, if you cheated on me, what are you going on about? We were only engaged for a week before I shipped out. When I met Ida, you and I hadn't seen each other in over two years. The long and short of it is that I fell in love with someone else."

"Spare me the romantic war story." Ellen dropped the act and stood up, looking at him with fiery eyes. "We've known each other our whole lives. I told you everything, always. You put a ring on my finger and made a promise and erased it all in a single letter. Then you come home with a wife and child and hardly speak to me? It would be easier to hate you if you'd stayed away. Did you know that I can't have children? No one talks about it, but even if they did, I can't tell them that I wouldn't want children with Allen anyway. The problem is I've always loved you, and I can't stop thinking about you, and it destroys me seeing you with your perfect wife and children." Her sadness appeared all at once. She put a hand on Sidney's chest. "I'm lonely." Her voice broke and Sidney wrapped his fingers over hers.

He would have liked to tell her that loneliness, like sorrow, could not be cured with distraction. Pleasure was a temporary relief. He squeezed her hand and gently removed it from his chest. "It was never my intention to hurt you," he said. "And I am sorry."

She turned her back to him. "Just not sorry enough," she said, stubbing her cigarette out in his sink.

Sidney walked her to the front door feeling groundless.

"We should never have gotten engaged," Ellen said, stepping outside.

"We were better as friends," Sidney said.

"Only I lost that too, didn't I?"

Ellen did not wait around for an answer. She walked down his steps, past his trimmed hedges, and was gone.

47

SIDNEY DROVE TO HIS parents' frustrated with how disorientated he felt. Ellen's visit had made him regress to the idiotic young man he'd been when dating her, which only highlighted how pathetic and vulnerable and lost he was. He needed to focus on what to tell his parents about Ida's phone call and how, exactly, he planned to find his wife.

What he did not think through was what he was going to tell his daughters. Pulling into the driveway, he sat with his hands on the steering wheel looking at his parents' too-big home, feeling overwhelmed by the prospect of facing them. Instead of getting out of the car, he stared at the picturesque lawn of his childhood home thinking of his brothers, their absence made worse by Ida's. He didn't handle loss well. Did anyone? It was this house, he thought. He wished his parents would sell it already. There had been talk of his sister-in-law raising his brother's boy here, but in the end, she'd moved home to New Hampshire, and now this place made no sense. His father agreed, but his mother had dug her heels in. She'd raised her boys here, she said, and besides, it was a house people slowed down to look at, and she wasn't going to trust a newcomer to keep it up. The Georgian architecture made people think of simpler times—imperative in this fast-changing world—Christmas trees and summer pageants, maple candy and antiques. Lexington was the birthplace of liberty and freedom. The destination of Paul Revere's famous ride. The Revolution's first bloodshed. They were Northerners. Yankees. American pride. Their family valued money, land, security, and God. His mother used to tell

Sidney and his brothers that they could live reasonable lives, or great lives, with what they'd been given.

She'd been so proud when they enlisted. Fighting the Germans was a noble cause. Was she still proud? Sidney wondered, finally getting out of the car and making his way to the front door. His brothers were killed for their bravery. He was alive because he'd hidden like a coward. Was one scenario better than another because of its virtue?

DINNER WAS CHICKEN cutlets, herbed potatoes, and peas. The Whipples sat around the table in golden sunlight. The windows were open, the screens secured.

The normalcy of the Sunday supper made Sidney want to crawl out of his skin. He hadn't told his parents about Ida's phone call because Bea attached herself to him the moment he arrived, and he didn't know what to say in front of her. His father's deeply concerned looks were also getting to him. Ed Whipple used to tell his sons it was a husband's duty to keep his wife happy. If she wasn't, it was the man's job to make it right, which was annoyingly abstract advice. Right now, Sidney wanted a father he could confide in, one who would listen. Ed was loving, just not understanding. He'd never understood Sidney. As a child, Sidney cried at all sorts of things. He'd get upset if he couldn't solve a math problem, or if he missed a baseball pitch, but mostly when he witnessed routine cruelty, teachers terrorizing students or male playground brutality. Sidney's tears were sudden and uncontrollable, and always caught his father off guard. All Ed could do was stand there and ask Sidney if he wanted to go throw a baseball or build a model airplane. His father told him he was too sensitive. He needed more resilience. "Buck up, buddy," he'd say. When Sidney grew bigger than the rest of the kids in his class and began beating everyone up, his father told him he had too much resilience. Then he'd say, "Why are you so hotheaded?" questioning Sidney without ever asking what was wrong.

Watching Ed methodically slice his chicken, with head down, eyes distracted, Sidney wished he could tell his father that he'd turned violent as a teenager to beat basic principles of morality out of himself so he could stop feeling them. The world was unjust. Unable to make sense of the indefensible, Sidney became the very thing he hated.

It was the war that changed him. The fighting had shown him real violence, and Ida had shown him real love, and between the two, he'd found an equilibrium. Why couldn't his father see that?

"Daddy? Did you hear me?" Bea was looking at Sidney.

"No, sorry. What were you saying?"

"That I baked a cake with Dierdre. She showed me how to separate an egg. It's an orange cake. I squeezed the oranges myself, and we made lavender icing."

Sidney nodded. "That's nice." He did not say that lavender sickened their mother. Didn't Bea know that? Lavender was a hot day in France. A leap from an open window. Ida in a heap on a marble floor.

Dora nudged Bea with her elbow, and Bea said, "Dora decorated it with nasturtiums."

"I can't wait to taste it," Sidney said.

"You shouldn't do that," Ed said.

"Do what?" Sidney was immediately defensive.

"Let Bea speak for her sister. If Dora wants to tell us something, she needs to do it herself."

"Edward." Isabelle waved her fork at him. "Leave the girl alone."

Ed dug into his potatoes. "I'm just trying to help. She needs to learn. I don't see why you're all coddling her."

"Dora speaks just fine," Sidney said.

"Only not to us," Ed said.

"Girls." Isabelle squinted at them as if about to reveal a secret. "While you were baking, I saw something strange in the yard. It looked . . . twinkly. Not like a firefly, more like . . . " She paused, searching the air with her eyes.

"A fairy?" cried Bea.

"Exactly!" Isabelle said. "I don't know what it was doing out there, but if you're finished, you can clear your plates and go inspect the bushes at the far end of the yard. That's where I saw most of the activity."

They did not look to Sidney for permission as they clattered forks and knives onto their plates and scrambled from the table.

When they left, his mother said, "All right, tell us what's going on."

Sidney pushed his plate away. "Ida called. She's in Los Angeles."

"Why Los Angeles?" Ed sounded as if there was no good reason for anyone to be in Los Angeles.

"I don't know," Sidney said.

"Not a clue?" his mother said. "Clues are needed. Los Angeles is a very big city."

"It seems unsafe, her being out there all alone." Ed's tone implied that this might be one of Sidney's failed-husband moments. "Did she say where she's staying?"

"No, Dad."

"How is she paying for anything?"

Getting up, Sidney said, "Ida is very self-sufficient" and cleared his plate to the kitchen.

What his father did not know was that Ida had more money than any of them. She'd just refused to touch it until now. A few days ago, Sidney discovered that she'd withdrawn three hundred dollars from an account they'd agreed would be left to Bea. What was so important that Ida would touch that money?

Out the window, he watched his daughters skip around the bushes. Bea's wispy arms and legs swung out at all angles. Dora followed, her short legs pumping up and down. They hadn't even asked about their mother.

Isabelle came up behind him. "Your father and I agree that you should go out there. Even if you don't know exactly where she is."

"That's what I've been thinking, but it seems crazy. Arrive in Los Angeles, and then what?"

"You'll figure it out. What will make you crazy is staying here doing nothing. How did Ida sound on the phone?"

"Good, that's what's upsetting. She sounded . . . calm. I feel like"—Sidney put a hand to his chest—"I can't breathe." He hated that he wanted to cry in front of his mother.

She touched his arm. "You're going to be fine, Sidney. You and Ida will work it out. She needs you, even if she thinks she doesn't. Did she say she was coming back?"

He kept his eyes on his daughters out the window. "She said she didn't know."

"Well, that's not a no. You'll need to put things in order, but you should go as soon as you can."

"What things?" He could walk out the door, get in the car, and drive across the country right now.

"Your children, for one."

"You can get whatever you need from the house."

"Me?" She nudged him aside and began filling the sink with hot water. "I'm not taking the girls."

"What? Why not?" He had unquestioningly expected her to.

His mother squirted soap onto a sponge, her hands veined and spotted brown. "I raised my children. I'm not raising yours, Sidney. Don't get me wrong, I love them as much as anything, but this is your mess, and they're your children."

"What am I supposed to do with them?"

"Take them with you."

"I can't take them on a trip like that. Dora won't even talk to me."

"She won't talk to me either."

"Why won't you watch them? They love you. I don't understand why you're being so unreasonable."

"Have you ever considered"—Isabelle said sharply, holding the dripping sponge over the sink—"that Dora doesn't speak to you because she hardly knows you? How much time do you spend with her? Do you read to her at night? Do you make her food and dress her and take her to school?"

"I work," Sidney said, incredulous.

Isabelle drowned a plate in soapy water. "All I'm saying is that mothers are expected to do things without a word of complaint. Maybe Ida needs a break, and this is your chance to give her one. I spent twenty-five years raising you boys before I went back to teaching. I imagine Ida sounded good because she was doing something for herself."

Sidney felt unprepared for this conversation. "I thought you liked raising us?"

"I loved raising you boys. It's not black and white, but I can tell you there are times when a mother feels like there's nothing left of her. Women are expected to sacrifice everything for their children, and they get very little credit for doing so. I realize it's inconvenient for a father to be involved. But from where I stand, these girls have no mother, which means you have no choice."

"I have no idea how to take care of them."

"They're just children. If you listen, they'll tell you exactly what they need."

His mother went silent. From the angle of her shoulders and the way she slapped the sponge around, Sidney knew there was more on her mind. Tactically, he picked up a dish towel and began quietly drying.

After a few minutes, she said, "What you can't see is that I am doing this for your own good. You have no idea what it's like to lose your children. Not that this is the same thing. I'm just saying, you need them as much as they need you." Her scrubbing halted.

Sidney put his hand on her shoulder. "Mom."

She shook her head. "No. We never talk about it. I lost my boys. I will never be the same. Their deaths dropped me to my knees"—she gulped back a sob—"but when I thought I'd lost you too . . . it was like my insides had been scooped out. It emptied me of everything. I felt like I'd been blown to pieces along with your brothers. I quit teaching. I spoke to no one for weeks. I told your father I wanted a divorce. I told Dierdre she was fired. I told Alice across the street that I'd rip every rose bush out of the ground if she didn't stop that goddamn snipping." Isabelle gave a choked laugh. She looked at Sidney, letting the dish in her hand drip water all over the floor. "I don't want you to leave. I don't want you, or the girls, to go anywhere. I want to hold you all right here where I can keep my eyes on you forever."

Sidney took the dish from her and set it in the sink before wrapping his arms around her. "I'm not leaving for good. My life is here." His mother felt small and frail against him.

Isabelle sniffled into his shoulder. "Your life is with Ida, wherever it leads you. She's important, Sidney. Did you know that when you left for the war, I didn't even like you anymore?"

"Mom!" Sidney released her.

"I loved you. I just didn't like you very much." Isabelle pressed her hand over his heart. "You were angry all the time." She turned back to the sink. "I don't see that angry man anymore. I see a man who believes in himself. A man willing to do what it takes. You and Ida are good for each other. You love each other. It's not complicated."

It felt complicated. Sidney sank into a chair. "I'm scared I won't find her, and I'm scared if I do find her, she'll turn me away. What will I do if she turns me away?"

"If she turns you away, you will manage. You will be a father. You will get by."

"I'm not a good parent," he said. "I don't even know how to properly slice a banana."

Isabelle laughed. "It's not bananas I'm worried about. Come, you can slice the cake, and we'll see how you do."

48

T HEY ATE CAKE AROUND the table in the gathering dusk. After, Isabelle packed up the girls, kissed them goodbye, and told them to be good for their father. Ed patted his son's shoulder, told him he'd help him change the oil in the car before he took it on the road, and then ducked into the living room to watch the news.

The girls needed no help brushing their teeth or buttoning up their nightgowns. Bea read Dora a bedtime story while Sidney waited in the hallway. It felt intimate and improper for him to be a part of their nightly routine. Normally, they kissed him goodnight downstairs before Ida marched them up to bed.

"Dad?" Bea said.

Sidney stuck his head through the bedroom door. The walls were powder blue, the curtains striped, the throw rug decorated with piglets and sheep.

"Yes?"

"You have to tuck us in."

He stepped all the way in. Dora looked up from her pillow with wide, curious eyes. Her father putting them to bed was an exciting new idea.

"Good night," he said, tucking the sheet up to Dora's chin. She squeezed her eyes shut, opened them quickly to see if he was still there, and then snapped them shut again.

Sidney smiled. She looked so much like Ida he felt a giving-way in the bottom of his stomach. How painful and natural it was to see the shadow of his wife in his daughter's face.

When Bea said, "Will you sit with me?" he eased onto the edge of her bed wondering whose shadows his eldest daughter carried, as she pinched her lips to one side, looking as shrewd as Isabelle. "Grandma says Mom is on vacation and that we're going to see her. Are we going to see her?"

"We are."

"When?" She sounded skeptical.

"Soon."

Bea sat up. "Let's leave tomorrow. Mom would want us to. I'm sure she misses us. It's no fun being on vacation by yourself." It was clear Bea did not believe her mother was on vacation but was pushing the lie along for the adults.

Sidney wasn't sure how much information you were supposed to give children. Ida was the one who always knew what to do. When she first gathered Bea into her arms, there was something so natural in it. That moment changed everything between them, and yet Sidney never felt resentful. A child like Bea might have torn them apart, but she did the opposite. If anything, she helped heal them.

"I have to figure some things out, but we will go very soon," he said.

"How soon?"

"I don't know, Bea."

Bea lay back down. "Will you turn on the nightlight before you leave?"

The nightlight was a paper globe of dancing cutout figures. When he clicked it on, the silhouettes froze mid motion on the wall over his children's heads. They looked like they were waiting for someone to clap their hands so they could dance again.

"Dad?" He was halfway out the door.

"Yes?"

"I love you."

"I love you too."

49

WHEN SIDNEY THOUGHT ABOUT that day in France, it was the German's face he remembered.

Crouched in the grass with a freshly caught rabbit, Sidney heard the thud of boots on dry dirt. The whistle flattened him to the glass wall of the orangery. Who was coming from the woods? Where was Ida? Where was Arlette? He twisted the knife in his hand, kicking himself for leaving his pistol inside.

Inch by inch, he eased around the side of the orangery.

The officer stood a few yards away, yellow hair, face chiseled, eyes squinty. Even from a distance, Sidney could see the barren blue core of the man's bleached insides. The sun beat down. The officer was high ranking. Sidney recognized the embroidered gold insignia on his collar, the roped shoulder straps, the winged eagle over his right breast pocket. It took Sidney a moment to register Ida's hand in his, her body stepping closer to the man's suffocating jacket, his hard belt against her stomach. When his full lips smothered Ida's, rage shot up Sidney's spine. His heart thundered against his ribs. He wanted to kill the man. He wanted to gut him like the rabbit.

He had not believed Arlette when she told him that Ida had been in a relationship with a German officer. "I don't know the details," Arlette said. "But I was told he slept under this roof and ate at this table. I was told that he killed people right out there." She pointed to the window. Under her scabbed face and patchy hair, Arlette's beauty was obvious. Leaning in with a hand on his forearm, she said, "I was warned against coming back here. I don't know if Ida can be trusted anymore." She was commanding, imperious. It made Sidney think that wealth and beauty looked the same no matter what part of the world you were in.

"You could just ask her," he said, certain Arlette had it wrong. German officers were stationed all over France. If one had stayed here, that wasn't Ida's fault, and he found it hard to believe she'd sleep with the enemy. If she'd been forced, he was sure she would have told him. They'd confessed everything to each other.

Arlette removed her hand from his arm. "Ida wouldn't tell me the truth if I did. She was in love with me once, and even then, she didn't tell me the truth. Our only hope is that she's in love with you now."

"Because then she'll tell me the truth?"

"Not necessarily, but she's less likely to turn us in if it comes to that."

When she said, "Keep Ida on our side, Sidney. Make love to her often," a flawed desire came over him. That she wanted him to seduce Ida to keep her quiet made him want to rebel against it. He wasn't going to be told by one woman to make love to another. It was emasculating. He'd make love to a woman when he wanted to, *because* he wanted to. It was bad enough he was cheating on his fiancée. His morals had been corrupted long before the insanity of this time and place, but Arlette's hubris made him want to prove her wrong. He didn't need to seduce Ida to win her trust. He already had it.

At least, he thought he did, until he saw her under the blazing sky kissing a German officer. A handsome one, which made him even angrier. There was no force involved. Ida slid her hand into that man's and stepped right up to him. It took everything Sidney had not to rush out and demand an explanation. An explanation that would get him killed, he reasoned, going cold and rational as he dropped the rabbit in the grass and snuck his way into the room under the eaves in the carriage house. Running wouldn't make any difference. If Ida wanted to turn him in, he'd be found just as easily in the woods. When he heard her voice, his anger slipped. When he saw her, it dissolved altogether. She was not turning him in. She was warning him.

"I love you. I need you alive," she said, and he believed her.

She was giving the German what he wanted, throwing him off their scent.

Sidney did not wait until nightfall. Jumping from the window, he landed hard, rolled onto his side, and found his feet, wincing at a pain in his ankle. The image of that man's hands on Ida, the way he'd pulled her against him, made him crazy. It was all he could do not to rush into the chateau, but he had been trained for crises. He did not have a gun. More soldiers were on their way. Exposing himself only exposed Ida. He'd get them all killed if he didn't keep his temper. The logical thing was to wait until dark, sneak in, and take the kraut by surprise.

The practicality of Sidney's thinking, as he crouched in a ditch near a small ravine in a foreign land, did not make him feel any less cowardly. When darkness fell and he found Ida curled on the marble floor of the chateau, his only thought was that she was unharmed.

"It's okay, I'm here," he said, lifting her from the floor, but it was too late. He had not kept his promise. He had not kept her safe. She'd done that all on her own.

WITHIN THE MONTH, the Allies had landed at the port and parachuted into the countryside. By the time French artillery opened on the old fort of St. Nicholas, the Germans were as much as defeated. On August 29, 1944, one month after Arlette's arrest, Marseille was officially liberated.

Sidney learned that the man who took Arlette was named Franz Kunstler. Ida said he'd been billeted at the chateau for a brief period of time but that she knew nothing about him, so Sidney put the kiss out of his mind. It was meant to protect him, and he could see that Ida didn't want to talk about it.

They were told by the local police that Herr Kunstler was in the city rounding up Resistance fighters, executing them with the urgency of a man taking his last breath. Between July 18th and August 12th, thirty-eight members of the Resistance were tortured, executed, and dumped into a mass grave. Among them were four Free French Forces officers, and one American intelligence officer. None of them, as far as Sidney and Ida heard, were women.

That they had done what they had to in order to stay alive made no difference. The timing of Arlette's capture a month before Marseille's liberation tightened the noose around their necks. Choked them a little tighter. They held on to the idea that if she had been put into a concentration camp, she might still be alive. They joined the throngs of people on the Canebière to cheer the troops, keeping an eye out for the only woman who could forgive them. The camps were closed. She could be anywhere.

THE WORLD CAME back into itself. Boots marched. Tanks rolled. Flags snapped. People cheered and wept. Strangers kissed. Babies bounced on hips and children darted between legs. No one stood still. They stepped over rubble and tore down Nazi posters. They pumped fists in the air and shouted until their voices were raw.

It was Sidney's first real glimpse of France, but it was the joy he felt seeing his fellow GIs that overwhelmed him to tears. In civilian clothes, they took him for a Frenchman until he shouted in English, and he was clapped on the back and swept up into the crowd, his hand holding tight to Ida's. She could finally shed the skin of Anna Bacri. They no longer needed to hide. Or blame themselves. War was cruel. There were wins and losses. They had their freedom. Their future.

Bursting, he took Ida's face in his hands and asked her to marry him.

In the rumble of the street, between the pulse of bodies and the heat of summer, Ida said yes.

They drank "sherry"—raw alcohol and caramel—in a dark bar filled with shiny-faced, pimpled American soldiers. Sidney buzzed. He told every fellow countryman he met that he was engaged, gathering hugs and high-fives and slaps on the back, as if every one of them was his best friend. People sang. Record players blared from open windows. Sidney pulled Ida into the cobblestone street and showed her how to dance the boogie-woogie. They tripped over each other, laughing so hard they cried.

Warmed by alcohol and the night, they forgave themselves. Or so he believed.

SIDNEY SENT LETTERS home, and they made plans. The destroyed city was being rebuilt, the ports restored, the war effort charging ahead. Liberty ships carrying trucks, tanks, ammunition, and soldiers arrived weekly. Buildings occupied by Germans were now occupied by Americans. Glen Miller sang from record players and soldiers drank the bars dry. Freedom came in the form of canned green beans and powdered eggs and tins of sardines. It was doughnuts and color movies—*The Wizard of Oz* and *Gone with the Wind* and *Snow White*. It was rude and loud and generous. It gave kids chewing gum and young girls jeep rides down the steps of the Gare Saint-Charles. It was bouncing mad and joyful. It was laughter and sex and jazz and comic strips and the honey taste of American cigarettes.

Freedom was also rage. Humiliation. Justice. Revenge.

Collaborators were dragged from their beds and executed without trial. Civilians found with German weapons were shot on the spot before they had time to explain. American provisions were pilfered. Men were arrested. Food was rationed and the black market thrived. Women accused of consorting with German soldiers had their heads shaved and swastikas drawn in lipstick on their foreheads. Some were beaten. Others smeared with tar. All were stripped to their undergarments and paraded through the streets by smiling Frenchmen with rifles.

It was three in the afternoon when they came for Ida. Two in jackets, one in a beret. The fourth wore a tie and smoked a cigarette. All were thin and jumpy. They knocked on the door. When Ida opened it, the man with the cigarette pulled her outside exactly as Franz had pulled Arlette.

"You are being taken for consorting with Franz Kunstler," he said, pushing her head down as he tried to shove her into the car. There was no humiliation in shaving someone in the privacy of their own home. They'd shame her in public with the rest of *les femmes tondues*.

With more force than the man anticipated, Ida yanked her head back and bit his hand, drawing blood. He slapped her. She screamed. Wild. Inhuman. She had not survived to suffer this.

Her screams brought Sidney running. When he saw the man's hands on Ida, he went wild too.

There was a crack of bone. The cigarette flew from the man's mouth. Sidney's knuckles found his jaw a second time, and the man stumbled sideways. Ida broke free. Fists and dirt flew. It was an unfair fight, three against one, but Sidney's pent-up rage came out like a bull in chains. He bucked and kicked. His ears rang and his heart pulsed and sweat poured down his face. It felt good hitting them, watching them scramble for their car and tear off down the road.

Panting, bloody, he pitched forward with his hands on his knees as the engine growled away.

Ida was crouched in the dirt. Her hair hid her face and her body shook with sobs. Spitting blood onto the stones, Sidney stubbed out the smoldering cigarette on the ground and pulled her into his arms.

That night, he found her in bed fully clothed, hair pinned up, makeup on.

She said, "Do not get into bed." She said, "Sit over there."

He sat in the chair where she pointed. The room was bright with moonlight. Through open windows, nocturnal creatures reported on the night.

In semidarkness, Sidney watched her kick the covers aside.

"You do not want to marry me," she said.

She was not a good person. She was broken. Defective. She went on to say that every name her mother ever called her was fitting. The beatings her father gave her, deserved. Stealing bakery items was only the beginning. The stolen hairpin from a co-worker, the money from her father, were symbolic, all leading to the day where she would betray her friend. It didn't matter who she was trying to save. She had failed. She had not fired that pistol. She had turned over the one person who gave her everything—escape, an identity, safety, a home—to a murderer.

The more disgust she heaped over herself, the more Sidney held on. He did not see a thief and a liar; he saw a woman willing to claw her way out. He saw the bravest person he'd ever met.

"Do you want to marry me now?" she demanded.

"More than ever," he said.

50

D ADDY?" SIDNEY PULLED HIS head up. Bea stood in his bedroom
doorway. "Are you okay?"

"I'm fine." He drew a hand down his face.

Bea came and sat next to him, dangling her legs from the bed. They
did not look at each other but kept their gazes on the opposite wall.
Everyone, even Sidney's parents, believed, unquestioningly, that this
pale blue-eyed child was his.

Bea said, "You can have my nightlight if you want. I used to be
afraid of sleeping alone too."

He wanted to hug her. Instead, he stood up. "I have a better idea."

"What?"

"Let's not sleep at all. Let's leave tonight. Right now."

"Really?" She jumped off the bed. "To see Mommy?"

"To see Mommy."

"Where is she?"

"California."

"That's far."

"As far as you can get on this continent."

"Will we drive all night?"

"We'll drive all week."

"When will we sleep?"

"Who needs sleep?"

"Dad." Bea leveled her eyes at him. "We will need to sleep."

"Then you'd better pack the nightlight," he said.

"Okay." She clapped her hands. This was exciting. "I'll pack a bag for Dora," she said with practiced maturity. Sidney was sure he seemed unstable. "Should I pack food?" she asked.

"We can eat on the road," he said, pulling his suitcase out from under the bed. Action invigorated him. It was a leap into cold water, a slap of the cheeks, a sprint to the finish line. They would leave in the middle of the night. They would drive to California. It would be an adventure. "Pack whatever clothes and toiletries you need. Maybe some books for the ride, or puzzles."

"You can't do puzzles in the car."

"Books, then."

"Lots of books!" Bea shouted, heading down the hall.

Sidney put a pair of shoes into the bottom of his suitcase and folded his suit jacket, slacks, and a tie over them. He couldn't remember the last time he'd taken a trip. To the Catskills? That was at least two years ago and for all of three nights. How long would he be gone? To be on the safe side, he packed five pairs of briefs and seven pairs of socks.

On their way out the front door, bags in hand, Sidney asked Bea if she'd packed her hat. Bea stopped in her tracks. Hats were his daughter's one rebellion and one of the only things Ida insisted on. The argument always began with Bea saying she didn't need one and Ida saying, "You're fair skinned. You'll turn pink as a lobster." Bea would reply that she'd rather be pink as a lobster, at which point Ida would plop a hat on Bea's head, and Bea would insist she could do it herself, and Ida would say "If that was the case, then you would have done it already" while Sidney and Dora stood waiting to go to the pool, or church, or wherever a hat was required.

Bea looked pleadingly at Sidney.

"Forget hats," he said. "I don't like them either."

Giving him a quick gleeful hug, Bea skipped out the door, hauling her bag to the car and climbing in next to Dora, who'd slept through all the packing. Sidney checked the house one last time, making sure windows and doors were locked before getting into the car.

"Ready?" He looked at Bea over the back of the seat.

She gave a hard nod. "Ready."

Cloaked in the late hour, his daughters looked small and fragile. Dora was curled up, arms and legs tucked in. Sidney thought of the first time he'd held her, her tiny face looking up at him from that tightly wrapped pink bundle. Born a month early and only six pounds, the idea of having to take care of anything that small and vulnerable had struck terror in him. A similar feeling was coming over him now. Why were they rushing away? The reasonable thing was to get a good night's sleep and leave in the morning.

"Dad?" Bea sensed he was changing his mind.

"Yes?"

"Are we going?"

"Yes. Yes, we are." Head up. Eyes forward. He could do this.

Sidney started the engine and pulled into the street. His headlights cut the fog. The white church swished past, the town hall, the diner that served fountain drinks with pink straws. Nostalgia came over him as he passed the curb where he'd skinned his knee as a kid, and then the common where his parents used to take him and his brothers for picnics.

Sidney glanced at Bea in his rearview mirror as he merged onto Route 128. She sat rigid, her eyes wide open as if afraid of missing something.

"You can sleep, Bea," he said. She blinked heavily but didn't lie down. "That wasn't a request."

"Okay." Relieved, she slid down next to her sister, propped her head on the seat, and promptly fell asleep.

51

I T TOOK TEN MONTHS for Ida and Sidney to leave France after the liberation of Marseille.

Ships were coming in, not going out. The war still raged to the east, and Marseille had become the official transit route for soldiers being sent to the front. Sidney, no longer MIA, was ordered to the camp at Calais to help with redeployment. His sergeant assured him he wouldn't be sent to fight as long as he proved himself resourceful with handling the locals. It was easy enough to stay sober, break up fights, and apologize for the soldiers who knocked on doors, asking respectable families if they had a "mademoiselle" available.

Twice a week, he met Ida at a local bar and was given permission to stay with her at the chateau on his official day off. Apart, they craved each other. It made their one night together sweeter. They stayed up late, smoked in bed, talked, slept lightly, and found each other again in the morning.

When the war officially ended, all Sidney could think about was taking Ida home.

He'd wrongly assumed she was as anxious to go as he was. Days after Charles de Gaulle announced that the German Third Reich had signed the unconditional surrender, Ida said, "I can't leave before Arlette comes back," as if he was an idiot for suggesting it.

It was early afternoon. Sidney was putting on his boots by the kitchen door. He was supposed to meet his sergeant at the docks, and he was late.

"Ida." He pulled his pants legs over the tops of his boots and went to her. She wore a baggy shirt that came down to her knees. It was a shirt Arlette used to wear. "Arlette would have come back by now."

"We have no proof she's dead."

He took her hand. "Thousands are missing. Lots of people don't have proof."

Calmly, Ida took her hand back. "This is not my house. It was put in Anna Bacri's name, and I am not Anna Bacri. If Arlette is dead, the house belongs to her mother, Lucienne Lellouche."

"How do we find her?"

"I was hoping Peggy Guggenheim would know where she was, but I haven't been able to locate Peggy's address in New York. Would you make some inquiries for me? She's a famous name. Your Americans are bound to know how to get in touch with her."

Sidney said he'd try his best.

Back then, he believed that they would leave Arlette behind in the chateau. She would stay with the furniture and the paintings and the rugs, in the bedrooms, in the clothes and linens, in the outbuildings and gardens. There would be nothing but her memory in Massachusetts, and memories fade.

What he did not count on was what they would take with them.

THE WOMAN ARRIVED at the chateau in a maroon Peugeot. It puttered to a stop near the stone wall bordering the drive.

Sidney and Ida didn't hear it; they were upstairs deciding what to take and what to leave behind. Sidney had found an address for Peggy Guggenheim, but so far, she had not responded to Ida's letter, and Ida had agreed to at least get on a boat to England. Two million soldiers were being demobilized, and more foreign girls had married GIs than the US knew what to do with. What Ida and Sidney thought was their unique romantic situation had turned out to be quite common. The problem, according to Sidney's sergeant, was that the Immigration Act of 1924 was preventing these women from getting visas.

"He said the thing to do is marry you as soon as I can," Sidney had told Ida, his hands, in that moment, cupping her bottom. "Since that can only be done in England, we'll get that far and figure out the rest as we go." When he asked her if she wanted to invite any family, she'd laughed. "They wouldn't come even if I did want them there, which I do not."

As soon as the mail was running, she'd smoothed out the pounds rolled in her socks and sent it all home, foolish enough to think a little stolen money wouldn't matter after everything they'd been through. When there was no response, she'd written to her neighbor Mrs. Dummerston, asking if her family had survived the war. Mrs. Dummerston was kind enough to reply. *You broke your poor mother's heart. What your family has been through with their boys off to war and their only daughter gone and disappeared on them.* Amazingly, all three of Ida's brothers had returned from battle and were back working with their father in the family business. *As you should be, young lady.*

Ida did not write back. Her brothers were alive, and not a single one had replied to her letter, not even Leon. She didn't need to go home to confront what she already understood. "You're my home now," she said to Sidney, agreeing to go to the US as soon as they were able to find a ship that would take them.

Ida was folding Sidney's uniform into a small trunk when the thuds on the front door reached them. She went rigid. Sidney squeezed her arm, assuring her that a knock on the door would not forever throw her into a panic.

"I'll see who it is," he said.

The woman was middle aged, petite, and freckled. She smiled a row of tiny white teeth at him and said something in French he did not understand. Sidney replied that he did not speak French, and she immediately switched to English.

"I'm not French either." She fidgeted, sliding a hand in and out of her skirt pocket. "I'm Swiss. I married a Frenchman thirteen years ago. My mother was English, my father German. I speak three languages now." Sidney noted the tiny diamond around her neck, her practical skirt, brown socks, and loafers. She wore no nail polish and her lips were a waxy pink. "I am looking for a woman named Anna Bacri. I was told she bought this chateau right before the war broke out. Do you know her?"

"What is this regarding?" The woman's nervousness put him on guard, as did the use of Ida's false identity.

"Can you at least tell me if she lives here?" The woman glanced at her car, and then back at Sidney. "Did you know the Lellouche family? I was hoping the new owner was somehow connected to them." She leaned forward, whispering as if conspiring could still get her killed. "Do you know what I really hoped, prayed for, was that Madame Lucienne Lellouche had hidden here during the war, and I'd find her safe and sound. She's not here, is she?"

"No." Sidney was growing more uncomfortable by the minute.

The woman kept on. "Your accent is distinctly American. How did you come to be here?" When he did not answer, her voice pitched higher. "Is the mistress of the house home? I really don't want to have to explain myself twice."

Sidney had the urge to shut the door in this woman's face, but the sudden tears in her eyes made him back off. "Are you all right?" he asked, unsure what to do.

"No, not really." Embarrassed, she turned her face away.

"Would you like to come in?"

"No, no." The woman shook her head.

Rescuing him, Ida stepped into the doorway. "How can we help you?"

In an anguished voice, the woman said, "Did you know the Lellouches? Did you know Arlette?"

Unhesitant, Ida said, "Arlette was my best friend."

Tears streamed down the woman's cheeks. Her chest heaved. "I'm sorry." She patted the air, fishing a handkerchief from her skirt pocket. "I don't normally cry. I'm made of thicker stuff. I just . . . there's a moment when it all hits you, you know?" She wiped the mascara from under her eyes and blew her nose, blinking rapidly. "It's so beautiful here. Why is everything so much sadder when beauty is involved?"

The woman did not want to come inside, so they sat on the patio under the peach tree, the branches heavy with thumb-sized fruit. It would be a good year for peaches. The grass was high, the weeds out of control. Through the brambles, perennials shot up in yellows and blues. Clouds floated overhead.

The woman's name was Leonie Busche. She had worked for the Swiss Red Cross at Gurs internment camp when Arlette was arrested back in '42. Leonie had recognized her name on the list of inmates. "Anyone who reads French newspapers knows who the Lellouches are," she said. "The first thing Arlette said to me was, 'Whatever you do, keep your name humble. They hunt the famous ones down like prizes.'" Leonie tugged at the handkerchief in her hand. "That Emile Lellouche's daughter ended up a Resistance fighter was no surprise. I kept an eye on her. It was favoritism, but I couldn't help it. Arlette had a way of drawing a person in."

She told them that the camp was separated into plots of thirty cabins with wire fencing running between each. The "cabins" were planks of wood nailed together and covered with leaky tarps. It rained more than it didn't. Feces mixed with mud that never dried. Toilets were makeshift. Food scarce. Sleep impossible on the hardwood floor. Guards manned the watch towers and roamed the perimeter with machine guns. They could be bribed.

"You have to understand," Leonie said, "there was only so much we nurses could do."

Arlette was relentless, Leonie told them, insistent on helping others to a fault. She held the children of weak mothers. Let old women lay their heads on her stomach to keep off the cold floor. What little food she had she gave away. Offering her body to guards for favors was a regular occurrence, the favors rarely for her: a last cigarette for a dying person, an extra ration of food for a sick child, a blanket for the elderly. When a guard hauled her behind the watch tower, the vengeful look on Arlette's face bordered on psychotic.

Or at least, that's how Leonie saw it. "She looked like she was winning every time. I implored Arlette to stop. It was bad enough she could die of dysentery or typhoid fever, but if she kept on with the soldiers, she was certain to get syphilis." Leonie bit her lip and looked into the sky. "I was so focused on keeping those women alive, it never crossed my mind that I'd come in one day and find them gone. When I heard she'd been deported, I didn't understand it. She wasn't a foreign Jew. She was French. She was as French as they come. I'd been waiting for her to be released, a woman like that, with her connections and wealth. I assumed she had someone who could get her out, and then—" Leonie batted a tear away and collected herself. "We were told the deportation was a result of general instruction given by the occupying authorities regarding the Jews. I knew it was bad she was being sent out of France; I just didn't know how bad."

Leonie looked at them as if she was somehow at fault. "I tried my best. I swear to you, I did what I could to find her. I wrote a letter to my father-in-law, who has some influence with the secretary of state to the vice president of the Council of Ministers and begged him to look into it. He said it was too dangerous. Merely implying I was connected to a woman involved in the Resistance could get me arrested. I was told to shut my trap." She gave a hard nod. "I did not. I wrote letters to every Red Cross worker I knew, trying to find out what happened to Arlette. My husband told me I was putting us in danger. He's a landowner in Oloron-Sainte-Marie. He saw my aiding the camps as charity work and allowed it, but he wasn't about to join the fight.

"Don't get me wrong, he hated the Germans invading his country, just not enough to risk his position by getting rid of them. If you ask me"—she was diverging—"social class is what caused this war. As long as the wealthy got to keep their fortune, they turned a blind eye. My husband didn't support the Germans directly, but he complied, and they protected him. That's why I admired Arlette. I used to think the poor fought because they had nothing to lose. Arlette had everything to lose and fought harder than anyone I've ever met."

It was clear that Leonie had no idea Arlette escaped off the train from Gurs. Sidney wondered if they should tell her but thought it might be best to keep Arlette's brief freedom to themselves.

Drawing something from her skirt pocket, Leonie said, "A few months ago, a woman in the French Red Cross sent me this."

On a white record card smuggled out of Drancy, Ida and Sidney learned that Herr Kunstler had taken Arlette to a detention camp where she was assigned to room 11.2. From there, she was put on a bus and driven to a train station in Bobigny and assigned to Convoy no. 57.

The card was handwritten, marked with a large blue letter B.

"What does that mean?" Ida pointed with a trembling finger.

"Rapid deportation," Leonie said.

Eventually, Ida and Sidney would learn that Convoy no. 57, containing 1,166 people, left for Auschwitz on July 26, 1944. It was one of the last trains from Drancy. When it arrived in Poland, ninety-two men and forty-seven women were sent to labor camps. The other 1,022 people were sent straight to the gas chamber.

Arlette was not one of the forty-seven.

That they did not have this information on that day in June didn't matter. The card confirmed what they already feared.

Leonie stood up, running a finger under the chain around her neck, tugging at it, the diamond catching the light. "My husband is waiting in Marseille. I told him I wouldn't be more than a few hours." Her face flushed with fresh tears. "Come with me, both of you."

They followed Leonie to her car, suspecting she had something of Arlette's, a letter or a sentimental piece of jewelry. Her real possession was so unthinkable they stared through the open car window, unable to wrap their heads around the small, plump child who lay curled on the maroon leather seat: frizzy blonde hair, flushed cheeks, bunched yellow dress. The girl slept with her arms flung over her head, one foot dangling, her tiny leather shoe unlaced.

"I named her Beatrix." Leonie spoke in a hushed voice so as not to wake her. "She was born August 7th, 1943. She's twenty-two months old." Numbers were helpful. Facts. Calculations. Sidney could see that this child was the sum total of Leonie's desperation. "I can't keep her. I simply can't. My husband won't allow it any longer. When I first brought her home, I promised him her mother was getting out and I'd return the child the moment she did. When Arlette was deported, he insisted I find the child's family. We've kept up a good lie that my sister fell ill and I agreed to take her baby, but my husband has reached his limit. He said he's put up with enough without an illegitimate Jew child to take care of. He told me if I didn't find her family, he would send her to an orphanage.

I lied to him," Leonie gasped, wringing her hands while Ida and Sidney stood in silent stupefaction. "I told him I'd found her grandmother. He thinks I've come here to leave the child. I prayed to God that Madame Lellouche was here. I didn't know what I'd do if she wasn't, but here you are. It's God's will. Who better to take the child than her mother's best friend?"

The sleeping child, this woman's hysterical voice, made Sidney want to back away. "How do we know she's Arlette's?"

"Because I was the one who helped birth her."

The sun sank, and the clouds turned pink as icing. Ida was the one who backed away, from him, from Leonie and the car. She backed all the way to the stone wall. Sidney kept his eyes on the child, waiting for her to come to life.

Under the melting sky, Leonie told them that Arlette gave birth on the wooden planks of a crowded cabin in Gurs by a single candle. Leonie and a nurse named Meret assisted her. The baby was born in four hours, which was helpful. The shorter labors were easier to hide. Arlette was not a screamer, which was also helpful. The fact that it was dark and late all factored in.

"We were told that newborns were to be 'disposed of.'" Leonie said this calmly, her hand pressed to her heart. "We were not officially ordered to murder them, but it was clear that that is what was expected. That they trusted we'd do it was maybe the maddest thing of all. We were sent to the camp to assist the dying and became experts in smuggling out the living. It was easy enough to strap the wee ones to our chests or tuck them inside our supply bags. A pinky in the mouth kept them quiet. The soldiers didn't care what we did with them anyway, just as long as we made them go away."

"My God, what did you do with them?" Ida's voice was stricken.

"There were seven babies born while I was there. Four were smuggled out of the country, the other two went to families willing to claim them as their own. Little Bea, I kept. When I brought her home and told my husband I'd been ordered to 'dispose' of the child, he couldn't refuse me. Saving a life was the right thing to do. He's a good man, my husband, just not a brave one."

"Did Arlette know you took her baby?" Sidney said.

"No. She said she didn't want to see her, or know her name, or know what was going to happen to her. She was very clear on that. In her circumstance, I can't blame her. Bea was a child born of violence, fathered by the enemy."

Ida was suddenly beside him, wrapping her arms around him and muffling a sob into his neck. Sidney stared through the car window. The child stirred. Her tiny legs kicked and her yellow dress rustled, and she sat up, blinking clear blue eyes at him. She did not smile, but she did not cry. Her expression was serene and unafraid.

Ida lifted her head, and Sidney opened the car door. Instantly, Bea flipped onto her stomach and scooted backward off the seat, landing on wobbly feet. Ida caught her hand, steadying her. Bea's other small hand shot up and found Sidney's.

Anchored between them, she took a balanced step forward.

52

AT A DINER IN Ohio, Sidney sipped his second cup of coffee and watched his daughters eat pancakes. He was strangely alert for having driven all night. They'd made good time. It was ten a.m., and they were somewhere outside of Cleveland in a place called Johnny B's, a flat teal-colored building with teal booths, teal stools, and teal countertops. Sidney joked that their food would come out teal. When their waitress—glossy lipped, her hair rolled into tubes and lacquered to a shine—came out with yellow eggs and brown pancakes, Dora looked disappointed. Bea said there was no such thing as teal food anyway, at which point they all tried to think of a single teal-colored food, and couldn't.

"There must be teal-colored fish in the ocean," Sidney said, and Bea said if there were, they would be too beautiful to eat. He agreed.

The night before, driving into darkness, the roads emptying, the trees ticking by, Sidney chided himself for not insisting the girls stay with his mother. He didn't have a clue what he was doing. At the New York border, he'd considered turning around, but the thought of going back felt worse than any mistakes that lay ahead, so he'd kept on.

Sidney loved being behind the wheel of a car. It never exhausted him. There was something both active and peaceful about it. Time vanished. His mind relaxed. When night slipped into a pale, promising morning, his confidence returned.

The girls woke to a red horizon.

Dora said, "Bea, the sky is bleeding." Then, making a glorious discovery, she said, "We're in our nightgowns!" At which point Bea patiently explained that they were meeting Mommy in a place called California and it was a very long way and they would need to sleep in the car.

"Are we going all the way in our nightgowns?" Dora asked.

"No, silly. Dad?"

"Yes?"

"We need our bag from the trunk so we can change."

"I'll get it when I stop for gas."

"I don't want to change," Dora said, and for a moment Sidney thought she'd spoken to him, but when he glanced back, she was looking at Bea.

Bea told her they couldn't go around in their nightgowns all day, and Dora pressed her face up to the glass and pouted.

With a hot cup of coffee in his hands and miles behind them, Sidney was optimistic. Sun spilled onto the shiny tabletop. Dora worked her pancake around her plate, soaking up her syrup, her shoes making gentle thumps against the bench. A fan whirred, saturating them in the scent of fried food. Bea had finished her breakfast and was looking around with delighted curiosity. What had he been so worried about?

Three hours later, driving with the windows down and the wind roaring, Bea leaned over the backseat of the car and shouted, "Dora needs to use the bathroom!"

"I told you two to use the bathroom before we left the diner."

"We did," Bea shouted. "She needs to go again!"

"How badly?" He didn't like losing time.

Bea slid back, and Dora whispered in her ear, and Bea shouted, "Bad!"

Sidney pulled over. There was nothing but cornfields on either side of them.

"Take her out there and don't get lost."

There was no movement from the backseat. Sidney twisted around to look at them. "What are you waiting for?"

Bea crossed her arms with a stormy expression. "I'm not taking her."

Until this moment, Sidney had not considered what might happen if Bea was disagreeable. "Take your sister out there right now," he said.

"No."

"Why not?" It was ridiculous he had to ask. Bea should do as she was told.

"What is she supposed to"—Bea widened her eyes and dropped her voice to a whisper—"wipe with?"

Sidney hadn't thought about that. "I don't know. Anything. A corn husk."

"Dad!"

He might as well have suggested Dora strip naked and run down the road. Bea turned her face to the window, arms tight. It was clear there was a limit to what she was willing to do.

Sidney's voice rose. "It's not that big of a deal. When I was in the war, I spent a week in the forest with nothing. A corn husk would have been a grand thing to wipe one's bottom with. Now get out there and help your sister before she wets her pants."

Bea gripped her arms tighter. "No."

Fuming, Sidney got out of the car and opened the back door. Dora slid out, her patent leather shoes hitting the gravel. "Go on." He waved his hand in the direction of the cornfield. Dora didn't move. "Are you going to start now? If you need to go, go, otherwise get back in the car and hold it until the next gas station."

With anxious eyes, Dora reached up and hooked her small fingers around his.

Sidney's heart flipped over.

He didn't like babying her, but he walked her into the stalks anyway, into the manure-scented shade and hard-packed dirt. Yanking a piece of corn from its stalk, he peeled the husk away and handed it to her. "Do your business," he said, turning his back.

The sound of trickling pee made him uncomfortable, so he whistled, twisting the cob in his hands, the unripe kernels smooth and glassy. After a minute, there was a tap on his arm, and he turned to see Dora smiling up at him and pointing to a circling flock of crows. The birds settled into the corn with earsplitting squawks, and Dora jumped up and down, so delighted you would have thought they were flamingos.

Sidney took her hand, the entire tiny appendage disappearing into his large palm. "We should get back to Bea."

With a little skip, she said, "Okay," as if she'd spoken to him her entire life.

53

※

SIDNEY HELD ON TO that single word for days. It was not a revelatory shift. It was a subtle acceptance. Dora hadn't said anything more to him, but Sidney could tell she might at any moment.

In Kansas, they spent the night in a motel, which revived Sidney enough to drive through the Rocky Mountains the next night, arriving to a red-hot morning in Utah. The logical thing would have been to drive through the mountains in the day and the desert at night, but Sidney didn't know how hot it would be.

Not wanting to stop for breakfast, they'd eaten hard-boiled eggs and crackers at the gas station, filled up the tank, and were back on the road by nine a.m.

The heat flattened them. He thought Utah was the worst of it, but when they crossed the southern tip of Nevada into the Mojave Desert, they were in trouble. It was nearing seven p.m. The sky was bright, the road ahead straight and flat and empty. Sidney had been up for twenty-four hours. He wasn't thinking clearly. He should have stopped at the last motel they passed. The car was low on gas, and he had no idea where the next stop was. Dora had been asleep for hours, and Bea kept whining that she was thirsty. Their soft drinks were long gone.

"Dad!" Bea suddenly cried. "Dora threw up."

Sidney pulled over, the wheels kicking up dust thick as smoke. He got out of the car and opened the back door. Waves of heat beat off the pavement. Dora's head lay in a pool of vomit. He pulled her into a sitting position. Her little arms were hot as fire, and her cheeks were an unnatural red. "Dora?" He tried to prop her head up, but her chin kept rolling onto her chest. He wiped the sticky hair from her forehead. "Dora, wake up." She didn't.

Bea scooted to the other side of the car. "It's all over my dress."

Laying Dora back down, Sidney grabbed a shirt from the trunk and tried to wipe up the vomit while Bea took a clean dress from her bag and changed by the side of the road, no longer worried about being seen. In a few days, his daughters' small world had become large and unrecognizable. They'd brushed their teeth in bathroom gas stations, had gone without washing their hair or changing their clothes, had slept in the car and eaten in towns with names no one could pronounce. Now they were in a land where lizards watched with beady eyes and bleached plants shot up like daggers from the cracked earth.

What Sidney felt, lifting Dora's hot body from the backseat and settling her into the front, was a loss of control. It was the same feeling he had the day she was born, when Ida was given a drug meant to help with pain that only made her thrash and scream harder. Sidney refused to leave her side and had to be pushed from the room by a white-capped nurse while a doctor strapped his wife to the bed. He'd paced the hall, wanting to tear the door down. When the nurse finally placed his infant daughter in his arms, he felt bewildered and powerless. Somehow this tiny creature had come from that pain and suffering, this helpless, impossibly small human he was meant to keep alive.

Getting back on that endless flat road, Sidney pushed the Plymouth to seventy-five miles an hour, afraid the car would overheat or he'd run out of gas. He'd topped off the oil in Nebraska, but that was two days ago. He hadn't checked the brakes or any hoses or belts. If the car made it in this heat, he'd have God to thank.

Sun blistered the horizon. The needle on the speedometer trembled. The car vibrated. Dora slumped against the door, limp and motionless. In the backseat, Bea was uncharacteristically quiet. The knot at the base of Sidney's neck spread to his shoulders. When he saw a speck in the distance, he stepped on the gas pedal. A sign came into view, BUN BOY, then a low, flat building with big glass windows. Sidney flew into the parking lot, the brakes squealing.

Bea was out of the car before he was, opening Dora's door, his eldest daughter's face washed of color. Most kids would have been asking a million questions. Not Bea. She was silent and stoic and efficient. By the time Sidney rounded the car, Bea had pulled her sister's dress down over her knees and propped her head up.

"I've got her," Sidney said, lifting Dora's feverish body.

Things happened quickly, then. A busty, perfumed woman at the front door took one look at Dora and shouted to an older woman, who set down the coffeepot and was out from behind the counter with her palm to Dora's forehead in seconds. "How long's she been like this?"

"A few hours," Sidney guessed. He had no idea how long Dora had been sick. She'd seemed fine at the gas station, but that was ages ago.

The woman instructed him to lay Dora in a booth and started pulling off her socks and shoes. "Marsha!" she called to another woman who was taking an order three tables away. The woman hurried over, freckled, young, with arched brows and pale lips. The older woman said, "Get a glass of ice water and a cold rag." She rolled Dora onto her side and began unbuttoning her dress. Without looking up, she said, "I'm Francine, that's Marsha, and that there"—she jutted an elbow at the woman who'd met them at the door—"is Betty." Francine was clearly the one in charge. Her cheeks were thin and strong, her skin weathered, eyes sharp.

Water, ice, and washcloths were produced, the three women working fast. Bea knelt in the opposite booth, watching as they dipped a washcloth and pressed it to Dora's forehead. Her dress was pulled down around her waist and another cold cloth was pressed to her bare chest. Pink fingernails ran ice cubes over Dora's cheeks. The ceiling fans blew hot air around. Customers looked up from their tables, everyone hushed and worried.

Sidney stood to one side, feeling useless. The smell of onion and hot oil and perfume made him queasy. After a few minutes, Dora's eyes fluttered open. The older woman smiled at her. "Hey there, baby doll." When Dora's eyes dropped shut again and her head rolled to one side, the woman whisked her from the booth.

"I should take her to a hospital," Sidney said.

"That very well may be, but the nearest hospital is sixty miles away, and the heat could kill her by then." Francine swept past him, all action. "We need to get her into a cold bath. Betty, get a room key. Marsha, get the other child a cold drink so she doesn't get heatstroke as well. You, come with me." She jerked her head at Sidney, and they rushed outside.

Across Route 66 was a long, flat motel. A bath was drawn in room 12, the white enamel tub stained yellow. Water coughed from the pipes and plaster crumbled from the walls. All three women had abandoned their posts at the restaurant. They ran cold water, undressed Dora, and eased her into the tub. Marsha and Betty propped her up while Francine palmed water over her chest and shoulders, clucking and cooing like Dora was an infant.

If it was improper for Sidney to be there, he didn't care. He planted himself in the doorway, cursing Ida. This was not what he'd bargained for. His wife was not a selfish woman. Unsettled and restless, yes, but self-centered to the point of abandonment? It didn't fit. It wasn't who she was. It was Arlette's fault. Always Arlette. If that photograph hadn't turned up, Ida wouldn't have left him, and he wouldn't have driven across a desert and put his daughter's life in danger.

Dora's eyes opened. She looked into the women's faces and whimpered, "I want Mommy."

Sidney stepped all the way into the bathroom, unsure which moved him more: that his daughter was awake or that she'd just spoken to strangers.

Kneeling on the brown bathmat, Francine said, "Your daddy's here. You gave him a right scare, baby doll."

Tears sprang into Dora's eyes. "I want Mommy," she said, but lifted her arms to Sidney.

Sidney squeezed between the women, the bathroom barely containing them all as he reached for his girl, hoisting her solid body against his chest.

"She needs sleep." Francine patted her back with a towel.

"And liquids," Betty said.

"A glass of cold milk," Marsha said.

Dora lay her wet head on Sidney's shoulder. He pushed past the flock of women into the motel room. Double bed, dresser, television set. "Where's Bea?"

Marsha said, "I told Max to make her a fountain drink. I'll send her over when she's finished."

Marsha and Betty slipped out while Francine propped a fan into the open window and plugged it in. "It's cooler if you blow the hot air out."

The fan clacked and whirred to life. Sidney laid Dora on the bed. She rolled onto her side, pulling the towel with her.

Francine put a hand on her forehead, and Dora closed her eyes. "She'll be all right. I'll bring the milk over for her. Other than that, try and keep her cool and let her sleep." She paused in the doorway, focusing on Sidney for the first time. "You all right?"

He sat down on the edge of the bed. "I don't know."

"It seems like you're a long way from home."

"I am."

"Your wife leave you?"

It was startling to be asked directly. For the first time, Sidney felt like a man whose wife really had left him. "Looks like it."

Francine nodded, opening the door to dusty golden sunlight. "You'll get through it, honey. We've all got our cross to bear." She said it as if she'd seen worse. "Come on next door for something to eat when you're ready."

Sidney didn't want her to leave. He wanted to lay down and close his eyes and have this woman take care of everything.

54

FOR THE NEXT THREE nights, Sidney slept on the pebble-brown rug of the Bun Boy Motel. After the girls fell asleep, he'd go outside for a cigarette, making it last, wishing he could watch television without waking them, or that he at least had a book to read, anything to distract him.

Lying on his flat pillow under his threadbare sheet, it occurred to him that he had no idea what he desired anymore. Not from Ida, but from his life. Existing for someone else was not living. Closing his eyes, he conjured up the feel of Ida's hair in his hands, the sound of her voice, the way she'd run her fingernails up the inside of his arm and nibble the tip of his ear. And then, he tried to imagine his life without her. A single bed. A closet for one. Three settings at the table. Could he raise his children on his own? Bea was old enough to take care of things when he couldn't manage. Maybe they wouldn't return east. Maybe he'd find a job in a seaside town and raise the girls in a bungalow on the beach.

Sidney stopped this line of thinking. He'd come all this way to find his wife. Why was he questioning it? He wondered if she'd tried calling home again, if she worried when no one answered. Yesterday he'd telephoned his parents. They both got on the line, firing questions at him. When he asked if Ida had called them, they said no.

In the lonely town of Baker, California—Death Valley, Sidney had learned it was called—on that bumpy rug that smelled of cigarettes, Sidney thought back to the one conversation he'd had with his wife since she left, and finally understood.

Ida had organized her life in service to Arlette. She had taken Bea from Leonie without question, promising she'd find Arlette's mother. When they discovered that Lucienne Lellouche never made it to America because of a faulty visa and was sent back to Spain, they went to Spain in search of her. When they learned that she died of pneumonia in a hospital in Madrid in 1943, Ida told Sidney she would only stay married to him if he agreed to raise Arlette's daughter as their own. They'd been married for three months—a hurried ceremony in a registry office in London—and had been taking care of Bea for six months.

It wasn't that Sidney didn't want Bea, despite how sudden it was, it was that he didn't want to lie, especially not to his parents. He told Ida he'd raise Bea if they told his family the truth.

Ida flat-out refused. It was their first real fight. They were standing on a street corner in Madrid. Bea had her arms wrapped around Ida's legs. Ida had hers folded over her chest.

"Why not tell people Bea's mother died in a concentration camp?" Sidney said.

"It's not safe."

"To admit she's Jewish?"

"Yes."

"The war is over."

"For now. Who knows what will happen to the Jews in the future."

"Ida, you're being unreasonable. This sort of thing doesn't happen in America. Why do you think we fought against it?"

"It took you Americans long enough. How many Jews died before you got involved? Peggy told me she was kicked out of a hotel in Vermont for being Jewish, and that was years before the war. People are cruel. They will be cruel to Bea."

"I know plenty of Jewish people. Why do you think they all escaped from Europe to the US? Bea will be completely safe with us."

"Do you want to explain to your parents, to Bea, that we killed her mother?" Ida was shouting. People were looking at them. "You want everyone to know how I stood there and watched while you hid in the woods as they dragged her away? How I got all of her money? Her

French chateau? Do you think anyone will believe I didn't do it on purpose?"

To shush her, Sidney pressed his hand to the back of Ida's head and pulled her into his chest. "Okay, okay," he said.

And that was that. Bea would be theirs.

The fan whirred in the motel window. A car drove by. Footsteps and laughter moved along outside.

On the phone, Ida had said the photograph wasn't a Man Ray. She said it was taken by Arlette. Did taking a photograph or printing a photograph give an artist the right to it? Either way, Ida saw it as a forgery. One more thing stolen from Arlette. One more injustice.

It helped to believe that Ida had not left because of him and the girls, but that she had left to vindicate her friend, and in doing so, exonerate herself. Sidney felt certain that if he found Man Ray, he would find Ida. Proving the photograph was Arlette's was Ida's chance at redemption, her way of reaching toward a future where they could live in some kind of balance.

He also understood that she would only return to them if she succeeded.

Sidney got up. The girls were tangled in the bed, arms and legs every which way. He felt Dora's forehead—clammy, but not hot—and went outside to smoke another cigarette. The sky was a boundless sheet of black. Moonless. Thick with stars. Sidney had never seen such a sky. The beauty of it, that vast space full of possibility, made him acutely aware of himself.

This wasn't only about finding his wife. It was about what he wanted for him and his daughters. For their whole family. For once, it was about choice, not obligation.

55

A WOMAN AT THE VILLA Elaine Apartments gave Ida the address, a bleach blonde named Stella who passed Ida knocking on Man Ray's door, and said, "You won't find Mr. Ray in there, darling. He's gone up the coast."

"Do you know where?" Ida asked.

"I do, as a matter of fact. Not that I've been invited up. I just water the man's plants. Come on in."

Stella's apartment was brightly lit—high windows, stuffed white furniture, movie posters adorning the walls. Digging through a kitchen drawer, she came out with a slip of paper held between red fingernails. "Here's the address, but good luck trying to get there. They don't even have telephone lines." She opened a window and lit a cigarette. "Can you imagine?"

As she rode along Highway 1, Ida could imagine, the land was wild, the houses few and far between, crammed onto hillsides, barely hanging on. She had stayed at a cheap motel in LA for three nights before getting on a bus in Glendale for the seven-hour bus ride to Carmel. The paunch-bellied man in the seat next to her had talked nonstop about his beagles. By the time they pulled into the seaside town, Ida could recite the names of all nine of his dogs. When they parted ways, the man told her she was welcome at his farm anytime, and the woman who'd sat behind her whispered that Ida was a saint to endure that man's babble. When they walked away, Ida felt strangely abandoned.

She learned from the receptionist at the nearest motel, a breathtaking woman with flowing hair and green eyes, that the only way to get to Big Sur without a car would be with the mail carrier, Fred Culver. "He'll give you a ride if you like, but he only goes on Tuesdays and Wednesdays." It was Thursday. "He's playing in the dance band tonight over at the El Dorado if you want to find him. He plays the bass viol like a champ." She shook out her hair. "I'll be there. I can introduce you. He's a dream, but he has a wife and four kids, so don't get any ideas."

Ida gave her a weak smile. Flirting was the last thing on her mind.

After five restless days in Carmel walking the beach, eating shellfish, and unsuccessfully reading a copy of *War and Peace* she'd found in the hotel lobby, Ida was finally seated next to Fred driving down the coast in his red pickup truck.

Fred was a dream. Not for his peppered hair and distinguished bone structure—he did look rather like a movie actor—but for his good-humored sociability. He told Ida he not only delivered mail but that he filled grocery orders, cashed checks, and carried all sorts of messages to folks up and down the coast. "Don't know what they'd do otherwise," he said, his duty to bring them the necessities of the modern world a serious one.

The drive was magnificent and terrifying. Ida had never seen anything like it. Mammoth rock faces plummeted down to waves that shot a hundred feet into the air. Trees grew at funny angles. Birds swooped at eye level. The thirty-five-mile drive to Big Sur took all day. Fred liked to talk, and folks were happy to see him. He conversed at gate posts and mailboxes. A few times, he was invited in for coffee, once for a bite to eat. Ida tagged along, everyone nosy to find out where she was from and who she was visiting. When she told them Man Ray, they smiled and nodded as if he received visitors all the time.

It was four o'clock by the time Fred dropped her at the top of the driveway to Anderson Creek. He refused to take any money for the ride, but said he'd be grateful if Ida would deliver the bag of groceries down the hill for him. He was hoping to get to the town of Lucia before dark. "I'll stop by tomorrow on my way back to Carmel to see if you need a ride north," he said. "If I time it right, I might just get an invitation to supper. Tell everyone I say hello!" He waved, shifted his truck into gear, and eased onto the treacherous road.

The dirt-and-dust driveway was steep and narrow, the house at the bottom large and white with a wraparound porch. Fred told her it was built as an infirmary for the men building Highway 1 back in '37, and now rented out to a woman named Margaret who hosted weekly dinner parties and housed artists from Los Angeles seeking a reprieve from the city.

The smell of sage and eucalyptus whipped past on a cool wind. After the heat of LA, it felt magnificent. In the yard, two women bent over a washtub, barefoot, hatless. One woman wore a scarf knotted at the top of her head and a shirt that tied around her neck and ended under her small breasts, revealing her flat stomach and narrow hips. Her pants were belted with a rope and rolled to her knees. The other woman wore a dress of varying pinks that swirled together like oil on water. Her body was full and curvy. Her long hair raven black.

The door of the house banged open, and a young woman came out with skin and hair as pale as driftwood. Three children dashed from behind her, a boy and two girls. Without breaking stride, the boy leapt into the washtub, splashed the women, leapt back out, and met the girls, who were laughing like hyenas as the three of them tore off into the woods, the girls' pigtails flying.

Watching them disappear, Ida was struck with a memory of Dora and Bea running ahead of her for a swim at Walden Pond just a few weeks ago. The memory made her throat ache. It felt, suddenly, like she'd been gone for months.

The pale woman approached her. She had a wide face with skin pulled taut over high cheekbones. "Ignore the children. They're hellions. Discipline is not in their vocabulary. I'm Lebska." She gave Ida a firm handshake and pointed to the other women. "That's Juliet and Margaret."

Juliet, the skinny one, raised her brows. "We're hellions too," she said, wringing out a wad of fabric.

"Here, let me take that for you." Lebska reached for the groceries in Ida's arms. "I see you came with Fred. Margaret, your food's arrived just in time." Looking at Ida, she said, "What did you say your name was?"

"Ida."

"Well, Ida, it's your lucky night. We're having an abalone-shucking party. Margaret's already made a red velvet cake, and there's a bottle of gin on ice. Can't ask for a better Tuesday, can you?"

Out of nowhere, Ida remembered that the girls had swimming lessons on Tuesdays. Would Isabelle remember to take them? With sudden urgency, she said, "Is Man Ray here?"

Juliet poked her head around a swath of linen. "What do you want with my husband? Has he done something awful?"

Margaret, scrubbing a ball of fabric against the washboard, said, "It wouldn't be the first time."

One of the girls suddenly popped out from a thicket of evergreens, shouting, "Letti is bathing! Tony saw her naked." Cackling with laughter, she flitted away again.

Lebska said, "My daughter likes to raise alarms wherever she goes. We have no running hot water, so we bathe in the hot springs. It's all very civilized." She laughed.

"Tony's seen all of us naked," Margaret added.

Juliet said, "He's the luckiest boy alive."

These braless, barefoot women with their unruly children and bohemian clothes kindled a part of Ida she'd stomped to death years ago. At one time, her life was going to be this gloriously eccentric. When a man appeared in the doorway of the house wearing a vest and a beret, it was as if Ida was standing on the patio at Villa Air-Bel.

"Henry?" Lebska turned to him. "Have you seen Man? This woman is looking for him."

"He's in his studio." Henry leaned against the doorframe. He had fanatical eyes and a mischievous mouth. He smiled at Ida. "Henry Miller, nice to meet you."

"Ida Whipple."

He looked like an illustrious farmer with his weathered tan skin and deeply lined face. White tufts of hair crested his small ears. "Have you come a long way, Ida Whipple?" He said her name with an English accent.

"I have come a very long way."

"From England?"

"No."

"But you are from England?"

"Yes."

"How do you know Man?"

"We met in Paris. I worked for Peggy Guggenheim."

A palpable silence fell. Margaret dropped the shirt she was scrubbing to the edge of the tub. Juliet came out from behind the clothesline. She had a strong face and alert eyes. Lebska looked in the direction the children had gone, and Henry chuckled as if someone had made a joke.

Margaret took the grocery bag from Lebska. "I'm going to get this food inside," she said, and the two of them eased around Henry into the house as if skirting a storm.

Juliet came toward Ida. Something had cooled. Did they have some complaint against Peggy? That wouldn't be surprising. "I'll take you to Man," she said.

Confused at this sudden shift, Ida followed her in silence. They walked down the path the children had gone and stopped at the bottom of a stairway cut into the hillside. High above them, a structure the size of a small shed reflected the sea in tiny paned windows. Juliet began to walk up the stairs, the muscles of her exposed back taut and sinewy. Ida hesitated, suddenly nervous about confronting Man. He was a great artist. Why would he forge a photograph? What if he denied it?

"Are you coming?" Juliet turned, and her eyes moved past Ida to someone walking up the path.

A woman called out to them. "I wouldn't disturb Man if I were you. I tried to get him to take a soak with me, but he's in a foul temper."

The path was steep, and the woman was breathless when she reached them. A towel was draped over her shoulders, and she wore a yellow sundress that clung to her wet skin. Shaking the water from her cropped dark hair, she stopped in front of Ida.

They faced one another, hearts pounding, faces bleached of color.

Arlette.

Ida heard Juliet say, "I thought you two might know each other," but it came from far away.

The ocean beat in Ida's chest. Thrashed in her ears. Pulsed in her limbs. She was salt and mineral smashed against rocks. She was seafoam. Evaporated particles.

The hillside closed in. The sky fell over Ida and the cliff crumbled away.

56

Ray was after Rawlings in the phone book. Sidney jotted down the address and handed the phone book back to the clerk at the Beverly Hills Hotel.

After what they'd been through, he'd decided to treat his girls to a luxurious stay in Hollywood. The room had two double beds, pink sheets, a plush chair, and a palm tree out the window.

So far, the glamour was lost on them. When they arrived last night, Bea and Dora grumbled that they missed the Bun Boy. Francine had let them pull their own sodas from the fountain. Max, the cook, showed them how to flip burgers. Marsha let them scoop ice cream, and Betty brought them to her house to play with her kittens.

There were no kittens at the Beverly Hills Hotel. Kids weren't allowed in the dining room after six p.m., and they were told not to touch anything in the lobby.

In their room, Dora kicked the shiny bedframe. "I want to see Mommy. You said we were going to see Mommy." Another kick to the bed.

"Stop that," Sidney said. He was still getting used to hearing her small voice directed at him. "We'll see Mommy soon." He tucked in his shirt and shot up his cuffs.

Bea lay on the bed with her hands propped under her chin. "Why do we have to stay with that strange lady?"

"Her name is Virginia, and she won't be a stranger when you get to know her." Virginia was a middle-aged housewife from South Carolina he'd met in the lobby. They'd struck up a conversation, and she'd agreed to watch the girls while her husband was at the racetracks. Virginia, overly concerned, had smiled at Bea and Dora and asked Sidney what he was doing on vacation with his children and no wife. Sidney told her his wife was joining them shortly.

"Where are you off to tonight, then?" Virginia had said, a little more accusing than he would have liked.

"To visit an old friend."

"I see." She raised her brows as if to indicate she knew all too well what was really going on.

Now, Bea said, "Daddy, who's your old friend?"

"A man I've never met."

"How is he your friend, then?"

"He's your mother's friend, which makes him my friend."

Dora said, "Will Momma be there?"

"I don't know."

There was a knock on the hotel room door. "Coming," Sidney called. He slid on his suit jacket and put a hand to Dora's forehead to check her temperature.

She pulled away. "Stop doing that, Daddy."

"She's fine," Bea said.

"I'm just making sure."

He was at the door when Bea suddenly leapt off the bed and threw her arms around him.

"Don't go."

He gave her a squeeze. "I will be back before you're asleep."

"What if you're not?"

"I will be."

"Promise?"

"I promise."

VILLA ELAINE APARTMENTS was not what Sidney expected. He'd pictured the famous artist living in a mansion with a metal gate and a circular driveway, not in an apartment two flights up with a sour smell in the hallway. Sidney knocked at number 13. No one came to the door. He checked the address, knocked again. It was only eight o'clock. Man Ray had to come home eventually, he reasoned.

From a pay phone on the corner of Vine and La Mirada, he had the hotel clerk put him through to his room and asked Virginia if she wouldn't mind staying longer. She told him to take his time. The girls were fine. They were eating pretzels and playing Parcheesi.

In the dimly lit hallway of the apartment building, Sidney sat on the floor with his back to the wall. His whole body ached. Since leaving home, the only bed he'd slept in was in a cheap motel in Kansas, and a hard flat one at that. Driving from Baker that morning, all he could think about was lying down in a comfortable bed again. Now here he was, upright on a wooden floor. His breath deepened and he dozed off, his head rolling forward. He heard music in his sleep. Something jazzy being played in the street. Behind closed lids, he was back in Marseille. The war was over and the street was filled with people. Ida's hand was in his, and then it wasn't. He reached back, but there were too many faces. Too much noise.

A car backfired and the bang jolted him awake. The hall light flickered off and on. He was slumped all the way over with his head on the floor. Sidney sat up and checked his watch. It was midnight. He'd slept a shocking four hours.

He roused himself and went back across the street to the pay phone. Virginia had left a message with the hotel clerk saying she'd put the girls to bed and had gone to her own room, but to ring if he needed anything. Sidney asked the clerk if he'd make sure his room was locked and told him he'd be back as soon as he could. The clerk said not to worry. Most parents didn't make it home until dawn.

Sidney hung up and tapped his pack of cigarettes. It was empty. Across the street was a building with a large sign that said Hollywood Ranch Market. The place was hopping. Music played from parked cars. People milled about the aisles buying everything from liquor to cereal. A woman in a short dress holding a bottle of scotch and a box of crackers leaned against the cigarette machine, smiling at him. She shook the bottle. "Want to join me, handsome?"

To be flirted with so openly was flattering and nerve-racking. Times had changed. Or maybe Californian women were bolder than New Englanders. "Thank you, but I'm married," he said.

The woman gave a throaty laugh and leaned in, her mouth right in front of his. "So presumptuous! I was only asking if you wanted to join me for a drink." She emphasized the word *drink*, puckering her lips. Her breath was minty, her eyes almond brown. Realizing just how young she was, Sidney recoiled, his daughters flashing across his mind. What if they grew up to wear revealing dresses and flirt with older men in brightly lit stores at midnight?

"So, how about it?" She smiled.

"Thank you, no," he repeated.

"Your loss." She strutted away and Sidney couldn't help looking at the bare backs of her calves as she moved down the aisle.

The machine coughed out a box of cigarettes. Feeling pathetic, he went back to his post outside Man Ray's door.

57

THE FOLLOWING AFTERNOON, IDA sat on a cliff with her head between her knees. Her husband's green army bag lay on the ground next to her with the wrapping paper tube sticking out of it.

Beside her, a ghost sat in a bed of pine needles.

The thundering in Ida's ears slowed to a low drum, and she dropped onto her back with her hands on her stomach. "You're supposed to be dead," she finally said.

"Arlette is dead." Her voice was alive. Her voice was exactly the same.

"I saw your deportation card. You were sent to Auschwitz. Your name was not on the list of survivors."

"Lists can be wrong."

Ida kept her eyes on the circle of sky between the towering evergreens. Her heart pulsed under her palms as if that powerful organ had fallen below her ribs and lay drowning in her stomach.

All the questions she had for Arlette fell away. All she could think of was Bea. Her Bea. The Bea she'd read *The Carrot Seed* to a hundred times, whose favorite movie was *The Little Princess*, who once drew red marker in her hair trying to look like Shirley Temple. The Bea who adored her little sister, who was honest to a fault, who told Ida not to wear yellow on the Fourth of July. The Bea who left snippings all over the living room when she cut out paper dolls, whose forehead Ida had touched the night she left, whispering, "I won't be gone forever, just for now."

To leave, Ida had to push her children to the back of her mind. She had to push Sidney even further. The night Arlette's photograph sucked her back in time, she'd wanted to become the girl who took flight from her home in England with her father's money. To rebel. To take charge. To run toward something unexpected. It had felt risky. Empowering. Like returning to a part of herself.

Now it felt redundant.

She might as well have been lying on the floor of a gallery in London. Her life was not sectioned off into pieces. There were not multiple versions of her. She was a single narrative.

And once again, Arlette had lured her to a destructive end.

Ida sat up. "Why didn't you come find me?"

Arlette looked toward the horizon. "I needed to start over."

"Without me?"

"Without everyone."

"Why?" Ida asked again, not that Arlette's answer would make any difference.

From the beginning, Arlette had given everything and taken everything.

Arlette held her knees close, her curved spine visible through her thin cotton dress. Past the trees and the cliff, the sun sank over the ocean. There was no fiery sunset, just the cool blues of migrating ocean and sky.

"My name held me back, even before it almost killed me. I was in Auschwitz. I will not tell you the means by which I survived because they are repulsive." She tipped her head and rested a cheek on one knee, holding Ida with her eyes. "It was not out of anger that I didn't come to find you. I wanted a rebirth. If it makes you feel any better, Man is the only person I've been in contact with from my past."

"It does not make me feel better." Ida reached for the wrapping paper tube. She pulled out the photograph and unrolled it over her legs.

This time, looking at the masked face of her younger self, Ida remembered what it felt like to be that hopeful, anguished girl. She wondered if Arlette felt it. This photo was their rebellious grasp at freedom, their attempt to create something that mattered for a future that did not exist.

But they were no longer those girls. They had grown into women who sat on a cliff in California trying to make sense of each other.

Arlette said, "How do you have this?"

"I stole it from my neighbor."

Arlette suddenly laughed, and the knot in Ida's stomach loosened the littlest bit. They were eight years and six thousand miles from their past, but Arlette's laugh was the same.

She then told Ida how she went back to the chateau three years ago and dug up the box they had buried. She needed the money, but more than that, she had wanted to test her resilience. Abandoning her past had not rid her of sorrow, and neither did returning to it. If her mother had survived, she might have rebuilt the chateau, or at least reclaimed it, but seeing it only confirmed for her that she wanted nothing to do with it. She didn't mind poverty. "But after a while, you owe too many people," she said. To pay off her debts, she emptied the chateau and sold everything off. Selling the chateau itself would have required explaining the forged documents and paying back taxes that hadn't been collected from a missing Anna Bacri in years. The chateau was in such a state of disrepair, Arlette was sure no one would buy it anyway. "So, there it sits. A last haunting memory."

There was another memory. A living one.

Ida listened in silence. She was trying to figure out how to tell Arlette about Bea. Did she wonder what had happened to her baby, all those years ago?

"You still haven't explained the photograph," Ida said.

"And you haven't explained how you got your hands on it."

"You first." Ida was not intimidated. Arlette did not make her feel less than or needy anymore. Whatever power she'd had over Ida was now gone.

"I printed it right up there." Arlette pointed to the studio on the hill above them. "I forged Man Ray's signature to prove a point."

"What point?"

"That my work is good and people will buy it."

"Or you just proved that Man Ray's name can sell anything."

"You don't think it's good?"

Ida wasn't going to indulge her with an answer. "Does Man know?" she asked.

"Are you mad? Of course not." Arlette rolled the photograph back up, slid it into the wrapping paper tube, and stuck it into Ida's bag. "And he's not going to."

"The gallery owner told me he sent Man a check."

Arlette shrugged. "Juliet keeps track of his money. I'm sure she assumed the payment was for a legitimate piece."

Noises reached them, voices, people gathering.

"Your turn," Arlette said. "In what universe did this photograph show up?"

Avoiding the topic of her children, Ida described Lexington, the party, Ellen. She told Arlette how she walked into Ellen's dining room in the middle of the night and took it right off her wall. They commented on how freakish it was, this photograph landing in Ida's life and bringing her here. Fate, divine intervention, luck. Whatever it was, they were meant to be reunited.

Bea clutched at Ida's heart.

Arlette stood up and brushed the leaves from her bottom. She offered Ida her hand and Ida took it, letting Arlette pull her to her feet. Ida felt strangely normal, hungry, and tired.

When Arlette hugged her, tight and hard, Ida did not resist. She held her arms around her friend, feeling her damp hair against her shoulder and trying not to cry. After everything, Ida still loved her.

When they pulled away, Arlette picked up Ida's bag and carried it as she had carried Ida's valise all those years ago in Marseille.

"Do you want to know why I really did it?" Arlette said.

"Did what?" Ida asked.

"Started over."

"Why?"

"Because I was convinced it would bring me success. Turns out, no one wants to buy Letti Carmichael's art any more than they wanted Arlette Lellouche's."

"Carmichael?"

"Americans think nothing of my French accent and Scottish surname. It's a mash of identities here. I rather love it."

"Carmichael is a terrible name for an artist," Ida said.

Again, Arlette's familiar bark of a laugh. "What do I call myself, then?"

"Lellouche is beautiful."

"Maybe I'll take it back."

What else will you take back? Ida thought as they walked along the path, the air cool, the leaves sweet scented.

58

EARLIER THAT MORNING, A woman leaned over Sidney, shaking his shoulder, her bright hair bobbing up and down. "Are you okay?"

Sidney yanked himself into a sitting position, wincing at the pain in his neck. "Good God, did I sleep here all night?" He pulled himself to his feet, his legs stiff, his right arm tingling. He blinked in the bright light.

"Honestly." The woman patted her hair. She wore a neat white suit with yellow heels. "I was going to call the police, but then I got a better look at you, and you didn't seem like your average drunk." She smiled. "You're far too put together to be a bum. Did your woman lock you out?"

Sidney's mouth was dry. He stepped back sure his breath was foul. "I'm looking for Man Ray. Do I have the right address?"

"Good Lord. Is everyone looking for Mr. Ray? There was a woman here last week asking about him. What, is he having a deal on portraits? I tried to get him to do my portrait, and he wanted two hundred dollars! I know for a fact he charged Elsie Littleton fifty dollars, probably because she's more famous than I am. He's a pompous fellow, if you ask me. Are you an actor?"

"Who was here?"

"What?"

"The woman. Who was she?"

"Oh, I don't know. Ilene, maybe? Sweet thing. Pretty. Dark hair. Very thin. Maybe Doris?"

"Ida. Was her name Ida?" Sidney had to hold himself back from shaking the woman.

"Maybe? Gosh, I don't remember. I gave her Man's address in Big Sur, but he and his wife are usually only up there for a week or so. They'll be back any day now."

Sidney was buttoning his coat, securing his loosened tie. "Can I get it? The address?"

She laughed. "I should start charging. Come on in. I imagine you're hungry, sleeping out here all night. I'd invite you for breakfast, but I'm supposed to meet my agent in an hour. Juicy little part coming my way, or so he says." She rolled her eyes and swung open her door.

Stella, Man's neighbor, insisted Sidney stay for a cup of coffee and gave him the address only after he agreed to escort her to her meeting. "My agent tells me what I need is a man to get my career off the ground. I know, I know." She slapped Sidney's arm, working her fingers down to the ring on his hand. "You're married. And if I'm guessing right, it's to that woman who was here. She's left you, and you're after her, and that's just about the damn sweetest thing I've ever heard. Or." She laughed. "You've left your wife, and that woman here was your mistress, and you're a rotten man and I should hate you. Either way, all I need is for my agent to see you dropping me at the restaurant door so I can convince him I've got a man, and he'll stop setting me up on dates with fat, old movie executives." She let go of Sidney's arm and nestled a hat on her head. "I'd say you owe me a favor for not calling those cops on you."

In the street, he unwrapped himself from Stella's grasp and used the pay phone for a third time. The hotel clerk promised he'd have breakfast sent up to his room with a message that he would be back soon.

This did not help matters. It was ten fifteen by the time Sidney made it back to the Beverly Hills Hotel. When he walked into the room, the look on Bea's face crushed him. Her lips quivered, and she clamped her teeth to keep from crying. Dora openly sobbed, her face buried in a pillow. A good parent would hug his children, reassure them. What Sidney wanted was to lock himself in the bathroom so he could think straight.

"You promised," Bea said.

Sidney slid off his tie. His night on another floor had left him with a searing pain in his neck. "I promised I'd be back and I am." He needed a hot shower and a change of clothes.

"You said *before* we went to sleep. Where were you?"

The last thing Sidney wanted to do was explain himself to his eight-year-old daughter. "Something came up."

"What?" Bea demanded.

"It's grown-up stuff, Bea."

"Mom is not coming back, is she?" Bea burst out, and Dora sat up, her face streaked, hiccups racking her chest.

"Of course she's coming back."

Darkly, Bea said, "Do you promise?"

Her tone was unacceptable. "You will not speak to me that way, young lady."

In a rush, Bea blurted, "I hate you." It did not have the effect she hoped for.

Sidney barred himself against the door. "Fine. Hate me." It was not his job to make his children like him. He wasn't entirely sure what his job was at the moment. All he knew was that he didn't want their tears, or this pinch in his neck, or the feeling of disappointment their accusing faces heaped on him. They were kids. They needed to sit down and be quiet. Couldn't they see he was barely hanging on?

Bea dropped to her knees, whimpering, "I thought you were never coming back. I thought you left us and I'd have to take care of Dora in this awful place all by myself. I don't want to take care of Dora anymore. I want to go home."

Seeing his daughter's careful balancing, her sturdiness, crumble, snapped Sidney out of whatever selfish exhaustion he was in. She was a child whose mother had left her, whose sister had fallen ill, whose father had taken her from everything familiar and left her alone, all night, in a strange city.

When Bea collapsed forward with her forehead pressed to the rug, Sidney knelt beside her and put a hand on her back. Dora slid off the bed and lay on the floor next to her sister. "Bea?" she whispered. Bea turned her head, and Sidney watched Dora wipe the tears from her big sister's cheek.

Their bond was remarkable. That there wasn't a single drop of familial blood between them made no difference. Sidney thought back to the day in Spain when he argued that Bea should be raised knowing who her true parents were. Now, he never wanted her to know. He didn't want his girls to think they were any less sisters because of it, or that he and Ida were any less Bea's parents. Not all truths needed revelation.

Sidney took his car keys from his pocket and wiggled his dog tags off the chain. "Sit up, Bea," he said. She straightened, sniffling and trying not to look at him. "Open your hand."

She turned her hand over, and Sidney placed his dog tag in her palm. Bea touched the thin metal, tracing her finger over his name and service number notched into it.

"What is it?" she whispered.

"It's a dog tag. Soldiers are given them when they go off to war. I haven't been without mine since the day I was issued them."

She looked at him. "Are you giving it to me?"

"Yes."

"Why?"

"To remind you that I will always come back."

"Can I have one?" Dora leaned into her sister to get a better look.

"It just so happens that I have two." Sidney handed Dora the second one.

The girls held them as if they were breakable. A lingering sob escaped Bea's throat, and Sidney propped a finger under her chin, knowing he was going to get this wrong, but trying anyway. "You shouldn't use the word *hate* unless you mean it."

"I didn't mean it."

"I know." He let go of her chin. "Do you know what I used to do when I was angry?"

"What?"

"Punch people."

Bea giggled. "Girls don't punch people."

"That's because they know better." Sidney stood up, uncramping his legs as he moved the his daughters' uneaten breakfast tray off the bed and spread out the map he'd picked up at a gas station.

Dora climbed onto the mattress, wrinkling the map as she poked her finger at a yellow line. "Where are we going now?"

"Up the coast of California." Marking the distance with his fingers, Sidney calculated it was over three hundred miles from Los Angeles to Big Sur.

Dora said, "Are we going to get Momma? I want to show her the pink hair ribbon Virginia gave me."

"I don't know," he said. He didn't want to lie to them, and the closer he got, the more he wondered what it would look like if he did not find Ida, or if she chose not to come home with them.

Bea leaned into his side, and Sidney put his arm around her shoulder.

In France, when Bea first looked at him through that open car window, the depth of her eyes astonished him. They were too blue, too wise, too trusting.

It wasn't hard to become her dad. It wasn't hard because of Ida. Together, they had set their guilt aside to raise a child that wasn't theirs. To love her. To do whatever it took.

59

❧

ARLETTE'S MIRACULOUS APPEARANCE, her ghostlike transient life, made Ida panic for her solid one.

In that house on a cliff, Ida felt like someone had chucked her into a cold body of water and told her to swim or drown. She moved from one dinner conversation to the next, from her plate of shelled abalone—chewy, salty—to her glass of wine—crisp, white—unable to shake off the shock of it all.

At midnight, Arlette grabbed Ida's hand and led her outside down a moonlit path. It felt like the time before children, before the war and Sidney. A time Arlette was trapped in and Ida wanted out of. She did not want to relive the past, and yet here she was, stuck in the company of Arlette and another band of artists.

They came to a clearing at the end of the path, and Ida saw two claw-foot tubs sitting on the cliff. Arlette removed a plug stuck in the side of the mountain like she was popping a cork from a bottle, and water steamed into the bucket at her feet. They filled the tubs, bucket by bucket, then stripped naked and climbed in. There was nothing sexual or sensual about it. Ida's adventure had come to an unexpected end. She felt frayed and tired. She missed her children. She missed Sidney. She had misjudged everything.

The water was hot and smelled of sulfur. The sky was bright and starless, the moon full as a belly. Ida thought of the tub in Kay Sage's apartment, all those glorious baths, the Seine rushing outside their window. It was a surprise to find that she did not miss that life anymore.

She lifted her steaming arms from the water. The heat made her light-headed. The ocean throbbed in her throat.

With her head back, eyes closed, Arlette said, "What do we do now?"

"About what?" Ida hadn't been able to tell her about Bea. The thought of losing her daughter turned her inside out. She would keep quiet. Say goodbye to Arlette. Leave forever. "I still have the money you put in my name," Ida said.

"Not that. I don't want it."

"Why not? It's yours."

Arlette flipped onto her stomach, splashing water over the edge of the tub. She rested her chin on her hand. Her skin was moonlight. Her eyes the night sky. "It's the past."

"*I'm* the past."

They looked at each other in silence. *Tell her*, Ida thought. *You have to tell her.*

"I did not forgive you for a long time," Arlette said.

"But you've forgiven me now?"

"Only as much as I've forgiven myself."

Ida didn't dare ask Arlette what she had to forgive herself for. A baby? Born at midnight and taken away?

A sudden voice came from the darkness. "Ida?"

There were footsteps in leaves, and Sidney stepped into the clearing.

IT WAS A hallucination: his wife in a tub at the edge of a cliff. Sidney hadn't slept properly in days. His mind was fuzzy and his body ached. It was a trick. The people on the porch of that house, smoking and talking and drinking, the cliff's craggy rocks and a violent ocean—all a dream.

Arlette was there, head raised, elbow bent on the edge of the tub, water rippling over her bare back. There was no mistaking her. For reasons unknown to Sidney, her existence did not astonish him. In a twisted way, it made perfect sense. She was their wreckage.

Steam rose. The ocean crashed. Thin clouds shifted over the moon, dipping his wife in and out of light, her breasts resting on the surface of the water, her flesh polished, face inert. Exhaustion swept over him. He wanted to lie on the ground and close his eyes. He wanted to climb into the tub and take his wife in his arms. Why didn't she speak?

The water rippled, and in a burst of moonlight, Ida reached out to him. Sidney stepped forward and took her hand. It was slippery and warm.

"How did you get here?" she whispered, like he might vanish.

"I drove."

"All that way?"

"Yes."

"Alone?"

"The girls are with me."

"Here?"

"They're asleep in the car."

Clutching his hand, Ida pulled herself from the tub. "I want to see them." Her voice was fraught, and it was then that the truth of their situation hit him. Arlette was here. In California. Alive. Not the Arlette of France. Bea's real mother, Arlette.

The cool air cloaked Ida's body in mist. Sidney wanted to grab her and run. To get in the car and drive as fast and far away as they could. In reality, things moved very slowly. He picked Ida's dress up off the ground and held it out to her. She stepped into it, and he put his hand on the small of her back as she lifted her hair off her neck so he could zip it up.

Ida looked at Arlette. "I have to go."

"I know," she said. "It's okay."

"You don't know everything."

A sad smile moved across Arlette's face. "I know more than you think." She turned onto her back and rested her head on the edge of porcelain with her face to the sky. "I know about Beatrix. I have always known. I know that you haven't tried to sell the chateau because you hope to give it to her one day, and that you have not spent the money I left you because you plan to give that to her one day too." She looked at Ida, her cheeks flushed and damp. "And I know that you love her enough to walk away from me."

Ida crouched beside the tub. "How did you know?"

"Leonie was not a hard woman to track down. I have known for years. Beatrix is the real reason I didn't find you." In her eyes, a plea, like she was the one seeking forgiveness.

Ida touched her shoulder, and Arlette slid her arm into the water and turned her head away. The worst thing was upon them. There was no going back.

"Your daughter is here," Ida said, her ribs cracking with pain. "You should see her."

From behind her, a sharp inhale from Sidney.

He took a step backward. These women were resolving something without him, unaware of his scraped-out heart. If he slipped into the trees and closed his eyes, he might wake up to a different ending. Or he could make his own ending, run up the hill and get in the car and drive away with his children.

He did neither of these things. Motionless, silent, he watched Arlette push herself from the tub, lift her dress from the rocks, and pull it over her head. They walked without speaking. The dark fragrance of eucalyptus washed over them. The moonlight cast long shadows. Sidney did not reach for Ida.

This was a moment neither of them had thought to fear or anticipate. In no scenario was Arlette alive. In no scenario did she come for her daughter. Her haunting had been in memories and guilt. If she collected Bea into her arms and took her away, what could they do?

The three of them moved past the light-splashed windows of the house, past voices and laughter up, the steep drive to the car pulled off the road, nose forward, windows open. The girls lay in darkness, their heads on a single pillow, feet tucked up, arms in. Ida wanted to climb into the backseat and curl up next to them, to hold them and rock them and tell them she loved them.

Silent sobs racked his wife's body, but Sidney couldn't comfort her. He felt shattered. Bea's lengthy limbs looked nothing like the chubby toddler he'd first laid eyes on, and yet his daughter's future had become just as vulnerable as it was that day.

When Arlette moved toward the car, Sidney did not try to stop her. It was not a choice. The part of him that wanted to block her view, to cover his daughter's body with his own, understood that this was how it was supposed to go. When Arlette put her arm around his wife's shoulder, he looked at these women linked from behind, mother to mother, and felt that he had never had any right to Bea at all.

"They are beautiful," Arlette whispered.

"They are," Ida said.

After a while, Arlette turned to Sidney, acknowledging him for the first time. "Let's not wake them just yet." She wrapped her arms around herself, shivering in her damp dress.

Just yet? Sidney was abruptly angry. Why did she get to decide? He looked at his wife, trying to understand why she let Arlette have so much control over her.

When Arlette started down the hill, Ida said, with no uncertainty, no waver, "It's going to be okay."

"How is it going to be okay?" He felt delirious.

Ida would tell him everything in time. All she could do now was try to portray the delicacy of the situation. She was not letting Arlette take control, not this time, but she knew enough to allow her the illusion of control.

There were things about Arlette that had not changed. This was obvious to Ida as she and Sidney followed her back into the glow of the house, into the gathering of people who had no idea what was taking place. Drinks were put into their hands. Slices of cake.

It was an unfathomable hour to be eating and drinking. Sidney managed not to draw attention to himself as he dumped his drink down the sink. He set his uneaten cake on the counter and watched Ida as she watched Arlette.

The cake crumbled under Ida's fork as she flattened crimson chocolate and sticky frosting onto her plate, watching Arlette rotate around the room with her too-bright eyes and high-strung voice. Arlette did not know what to do with the reality of her daughter, so she was doing what she always did, lighting up, moving toward distraction.

❧

IT WAS THREE in the morning when they made their way back to the hot springs. Arlette had insisted, and she now walked with her arm linked through Ida's like a schoolgirl's. Sidney followed in a silent stupor, his eyes heavy with exhaustion, his heart raw. He had really begun to think he might never sleep again.

When they reached the clearing, Ida sat on a rock, and Sidney sank to the ground. Silently, Arlette shed her clothes and climbed back into the tub. The water had cooled, but Arlette didn't care. It was important that she get back in. Ida saw that she needed to do this. To roll back time and return to the moment before she laid eyes on Bea.

At the car, Arlette had not wept. She had not pulled open the door. She had not curled her daughter into her arms. She had not even reached through the window to touch Bea's ankle. When she put her arm around Ida's shoulder, an understanding passed from one woman to another. Love is unpredictable. It is complicated. It does not always show up where it should, or how it should.

Ida looked at Sidney with his hands propped behind his head. He hadn't yelled at her, or told her she'd destroyed their lives, or that this was all her fault. He was watching her in silent trust, waiting for her to finish what she'd started.

Ida got up. There were tears in Arlette's eyes, and it struck Ida that in all the years she'd known Arlette, she'd never seen her cry.

"She looks nothing like me," Arlette said.

"She has your confidence." Ida wanted to reassure her, to give her something. "And she likes to tell me what to do."

Arlette smiled. "I hope you have learned to do exactly as you please anyway."

"Sometimes. Not always."

"That is why you are a good mother. I have never learned to please others."

The fog thickened, and a veil of mist moved between them. Ida could no longer make out Arlette's expression.

"I need to say goodbye," Ida said.

"I was never very good at that either," Arlette said. "Ida?"

"Yes?"

"Promise you will keep the photograph of us and show it to Bea one day? Tell her you once knew an artist named Arlette Lellouche?"

"By then she'll have already heard of you." Ida turned to Sidney. Filled with uncertainty, she reached for him. He deserved to be a part of this.

Sidney lifted himself from the ground and took his wife's hand. Arlette was already disappearing behind the rising fog. "We will tell her when she's old enough to understand," he said, and Arlette gave a small nod.

For the last time, Ida and Sidney walked down the path along the cliff in Big Sur. They had no idea what lay ahead, only that their daughters were waiting for them.

They liked not knowing. Maybe they would stay in California and become unpredictable.

What they knew, for certain, was what they were leaving behind.

Arlette, a speck on the cliff, human and small.

Ahead of them, an opening in the trees, their future a pool of light.

60

⟨ornament⟩

THEY WATCHED THE SKY lighten from the beach. Too tired to keep driving, Sidney had pulled into an empty parking lot overlooking the ocean at four a.m. For a while, he and Ida sat in silence, listening to the measured breathing of their children. They were both exhausted and unable to sleep. There was so much Sidney wanted to say, but he was at a loss for words. All he could do was put his arm around Ida. She did not resist. She slid across the seat and folded into him, and he began to cry.

"I'm tired," he laughed, embarrassed by his tears.

"Me too," she said.

The girls stirred, and Ida put a finger to Sidney's lips. He held it there and kissed it. Scooting away, Ida pulled her sweater over her head and got out of the car, beckoning for him to follow.

He would have liked to make love to her on the beach under that clouded moon, but Ida was ready to talk.

Wrapped in Sidney's arms, their legs tangled in the sand, she told him the truth about what happened at the chateau. The memories did not drown her as she'd imagined. Time had made them less vivid. It helped that her back was against him and her eyes were on the dark water. To face him would have been harder. The rhythmic crash of the waves was soothing, the white foam curling toward her toes peaceful. The violence felt very far away, diminished to a excavation of words.

She told Sidney how she'd been kneeling on the hearth, staring at the remains of her scorched career when he walked into the living room. It was not lost on her, she said, that he came into her life the moment her violin went out of it. "If you hadn't, I don't think I would have sur-vived. I wouldn't have wanted to."

Sidney was overtaken by sadness at what his wife had witnessed, and by the knowledge that she harbored this secret, abandoned talent. It was like he'd missed a whole part of knowing her. "You could play again," he said.

"No. I don't even want to. It's not who I am anymore." When she said this, she realized it was true. She had not reinvented herself; she had just changed.

"Who are you now?" Sidney said, not for his own intentions, but because he wanted to understand hers.

"I don't know anymore, but maybe that's the point."

She turned around and hiked up her dress in order to wrap her legs over his. Sidney kept his hands on her hips and waited for her to say more.

"What I do know is that I don't want to go back to Lexington," she said. "But I'm afraid you and the girls won't want to leave."

He smiled. "We've already left."

They said nothing more. They did not need to. They were balanced in the liminal space between the past and future, tethered only to each other.

The girls found them lying on the beach watching the morning sky unfold. Popping from the car like Cracker Jacks, they ran, unrestrained, toward their mother, kicking up sand as they tumbled into her. Ida kissed their heads and hands and cheeks, overwhelmed at her desire to smell their hair and press her palms against their skin.

"Daddy, I'm ravishing," Dora said.

"You mean ravenous," Bea said.

"You all three are ravishing." Sidney stood, swinging Dora onto his shoulders.

Hearing Dora speak to Sidney brought tears to Ida's eyes. She had missed so much in a few weeks. Her neat daughters were barefoot and wrinkled and their hair looked like it hadn't been brushed in days, which made Ida smile. She shook the sand from her clothes, watching Sidney latch a protective hand around Dora's leg as he reached down and helped Bea to her feet. The ease between the three of them was re-markable.

It was impossible to express how moved Ida was by the simplicity of her travel-worn family on a beach in rumpled, sandy clothing. Maybe her history had piled up behind her and pushed her to this point merely so she could find the sacred in the ordinary.

Bea slid her hand into her mother's. "Are you hungry, Mommy?"

"Ravenous."

"Daddy knows all the diners."

"All the diners?"

"Every diner in the greater United States of America," Sidney said, linking his hand to Ida's and walking them to the car.

Acknowledgments

T HE INSPIRATION FOR THIS novel came from a photograph of my grandmother Margaret Neiman, taken by Man Ray. Without her bravery, her willingness to have her body photographed in all its bold beauty, this story might not exist. I am deeply grateful to her, and to Man Ray for giving me the gift of my youthful grandmother through his art, as well as to Juliet Ray for partnering with them both and awakening the character of Arlette.

Thanks to my mother for keeping the stories of our family's past. Peggy Guggenheim for collecting and saving valuable art from the Holocaust and documenting her efforts in *Confessions of an Art Addict*. Thank you to the artists who stepped into my pages, however briefly, in order of appearance: André Breton, Samuel Beckett, Bram van Velde, Victor Brauner, Djuna Barnes, Kay Sage, Yves Tanguy, Constantin Brâncusi, Man Ray, Max Ernst, Victor Serge.

To my early readers, Ariane Goodwin and Heather Liske, thank you for your keen eyes, attention to detail, and thoughtful critique.

I could not write historical fiction without the extensive research of others. Thank you to these authors for their works of fiction and non-fiction: *Villa Air-Bel*, by Rosemary Sullivan; *Art Lover*, by Anton Gill; *Out of This Century: Confessions of an Art Addict*, by Peggy Guggenheim; *Brideshead Revisited*, by Evelyn Waugh; and *Suite Française*, by Irène Némirovsky.

No matter how many stories I hear of WWII, the strength and bravery of those who survived, and those who did not, astounds me.

Suite Française was an invaluable resource for me while writing this novel. Némirovsky died in a concentration camp and never lived to see her work published. Stories like hers are how I can tell stories like mine. To this brave soul, I am profoundly grateful. And to the real-life heroes who appear in this book, ones who risked their lives helping refugees escape Vichy France, Varian Fry, Lena Fischmann, Theo and Danny Bénédite, the world thanks you.

Thank you to my powerhouse team at Atria and Simon & Schuster for all of their hard work and support: Chelsea McGuckin, Liz Byer, Shelby Pumphrey and Paige Lytle, Dayna Johnson, Debbie Norflus, Davina Mock-Maniscalco, Natalie Argentina. Thank you to Trellis Literary Management, to Elizabeth Pratt and Allison Malecha for working diligently behind the scenes.

To the two outstanding women who make all of this possible: my agent, Stephanie Delman, for reading the thousands of words I write and for her absolute dedication and support, and my editor, Laura Brown, for seeing the scope of this book, and for her belief and trust in me.

Thank you to my family for always being there.

And finally, thank you to my readers. You are who give this book life.

About the Author

SERENA BURDICK is the *USA Today* bestselling author of *The Girls with No Names*, *The Stolen Book of Evelyn Aubrey*, *Find Me in Havana*, and *Girl in the Afternoon*. She studied creative writing at Sarah Lawrence College and holds a BA from Brooklyn College in English literature and an AA from the American Academy of Dramatic Arts in theater. Find out more at SerenaBurdick.com.